From stage actor and international te
bestselling author, Judy Nunn's career
Her first forays into adult fiction re
as her 'entertainment set'. *The Glitt*
Araluen, three novels set in the worlds of television, theatre and
film respectively, each became instant bestsellers.

Next came her 'city set': *Kal*, a fiercely passionate novel about men and mining set in Kalgoorlie; *Beneath the Southern Cross*, a mammoth achievement chronicling the story of Sydney since first European settlement; and *Territory*, a tale of love, family and retribution set in Darwin.

Territory, together with Judy's next novel, *Pacific*, a dual story set principally in Vanuatu, placed her firmly in Australia's top-ten bestseller list. Her following works, *Heritage*, set in the Snowies during the 1950s; *Floodtide*, based in her home state of Western Australia; *Maralinga*, set in South Australia during the British atomic weapons tests; and *Tiger Men*, a sweeping family saga set in Tasmania, have consolidated her position as one of the country's leading fiction writers.

Judy Nunn's fame as a novelist is spreading rapidly. Her books are now published throughout Europe in English, German, French, Dutch and Czech.

Judy lives with her husband, actor-author Bruce Venables, on the Central Coast of New South Wales.

www.judynunn.com

By the same author

The Glitter Game
Centre Stage
Araluen
Kal
Beneath the Southern Cross
Territory
Pacific
Heritage
Floodtide
Maralinga
Tiger Men

Children's fiction
Eye in the Storm
Eye in the City

JUDY NUNN

Elianne

WILLIAM HEINEMANN: AUSTRALIA

A William Heinemann book
Published by Random House Australia Pty Ltd
Level 3, 100 Pacific Highway, North Sydney NSW 2060
www.randomhouse.com.au

First published by William Heinemann in 2013

Copyright © Judy Nunn 2013

The moral right of the author has been asserted.

All rights reserved. No part of this book may be reproduced or transmitted
by any person or entity, including internet search engines or retailers,
in any form or by any means, electronic or mechanical, including
photocopying (except under the statutory exceptions provisions of the
Australian *Copyright Act 1968*), recording, scanning or by any information
storage and retrieval system without the prior written permission of Random
House Australia.

Addresses for companies within the Random House Group can be found at
www.randomhouse.com.au/offices.

National Library of Australia
Cataloguing-in-Publication Entry

Nunn, Judy
Elianne/Judy Nunn

ISBN 978 1 74275 838 1 (paperback)

A823.3

Cover image of Queenslander courtesy Garth Chapman Queenslanders,
other images courtesy Bigstockphoto, stock.xchng and Josh Durham
Cover design by Josh Durham/Design by Committee
Internal design and typesetting by Midland Typesetters, Australia
Printed in Australia by Griffin Press, an accredited ISO AS/NZS 14001:2004
Environmental Management System printer

This book is dedicated to the people of Bundaberg and to all those Queenslanders who suffered such hardship in the floods of 2011, only to be revisited by the even more catastrophic floods of 2013. Like the rest of Australia, I marvel at the bravery and spirit of mateship displayed in the face of such adversity.

Chapter One

1964

Some people didn't like the smell. Some people found it overly rich and cloying, some even used the term 'sickly'. But they were strangers, visitors from the city.

There had always been visitors to the mill. Overseas dignitaries, politicians, even the odd prime minister had enjoyed the lavish garden parties and general hospitality on offer at Elianne. At times there might be dozens of them, strolling about the grounds of The Big House, or lolling in the wicker chairs on its broad verandahs and upper balconies, while the more active opted for tennis and bowls on the grass courts and greens.

In earlier times, before dirt tracks became accessible roads, and before motor vehicles were the ready form of transport, guests would stay for days on end. The arduous trip by horse and carriage demanded its reward, and Elianne had much to offer – not least of which was the mandatory trip to the nearby mill. The intrepid would climb to the lofty heights of the lookout tower and drink in the panorama of cane fields, stretching like a vast green ocean to the horizon while those without a head for heights would be taken on a tour of the massive metal complex with its varying levels and intricate steel walkways, its giant vats and machines and eighty-foot-high ceiling, and they would marvel at the magnitude of its scope and industry.

During the crushing season, from mid-year until December, the cacophony of heavy machinery was overwhelming as the mill's giant rollers and presses smashed and mashed and ground the cane through every stage of its transition to raw sugar. Nothing was wasted. The fibre that was left from the crushing was burnt in the furnaces to generate steam power; the mud filtered from the cane through the presses was returned to the field as fertiliser; and after the painstakingly long crystallisation process, the molasses residue was mixed in with the stock feed or sent to the distillery for the making of rum. The whole exercise was highly efficient as men and machines went about their tasks with precise teamwork.

The mill was a busy, buzzy place during the crushing season, like a beehive where each worker knew precisely the purpose he served. The men took pride in the fact they were Elianne workers. They thrived on the noise and the industry and the smell of the mill, the very smell that some of those from the city professed to find 'sickly'.

Kate and her brothers loved the smell of the sugar mill. They found the toffee-scented air heady and intoxicating. It was the smell they'd grown up with, all three of them. It was the smell of home.

I've missed it, Kate thought, breathing in the richness as she wandered through the cathedral-like metal maze, where the giant mechanical monsters now sat eerily silent. Even during the slack season the smell is here, she thought, it's always here. It's been here for as long as I can remember.

She hadn't realised how much she'd missed the mill and the plantation over the past year. She'd been too distracted. Her life had undergone such a radical change. She remembered how she'd anticipated with relish every homecoming from boarding school in Brisbane. Every end-of-term holiday, every long weekend had seen her eagerly embrace the familiarity of her childhood. The cane fields shimmering in the heat; the smell of the mill and the easy friendship of the workers, so many of whom were like family; the horse races with her brothers along dusty dirt roads; swimming in the dam and the way, knees clutched to chests, they 'bombed' each other off the end of the jetty; tin canoes and excursions up and down the river; laden mango trees climbed to see who could shake down the most fruit; and on and on it went, the list was endless.

But this homecoming was different. Something had changed. After a year at university, this homecoming had taken her by surprise. It was more intense, more meaningful. The past seemed more precious than ever, as if she were somehow threatened with its loss. Perhaps it's because *I'm* different, she thought. Perhaps it is *I* who has changed, and things will never be the same again. The notion was disturbing, even a little sad, but also strangely exciting.

Although the mill appeared deserted, Kate was aware she was not alone. The gentle clink of tinkering could be heard as here and there mechanics cleaned and serviced the machinery. But the delicacy of the sounds only served to highlight the stillness. At least it seemed so to Kate. She loved the mill most of all during the slack season when it lay dormant, quietly exhaling its treacly breath, biding its time before the next crushing frenzy.

'*Buongiorno*, Kate. Welcome home.'

The voice that jolted her from her reverie came from behind the massive filter press nearby; it belonged to Luigi Fiorelli. He rose to reveal himself, burly, grease stained and good natured as always.

'Is good to see you,' he said with a huge grin and a wave of the grimy rag he held in his hand.

'Good to see you too, Luigi.' She smiled and returned the salute.

'How you like it down South, eh? You have good time down there?' His tone was highly sceptical. During his eighteen years in the southern cane fields of Queensland, Luigi had travelled no farther than Bundaberg, on the other side of the river just fifteen miles from Elianne. He hadn't even made the trip to Brisbane, which, although two hundred and forty road miles to the south, was easily accessible by both rail and road. He didn't like big cities, he said, which was perhaps an odd remark from one who'd been brought up in the backstreets of Naples. But then his brothers, also Neapolitan by birth, were of exactly the same mind. The Fiorellis stuck to their farms and to Elianne, never travelling any further afield than Bundaberg. Why bother, they would say, and many felt the same way. Bundaberg, affectionately known to all as Bundy, had been successfully servicing the area for nigh on a hundred years.

'Yes, I had a very good time down south, Luigi,' Kate replied. 'I like university very much.'

'*Si, si,* sure, sure, university is fine, very good, but *Sydney* ...' Luigi was now openly scathing '... you don' like *Sydney*! You can' tell me you like *Sydney,* Kate.'

The thought was clearly anathema to Luigi, but Kate made no reply, maintaining instead an enigmatic silence.

Luigi Fiorelli had emigrated from Italy with his three older brothers in 1946, following the war. His brothers had become market gardeners, starting out with tomatoes and zucchinis, and also tobacco, or 'tabac' as they called it. Over time, and with application to the all-powerful Colonial Sugar Refinery, they had converted their modest acreage to cane, but twenty-two-year-old Luigi had followed an altogether different path. A skilled mechanic, he had applied for a position at Elianne. He was forty now, and one of the estate's senior overseers, responsible for the repairs and maintenance of all mill machinery. He preferred to do more than supervise, however, and was invariably to be found in his overalls working alongside those under his command. 'How a mechanic is to be a mechanic without he get his hands dirty, eh?' he would say. Luigi's command of English had improved immeasurably over the years, but his accent and disregard for syntax hadn't changed very much.

The Fiorelli brothers and their families remained inextricably linked to Elianne. Luigi, his wife and two teenage children lived on the estate in one of the many comfortable cottages made available by the company to the mill's most valued employees. The three older brothers, now independent growers and each also with a family, relied upon Elianne for the crushing of their cane, delivering it to the collection points each season, from where it would be taken by cane train to the mill.

The mill was essential to the livelihood of the entire district. The estate itself was home to many, and for some, like Luigi, it was their whole world. Kate's continued silence, which appeared a comment in itself, now plainly shocked him.

'You don' say to me I am wrong, Kate. A girl like you who is born right here at Elianne? Your ancestors who build this place,' he stretched out his arms as if to embrace the mill and all it stood for, 'how you can like Sydney? Is not possible.'

Kate laughed. 'I'm ashamed to admit, Luigi, that yes, I like Sydney very much.' Her eyes, beguilingly green and mischievous at the best of times, held a cheeky challenge as she added boldly, 'In fact I *love* Sydney.' She clutched a dramatic hand to her heart. 'I love everything *about* Sydney.' She enjoyed teasing Luigi, whom she'd known as a colourfully avuncular figure all her life, but there was nevertheless a touch of defiance in her statement. Such a comment, even in jest, would annoy her father immeasurably, and indeed others of his ilk. Like many powerful businessmen, particularly those in the sugar trade, Stanley

Durham did not see eye to eye with the politics of the South. Queenslanders were a breed apart, he believed, and needed a different set of rules to live by; they always had.

'Oh, this is most terrible.' Realising he was being teased, Luigi joined in the joke, pounding his forehead with the butt of his hand in typically Italian fashion. 'You turn into a Southerner. *Mamma Mia*, what we tell your papa?'

'I suggest we keep it our little secret, Luigi.'

'Very good, very good,' an exaggerated shrug of resignation, 'I say nothing to Stan that his daughter is a traitor.'

'Yep, best we keep Stan the Man out of it I reckon.'

Kate blew him a kiss, and Luigi saluted her once more with his oil rag. He watched as she turned, flicking her auburn hair back like a horse might its mane. Then she walked out of the mill with that easy, confident stride of hers. There was still the tomboy in her, he could see that, still the physical assurance that she could outride, outswim and outrun many a male her age. Growing up in a man's world she'd always been competitive, never one content to sit among the women on the sidelines of life. But he'd recognised the change in her the moment he'd seen her enter the mill, well before he'd made his presence known. No more the lanky teenager, Kate Durham had become a woman.

He plonked himself down on the wooden crate and resumed his work. The fact was hardly remarkable, he told himself. Kate would be eighteen in mid-January, barely one month away. But the change was confronting nonetheless. It wasn't just the way her body had matured, which was to be expected – there was a sexual awareness about her, he could sense it. She's probably lost her virginity in Sydney, he thought disapprovingly. Luigi's own daughter, Paola, was just three years younger than Kate and he dreaded the prospect of her falling for some lusty young buck after nothing but sex. Paola would marry when she'd met the right man, and she would be wed a virgin; he'd kill any bastard who attempted to deflower her.

Luigi wondered how Stan would react if he discovered his daughter was no longer a virgin. Indeed he'd wondered from the outset why Stanley Durham had allowed his daughter to travel so far afield for her education. Surely Kate could have gone to university in Queensland. She would still have been away from home of course, that was unavoidable, but at least she wouldn't have been influenced by the decadence that abounded in the south. Sydney was a den of vice; everyone knew that.

Luigi had never voiced such misgivings, however – it was hardly his place to do so. He and Stan were friends certainly, but Luigi Fiorelli, an intelligent man, was well aware there were limitations attached to such a friendship. Ah well, he now told himself, it is none of my business, and he shrugged and got on with his work.

Stanley Durham made a point of initiating close ties with his workers, particularly his key employees, who called him by his first name. Those of long standing like Luigi were indeed considered friends, and often asked up to The Big House, although such offers were never extended when visiting dignitaries were ensconced there.

Stan chose not to play 'the Boss' among the general hierarchy of Elianne, but rather the skipper of the team. His workers called him Mr Stan to his face, but he was indirectly referred to by all as Stan the Man, a term which rather pleased him, for he saw himself as a man's man and a leader of men. But if the truth were known 'Stan the Man' was just another term for 'the Boss', because that's exactly what Stan Durham was. He was very like his grandfather, who had built Elianne out of nothing; in fact Stan the Man was Big Jim Durham all over again.

Kate set off at a leisurely pace on the mile-long walk to The Big House. The day promised to become a scorcher, but at the moment a mild breeze alleviated the discomfort; even at its most intense, the weather was never as oppressively humid as it was further to the north, where the swelter of the tropics could be overwhelming. In any event, Kate loved the heat of midsummer. Many from the South considered it insufferable, but personally she couldn't understand how others could withstand the cold as they did. Sydney's climate was supposedly temperate and yet she'd found the winter quite uncomfortable. She dreaded to think what a Melbourne winter would be like, or worse still a Tasmanian one.

She crossed the rail tracks to where she'd left the dogs sitting patiently beside the mill dam. The moment they saw her approach, they jumped up, tails wagging, but they didn't leave the spot, waiting for her to come to them instead. Cobber and Ben were well trained and knew that the dam was as close to the mill as they were allowed to go.

'Good boys,' she said. As she reached them then continued down the dirt road, the dogs raced on ahead, Cobber having trouble keeping up with Ben, although it didn't ultimately matter as Ben kept circling back to round him up.

Cobber was an eight-year-old Golden Labrador just beginning to show his age and Ben was a hyperactive Blue Heeler who happily rounded up everything he saw except stock. The family had inherited Ben, now four, as a pup from a local farmer who bred working dogs. 'He's no use to me,' the farmer had told them, 'he got kicked by a steer and won't go near cattle.'

It's so good to be home, Kate thought as she watched the dogs at play, Ben circling back to nip at Cobber's heels as if to speed him up, Cobber accepting the bullying good-naturedly; the two were great mates. Ostensibly the dogs belonged to the family, but everyone considered them Kate's as she'd trained them and they simply adored her. Kate had always had a way with animals.

She walked on enjoying the burn of the mid-morning sun on her bare shoulders. She was wearing a light cotton shift with shoestring straps, and the heat's caress through the dress's thin fabric was more than pleasurable. It was sensual, somehow arousing – a little erotic even. She smiled and quickened her pace, chastising herself. Good God, girl, is there anything these days that *isn't* arousing, that you *don't* find erotic? Pull yourself together and stop thinking about sex.

Luigi Fiorelli was wrong in his reasoning. Kate had not lost her virginity in Sydney. But she had come very close to it, and she certainly intended to do so upon her return in the New Year.

Now as she strode down the road and past the stables, she thought of Jeremy, recalling with fierce clarity that night he'd first kissed her. It had been nearly three months earlier, and the first real kiss she'd ever known. She'd considered herself quite an experienced kisser, but she'd obviously been wrong, for this was something entirely different. This was not the experimental brush of teenage lips at school dances in Brisbane, nor was it the clumsy fumbles of local boys, easily fought off, in the back row of Bundaberg's Paramount picture theatre on a Saturday afternoon. This was the tenderest exploration of mouths. She could still recall her wonderment at the fact that she hadn't found his tongue repulsive. She could relive, and had done many times, every moment of her surrender to an intrusion that was at first shocking, then fascinating, then amazing as in her boldness she'd parted her lips that little bit more, allowing him easy access, even flickering her own tongue over the delicate tips of his teeth.

She could have given herself wholly to him in the back room of that poky East Sydney flat while the party raged next door. And indeed in a way she had given herself to him. The promise had been there – they'd both recognised it. But Jeremy had not rushed her. Twenty-year-old Jeremy, a second-year Arts student, mature and experienced, but also infatuated, was, Kate knew, not after a one-night stand. Jeremy wanted a full-on affair and aware she was a virgin he had no wish to frighten her. He'd been content to bide his time. Over the ensuing weeks, he'd progressed a little further – his lips travelling down her neck; his hand straying lightly over her breast, sending shivers through her body – never too invasive, but steadily more intimate. To Kate, however, it was the indelible memory of that first kiss that remained the true turning point. She'd made her decision. Jeremy would be the man to whom she would surrender her virginity.

The week before her return to Queensland for the Christmas holidays she'd visited a doctor and put herself on the contraceptive pill for that express purpose.

'I'll see you in the New Year,' she'd whispered as he'd kissed her goodbye at the train station, and they'd both known exactly what she meant.

Having passed by the cookhouse and mess hall, and then the bakery, Kate reached the village green, with Elianne Hall to her right. The estate's village green and hall had been social centres throughout the whole of her childhood, as they had throughout the childhoods of many of her contemporaries, and also those of generations past.

She came to a halt, once again chastising herself, but this time in a more serious vein. I really must put Jeremy and sex out of my mind, she thought crossly. She'd been away from Elianne for close on a year and yet her head was full of the impending loss of her virginity. If she went on like this she'd ruin her entire holiday.

She sat on the hall's front step, Cobber flopping contentedly at her feet, Ben as ever wandering off to explore. Looking out across the village green she recalled the many fetes and picnics, where teams of small children had competed in every imaginable event contrived to excite and enthral the young. Workers' children of all colour and creed: Australians, Italians, a few Kanakas and Chinese, English, Scots, here and there the odd Scandinavian and German, here and there several Torres Strait Islanders. She could see them all now, herself included, running themselves ragged in three-legged races, staggering clumsily about in hessian sacks and hauling on twenty yards of rope as if their lives depended upon winning the tug o' war.

The same fetes and picnics and parties continued to this very day. The numbers had dwindled somewhat of late, but Stan the Man insisted tradition be upheld. She'd been home for just one week, and on the Saturday following her arrival there'd been a pre-Christmas picnic attended by at least twenty families. She and her younger brother Alan, who was home from boarding school, had handed out the presents and the toffee-apples, while Neil, soon to turn twenty, the oldest of the three and heir apparent, had awarded the prizes, a job that had always been the domain of their father. These days, however, Stanley Durham, while remaining as dominant a figure as ever, preferred to sit on the sidelines like a benign monarch, surveying his realm, his subjects and his family with pride.

The Durham siblings, although no longer among those youngsters so fiercely competing, had shared in the recognition, and taken pleasure in the knowledge that some things hadn't changed, and some things probably never would. Kate smiled now as she recalled their exchange. Not one word had been spoken, but the glances they'd shared had said everything. They'd been children again: ten or eight or six, no matter, the two-year age difference between each of them had never formed a barrier. Throughout the whole of their childhood, they'd been the three musketeers, and she, in the middle, had been the lynch pin. Kate loved her brothers dearly.

And as for the hall, she thought, turning to look over her shoulder, well the hall hasn't changed one bit. The building indeed seemed to belong in a time warp – it had been the same for as long as she could remember.

Elianne Hall, as it was grandly known, was really just a vast timber-framed building with a tin roof, but for the mill's workers and extended family it had been a vital hub for generations. Here every form of festivity had taken place, concerts and parties for all occasions, along with birthdays, weddings and wakes. The hall also served as a Sunday school, and not only for the workers' children. Attendance by the Durham siblings had been mandatory.

Again Kate wondered why everything seemed so poignant. Is it just because I've been away so long? she asked herself. Or is it because I've changed? Everything else appears to have remained much the same. It must surely be me.

She stood. Time to go home. She was hungry now – she'd skipped breakfast for an early-morning walk down by the river.

Cobber, who'd been dozing in the sun, stretched and joined her as she set off. Ben was nowhere in sight, but she didn't need to call him. Within minutes he'd appeared and was racing on ahead.

Across the village green, she could see several girls around fifteen years of age wending their way homewards along the rough bush track. They were animatedly chattering as they returned from their morning stints at Elianne's cattle yards and dairy a half a mile away. Kate gave them a wave and they waved back. She knew each one of the dairymaids: two were the daughters of the dairy farmer himself, and the third was the butcher's daughter, who was earning extra money during her school holidays. Their fathers were not seasonal itinerate workers, but lived on the estate running their businesses year-round as many did.

During the crushing season, several hundred mill and field workers were employed at Elianne, the cookhouse working round the clock to provide dawn breakfasts, packed lunches, smokos, evening meals and shift dinners for the hundred or so accommodated in the single men's barracks. Throughout the slack season, however, Elianne remained a self-sustaining village catering to the families who lived on the estate. It boasted a general store, a bakery, and a butcher's shop that was regularly supplied with fresh meat from the nearby piggery and cattle slaughter yards.

With only two thousand acres of the property under cane, the majority of the mill's produce came from local farmers, some of whose children worked on the estate alongside others who travelled by foot or bicycle from the settlement of South Kolan, only two miles away. Given the affordability of vehicles and the easy access of modern roads, there were also those who now commuted from Bundaberg, but despite the changes wrought by progress, Elianne remained a community, and a vibrant one at that. Elianne was a family to which people were proud to belong.

Kate walked on down the road, passing the attractive cottages of South Mill Row with their front verandahs and pretty little gardens. One of these was home to Luigi Fiorelli and his family. There were several such rows of cottages on the estate, but the others offered far more basic accommodation than those of South Mill Row, which were reserved for the permanently employed and most valuable of workers. Indeed, the hierarchy of Elianne could be immediately detected in the architecture of the housing allotted to its employees. To the north of the mill were the single men's barracks, to the east and the west the rows of rudimentary cottages reserved for married workers, and then there was South Mill Row. After that there followed a further distinctly upwards curve, for the homes allotted to Elianne's senior staff were a different matter altogether. There were at least a half a dozen of them dotted about the estate, gracious affairs of striking design: stilted wooden, Queensland-style houses with broad verandahs, perfectly suited to the climate.

None, however, was as grand as Durham House. Always referred to simply as The Big House, the Durham family home was nothing short of magnificent. The Big

House appeared three stories high, but it wasn't really, this was just an illusion. The attractive white-painted lattice work flanking the broad stairs that led up to its first-floor verandah masked only storage space and a laundry, for this house too stood very tall on its stilts. Its elevation gained impressive views on all sides both of the river a quarter of a mile away and also of the plantation. From the balconies of The Big House the cane trains could be regularly observed during the crushing season, even at night, lights gleaming in the distance, feeding the hungry mill the hundred and fifty tons of cane it devoured every hour.

Painted white with railings of green, and surrounded on all sides by wooden verandahs and upper-storey balconies, the house lounged in its landscaped gardens and tennis courts like an indolent giant. It was too huge and too opulent to be elegant, but also too beautiful to be crass, the finishing touches of oak doors and wooden-framed French windows saving it from even the harshest of critics. Hilda Durham had seen to that.

Stan the Man had had the house designed along the lines of the original Elianne House, built by his grandfather in 1890, which, since the death of old Big Jim Durham twelve years previously, had served as home to Ivan Krantz and his family. Ivan was the estate's managing accountant and company secretary. The only adjustment Stan had made to the original design of the house, or so he'd said at the time, was to quadruple the size of the place and add another storey with balconies.

'The same only bigger,' he'd assured his wife shortly before Neil was born. Hilda had loved the old house. In fact, she'd loved Elianne House far more than the modern residence Stan had had specially built as their marital home. 'We'll need the extra space with family on the way,' he'd insisted, when she'd queried whether the size he envisaged might be a little vulgar, 'and of course there are always the visitors. We must be able to accommodate our visitors in style. They expect it my dear, just as they did in Big Jim's time.'

It had been Hilda who had had the final say, however, particularly with regard to the interior. The grand oak staircase leading to the upper floor had become a principal feature, as had the wooden panelling in the main dining room and the various sitting rooms. Doors with frosted-glass panels featuring original designs, crystal chandeliers, wall-bracket light fittings of brass, lead-light and stained-glass windows, together with Hilda's personal selection of objets d'art and paintings had completed the final touches. Stanley Durham very wisely never questioned his wife's taste.

Kate bounded up the front steps three at a time, the dogs flopping on the verandah; they were not allowed inside the house.

The family was having morning tea in the smaller downstairs drawing room as she'd presumed they would be. Or at least as she'd presumed her mother would be. Hilda insisted upon morning and afternoon tea being served in the front drawing room. Even if no one else attended, and they very often didn't, Hilda would quite happily sit there, sipping away at her tea and nibbling at her cake or scones. She never demanded anyone join her; the ritual was all she required.

To Kate's surprise, everyone was there, her father lounging in his favoured armchair, her mother perched as always in her carver at the table and Neil and Alan seated on hardback chairs demolishing the slices of sponge cake that young Ivy the maid had just passed around.

'Morning all,' Kate said, looking a query from one to the other. She hadn't expected to see her brothers.

Hilda signalled Ivy to fetch a fresh pot of tea and Stan signalled his daughter to sit.

Kate did so. 'What's going on?'

'Dad's called a family meeting,' Alan replied with a typically nonchalant 'don't ask me' shrug.

'What about?'

'Change.' Neil dived in diplomatically before Alan could offer another careless shrug. His younger brother's nonchalance had a way of irritating their father. Placing his side plate on the table and giving his mouth a perfunctory dab with his linen napkin in order to appease their mother's constant plea for good table manners, he stood. 'Dad decided to leave it a week or so for you two to settle back in before calling this meeting to discuss some developments undertaken by Elianne Pty Limited.' Neil's address to his siblings was solemn and Kate and Alan exchanged looks. Home being 'Elianne' and the family business 'Elianne Pty Limited' Neil was wearing his 'Company Hat'. Normally they would have teased him about it, but not today, not in front of their father.

'There have been a lot of changes over the past year or so ...' Neil cast a look to Stan whose brisk nod conveyed the unmistakeable order to carry on. Stanley Durham was very proud of his eldest son. Since completing his boarding-school education three years previously, Neil had been drilled in every area of mill management and was proving the perfect heir to the throne.

'Given your time away at uni, Kate,' Neil continued, 'you may not be fully aware of the fact that we're in a state of transition, and that there is indeed further change in the air.'

Change in the air. Recalling her earlier reflections, Kate found the phrase extraordinarily apt. Perhaps it isn't me after all, she thought.

'In the field, the mechanisation of cultivation and harvesting and loading is revolutionising the sugar industry ...' Neil's focus remained principally upon his sister. There was no need to talk mechanics with his younger brother. At fifteen, Alan knew more about the specifics of any given machine than Neil would ever know. Having been obsessed with machinery from the age of ten, Alan spent every moment available to him in the mill or in the maintenance workshops with the man he adored above all others, his friend and mentor, Luigi Fiorelli. Alan was a born mechanic.

Kate nodded. Neil was telling her nothing she hadn't registered. How could one fail to observe the recent changes brought about by mechanisation, particularly those wrought by the harvester. The mechanical harvester was already replacing whole teams of manual cane-cutters. The very face of the industry was being transformed.

'Several other major mills that service the southern cane fields are expanding,' Neil explained, now addressing himself to Alan. 'They're increasing their crushing tonnage and also their rate of crushing per hour. Elianne must follow suit.'

Ivy had arrived and was setting the fresh pot of tea on the table. Hilda raised a delicate hand, indicating that she herself would play 'mother' and, as Ivy left, Neil continued without pausing to draw breath.

'... And to this end, it is our intention to purchase substantial new mill machinery –'

'What sort of machinery?' Alan interrupted, his attention instantly captured.

'Four new Broadbent high-grade centrifugals, two new Thompson four-drum water tube boilers, and a Saranin design vacuum pan.' Discarding the 'Company Hat', Neil's tone was suddenly boastful and his grin boyish as he listed, like a series of prizes, the proposed acquisitions, knowing how very impressed Alan would be.

Alan was. With duly raised eyebrows, he returned his brother's grin, looking exactly like a younger version of Neil. Much as the two differed in temperament, they shared the Durham look – the look of their father and his father before him, both chisel-boned, dark-haired, impressive men.

'Where's the money going to come from?' Alan said, intrigued. 'They'll cost a lot. Machines like that don't come cheap.'

His remark was more a comment than a query but,

delivered in his customary laconic fashion, it annoyed his father.

'That's no concern of yours, boy,' Stan growled. 'Ivan has everything in hand. He's issuing limited shares in the company and selling them to raise the necessary capital. He and your brother and I have had endless discussion regarding the mill's expansion and investment. It's hardly your place to question our decision.'

Alan gave another shrug that appeared careless, but really he was just giving up. He hadn't been questioning the decision at all, but there was no point in arguing. Father and younger son did not understand each other and never had.

Once again it was Neil who sprang to the rescue, as he invariably did. 'With the increase in milling efficiency, we'll be saving in other areas,' he explained. 'For a start, there'll be fewer workers needed on each shift to operate the mill, and that's just one of the expense-saving factors. Ivan says that –'

Stan decided it was time to take over.

'Which brings us to other major areas of change,' he said as he rose from the throne of his armchair. 'Thank you, my dear,' he accepted the fresh cup of tea his wife offered him, 'and thank you, Neil.' It was a signal for his son to sit, which Neil did, but not before delivering the cup of tea his mother had poured for his sister.

Stan sipped his tea, waiting until everyone was settled. He liked to make an impact and was accustomed to receiving the undivided attention of any audience he addressed, which was why the occasionally offhand manner of his younger son so annoyed him. He considered it disrespectful.

At fifty years of age, Stanley Durham gave the impression of being a big man, one who towered over others. But standing just short of six feet, he was not overly tall by Queensland standards. Perhaps it was the way he carried himself with such pride. Perhaps it was the strength of his build, or his dark, brooding eyes and handsome head of hair, now flecked with grey. Whatever the chief contributing factor may have been, Stanley Durham's overall image was that of a 'larger than life' man. It was certainly the way he saw himself. It was the way he *wished* to be perceived and therefore the way he *was* perceived.

Assured of his family's full attention Stan now made his dramatic announcement.

'Ivan Krantz will be leaving Elianne at the end of next month.'

A moment's silence followed as Kate and Alan exchanged looks of bewilderment. Ivan had been the mill's accountant and company secretary for the past twelve years. He and his wife and son had lived in old Elianne House all that time. The Krantzes and the Durhams had been as close as two families could be. Why would Ivan choose to leave the mill, and particularly now, after instigating such changes?

'You're being naughty, Stanley. You mustn't tease.' Hilda's rebuke was mild. She was a gracious woman who, even in the admonishment of her children, never raised her voice. To Hilda, decorum always remained the order of the day.

Stan laughed. He'd enjoyed the effect of his statement, his intention having been to confuse and bewilder. 'No, no, you misunderstand,' he said expansively. 'Ivan's not leaving the *mill*, he's just moving from the estate into Bundaberg. He'll remain Elianne's company secretary and he'll still be personally handling our business.' Stan was obviously happy with the arrangement, and genuinely pleased for his friend. 'Ivan and young Henry are setting up offices in Bourbong Street, right in the centre of town, and Elianne is to be their very first client.'

Twenty-two-year-old Henry Krantz, much to his father's pride, had recently returned from Brisbane a qualified accountant. 'The lad topped his entire course, Stan,' Ivan had boasted, 'what better junior partner could a man wish for, I ask you?'

'To Krantz & Son,' Stan raised his teacup high and the others found themselves automatically saluting with their own cups. 'Good luck to them, I say.' He took a hefty swig of his tea and dumped his cup and saucer on the table. 'Times are changing. Expansion is on the rise and good accountants are essential. I've no doubt Ivan and Henry will do very well. With Elianne as their first major client, others are bound to follow ...'

Stan might have continued a little longer in the same vein, but he made the mistake of glancing at his wife, whose attention was no longer focused upon the tea. Hilda, so often vague and distracted by the niceties of life, was looking intently at her husband, demanding he make the further announcement, which to her was the most important one of all.

In response to his wife's unspoken but unmistakeable request, Stan halted. He cleared his throat. 'Ivan's move into town will bring about another change,' he said with a slight hesitation, which was not like him. But even when delivering news he was aware would not be received favourably, Stan Durham chose to make an impact.

'Old Elianne House is to be demolished,' he announced in a manner that defied dissent. Then he waited for the argument that would follow.

There was a further silence. Hilda's eyes were no longer upon her husband. Instead she was studying her daughter. Kate would surely be shocked to the core. Kate had inherited her love of the old home. And why would she not? Hilda wondered. The house had been built by her great-grandfather for the woman he worshipped. Elianne Durham, the woman after whom Big Jim had named his plantation and his mill and his entire estate.

'Elianne House is more than your heritage, Kate,' Hilda had told her daughter many times over the years, 'Elianne House is a symbol of love.'

Now, as she studied her daughter, Hilda awaited the explosion. Kate did not readily bend to her father's will like Neil, nor did she close herself off from him like Alan. Kate met her father head on, and confrontation between the two could be volatile.

But it appeared no explosion was to take place.

'Why?' Kate asked quietly. She was indeed taken aback, perhaps even shocked, but above all she was mystified. 'Why would you want to demolish a beautiful old home like Elianne House, a home that's been a part of your family for generations?'

'Who am I going to put in there, Kate? You tell me that.' Although his daughter's tone had not been accusatory, Stan's response bore a touch of belligerence. He'd known from which quarter the argument would come and he was quite prepared to do battle. 'Ivan's not the only one shifting into town, you know. These days many of the senior staff members are opting to commute from Bundaberg. We have other homes that are already going begging. Would you suggest I let Elianne House out for a pittance to one of the workers and his family? I can promise you, it'd go to wrack and ruin if I did.'

'But why demolish it?' Kate insisted. 'That's surely a little drastic. Couldn't we just leave the place empty?'

'A valuable piece of real estate sitting untenanted and requiring upkeep,' her father scoffed. 'That hardly makes financial sense, does it?'

'No, I suppose it doesn't.' Kate had the distinct feeling she was on the losing side. 'But perhaps the house could be sold and transported? I mean to destroy all that beauty ... The woodwork, the lead-lighting, the stained-glass panelled doors ...'

'The house is not in a fit enough state to be transported, Kate – we must be realistic.' Stan was no longer belligerent; there was no need. The battle was over. 'And I didn't say we were *destroying* it my dear, I said we were *demolishing* it. There is a distinct difference.'

'And that is ...?'

'The house will be dismantled. The features you mention are worth a great deal these days. The timber alone will fetch a fine price.' Stan threw in the clincher. 'The house is of far more value in pieces than it is whole, I'm afraid.'

'I see.' There was nothing Kate could say to that.

Hilda couldn't help but feel a sense of disappointment as she witnessed her daughter's acquiescence. She hadn't expected Kate to win the battle certainly, but she'd expected her to offer a more forceful opposition. Surely Kate could have taken a stronger stand, given everything the house represented: the past, Grandmother Ellie and Big Jim, the great love they'd shared ... She looked about the drawing room.

'More tea?' she offered. 'Neil, Alan, you must surely be ready for another cup.'

Kate was aware that she'd disappointed her mother. It was regrettable, but inevitable. She would certainly have done battle for the house on aesthetic grounds if its preservation had been practicable, but she could not fight for its symbolic significance the way she knew her mother would have liked. Unlike Hilda she was not a romantic. She probably never had been. As a little girl, her mother's stories of Grandmother Ellie and the past had enchanted her. But then so too had fairy tales. She'd long since grown up, and more and more these days she'd come to realise that, although she loved her mother dearly, Hilda Durham lived in a fantasy world.

'Well that's it,' Stan said, clapping his hands together loudly by way of a finale, 'family meeting's over. Let's call Ivy in: we need more cake.'

That night, shortly before dinner, Kate visited her mother in the upstairs sitting room that was Hilda's personal domain. She was seated as usual by the window that looked out over the balcony and the rear garden, browsing through a copy of *Tatler*, her dry sherry digestive on the coffee table next to her.

'Do come in, darling,' she said, putting down the magazine.

Kate entered and pulled up a chair beside her mother's. 'I'm sorry, Marmee.' It was the name they'd adopted by mutual consent when, aged ten, Kate had first read Louisa May Alcott's *Little Women*. Hilda loved the way her daughter called her Marmee.

'Good heavens, what on earth are you sorry for?'

'For disappointing you as I did.'

'But my clever, clever, Kate, how could you possibly disappoint me?' Hilda appeared bemused. 'I am so very proud of you.'

'Old Elianne House,' Kate prompted. Her mother seemed to have forgotten.

'Ah yes. That.' Hilda gave a slight shrug and looked out the window. 'You wouldn't have won, anyway.'

'I know.' Kate sensed that her mother wasn't really seeing the balcony, or the gardens stretched out below.

'How sad to think that a symbol of such love should be sold off piecemeal,' Hilda said quietly, more to herself than to Kate.

'Yes, I suppose it is.' She's not here at all, Kate thought, she's off somewhere in the past again.

Kate had spent her childhood wondering why her mother dwelt so much in the past. Was it in order to escape the present? But her mother led an extremely comfortable life, so why the need for escape? Then two years previously, and for some unfathomable reason Kate associated the occasion with her sixteenth birthday, the thought had suddenly struck her. It might simply be the drink. No one had ever mentioned Hilda's drinking, and no one had ever seen her inebriated. But the digestive dry sherry had always been a daily habit and the medicinal brandy not an irregular occurrence. Kate had wondered ever since how many digestive and medicinal measures her mother might secretly imbibe. Perhaps the past wasn't her mother's escape at all: perhaps the liquor was.

'She was over seventy when I first met her,' Hilda said, continuing to stare out the window, 'but still so beautiful, so very beautiful.'

Here we go again, Kate thought, Grandmother Ellie. Kate could even vaguely remember her great-grandmother, a slim, regal woman with white, white hair. She could remember Big Jim too, just, although he hadn't been particularly big then, a rather withered man, she recalled, who seemed terribly, terribly old. They'd died the same year, when she was five.

'Of course I knew who she was,' Hilda went on, 'everyone knew who she was. I'd seen her picture in the paper – Elianne and Jim Durham were famous. But I never dreamt I'd marry into the family. I never dreamt I'd come to know her as I did.'

She's really rambling tonight, Kate thought. It's probably because of the family meeting and the talk of the old house's demolition. Or perhaps it's simply the sherry, who can tell?

'You're so like her, Kate.' Hilda turned from the window. 'You've grown into your beauty, my darling, just as I said you would.'

Kate was startled from the complacency of her thoughts. Her mother's eyes were not vague, but highly perceptive.

'Do you remember how I used to tell you that you would be beautiful?'

'Yes, of course I do,' Kate replied a little brusquely. She could recall only too well her mother's constant attempts to be a guiding influence in a masculine world and to make her aware of her femininity. 'You will be beautiful one day, Kate,' Hilda would say, 'do not doubt yourself, my dear.' But Kate had not doubted herself for one minute. She'd needed no confidence booster, and she certainly didn't need to be beautiful.

'You still don't believe me, do you?' Hilda smiled her pretty smile. 'But you will soon. One day, very soon, you'll know that you're beautiful.'

Hilda had recognised every nuance of the change in her daughter. Kate's physical blossoming had been evident at first glance, but she'd also sensed the restlessness in the girl. Kate is still a virgin, Hilda had thought. She hasn't discovered her true womanliness yet. But she wants to. She aches to.

'You look so like the pictures of Grandmother Ellie as a girl.' Hilda studied her daughter fondly. 'The same green eyes and auburn hair.' She smiled again, and reaching out her hand, she stroked her fingers along the curve of Kate's cheek. 'It's a very effective mix with the Durham bones, I must say.' Her smile faded and her fingers rested where they were as her eyes locked with her daughter's. 'I do hope you will find a great love, my darling, one as fulfilling as Grandmother Ellie's.'

Kate felt uncomfortable, exposed somehow. Her mother, far from being in her customary distracted state, seemed altogether too knowing.

'I think it's time we headed downstairs for dinner,' she said and she stood. 'We don't want to keep the others waiting.'

'Goodness me, no.' Hilda glanced at the antique mantel clock, which still kept perfect time. A lovely piece in cherry wood with brass-fitted face, it had belonged to Grandmother Ellie and was one of her favourite possessions. 'We certainly don't want to keep them waiting.' She drained the last of her sherry, delicately patted the corners of her mouth with a lace handkerchief and rose to her feet. 'After Christmas, when Ivan leaves,' she said, 'we shall do a tour of Elianne House, you and I. No one else, just the two of us, and we shall bid our farewells.'

Our farewells to what, Kate wondered, the past? Her mother wore that distant expression again.

'Yes of course, Marmee, that's exactly what we'll do.'

Chapter two

It had become the custom on Christmas Day for Stanley Durham to host an extravagant luncheon for his senior staff and their families. The formal dining room of the Big House seated twenty-four to table with ample space for the addition of a further table near the servery to accommodate the younger children. Despite the heat of midsummer, the fare was traditionally British and, as ceiling fans whirred high overhead, guests feasted on roast turkey, ham, baked vegetables and gravy, followed by hot plum pudding with brandy sauce. The one concession to the Antipodean climate was the inclusion of huge bowls of tropical fruit salad and ice cream, which always went down very well.

The guests were waited on by household staff. The word 'servant' was never used in the Durham home, Stan favouring the more egalitarian approach. The cook and the household staff, three in all, were only too happy to work on Christmas Day, given the huge bonuses they received in recognition of their services. Besides, they had the evening off, which they celebrated with their own dinner and festivities in the staff quarters. Hilda was insistent no one remain on duty that night. She would make sandwiches for the family herself.

This Christmas, however, Stan had decided to adopt a different routine. The meal was to be the same and the service the same, but the numbers would be fewer and the company different. This Christmas was to be a more personal occasion.

'Half of the mill's senior staff lives in Bundaberg these days, anyway,' he'd said to Hilda, 'let's just keep it to us and the Krantzes, shall we? With Ivan's move to Bundy it may well be the last Elianne Christmas he and his family will have with us.'

'Why don't we ask the Fiorellis too?' Hilda had replied. 'They've been here even longer than the Krantzes and they've never once been invited to Christmas lunch.'

Stan had applauded the idea. 'An excellent suggestion, my dear,' he'd said, 'an excellent suggestion indeed.'

They were thirteen to table. For smaller gatherings such as this, the seating capacity of the formal dining table could be halved upon removal of the specially designed centre section, so with an extra chair added to one side they were comfortably accommodated at a twelve-seater. The guests numbered three Krantzes and four Fiorellis, and there were six Durhams in total, the sixth member of the family being Stan's father, Bartholomew.

Seventy-four-year-old Bartholomew had had a stroke three years previously, following the unexpected death of his wife from a heart attack. Since that time he had not spoken one word. Whether this was because he was unable to speak, or whether it was because he chose not to, no one really knew, for he'd made a good physical recovery. His movement was slow and measured, but he could adequately tend to his own needs – in fact he preferred to do so, politely eschewing help when it was offered. Bartholomew Durham lived a quiet existence in his quarters on the first level of The Big House, and appeared to have all of his faculties about him. He was certainly capable of communication, he just could not, or perhaps would not, speak.

'The poor man,' Hilda said time and again of her father-in-law. 'Tragic that history should so repeat itself. It was exactly the same with his father; when Grandmother Ellie died, Big Jim just gave up, he couldn't live without her.' True to form, Hilda saw epic romantic drama in the situation, and to some degree she was right. The death of Bartholomew's beloved wife, Mary, had indeed devastated him. It had not, however, robbed him of his life, merely of his speech.

'Would you like some more ham, Grandpa?'

Seated beside her grandfather, Kate had noticed that, although he'd barely touched the turkey on his plate he had slowly and methodically devoured his ham. The fact did not in the least surprise her. She was aware of her grandfather's penchant for ham, which he always ate with a liberal serve of hot mustard.

Bartholomew nodded, and she served him another slice from the nearby dish. Christmas luncheon was always a relaxed affair. After the guests had been individually served, fresh platters of meat were carved and set out on the table in order for them to help themselves.

Kate placed the pot of hot mustard in front of her grandfather and as their eyes met he smiled. His smile was lopsided, his lower lip a little slack as a result of the stroke, but his eyes were beautiful. Kate loved her grandfather's eyes. A soft, gentle brown in a once-handsome face, they were intelligent, communicative. Bartholomew spoke with his eyes. At least he did to Kate.

She removed the lid of the mustard pot and watched the laborious care with which he served himself. His dexterity reduced as it was, Bartholomew went to great pains to avoid being clumsy, careful never to spill or to drop things. It's like watching a film in slow motion, Kate thought, but she knew better than to offer any help.

Kate shared a special relationship with her grandfather, particularly since his stroke. She knew that he appreciated her practicality and that he abhorred both pity and sentimentalism. She sensed that he found her mother's tragic assessment of him galling, and she was quite right, he did. Bartholomew was a modest man. He always had been. Unlike his son Stanley, he did not see himself as 'larger than life' and had no desire to be the centre of attention.

Kate found her grandfather's situation strangely poignant. His daughter-in-law romanticised him to the point of embarrassment, and his son barely recognised his existence. Even before the stroke, Stan the Man had never seemed to have much time for his father, a fact that had always been a source of puzzlement to Kate. They were men of vastly different temperament, certainly, but given Stan's demands for respect it seemed odd that he showed so little for his own father. Whenever he spoke of the past and the old days of Elianne, as Stan very often did, it was always his grandfather, Big Jim, who featured, not Bartholomew. And yet both Kate and her brothers had heard from any number of sources that Bartholomew Durham had been a clever businessman, one who really knew the sugar industry. It would appear that Bartholomew, quiet and unassuming as he was, had been overshadowed by Big Jim, even in the eyes of his own son.

Champagne flutes and beer glasses were clinked and raised throughout lunch as toasts were proposed, first by Stan Durham, then by Neil. They drank to the success of Krantz & Son, and they drank to the Krantz family's impending move to Bundaberg. They drank to loyalty and friendship, and then, upon Neil's proposal, they drank to the new mill machinery, which was due for delivery in mid-January. Luigi and Alan exchanged excited glances at this point.

Finally Ivan decided it was his turn. 'I wish to propose a toast to Kate,' he said, rising from his chair.

Ivan, although second-generation Australian, was of German extraction. His grandfather had arrived in the area in 1890, contracted to work on the construction of the railway bridge that was to be built over the river connecting

North Bundaberg to the township. Following the bridge's completion, however, Gustave Krantz had stayed on. He'd married the daughter of a German timber man, and settled in Bundaberg working for Wyper Brothers, the hardware merchants. His only son had eventually married and moved south, where Ivan had been born.

Despite the fact that he'd been born, raised and educated in Brisbane, Ivan considered his grandfather's history qualified him as a local, a view with which the others were in complete accord. Ivan Krantz was a bona fide Bundy boy to the locals, and to those who lived on the estate he was one of the Elianne family.

'I speak on behalf of your friends, Kate.' Ivan looked about the table at his wife and son and the Fiorelli family. 'We are, all of us, so very proud of you,' he said, the others obviously in full agreement. 'Your father told me some time ago that your acceptance into Sydney University was an extraordinary accomplishment, and now he tells me that you've completed your first year with distinctions in all subjects. What a remarkable achievement. We salute you.'

Ivan raised his glass in formal salutation. He was a dapper man to whom appearances were important. Ivan believed an accountant should look like an accountant. And Ivan did. He was by no means humourless, simply practical, a quality which Stanley Durham respected. The two understood each other implicitly and were the best of friends. Stan the Man also believed in the importance of appearances.

'To Kate,' he said.

'To Kate,' they all echoed, and Kate smiled from one to the other, acknowledging the tribute.

'I must say,' Ivan added jokingly when they'd drunk to the toast, 'I salute you also for besting your father. Few who do battle with Stan manage to come out on top.'

There was general laughter all round as Ivan offered a further mock toast and sat.

Ah, Luigi thought, so that explains things. The fact that Stan Durham had permitted his daughter to go to Sydney had been a source of mystery to Luigi, but clearly Stan had not been in favour of the idea at all. Kate's triumph, therefore, was certainly no mean feat.

'*Si, si,*' he agreed, joining in Ivan's joke. 'Is not many win a fight with Stan, this is most true.'

Luigi did not realise, in that instant, that he had crossed the line. Nor, for that matter, did Ivan.

Stan felt a surge of anger as he watched them, chuckling away, sharing their joke from one end of the table to the other. Seated at the head as he was, he had chosen to place Ivan beside him to his left and Luigi in the more prestigious position at the far end of the table. His intention had been to avoid any element of hierarchy or snobbery and assure the Italian of his equality among friends.

And this is how I'm to be repaid, he now thought. I'm to be mocked in my own house at my own table! He wasn't sure who had angered him most, Luigi for his presumption or Ivan for relaying information given him in private and, even more unforgiveable, relaying it incorrectly.

'I was not "bested", I can assure you, Ivan,' he said coldly. 'And I can assure *you*, Luigi, that there was no battle fought. As you just mentioned yourself, Ivan, and as I recall telling you at the time, Kate's acceptance into Sydney University was an extraordinary accomplishment.' Stan decided it was Ivan who'd angered him most. Ivan should have known better.

The table fell silent. Stanley Durham's displeasure was so evident that even Paola Fiorelli and her younger brother, Georgio, registered something was wrong, although they had no idea what it could be.

Their father Luigi was also unsure. Luigi realised he must have overstepped the mark somehow, but his relationship with Stan had always involved a degree of jocular familiarity. What had he done to offend? He had been honoured that he and his family had been invited to the Big House and he'd warned his children to be on their best behaviour, accustomed as they were to the big rowdy Christmas parties shared each year with their uncles and cousins. And yet it was now he who was in the wrong. How had this happened? Luigi was puzzled.

Ivan Krantz was not. Ivan realised he'd made a mistake. He regretted the fact, but thought, Good Heavens above, it was only a joke. Why is Stan so touchy?

'Sydney University's Veterinary Science course, upon which Kate has embarked, has the strictest intake quota.' Placing his hands on the table before him, Stan addressed the gathering as if he was giving a lecture, and indeed he was. 'Kate's matriculation – at the age of *sixteen*, I might add – was so impressive that her application for enrolment was accepted over dozens of students who were a year her senior. She has been offered a Commonwealth Scholarship to the most prestigious university in the land! What father could fail to be proud of such academic achievement?' He paused fractionally as if defying anyone to differ, which of course no one did. 'My daughter went to Sydney with my full blessing and approval.'

'Of course she did, dear.' Hilda, seated beside him, thought how frightfully pompous he sounded, but she placed her hand over his in a gesture of solidarity. 'Kate has always had your total support. She knows that, we all do.' Glancing across to Ivy, who was standing at the servery awaiting instruction, Hilda signalled the girl to start clearing away the dishes. Then she turned once again to her husband. 'Shall we have a little more champagne before the pudding?' she suggested.

'We shall indeed.' Stan gave a wave to Max, who was also standing by awaiting orders. Max was the most senior of the household staff and served as butler, although the term was never used. Max was simply Max.

Hilda's calming influence had had the desired effect

and as Max disappeared to fetch more Dom Perignon the awkward moment passed.

Hilda and Kate did not look at each other. In fact they assiduously avoided any form of exchange, wary of betraying Stan in his lie. Both remembered, only too vividly, the confrontation between father and daughter.

'Don't you realise what an *honour* it is for me to be accepted into Sydney Uni, Dad?' Kate had pleaded desperately. 'Particularly being a Queenslander. Sydney rarely accepts Queensland Vet Science students: their course is hugely overcrowded. Queenslanders always go to Brisbane –'

'Then why don't you?'

'Because Sydney has *accepted* me, that's why!' Kate had wanted to scream in her frustration. Why was he being so obtuse? 'Because my matriculation marks were the highest. Because they believe I'm academically gifted. Because among the applications they received from all over the country they chose to accept *me*! Why do you want to stand in my way? You should be *proud* of me. Shouldn't he, Marmee? Tell him for God's sake. He should be proud.'

'Let her go, Stanley,' Hilda had said. 'Let her go to Sydney.'

But Stan hadn't even glanced at his wife. He was annoyed. 'What's wrong with a Queensland university? You're looking down on your own kind now, are you, girl? You think you're too good for us.'

'That's not true at all.' Dear God he was being tiresome, she thought, tiresome and pigheaded. She was a Queenslander to her bootstraps and proud to be so, as he damn well knew. 'Townsville would offer as good an education I'm sure,' she said wearily, 'it's just that –'

'Then that's where you'll go.'

'No it's not, Dad.'

They'd stood their ground, facing each other off like a pair of duellists. She is openly defying me, Stan thought. How *dare* she! 'You'll bloody well do as you're told, girl.'

'No. No I won't do as I'm told,' she calmly replied. 'We're talking about the next five years of my life. It's my right to choose where I live those years.' That was the real truth of the matter, Kate realised. She was flattered to be accepted into Sydney University, it was true, but the city itself was the major attraction. She'd never been further south than Brisbane, and even then she'd been locked away in a boarding school. She wanted to experience life in a big city with all it had to offer. Much as she loved her home, Kate wanted to become part of a world that was far removed from Elianne. 'I'm sorry, Dad,' she'd said, 'but I'm going to Sydney Uni with or without your permission, and there's nothing you can do to stop me.'

'Oh isn't there?' he'd sneered. 'And what about money? You think you can live without an allowance, do you?'

'Certainly, if need be. I'll get a job waiting tables or serving in a shop – a lot of students do.'

Stan had known then that he'd lost the battle, that she'd go to Sydney, that he'd give her an allowance – no daughter of his would wait tables or serve in a shop!

The general buzz of conversation had returned to the table, and from her central position beside Bartholomew, Kate looked down towards the far end where her father was now chatting to Ivan. Or rather Ivan was chatting to her father. Perhaps the poor man is apologising for his faux pas, Kate thought, although why he should feel the need was beyond her.

Kate understood why her father had been so over-defensive. He was not accustomed to admitting defeat. He'd even claimed non-surrender as a family dictum. '"Never say die", that was Big Jim's motto,' Stan had boasted over the years. 'Never give in. Never admit defeat. That's the Durham way.'

As Kate studied her father, he turned to meet her gaze, either sensing he was under scrutiny or expecting to be, or perhaps both. Their eyes met, and the smile they shared was instantaneous. Both recognised the truth. Stan's declaration, pompous though it was, had been more than a matter of self-preservation. Stan *was* proud of his daughter. He was immensely proud. And his daughter knew it.

'Did you see them in Sydney, Kate?'

'See who, what?' Kate's attention was diverted by her brother Alan. Seated opposite her, Alan was flanked on either side by Paola and Georgio Fiorelli. The three, who had been friends their entire lives, were engaged in earnest conversation.

'The Beatles,' Alan said in a way that seemed to intimate she hadn't been paying attention. 'A gang of us tried to see them in Brisbane, but the teachers wouldn't let us out of school. They thought we'd be caught up in a riot.'

'Did *you* see them, Kate?' Paola asked eagerly. She was an attractive girl, with thick dark hair tied up in a pony-tail.

'Not in performance, I didn't go to the Stadium, but yes I did see them.'

'Really?' Paola was wide-eyed with excitement. 'Did you get to *meet* them?'

'Hardly.' Kate laughed. 'I stood outside the Sheraton Hotel in the pouring rain with hundreds of others.'

'Ringo wasn't there though, was he?' Alan said assertively, as if trying to catch her out.

'No, he was ill in hospital according to the newspapers. There was a replacement drummer, I don't know –'

'Jimmy Nicol.' Alan nodded knowingly. Then he added in an aside to Paola, 'Ringo joined them in Melbourne for the rest of the tour.'

He's showing off, Kate thought, and she wondered why. It wasn't at all like Alan to show off. Quietly confident in his own right, Alan usually left others to claim centre stage.

'Ringo was with them when they came to Brisbane,' Alan said to Paola. 'I would have seen him if only they'd let us out of school. Ringo's my favourite.'

'Paul's mine,' she replied.

'Me and Paola saw *A Hard Day's Night* at the pictures in Bundy,' thirteen-year-old Georgio piped up.

Alan was caught out. He hadn't seen the film yet. 'Ringo came up with that title, you know.'

'Did he?' Georgio was successfully distracted by the non sequitur.

'Yep, *A Hard Day's Night*, they got the title from something Ringo said. He's a lot smarter than people give him credit for.'

Alan continued to ignore his sister as he led the discussion into which member of the Beatles was the most influential, but Kate didn't mind. The reason for her brother's uncharacteristic behaviour was becoming patently obvious. Alan was out to impress Paola. How interesting, she thought. The two had grown up in each other's company, sharing each other's childhood, attending primary school together in South Kolan, but during this past year there'd clearly been a shift of balance in the relationship. It was not difficult to see why. Fifteen-year-old Paola was now a very pretty girl, and fifteen-year-old Alan had noticed.

The Christmas pudding arrived, huge and impressive, carried on a giant silver platter by none other than Cook herself. Cook's name was actually Maude, but the only person who called her Maude was Max, for the simple reason that Max was married to her. To everyone else she was known always as Cook. It was a term of respect. Cook was far more than a name: it was a title.

The appearance of Cook and the pudding drew a round of applause from the guests and successfully called a halt to Alan's dissertation on John Lennon. Kate smiled to herself. It was touching somehow to see her little brother so fiercely asserting his masculinity. She hoped that Paola was impressed.

Two weeks later, just after breakfast, the family and all five household staff members assembled in front of The Big

House for the presentation of Kate's eighteenth birthday present. Bartholomew Durham actually allowed himself to be assisted down the front stairs by his daughter-in-law in order not to hold up the proceedings. Kate herself was blindfolded and shepherded by her brothers, one on either side, out the main doors and down the stairs to the large circular driveway, the dogs following and joining in the excitement. There, Neil whipped off the blindfold and they all sang 'Happy Birthday' while she stared open-mouthed at the brand new Holden Premier Sedan in gleaming gun-metal grey with white roof, bucket seats and leather upholstery.

'Happy birthday, Kate,' Stan said as he handed her the keys.

When hugs had been exchanged and the general delirium had died down, the staff departed and Bartholomew wended his way back up the stairs, independently this time, at his customary snail's pace. It was then that Stan, with a glance at his wife, attempted to put a proviso on the gift.

'We thought it might perhaps be best if the car stayed here at Elianne –' he started to say, but he didn't get any further.

'Don't be ridiculous, Dad.' Kate laughed out loud, as if he'd actually been joking. 'You can't give me a car and then tell me not to drive it.'

Yes, Stan supposed, that did sound a bit silly – it had been Hilda's idea and Hilda was often unrealistic. Kate was an experienced driver, after all. She'd been driving on the estate since she was fourteen years old, as had all three of his children – indeed Alan had been driving since he was twelve. But a sense of trepidation remained nonetheless. The traffic in Sydney was horrendous. On the numerous trips he'd made himself over the years, he'd always hired a chauffeur-driven limousine. Never once had he chosen to drive the city streets himself.

Kate was aware of her father's misgivings, and also of the reasons for them. Of course Stan Durham would find Sydney traffic daunting. He was the product of a time that had moved more slowly than the sixties, and he was accustomed to wide, open spaces.

'I'll be careful, Dad, I promise.' She gave him another hug. Then she added cheekily, 'It's only a city you know, like Brisbane but bigger,' and Stan felt thoroughly patronised.

Kate turned to her brothers. 'Do you want to come for a drive?'

'Rhetorical question,' Neil said with a grin. 'Where'll we go?'

'Where do you *want* to go?' She looked from one to the other.

'Bargara,' Alan replied boldly, knowing it was probably further than she'd intended. 'We could go for a swim.'

'Rightio. Grab your togs.' Then the thought occurred that it might be a courtesy to check with her parents. 'Is that all right?' she asked.

'Of course, dear,' her mother replied, 'just so long as you make sure that you drive very, very carefully.' Hilda herself had never driven a vehicle in the whole of her life. She didn't know how, and had no desire to learn. 'If you're going to loll around on the beach,' she added, 'you might want to take along a picnic lunch. I shall ask Cook; I'm sure she'll be happy to prepare some sandwiches.' She started towards the stairs. 'Now I really must go inside, Stanley, it's becoming altogether too hot out here in the driveway.'

'Make sure you're back by late afternoon,' Stan called over his shoulder as he joined his wife. 'Cook's planned a special birthday dinner.' Even Stan the Man deferred to Cook.

As her parents left, another thought occurred to Kate.

'Hey, Alan,' she said, 'why don't you ask Paola to come along?'

'All right,' he replied, doing his best to sound casual, 'good idea.'

'Better ask Georgio too.'

'Yep,' Alan said regretfully.

But as fortune would have it, Georgio was playing football that afternoon, so Alan and Paola had the back seat all to themselves.

They drove the fifteen miles to Bundaberg, crossing over the old bridge that forded the Burnett River and into the centre of town. Solid, grand and ornately designed, the old Burnett Bridge had served Bundaberg's traffic since the birth of the century.

A number of heads turned as they drove up and down the main road; Neil waved through the open passenger window to the people he knew. 'You can feel the envy from here,' he said.

'Yes, she's a bit conspicuously new, isn't she,' Kate smiled and gave the steering wheel an affectionate caress, 'I might have to muddy her up a bit.'

They paraded up and down the entire length of Bourbong Street, Bundaberg's massively broad main thoroughfare, where vehicles were parked down the centre of the road and on both curbsides, and where bustling shops and businesses did a roaring trade. They passed pretty Buss Park and the elegant stone building that was the School of Arts, and they passed the imposing clock-faced tower of the post office. Rising above the general cityscape like a giant exclamation mark carved out of stone, the post office clock tower was the unmistakeable symbol of Bundy.

Then in only a matter of minutes they were out of town and on the road to Bargara, the coastal settlement that lay nine miles to the east.

The day was hot and they drove with the windows down, the warm wind whipping their hair. None of them minded – they loved the heat. The landscape they passed through was the familiar flat, open plains of cane country. Here and there some fields lay fallow, rich and red-brown, but mostly they were surrounded by a waving green mass of sugar cane in various stages of maturity.

Several miles before reaching the coast, however, they passed an anomaly in the landscape. There it was to their right: the Hummock, rising incongruously two hundred feet above the sea of cane, the only hill in the entire district.

'Dad and I took a bloke from Sydney on a sightseeing tour a month or so back,' Neil said, 'and he reckoned it looked like a pimple.'

'A pimple,' Alan piped up from the back seat, 'you're joking.'

'No, I'm not. "A pimple on the face of an otherwise unblemished landscape", those were his exact words. He was a journalist,' Neil added as if that explained everything, 'doing a story on the sugar industry. He was just trying to sound smart, that's all.'

'I hope you set him straight. Did you tell him it was once an active volcano?'

'No, I was a bit more precise. I told him it was a cinder cone and the reason these lands were so fertile. He ended up putting that in the article, but he couldn't resist adding the pimple on the landscape quote as well, trying to be smart like I said – thinks he's Ernest Hemingway.'

'Well it's our pimple,' Alan replied tersely. 'It's our hill, the only one we've got, and we like it.'

'I think it's pretty,' Paola said, turning to catch a last glimpse of the Hummock through the rear windscreen.

Bargara, fronting the Coral Sea, had been a popular seaside resort for decades, a holiday-maker's haven where grassy slopes fringed long, sandy beaches and swaying coconut palms and pandanus trees gave a flavour of the tropics.

'Where to?' Kate asked. 'Neilson Park?' Neilson Park was the surf beach particularly favoured by the young bloods. It boasted a long-established Lifesaving Club of which the locals were justifiably proud.

'Yep,' her brothers chorused; both were keen body surfers.

Immediately upon arrival, they stripped down to their bathing costumes and headed for the water, or rather Kate and her brothers did. Paola chose to sit on the beach and watch. Unlike the Durham siblings, she was not confident in the surf.

After ten minutes or so, Alan jogged up from the water's edge.

'Aren't you coming in?' he asked, plonking himself down on the sand beside her, inadvertently spraying her with water as he flicked back his wet hair.

'It's a bit rough for me,' she said apologetically.

He looked at the waves. 'Really? You've got to be joking.' The surf was extremely mild.

'I'm not a very good swimmer,' she admitted, shame-faced.

'Oh. I didn't know that.' Alan was surprised. They'd been to the beach together on family picnics a number of times over the years and he'd never noticed Paola was a poor swimmer. But then, he thought, there was probably a lot he hadn't noticed about Paola.

'I usually avoid the surf. That way people don't find out.' She gave a rueful shrug. 'I look Italian enough as it is,' she added, 'and being a lousy swimmer's so terribly un-Australian.'

He didn't get the connection. 'What's wrong with looking Italian?'

'Nothing I suppose.' She shrugged again, carelessly this time. Then with a sudden change of heart, and much to her own surprise, she found herself confessing. 'Well yes, there is actually. I was born here. I'm Australian. I get sick of people calling me a dago and thinking I'm a foreigner just because of the way I look.'

There was a pause before Alan's response, which strangely enough popped out with the greatest of ease. He didn't feel in the least self-conscious.

'I love the way you look.'

'Do you?' She flushed with pleasure. 'Do you really?'
'Yep. You look just like Natalie Wood.'
Paola burst out laughing. 'Natalie Wood's not Italian.'
'She looks Italian.'
'Natalie Wood's about as American as you can get.'
'She's not actually.' Alan's tone held an air of superiority. 'She's Russian-American – I read that in a magazine somewhere.' Then he added with a ring of triumph, 'So what about that? Natalie Wood's Russian-American and you're Italian-Australian. You should be proud of your ancestry, Paola. I'll bet *she* is.'

'I am.' Paolo flushed again. She was very prone to flushing, but this time it was with guilt. She felt she'd betrayed her family in admitting her private secret to Alan Durham, and she wished now that she hadn't. 'I am proud,' she said, staring down at the sand.

'Of course you are.' Alan cursed himself. He'd been clumsy and hurtful. His intention had been to offer encouragement, not criticism. He reached out and took her hand, unsure of what he should say to make amends.

She looked up from the sand and met his gaze.

'I meant it as a compliment, you know. When I said that you look like Natalie Wood?' He thought how terribly lame and pathetic he sounded.

Paola could see the desperation in his eyes. 'I know you did.' She smiled. 'And I'm flattered. Thank you.' *I love the way you look too*, she thought, *so solemn and serious, and yet when you smile so like a little boy.*

Alan breathed a sigh of relief and then stood abruptly, pulling her to her feet. 'Right,' he said, 'let's go to The Basin and I'll give you a swimming lesson.' A mile and a half around the point, past the holiday bungalows and the golf course and the rocky outcrops of basalt that typified the area, another long sandy beach boasted a still-water tidal swimming pool. Many years previously, Kanaka workers had erected the low-slung wall of black boulders that encircled the pool and 'The Basin' had been a favourite choice for families with small children ever since. 'Come on,' he said, releasing her hand and picking up his towel.

'No, no,' she insisted, 'I'm perfectly happy here. Really I am.'

'Well I'm not. I want to go to The Basin.'

'That's absolute rubbish, Alan,' she said, calling his bluff. 'You don't want to swim with a bunch of little kids.'

'Of course I don't. I want to swim with you.' He dumped his towel back on the sand. 'Won't be a tick, I'll just tell the others.' And Paola watched as he jogged off.

Alan swam out to where Kate and Neil were standing chest-deep waiting eagle-eyed for the next wave.

'Paola and I want to go to The Basin,' he said.

'Oh, all right,' Neil was puzzled, obviously wondering why, but good-natured as always, he was happy to oblige. 'One more wave in and we'll join you.'

'No we won't.' Kate's look to him was so laced with meaning that Neil was baffled and suitably silenced. 'We'll meet up with you at The Basin in a couple of hours, Al, say about one o'clock. I'll bring the car around and we'll have lunch there.'

'Right you are then.' Alan swam off, catching a small wave that took him halfway to shore.

'What was that all about?' Neil asked.

'I think they want to be alone.'

'*What?*' Her brother's expression was comically incredulous. 'You mean *Alan and Paola* ...' The rest was left unsaid.

Kate nodded. 'I can't answer for her, but *he's* keen, I know that much.'

'Well, well, little brother's growing up, eh?' Neil grinned. 'I must say he shows good taste. Paola's become quite a looker.'

'Don't you dare tease him,' she warned.

'As if I'd do such a dastardly thing,' he replied with mock innocence. Then he noticed the waves looming out to sea. 'Hey, there's a good run coming up.'

The conversation stopped right there as the bigger waves started to roll in. But Kate knew there'd been no real need to sound a warning: Neil was always sensitive to the feelings of others.

They joined up for lunch, the four of them devouring Cook's ham and pickle sandwiches, and, after a dip in The Basin to wash off the yellow stain from the ripe mangoes that had followed, they packed the car and set off on the drive home.

Neil was at the wheel this time. Kate had promised Alan a drive too, although they'd need to wait until they were back on the estate as he was under-age, but Alan, oddly enough, hadn't appeared all that interested.

During the drive, Alan and Paola were quiet in the back seat, but Kate had noticed as she'd climbed into the passenger side that they were holding hands. Of course, she told herself, he doesn't need to show off any more. How completely together they are in each other's company, she thought, how content and at one. Is it possible, she wondered briefly, for fifteen-year-olds to be in love?

Beside her, Neil glanced in the rear-vision mirror. Well, well, he thought, little brother has a girlfriend.

The Krantzes' move to Bundaberg was slow and methodical, but also highly efficient, in keeping with Ivan's approach to both business and life. The offices of Krantz & Son had been well set up in advance and the home he'd bought on the outskirts of town was well-appointed with new furnishings, the plan being that once he and his wife and son had made the move, they could take their time picking through those of their possessions that remained at old Elianne House. Stan had assured them there was no rush as the house was to be demolished, and Hilda had been only too grateful that the old home was to be spared that little bit longer, perhaps in the naive hope that there might be some last-minute reprieve.

It was early February before the house was finally deserted and plans were set in motion for its demolition.

'How fortunate you are not to be here for that saddest of days,' Hilda said as Kate pulled the Holden up in the driveway of old Elianne House. Kate was leaving for Sydney in two days. She'd decided to go back several weeks early in order to find a place of her own. She'd given ample notice before the holidays that she would not be returning to the flat she'd shared with three fellow students, although she'd not told them why. She'd had her reasons at the time and she still did. Now more than ever Jeremy was beckoning.

'You won't have to stand by and watch it you know,' Kate said as the two of them climbed out of the car. 'You could plan a trip into Bundy on that saddest of days.'

'It would not ease the pain, Kate,' Hilda said a little tartly; sometimes her daughter's practicality was annoying. 'I would know it was happening.'

They walked up the front steps together. The old home, so similar in design to The Big House, was a Queenslander built on stilts and surrounded by wide verandahs, but the living area was restricted to one floor only with storage space beneath. Indeed, Stanley Durham in having The Big House designed along the lines of the original had been true to his promise: 'the same only bigger'.

'To think she brought up three children here,' Hilda said, running her fingers reverently over panelled surfaces and carved wooden fixtures. 'Married so young, half-French as she was and new to the country, how foreign it must all have seemed ...'

Kate had prepared herself for a running diatribe about Grandmother Ellie and the past.

'And oh, the tragedies she suffered,' Hilda continued. 'Well, they both did of course: they shared the heartache.

Losing two sons in the Great War, just imagine the pain.' She floated through to the next room like a wraith, her hand trailing over surfaces as if making contact with another life.

Kate couldn't romanticise the house herself. Pretty as the detail and the fixtures were, the house now empty and unlived-in was just a house. How interesting, she thought as she followed her mother, that the rooms are so much smaller than I remember from my childhood visits.

'It was their great love that gave them the strength to carry on.' Hilda suddenly stopped floating and they came to a halt in the main drawing room. 'Throughout all of their trials, Big Jim and Ellie always had each other.'

Kate couldn't help but register the note of regret in her mother's voice. Why? she wondered. What did her mother regret?

'Ellie lived the whole of her married life in this house,' Hilda said. 'The early days in particular must have been so very happy.' She remembered how happy she'd been in the early days of her own marriage. But things had changed when they'd moved into The Big House. That was when the babies had arrived and Stan had become unfaithful. Nothing serious, just dalliances, only two, and neither had lasted long. She'd supposed that many men with children needed dalliances in order to keep them distracted from the mundane aspects of parenthood. But she'd been so shockingly disillusioned. How she'd longed for a great love like Ellie's and Big Jim's, a love without dalliances, a love where fidelity was sacred.

'Are you all right, Marmee?' Kate asked, concerned. Her mother's silence was puzzling, and she looked worryingly sad.

'Of course I'm all right, my darling.' Hilda painted on a bright smile, 'just saying goodbye to the past.' My own or Ellie's? she wondered momentarily. 'That's always a little affecting.' She looked about the drawing room. 'Despite her share of tragedy, Grandmother Ellie was very happy here. She told me so. I remember the occasion well. She was sitting over there, on the little pink sofa that used to live by the window,' Hilda's voice took on a distant quality, 'and she told me that the isolation hadn't bothered her at all. She told me that she hadn't minded in the least being marooned out here in the middle of nowhere.'

Kate had the sudden feeling that her mother was referring more to herself than she was to Grandmother Ellie. Did *Hilda* feel marooned out here in the middle of nowhere? When she was first married she may well have done, Kate thought, for isolation would have remained very much a governing factor in the forties. Was that why she drank?

Hilda snapped out of her pensive mood. 'The women were so terribly alone in those early days,' she said, and once again she was on the move, gliding off towards the dining room.

Kate followed in silence.

'It's different for you modern young things,' she continued with an airy wave of her hand. 'You have your independence with the roads as they are and your very own cars.'

Kate didn't state the obvious. Her mother was only forty-four. She could learn to drive if she wished. Independence was hers for the asking. But Hilda Durham refused any form of driving tuition. She was accustomed to being chauffeured and preferred things that way, even though it made her reliant upon others.

They wandered around the house for a further fifteen minutes, Hilda chatty and animated, refusing to give in to another maudlin bout.

'Well I suppose that's it,' she said finally. 'I do believe we've successfully farewelled the past, wouldn't you agree?'

'Yes, I would.'

They walked down the front stairs to the car.

'There's a trunk load of Grandmother Ellie's old books under the house,' Hilda said. 'They'll need to be cleared out of course and donated to some charity or other. Would you like to look through them before I have Max take them into town?'

'Yes, I would.'

'Half of them are in French, so you're the only one who'd be able to understand them anyway,' she said with a light laugh. At school Kate's language of choice had been French, and like the rest of her subjects her matriculation results had been excellent. 'Goodness knows what we'll do with that particular lot,' Hilda added as she climbed into the passenger seat, 'I suppose Max will simply have to find a French charity.'

'I'll come back tomorrow and go through them.' Kate started up the engine. 'There might well be some I'd like to keep, particularly among the French editions.'

As they drove off, Hilda gazed back at the old house. 'Yes,' she said her mood again pensive and her voice distant, 'I remember Grandmother Ellie loved her books. They were very precious to her. She was always reading. Perhaps it was her form of escape.'

Once again, Kate sensed that her mother wasn't really talking about Grandmother Ellie.

The following morning, rather than walking as she would normally have done without the need to chauffeur her mother, Kate drove to the old house once again. It would save her carrying home any of the books she might choose to keep, and they could simply stay in the boot of the car ready for the following day when she would set off on her drive to Sydney.

She discovered the trunk sitting in a protected corner in the storage area beneath the house, surrounded by a number of empty packing cases. It was not locked and she opened it without any difficulty.

She'd expected that after twelve years, damp might have set in and that the books might be mouldy, but they certainly were not. The trunk was airtight and the books had been packed with great care, wads of folded tissue paper resting between each layer as if protecting items of the most delicate crystal. Kate found the degree of care taken touching. Following Ellie's death, the trunk would have been packed upon Big Jim's orders, he could possibly even have packed it himself, although that was doubtful, she thought, for he'd been over ninety when Ellie had died. But either way, the intention was obvious. Big Jim had wished to preserve his wife's precious books in respect for her memory.

Kneeling on the ground, Kate lifted the books from the trunk one by one and placed them on the tissue paper that she'd spread out beside her. There were publications in both English and French, and she made a separate pile of each. It was the French editions she was most interested in for they were harder to come by.

Despite the gloom beneath the house, enough light shone through the wooden lattice work for her to read the authors and titles with ease. Balzac, Dumas, Hugo, collections of poetry by Voltaire and Baudelaire ... Grandmother Ellie certainly enjoyed her French classics, Kate thought. There were several de Maupassant and Zola, and then moving into the twentieth century, Colette, André Gide ... There were also French translations of other great European writers: a copy of Tolstoy's *Anna Karenina* and Dostoevsky's *Crime and Punishment*.

Kate was fascinated. The fact that her great-grandmother had been an eclectic reader as well as an avid one came as no particular surprise, but the condition of the books did. Some were admittedly more worn than others, but considering their age, most were in a pristine state. She checked the publication dates and discovered that many were much later editions than she would have expected. Some had been published in the 1930s and even the late 1940s, when her great-grandmother would have been elderly.

Again, Kate found the fact touching. Big Jim had obviously gone to a great deal of trouble and expense to import French editions for his wife throughout their marriage. Yet Ellie was bilingual. She could just as easily have read the English translations that were readily available in Australia. Big Jim's gesture seemed to Kate an act of genuine love.

There were two books that did show definite wear and tear, however, one an English edition, the other French. Charlotte Brontë's *Jane Eyre* and Victor Hugo's *Notre-Dame de Paris* were decidedly dilapidated. Old favourites perhaps? Kate opened the flyleaf of both. Inside was inscribed *Elianne Desmarais*. Old favourites, indeed, she thought. Ellie must have brought them with her from the New Hebrides. No doubt they symbolised the dual cultures she'd inherited from her English mother and French father.

There were no more books as such left in the trunk, but sitting in the bottom was further material that looked like business accounts. They were ledgers, at least a dozen of them. She lifted one out and opened it, expecting to see some form of book-keeping, but the ledger's columns, normally reserved for figures, were ignored. The page was instead covered in the written word, and the written word was French. She squinted in the gloom. She could just make out a date at the top. *10 juillet 1895*

Kate took the ledger outside into the sunlight. She sat on the front step and read the first paragraph slowly, translating as she went.

Today there was such excitement. Our steam locomotive engine, which Jim acquired from the government, has finally arrived. It is a Neilson A10 locomotive, or so he informs me. Apparently the government has moved on to more sophisticated models. I have never seen Jim so enthused. He says it will change our lives and I am quite sure it will, but for my part I find it a rather messy thing, belching steam as it does, and noisy too. I shall miss the Clydesdales hauling the trucks along the tracks, such beautiful creatures. But of course we must move with these modern times ...

Grandmother Ellie's diaries, Kate thought. Oh my God, the ledgers are Grandmother Ellie's diaries. She couldn't wait to tell her mother. She would translate them for her, read them out loud, and Hilda would hear Grandmother Ellie's voice, she'd hear the voice of the young Ellie about whom she'd always fantasised.

Kate was thrilled by the prospect. This would give a reality to her mother's preoccupation with the past. No longer would Hilda Durham need to disappear into her fantasy world: she could experience the real thing.

She returned to the trunk, gathered up all the ledgers and brought them outside. The diaries would need to be sorted through for they were obviously not in sequential order.

Spreading them out on the front steps, she checked the dates – where she could find them for many entries were undated – then she placed the ledgers in sequence and looked at her watch. It was a good hour or so before lunch would be served at The Big House. She couldn't resist.

13 avril 1888

Once again Kate read slowly, translating each word with care.

I write this in the empty ledgers that Jim is happy to supply. He thinks that my scribbling will keep me happy, distract me from the loneliness of my surrounds, and I can only pray that he proves right. My scribbles will of course remain in French. There is no one in the household acquainted with the language and I intend to be honest. I must. Otherwise this exercise will be fruitless. Only truth can provide the escape I need ...

Chapter Three

My father sold me to James Durham. Papa denies this of course, but I know it to be true. I openly accused him ...

'Don't be ridiculous, child.' André Desmarais scoffed at his daughter's accusation. In fact he did more than scoff, he threw back his huge bearded head and laughed out loud. 'What a fanciful creature you are, *ma petite*. James Durham loves you. He's loved you from the moment he first met you, he told me so. He's simply been waiting for you to come of age. And he's a wealthy man – he will make a great match, you couldn't do better for yourself.'

'I am to interpret that as a denial, I presume?'

'Of course you are.' In the light of her coldness, André realised he could not afford to be glib. 'Now you listen to me, Elianne, I am agreeing to this marriage for your own good. James Durham can offer you a life of privilege in Australia, a life no prospective suitor from around these parts could provide. It is your future I am thinking of. Why otherwise would I deprive myself of my only child? With your mother now gone who will look after me in my declining years?'

'A noble sacrifice indeed, Papa,' her tone remained icy. 'So no money is changing hands?'

'Not one sou, I swear it.'

Elianne knew better than to push the matter any further; her father would continue to deny a transaction was taking place, and perhaps he wasn't even lying. Perhaps no money was changing hands, at least not in the physical sense. But she wondered just how much of the considerable financial debt he owed James Durham might be dropped upon his agreement to her marriage.

'Very well,' she said with a disdainful shrug, 'if you are happy for your daughter to wed such a man, who am I to disobey your wishes? I don't care either way personally, but I warn you, you are the one who will bear the shame.'

For all her disdain, Elianne did care, but she was not about to share the fact with her father. The truth was she found James Durham attractive, despite her aversion to his rumoured background. Furthermore, his offer of marriage held definite appeal, for since the death of her beloved mother, Beatrice, life on the coconut plantation had become intolerable. These days, her father kept open house for his raucous drunken gambling companions, rough men employed by the Compagnie Calédonienne des Nouvelle Hébrides to oversee the company's extensive interests in the islands. The men would invariably stay overnight, and no longer were they accommodated in the nearby guesthouse as they had been in Beatrice's time, if indeed they'd been invited at all. Rather, they would stay in the main house. A comfortable sprawling bungalow, the main house had a number of guest rooms, and Elianne was forced to endure the men's company at close quarters. She detested the way they ogled her. But she detested far more the way her father allowed it. Her father actually appeared proud that his friends lusted after his daughter.

Elianne detested everything about her father, whom she considered the vilest of ingrates. The reason André Desmarais's copra plantation had thrived in previous years had been due to the financial acumen of his astute English wife and the expertise of his hard-working French overseer, both of whose efforts had been not only unappreciated, but barely even recognised. And now, since Beatrice's death, the ever-loyal Michel Salet was faced with an ongoing battle to prevent his employer, whom he also considered his friend, gambling away the last of the company's profits. Elianne knew her father to be a liar, a hypocrite and a thief, and much as she would miss her friends on the plantation and in the small township of Port Vila, James Durham and Australia offered a welcome escape.

'It is you who will suffer the humiliation of having married your daughter off to a blackbirder, Papa,' she continued, 'and you know the contempt with which such men are held in society these days, not only in Vila, but –'

'James Durham is hardly a blackbirder,' André interrupted testily, offended by the term, as she'd intended he should be. 'James Durham is a wealthy plantation owner who has recently built his own sugar mill! Good God, child, a man in his position does not kidnap and enslave island workers! He employs indentured labour through government-appointed agents as the law dictates.'

'But he *was* a blackbirder, wasn't he, Papa?' Determined to have the last word, Elianne continued to needle her father, experiencing a perverse form of pleasure in his annoyance. 'I believe that's how he came by his fortune, is it not? Some years ago as a young man –?'

'He would need to have been a very young man indeed, Elianne.' Once again André interrupted his daughter, but this time in a patronising fashion. 'Considering he is not yet thirty years of age. His wealth, as you very well know, comes directly from his moneyed English family, who financed his interests in the colonies.'

'Yes, so he has told me,' she replied sceptically, 'but I have heard other stories. Pavi Salet says that not so very many years ago the islanders feared James Durham. Many accept employment from him now, I know, but he was not always respectable, Papa, as I'm sure you're aware. I've heard that as a very young man he was ruthless and brutal and that the islanders lived in fear of him. They called him "Big Jim".'

'Well of course they called him Big Jim, you stupid child,' André exploded. Her needling was successfully pushing him towards the limits of his patience. 'He's a big man and they're simple-minded blacks, what else would you expect them to call him?!'

'Pavi was twelve years old when his uncle and others of his family were taken from Ambrym,' Elianne continued, unfazed by her father's outburst. 'Pavi himself was here at the plantation when it happened, but he told me that upon a trip home with his mother, his aunties had sworn it was Big Jim who led the raid on the village.'

'That's enough, Elianne!' The angry light in her father's eyes warned her she'd gone too far. 'You're speaking of the man you're about to marry. I will not have you quote to me the lies you've heard from an ignorant savage.'

But André had in turn angered his daughter.

'That ignorant savage, as you call him, Papa, happens to be the son of your good friend, Michel Salet, who –'

'Who married a savage,' André snarled, 'which makes him a black-lover, and his son a savage just like his mother.'

For the first time in their exchange, Elianne found herself at a loss for words. Her father and his friends often spoke in a derogatory manner of the islanders, which she found offensive, for there were many loyal, hard-working natives employed at the plantation. Over the years, though, she had become inured to the bigotry that surrounded her. Now, upon hearing Pavi referred to in such a way, she was shocked.

'Pavi is my best friend,' she said after a pause, her expression bewildered, her tone disbelieving. 'We grew up together. We shared the same tutor.'

'Your mother's idea.' André nodded, thankful that he'd made an impact and finally gained her attention. 'Beatrice and Michel were always as thick as thieves. I gave in to her whim and allowed the two of you to be tutored together, but I should never have let it happen. You can't let crossbreeds mix with whites like that; it simply doesn't work.'

She was looking at him oddly: it was clear she didn't understand. 'You're seventeen years old, *ma petite*,' he explained, 'you cannot mingle with the blacks the way you did as a child. They're an inferior race, you must understand that,' he smiled as if to soften the blow, 'even one who is the son of a Frenchman.'

'A Frenchman who is your friend,' she said, still with an air of bewilderment.

'That is so,' he agreed, 'but friendship does not alter the fact that his son is black.'

André had never once considered Michel Salet his friend. He'd employed the man because of his expertise in the production of copra, and he'd allowed the semblance of a friendship to develop, but how could one claim as a friend a man who'd married a black? Michel had debased himself. Sleeping with native women was perfectly acceptable, even keeping a black mistress was not frowned upon, but one did not marry them and raise their children as white.

'I have nothing against Pavi,' he assured her. 'My God, the boy has such a way with horses I don't know what I'd do without him. He knows his place, what's more. Despite his education, he's made no attempt to rise above his station and of even greater importance he's chosen to marry one of his own kind.' André's smile was magnanimous. 'I hope he and Mela find great happiness in their union.' André Desmarais very much approved of young Pavi's engagement to his housemaid. It would prevent further cross-breeding.

Interpreting his daughter's silence as submission, and relieved their argument was over, he kissed her gently on the forehead. 'Just think, Elianne, you will be eighteen in the New Year. In little more than one month, *ma petite*, you will be eighteen, and then you will be married. Just think of that. How your life will change.'

'Yes, Papa, it will.' Now more than ever, Elianne longed for that change.

Upon leaving her father, she went directly to her room, where she donned a practical straw bonnet, tying the ribbon securely beneath her chin. She relied solely upon bonnets for protection from the sun, preferring to walk without the impediment of a parasol. Then exchanging her light satin slippers for her walking boots, she set off to find Pavi.

She checked the stables first. Pavi's natural way with animals had seen him recently promoted to stable manager and as such he was indispensable to her father. He wasn't there, however, so she set off through the plantation, knowing where he was most likely to be.

As she strode along one of the many avenues that led through the endless rows of coconut trees, the heavy cotton fabric of her ankle-length skirt swished busily against the undergrowth. For practical purposes she eschewed the bustle, which remained the fashion of the day, but the neatly nipped-in waist of her skirt and the fullness of her petticoats only served to accentuate the elegance of her figure.

She kept up a comfortable pace; she enjoyed walking. High above her, the leaves of the palms billowed like green explosions against the clearest of blue skies, but she knew that the weather might well become unpredictable. The day was blisteringly hot and still now, but this was December and a tropical storm could sweep in with little warning.

The processing area, towards the western perimeter of the plantation, was a twenty-minute walk from the house, and as she stepped out from the trees and into the clearing she saw Pavi at the drying racks. He was working alongside his father as she'd expected he would be. A number of native workers were squatting on the ground preparing the coconuts, some clearing away the husk, others cleaving the nuts in half on chopping blocks and draining them of their liquid. Michel and Pavi were spreading the halved coconuts out on the racks, meat side up, to dry in the sun, while beneath the structure nearby several other workers were tending the kilns. For the drying process, which was essential in the production of copra, Michel Salet chose to employ a mixture of both methods, invariably achieving the perfect balance.

Father and son greeted her upon approach, and a number of the workers gave her a wave.

'*Bonjour mam'selle*,' some said, or, "'allo missy,' in the local Pidgin English. Elianne was popular with the workers.

'Are we safe with the weather, Michel?' she asked, gesturing at the coconuts laid out on the racks.

'Yes, quite safe,' he assured her, 'until tomorrow afternoon I would say. We will transfer them to the kilns then, just to be sure.' Among his many other talents, Michel Salet was a walking barometer.

'May I borrow your son for half an hour?'

'Of course you may, Elianne.' Michel smiled and turned to his son. 'Take your time, Pavi, we have plenty of workers.'

'Thank you, Papa.'

Pavi, who had been working bare-chested, donned his shirt as a measure of respect for Elianne and they set off through the trees. Like many of mixed race, he was a good-looking young man, olive-skinned and fine-featured.

They walked for ten minutes through the rows of coconut palms to the edge of the plantation, where they emerged from the trees into a rocky clearing. Here the land sloped down to the valley, and in the distance beyond the lush tropical vegetation was the blue of the sea. It was a favourite place of theirs.

They sat on the rocks and looked out at the view. They hadn't spoken as they'd walked: there'd been no need. They were comfortable with silence. Sometimes they would gaze at the view without saying a word, other times they would ignore its beauty altogether and talk non-stop. The two were very much at ease in each other's company.

Today though was a day for talking, and it was Elianne who broke the silence. She couldn't wait to tell him her news. 'You're not the only one about to be married, Pavi,' she said.

Pavi stared at her in surprise. He'd not known that Elianne was being courted. He had courted Mela for a whole eight months before they'd announced their betrothal. They'd been just seventeen. Now eighteen and lovers, they both yearned to be wed so that their trysts need no longer be conducted in secret.

'You're to be married,' he said, 'really?'

'Yes, really,' she said.

She launched into her story, his eyes growing wider and wider with surprise as she recounted the exchange that had occurred between her and her father.

'You declared James Durham a blackbirder,' Pavi winced comically, 'that was perhaps not a wise thing to do.'

'I know,' she admitted. 'I hope I haven't caused trouble for you, telling Papa about your aunties and Big Jim.'

Pavi shrugged. 'He'll just think it's the gossip of silly black women.' Although Elianne had omitted any mention of her father's comments about 'ignorant savages' Pavi was fully aware of André Desmarais's contempt for the islanders.

'On the contrary, I had the distinct impression that it came as no great surprise. Papa was angered and denied any truth to the rumour of course, but he knows there's something questionable in James Durham's past, I can tell. He protested a little too vehemently.'

'How do you feel about this marriage, Elianne?' Pavi eyed her keenly. Her happiness was all that mattered.

She searched for a truthful answer. 'I will be sad to leave Efate, and sad to leave you, Pavi, but I will not be sad to leave Papa.'

'And James Durham? The man himself, how do you feel about him?'

Again she answered truthfully. 'I have to admit that, despite the rumours, I have always found him to be charming.'

She is attracted to him, Pavi thought. I can see it in her eyes. She could love this man. 'Then do not listen to the rumours,' he said, 'they may well be hearsay. And even if they are not, James Durham would have been very young in those days and obeying orders from others. Men change with time.'

She smiled gratefully, feeling somehow absolved of a crime she had not yet committed. 'I shall miss you so, Pavi.'

'And I you. But we have left our childhood behind, Elianne. It is time to move on.'

James Durham arrived in Port Vila three weeks later. André picked him up at the docks in a horse and trap and transported him to the plantation. His visits as a rule were of only two or three days' duration, but this time he planned to stay for a full fortnight while preparations were made for the wedding. It was his intention that these two weeks should serve as an opportunity to become better acquainted with his future wife, and she with him. He had informed the Frenchman that he would not stay in one of the guest rooms at the main house as he usually did, for propriety demanded he should not sleep under the same roof as his fiancée. Instead he would reside at the modest guesthouse a quarter mile away. Upon his further instruction the guesthouse, which was normally reserved for those visitors considered of secondary importance, was to be freshly refurbished as that was where he and his wife would spend their wedding night. James himself would pay for the costs incurred.

All of these arrangements had been set in place during his trip to Efate a good month previously, when the two men had come to their arrangement. The debt that André Desmarais had accrued over the past two years, a debt which could have crippled him had James chosen to demand immediate payment in full, was to be cancelled upon the marriage agreement.

'Do you think she will accept me?' James had asked.

A giant of a man, with a build that matched the six feet four inches of his height and a nature that appeared fearless, James Durham had seemed curiously unsure of himself.

'Hah! Why should you doubt it?' The Frenchman had scorned the very notion. 'What woman of sound mind could possibly refuse the life of privilege you offer?'

'But perhaps she would not welcome me as a husband. Perhaps she thinks me too old – I am more than a decade her senior.'

'An excellent age difference in a marriage,' André had assured him, 'and you're wrong, my young friend. She likes you very much.' Then he'd added suggestively, 'I've seen the twinkle in her eye when she's in your company, believe me I have.' André had seen no such thing, but then he hadn't been looking. James Durham's offer, welcome and timely as it was, had been completely unexpected. 'In fact I get the distinct impression that she may be in love with you.'

James had known the man was lying, but he'd left Efate praying the old rogue would prove right and that Elianne would accept him. He'd been besotted with the girl from the instant he'd met her, a green-eyed beauty of fifteen, blossoming on the threshold of womanhood. He'd vowed then and there to make her his wife, and he'd been quite content to wait until she was of age. The wait had in fact proved convenient. It had allowed him time to steadily embroil her father in debt, which had not been difficult given the Frenchman's propensity for gambling and his careless ineptitude under the influence of alcohol. James himself could drink any man under the table, not that he ever tried, for he had no wish to best others in such a common pursuit, but many a wager and many a card game had been won taking advantage of those who could not hold their liquor. André Desmarais had been easy game. The only possible obstacle to James's plans had been Elianne herself. Would she have him?

She would, as it turned out. And now James Durham had arrived in Efate triumphant and ready to claim his bride. But he would do so properly; all must be in order. He had determined to court his fiancée and put her at her ease. She would no doubt be nervous at the prospect of marriage to a man she barely knew, and the thought of life in a foreign land must surely be daunting.

'Would you care to walk with me, Elianne?' he asked as Mela cleared the teacups from the sitting-room table.

'Yes, James, but not just in the garden. May we go further afield this morning?' He'd been at the plantation for two days now and both mornings they'd promenaded about the front garden.

The garden, which had once been Beatrice's pride and joy but had become overgrown and jungle-like since her death, was now returned to its former glory in preparation for the wedding. The small central fountain bubbled again, the vines of the arbour were neatly trimmed, and hibiscus, frangipani and jasmine blossoms provided both colour and fragrance. Elianne loved the garden's resurrection, but she found the exercise of promenading around its paths in a pretty bonnet with matching parasol most unsatisfactory. Furthermore, the conversation she and James had shared as they'd walked had been as mundane as that conducted over the dining table at meal times. She appreciated his show of propriety, but she was becoming bored.

'Of course we may go further afield,' he agreed, 'if that is what you wish. Where would you suggest?'

'I'll show you. Please wait here while I change into my walking boots.' In her bedroom, she conceded an attractive feathered bonnet that matched the powder-blue of her day dress, but she did not take a parasol. This was to be a proper walk.

They strode out together, along the track and into the plantation, Elianne dictating the pace. He had thought there would be need to severely restrict his stride, but there was not. He towered over her, certainly, but she was well above average height, long-legged and healthy like a thoroughbred mare; he loved the way she moved.

He cast a covert glance at her as on and on they marched. She seemed tireless, the swish of her petticoats emphasising the athleticism of her legs beneath the pretty pastel skirt. They'd been travelling apace for a good twenty minutes now and she was not in the least out of breath. The fact pleased James immensely. Not only was she beautiful, she was strong and fit. She would bear him fine children.

Elianne took him to the special place she and Pavi shared overlooking the valley and the sea. She did not consider her choice disloyal. There were many beautiful vantage points she could have taken him to, but she'd deliberately chosen this one because it imbued her with a sense of power. She wanted to know the man she was to marry.

'I come here often with my best friend,' she said as they settled themselves on the rocks.

'Oh yes? And who is that?' He didn't even look at the view. The view held no interest for him.

'His name is Pavi. Pavi Salet.'

She studied his face, a strong face, albeit a little on the stern side, she thought. Granite-jawed and steely-eyed, he looked older than he was, more like a man in his mid-thirties, but she found him rather handsome nonetheless. She particularly liked the fact that, apart from his healthy moustache, he was clean shaven. Her father's friends were all bearded, and although she was aware that beards were quite the fashion of the day, she had come to associate them with rough men.

'Pavi Salet,' he said. 'Michel's son?' James was well acquainted with André's overseer. Michel had dined with them at the main house only the previous night, as he had done many times during James's past visits.

'Yes, that's right. Have you never wondered why Michel's wife and son are not invited to dine?'

'I must confess I hadn't really given the matter much thought.' Was it her intention to be provocative? Of course he knew why the man's wife and son were not invited.

'Michel's wife is black,' she said 'which means that Pavi is a half-caste.'

'I see.' He kept his response enigmatic in case she thought he hadn't known that, but he was bewildered. Where exactly is this leading? he wondered.

'Papa despises black people, even his own loyal workers. He disapproves of my friendship with Pavi.'

Ah, perhaps that's it, he thought, perhaps she's testing me. He had no particular antipathy towards the blacks himself, so long as they put in an honest day's work. His relationship with those he employed at his plantation in Australia was in fact excellent: he looked after them well and they worked hard in return.

'I am of the firm belief,' he said, 'that a person's choice of friend is no one's business but his own.' He knew instantly by her reaction that it had been the right response, so he went one step further. 'Indeed I have many friends amongst the Kanakas I employ at Durham Estate.' He said it without a qualm, for despite a degree of exaggeration it was not altogether a lie.

His easy manner inclined her to believe him, although as always the mention of 'Kanakas' grated a little. She knew that the term had been in general usage for many years by plantation owners and blackbirders who preferred a common label for all island labourers. And yet Pavi had told her the word 'kanaka' simply meant 'man' in the Hawaiian language. He considered its general use demeaning, and Elianne agreed, particularly as the term had now been adopted by the colonial authorities. 'Kanaka' had become official parlance among government regulators and agents responsible for contracting labourers from many different regions in the Pacific. It was ignorant and patronising, she thought, they should have known better.

She did not broach the subject, however. What would be the point? Besides, she was enjoying her conversation with James Durham. So much so that she decided to take a very bold step.

'I've heard that the islanders call you Big Jim,' she said.

'That's right.' *How can she possibly know that?* he wondered, 'all my Kanaka workers call me Big Jim; it's a term of respect.'

'No, I don't mean your workers; I mean the local islanders, here in the New Hebrides. I've heard you're known to many as Big Jim.'

'You've heard that? Have you really?' *She is being unashamedly provocative now – how very interesting,* he thought. 'Ah well,' he said with a nonchalant shrug, 'word does tend to get around. Many of my Kanakas come from this region.'

Was he being deliberately mysterious? He certainly wasn't giving anything away, but then she had hardly expected that he would. 'So you consider the nickname flattering?'

James saw in the green eyes that were boldly appraising him something beyond their obvious challenge, something mischievous. *She's flirting with me,* he thought, *she's playing a game.*

'Yes, I consider the nickname very flattering,' he replied. 'In fact I've embraced it wholeheartedly. At home, everyone calls me Big Jim.'

'Am I to call you Big Jim?' she asked.

'No.' He was enjoying her flirtatiousness. Women did not flirt with men unless they found them attractive and he wanted her to find him attractive. But he did not join in the game. He did not play games. 'You are to call me Jim.'

'Very well, Jim.' Elianne smiled, her eyes not once leaving his. She was aware she was flirting. She had never before flirted and she didn't know why she was doing it. She didn't even know exactly what it was she was flirting with. Was it the man himself, or was it the danger he represented? She seemed somehow to be daring herself. 'And what will you call me?' she asked.

'What would you like me to call you?'

'I don't know.' For a moment her bravado appeared to desert her. 'I have had only one nickname in the whole of my life.'

'And what was that?'

'My mother called me Ellie.'

She looked away, but not before he'd seen the sudden flash of vulnerability. In that instant, she had looked so very young, so very young and so very defenceless.

'Then I shall call you Ellie, if you will allow me.'

But she said nothing. She simply remained staring at the ground, and he didn't know how to interpret her reaction. Was it acquiescence, he wondered, or did she consider his suggestion the height of impertinence? He reached out and took her hand. 'I will care for you, Elianne. You are mine now. You will be safe with me always, I promise.'

She looked up, her eyes once again meeting his, the vulnerability gone and replaced by something else.

'May I call you Ellie?' he asked.

'You may.' She liked the feel of his hand, the strength of it, and the way he said 'Ellie' with such a proprietary air. He was one of those masterful men, she thought in a sudden flight of romantic fancy, one of those heroes from the novels that she and her mother had so eagerly devoured. He was dangerous and mysterious and commanding all in one, he was Darcy and Heathcliff and Rochester, and she desperately wished that he would kiss her.

James recognised her youthful longing. I could have her, he thought. Innocent as she is, I could have her right here and now if I wished, she's mine for the taking. The prospect aroused him immensely and he was sorely tempted. But he resisted the urge. To succumb to such a desire would be to deprive them both of their future, for he could not marry soiled goods, even his own soiled goods. She will come to me intact on our wedding night, he told himself, my perfect bride, my Ellie. He released her hand.

'It's time to go,' he said and he stood.

She stared up at him, his abruptness taking her by surprise.

'Ellie?' He offered his hand once again, but this time only in order to assist her to her feet. When she was standing beside him, he relinquished his grasp, which rather disappointed her.

During their walk back to the main house, Elianne pondered the strength of her attraction to James Durham. Was it just girlish fantasy inspired by the romantic novels she'd read, was it really that simple? Or had she perhaps been affected by the stories she'd heard of Big Jim and the fear he instilled in others? Whatever the reason, she was certainly drawn to the man, and it seemed the danger she sensed in him was the principal attraction. But was that too, she wondered, merely a figment of her imagination?

She found out five days later that it was not.

André Desmarais had returned from Port Vila late that afternoon with two of his friends in tow. Bored with the niceties of the past week, he was looking forward to a night of cards and presumed that James Durham, a keen poker player, would join them at the table.

The men had had several mugs of rum in town, and André ordered his young maidservant, Mela, to fetch a fresh bottle and glasses. They'd have a few more drinks, he said, and then dine early before devoting the rest of the night to poker.

'Bring some bread and cheese too,' he shouted after Mela as she left the room.

James and Elianne were out walking. They walked twice a day now, favouring the early morning and the late afternoon in order to avoid the midday heat. Sometimes they strode vigorously through the plantation, enjoying the exercise, and sometimes they ambled along holding hands and talking. Elianne would speak of her past, of her mother and her childhood, all of which James found most interesting, but his own past never featured in their conversation. There was never any mention of his 'moneyed English family', which led her to believe they were perhaps, as she had suspected they might be, a fabrication. When James spoke, it was always of the future and the wonderful life they would share on the plantation.

'I shall build you the grandest house, Ellie,' he would say. 'The mistress of Durham Estate must have the very best. We shall call it "Elianne House".'

This afternoon he had gone even further. He planned to build a community hall for his workers and their children, he'd told her, a hall where they could socialise and feel part of a giant family, and he would call it Elianne Hall. Then the idea had occurred. 'We shall call the whole estate "Elianne",' he'd declared with passion. 'In honour of my wife, in honour of you, Ellie, the house, the hall, the mill, the plantation: all will be known as "Elianne".'

She'd laughed. She hadn't believed him for one moment, but his enthusiasm was disarming, boyish even. James had laughed along with her, glad to see her happy. But he'd meant every word he'd said. He would build an empire, and she would be his empress. James was delighted with the courtship. Things were proceeding perfectly.

It was approaching dusk when they returned home, by which time André and his friends had downed several more glasses of rum and were in a mood to make merry.

James heard them from the front verandah. I know those voices, he thought. Then, opening the door, he and Elianne stepped into the main living room, where the men were gathered at the central table.

'James, come in, come in.' André, whose back was to the door, had noted his friends' glances and turned to wave a beckoning arm, 'we've been waiting for you,' and he added to the others, 'we could play a few hands before dinner, what do you say?'

The other two clearly thought it an excellent idea. They called a greeting to James, and one of them said, 'Come join us, *mon ami*.'

Yves and Alain, James thought, of course I know them: scum who worked for the Compagnie Calédonienne des Nouvelle Hébrides. He'd played many a poker game with them over the past two years, on several occasions even in this very house. But they had no right to be here now. Already he could see the way they were looking at Elianne – he'd seen it before, how they gloated over her body, undressing her with their eyes. Filthy pigs, he thought. No one looked at his future wife in that manner. James wanted to kill them.

'Go to your room, Ellie,' he muttered; and leaving the door open behind him, he crossed to the table.

Elianne moved off towards the arch that led to the east wing of the bungalow, but she did not go to her room: she stayed to watch the proceedings.

André rose and pulled another chair up beside his. Drunk though he was, he adopted a façade of courtesy and waited for James to sit, but he was ignored. Instead, James stood glaring across the table at the two Frenchmen.

Thickset, with rough beards and ill-kempt, matted hair, they wore open-neck shirts and scarves knotted at their throats. They looked like the thugs he knew them to be.

'In passing the stables on my walk, I noticed no strange horses or drays there,' he said coldly. 'How do you intend to return to Vila?'

'I shall drive them back in the morning, James.' André was drunker than his friends and had failed to read the warning signs, but Yves and Alain were fully aware of the Englishman's hostility. They couldn't fathom the reason for it, however, and exchanged mystified shrugs.

James turned to André. 'And where exactly do you plan they should stay the night?' he demanded, although he already knew the answer.

'Oh, you need have no fear,' André said with a laugh, 'they shall not impose themselves upon you. The guesthouse is yours, my friend, as we agreed.'

'That does not answer my question. Where do you intend they stay?'

André finally registered that something was not quite right. 'Why, here of course,' he replied, puzzled, 'here in my house. They are my guests.'

'They will not stay in this house,' James said. 'They will not stay under the same roof as my future wife.'

'Ah.' André was befuddled. Did James mean that Yves and Alain should stay with him at the guesthouse? If so, what a surprising suggestion; it was the last thing he would have expected. What in God's name am I to do? he asked himself. He could not afford to offend his benefactor and future son-in-law, but surely he must make some sort of stand. He was master in his own home, and these were his guests after all. He started to dither.

'Well, perhaps when we have dined and played cards –'

'These men will not dine with my fiancée,' James gazed directly at Yves and Alain, 'these men will leave this house now.'

Yves, the bigger of the two, held his hands out in a gesture of innocence; he was genuinely bewildered. 'Why is you anger, *mon ami?*' he said, 'what is we do?' Beside him, Alain nodded. Yves was always the spokesman; Alain's English was not good.

'I am not your *ami*,' James replied tersely, 'and you will do as I say. You will leave right now.'

'But James.' André felt he really must say something by way of protest. 'This is my house. These men are my guests –'

'And they are leaving.'

Yves stood. He was a big man. Not as big as James, but, sturdily built and handy with his fists, he took orders from no one. He did not like the Englishman's tone.

'This house is not your house,' he said. 'You hear what André say. This house is his house, and we is his guests. You do not tell us we go.'

'Yes I do. You will go now or I will throw you out.'

Yves gave a bark of laughter and glanced down at Alain, who rose to stand beside him. Together they confronted the Englishman.

'We is two, *mon ami*,' Yves sneered, 'you is one.'

James made no reply, but, taking a hold of the heavy wooden table that separated them he flung it aside with ease, two of the chairs crashing to the floor. Then he grasped the scarf that was knotted at the Frenchman's throat and before Yves knew it he was being barrelled towards the open door.

Caught by surprise and off balance, the Frenchman would have been hurled out on to the verandah, but as James released him he managed to grasp a hold of the doorframe, where he steadied himself and turned, prepared to do battle.

In that instant, Alain charged. He sprang onto James's back, clinging like a monkey with his legs wrapped around the Englishman's waist and one arm about his neck in a choker hold.

James reached up behind and, grasping fistfuls of the man's hair, he bent forwards in one swift movement, hauling Alain over his head and slamming him down on the floor in front of him.

Alain lay on his back, winded and wondering how he'd got there. He gazed in bewilderment at the Englishman towering high above him. It was the last thing he saw before James's boot found its mark. The sound of his skull cracking was clearly audible.

Yves looked down at his dead friend, at the eyeballs that stared up in such wide, comic surprise. He too was astounded. Alain was dead, and in only a matter of seconds.

The fight having left him, the Frenchman would have gone peacefully, but it appeared he was not going to get off so easily. Even as he looked up from the body to the Englishman a fist slammed into his face, breaking his jaw.

He started to slide down the doorframe, but hands grasped him around the throat, holding him up, taking his entire body weight as fingers of steel began steadily to throttle him. He struggled to prise the fingers free, but their grip was vicelike. He struck out at his assailant, landing blows to the body, but the blows were meaningless: he could have been punching the air.

Yves looked into the eyes of the Englishman. They were cold, emotionless. The Englishman was killing him effortlessly and without a qualm.

Both André and Elianne had been struck dumb by the speed of the events. They'd remained frozen where they stood, barely able to believe their eyes. Now galvanised into action, they begged James to stop.

'No more, James, no more, I beseech you,' André pleaded, desperate and terrified. '*Non, non, oh mon Dieu.* No more. No more, I beg you.'

'Stop it,' Elianne called out. 'Leave the man be, Jim, leave him be.'

It was the sound of her voice that brought Big Jim to a halt. He hadn't known she was still in the room.

He released his grip, but as the Frenchman once again started to slide down the doorframe, he held him up by his neck scarf like a rag doll, and Yves, already gasping for breath, was forced to remain on his feet or risk being choked to death.

James leant his face close to the Frenchman's. 'Do you want to live?' he asked quietly.

Hauling the air back into his lungs, his shattered jaw a bloody mess, Yves was unable to talk. He nodded.

'Then I shall tell you what you will do. André will drive you and your friend back to the outskirts of town where he will leave you both. You will then have the option of inventing some accident that befell your friend or, if you prefer, you can simply leave him to be discovered tomorrow morning. The choice is yours.' James knew only too well the choice the Frenchman would make. Yves would have no wish to be embroiled with the law. He would leave his dead friend on the roadside. There was no honour among men such as these. 'Are you happy with that arrangement?'

Yves nodded.

James released his hold on the man's neckerchief. 'André, fetch a horse and dray,' he ordered. 'Ellie, go to your room.'

Both obeyed instantly.

The following morning, no mention was made of the incident. It was as if it had never happened.

Elianne's eighteenth birthday came and went with little fanfare, for the main celebratory event was to take place two days later, when she and James Durham were to be wed by the Reverend Pidd.

The Reverend Pidd had had a long-time connection with the Desmarais family, particularly Elianne's mother.

A staunch follower of the Scottish missionary, John Gibson Paton, Raymond Pidd had been a regular visitor to the plantation during Beatrice's time, no doubt believing his presence served some significant religious purpose, although Elianne rather doubted that it did. She strongly suspected Beatrice encouraged the Reverend's visits as a welcome excuse to socialise at close quarters with a fellow countryman, the majority of her husband's friends being French.

The marriage took place in the garden, the ceremony conducted beneath the arbour while the twenty or so guests congregated about the small central fountain – an intimate affair, as planned, in a picturesque setting.

Elianne looked out at the gathering, pleased to see the faces she knew, and most particularly pleased by the mixture of brown and white. None of her father's riff-raff gambling companions were present and alongside the several English and French expatriates, businessmen and their wives whom she and her mother had befriended over the years were a number of islanders and their children. These included the house servants, with whom Elianne was extremely close, several of the senior workers whom she considered her friends, and of course Pavi Salet and his family.

André had raised no objection when his daughter had expressed a wish that her islander friends should be present. He hadn't dared, for Elianne had had James's support.

'Whatever you wish, my love,' James had said. 'A wedding day belongs to the bride. Do you not agree, André?'

'Yes, yes, indeed I do.' André would have agreed to anything James Durham said. The man put the fear of God into him.

André Desmarais was still haunted by that night. He hadn't arrived back at the bungalow until four o'clock in the morning after dumping the body by the roadside and watching briefly as Yves skulked off into the darkness.

He'd been living in dread of discovery ever since. The sooner the Englishman left Efate the better.

As the Reverend Pidd read out the vows, Elianne couldn't resist stealing an occasional glance at Pavi, who was standing to one side directly in her line of vision. He was with his father and mother and his little sister, twelve-year-old Simone. His fiancée, Mela, was beside him, and they had their arms about each other's waists. When Elianne first glanced at him, Pavi did not catch her eye – he and Mela were too absorbed in each other. But from the looks the two exchanged it was plain that neither was inattentive to the ceremony. Every word of the vows held a special meaning for Pavi and Mela, who were to be married themselves in barely a fortnight.

How in love they are, Elianne thought, how perfectly in love.

Then, as she repeated her own vows, she looked up into the eyes of the man she was marrying. Soon I will have a love like Pavi and Mela's, she thought. She was glad to be married to such a man as Jim Durham, regardless of the rumours that surrounded him, regardless even of the brutality she had witnessed. He excited her. She wanted to be his. And he loved her; she could feel it. Her glance darted once again to Pavi and this time their eyes met. He smiled and beside him, so did Mela. They were happy for her.

The Reverend Pidd made the pronouncement, Elianne heard the words 'man and wife', and as the gathering applauded, James Durham kissed her.

The reception was informal, guests milling about the garden and the front verandah where a lavish buffet was provided. James had spared no expense, importing the finest champagne and gourmet fare.

It was now that the schism between black and white became truly evident. The house servants returned to their duty, serving drinks at the buffet table, clearing away plates and fetching fresh ones, while the expatriate and other islander guests kept very much to the company of their own kind. That is with the exception of Michel Salet and the Reverend Pidd, both of whom mingled freely, particularly the Reverend. He always delighted in socialising with converted islanders, whom he considered a part of the giant Christian family personally bound by God's love.

The one who mingled with the greatest of ease, however, was Elianne, who insisted upon serving her guests. Standing beside Mela at the drinks table, exquisite in her lace bridal gown, Elianne poured champagne for the expatriates and fruit juice for the islanders, none of whom drank alcohol. She chatted away in English and French and shared a joke in Pidgin with several of the islander children. People were drawn to her, comfortable in her presence, unaware that they were gradually mingling with those who belonged to a different social stratum altogether.

James watched his new wife with pride. He was mesmerised, unable to drag his eyes from her. Beside him, someone was offering congratulations, but he paid them no heed and he or she drifted away. She is magnificent, he thought. She is magnificent and she is mine. Look how they love her, every single one of them. That is how they will love her at the plantation. I have found my perfect queen.

Elianne felt his gaze and, turning to him, she saw clearly the naked pride and elation, which he made no attempt to disguise. Instead, he raised his glass in a tribute to her. The smile she returned him was radiant.

The wedding festivities did not last into the night. With the need to travel either back to Port Vila or to their neighbouring properties some distance away, the expatriates were keen to leave while there was still daylight for at least part of their homewards journey, and those who lived on the plantation, aware of a sense of propriety, slowly drifted back to their cottages.

It was approaching dusk as the last farewells were made by Michel Salet and his family. Michel shook James's hand

and embraced Elianne, wishing them both a long and happy life together. The couple were to be leaving early in the morning, André driving them into Port Vila where they would board the ship bound for Bundaberg.

Michel's wife, Sera, a shy woman at the best of times, stood behind her husband, bobbing a form of curtsy to James, whom she obviously found daunting, and nodding her best wishes to Elianne.

Elianne, however, was not prepared to let Sera, of whom she was extremely fond, go unrecognised. She hugged her warmly, Sera returning the hug. Then Elianne hugged young Simone, and then Mela, and then finally Pavi.

André cast a wary glance in James's direction, wondering how the Englishman felt about his new wife embracing blacks in so unashamed a fashion. But it appeared the Englishman had no qualms whatsoever. In fact to André's utter surprise, the Englishman offered his hand to Pavi Salet.

'Congratulations on your own forthcoming nuptials,' James said as they shook hands, 'I wish you both every happiness,' and he smiled at Mela.

'Thank you, sir.'

James stood to one side while Elianne and Pavi exchanged faithful promises to write to one another. Then he waited patiently while Elianne comforted young Simone, who had become suddenly tearful at the prospect of missing her. James was in no hurry. It would not be seemly to bed his new wife during daylight hours anyway.

Darkness was falling when the bride and groom finally retired to the guesthouse, which had been prepared for them. The oil lamps had been lit and, beneath mosquito netting, a cold supper had been set out on the table.

James swept her up into his arms and carried her over the threshold as if she weighed no more than a feather, and Elianne laughed with delight at the sheer romance of the gesture.

By unspoken mutual consent, they ignored the supper, Elianne retiring to the spare room where her nightgown and toiletries had been laid out. There was also freshly folded bed linen and a second nightgown, together with a pitcher of warm water and a basin on the wash-stand. All was in readiness. Nothing had been overlooked by André's highly practical housekeeper, who served also as midwife to the local workers' families.

In the master bedroom, James stripped himself naked. Then he dimmed the lamps to a minimal glow, pulled the light coverlet over himself and lay waiting for her.

Elianne prepared herself. She was not afraid. She longed for James to make love to her. She longed to discover the mystery of sex. But despite her partiality for romance, she was not naïve in her expectations. She had been witness to the brutality of both sex and birth, she had seen animals mating and she had helped deliver calves, she did not delude herself. There would be pain this first time, she knew it, but she had determined she would not cry out.

In her nightgown, her body washed and perfumed, her hair freshly brushed, she crossed the hallway to the master bedroom opposite. She was aware of his eyes upon her as in the semi-gloom of the room she made her way to the bed. She slipped beneath the coverlet. Aware instantly that his body was ready for her, she steeled herself for the moment, expecting first to feel the touch of his lips on hers or the caress of his fingers on her body, something tender by way of preparation. But there was no such touch, no such caress. Instead, hands hauled up her nightdress and within seconds he was forcing his way into her.

The pain was intense. With each thrust she felt she was being ripped apart, but true to the promise she had made to herself, she did not cry out.

How long it lasted, Elianne could not possibly say, but finally, thankfully, it was over and he pulled away from her, sated, to lie on his back, his chest still heaving from the force of his own passion.

When he'd regained his breath, he turned to face her. 'I am sorry that I hurt you,' he said. 'You're a brave girl, Ellie, not to cry out.'

'I had expected pain,' she said, trying hard not to show her disappointment, and wondering if perhaps this had been a deliberate test of her strength. 'My mother had warned me that the first time is painful.' She rose from the bed. 'I must wash myself and fetch fresh linen.'

She went into the spare room where she stripped off her bloodied nightgown. It will be better next time, she told herself as she poured water into the basin and washed the blood from her body.

Behind her across the hallway, she saw through the slit in the door that the lamps of the master bedroom had been turned up.

She donned the fresh nightgown and returned to discover him standing naked by the bed looking down at the blood-stained linen, and in that moment he appeared to Elianne like a victor after a kill. Where is the tenderness? she wondered. There is no tenderness. There is only triumph.

Then his hands were about her waist and she felt herself lifted off her feet.

'Oh Ellie,' he said, 'oh my own Ellie, how I shall love you!' He held her up before him like a goddess. 'What a life we shall have, my dearest.'

Yes, she decided, he had been testing her strength. He loved her. He worshipped her. It will be better next time, she told herself.

Chapter four

I have now been married for three months, and no longer am I Elianne – that name belongs to a grand estate. I am simply 'Ellie', which, strangely enough, I find endearing. My nickname is perhaps the one tender element in the whole of my marriage and I cling to it.

Kate read on, her eyes riveted to the page, her mind teeming with images, she could see this girl, she could hear her voice. Elianne Desmarais had ceased to be a remote ancestor, or even a younger version of Grandmother Ellie as conjured up by the romantically inclined Hilda Durham. She was just Ellie, eighteen years old: the same age as Kate.

I do not doubt my husband's love for one moment; indeed the very force of it can be terrifying. My husband would not hesitate to kill any who threatened me and were it necessary he would lay down his own life in the process. These are grave responsibilities to bear and I find myself treading warily.

Jim often asks me what I'm scribbling about and I usually say 'My scribblings are about us, dearest. I scribble about you and me and our love.' That makes him happy. He does love me, of course he does, but in the only way he knows how, which is not a love I recognise as such. I am a possession to Jim — he owns me. Our coupling remains devoid of tenderness. He takes me in triumph, like a prize he has worked hard to win and has a right to lay claim to ...

Kate was amazed, not only by the naked candour of Ellie's writing, but the fact that the relationship between husband and wife appeared to differ so completely from the great love supposedly shared between Grandmother Ellie and Big Jim. Were the stories she had been fed over the years born purely of her mother's need for romance? But then she recalled the vague childhood images of Grandmother Ellie. Elegant, serene, she'd seemed a woman with a love that had sustained her through tragic times, and her support for her husband was known by all to have been absolute. Surely, Kate thought, these early writings were the result of a young woman's loneliness, perhaps fed by disillusionment. Perhaps, like Hilda, Ellie had been overly romantic in her expectations, both of her husband and the new country to which she had been transported. Surely she must have adjusted over time.

And there was certainly a great deal to adjust to, Kate thought, listing the discoveries she had made herself in this one short hour of reading. If Ellie was right, Big Jim had cancelled her father's debt in order to buy her. He'd been a blackbirder in his youth, or so Ellie had been told. He'd ruthlessly killed a man in cold blood, and Ellie had witnessed the event.

Kate found it difficult to comprehend. This was the Durham patriarch whom everyone revered, indeed considered a hero. This was the very man upon whom her father had modelled himself. She was confused. Who was she to believe? The legends passed down over three generations or the scribbles of a young woman nearly eighty years ago?

She checked her watch. A special lunch was planned at The Big House, a farewell in her honour, as she was leaving for Sydney early the next morning; she could not afford to be late. Ten more minutes, she told herself, just ten more minutes. But she would not read on from where she had left off, barely a quarter of the way through the first ledger. She could not reveal findings such as these to her mother. She would flick through the final ledger and discover the matriarch Ellie had become, the woman whom Hilda Durham had so worshipped. Then she would feel confident in telling her mother of her find, and she would promise to translate the writings of Grandmother Ellie, or at least a selection of them.

Kate opened the last of the ledgers. In sorting the books into sequential order, she had noted that the first entry in each was dated, after which Ellie rarely recorded a date unless it marked a specific event. The books were not diaries as such: there was no particular form to them and the entries were sporadic, random thoughts for the most part. Indeed Ellie's 'scribblings' as she called them.

The opening date in the final ledger served a dual purpose, for it did most certainly record a specific event. Kate felt the faintest shiver run down her spine as she read of the birth of her father.

1ᵉʳ septembre 1914

What a momentous occasion! Bartholomew's dear wife, Mary, has borne him a son, Stanley James Durham. Jim is so overjoyed that his first grandchild has proved a male, one would swear he had fathered the boy himself. He struts about like the proudest of peacocks, while Bartholomew and I look on with amusement.

It pleases me that my gentle Bartholomew appears finally to have done something right in his father's eyes. Jim has always been such a hard taskmaster. For my part, I hope the arrival of baby Stanley will prove a distraction from what lies ahead. I know Jim is proud Edward and George have signed up, he boasts of his sons fighting for King and Country and says he wishes he could go himself. But although it will be some time before they leave for the front, surely he too must worry about the possible outcome. Even now while my boys are safely at training camp, the horrors of war play on my mind and I am filled with trepidation.

Oh dear, Kate thought. She knew all too well the next specific event that would be recorded. Edward and George had met their deaths side by side on the beach at Gallipoli. Along with hundreds of others, they had been mown down during the initial landings on 25 April 1915, the day that was to become forever known as Anzac Day.

She moved on a dozen or so pages and there it was. The entry had been made two weeks after the family had received notification.

Jim is inconsolable. His grief is frightening to behold. My own heart breaks as I think of my darling boys dying in that Godforsaken place. My heart breaks for all our darling boys; the whole country is in shock, but I must somehow stay strong. Jim needs me as he has never needed me before. I am all that stands between him and insanity . . .

Kate stopped reading. She would address this harrowing material with the respect it deserved at a later date, she decided, but here clearly was an example of the love and support that epitomised the relationship between Grandmother Ellie and Big Jim. She felt more secure now in telling her mother about her discovery of Ellie's writings. Hilda Durham would weep to hear such words from the woman she so admired.

Another quick check of her watch told her she should be going, but unable to resist the compulsion, she flicked on still further.

The birth of Bartholomew's daughter in 1917 was clearly a salve to Ellie.

Our dearest Mary has given birth to a daughter, Julia May Durham. To have a little girl join the ranks of our family is to me a great joy, particularly after losing baby Beatrice all those years ago. How I longed for a daughter.
   Julia's arrival offers little comfort to Jim, however. Perhaps if our second grandchild had been another boy, things might be different — male heirs are all-important to Jim, and grief continues to weigh upon him immeasurably ...

Kate was saddened for them both, for Jim still burdened by grief two years after the death of his sons, and most particularly for Ellie, who had apparently lost a baby daughter. How strange that none of us knew that, she thought. Ellie must have kept the fact a secret even from her own children, for no member of the family had ever spoken of it. Hilda would certainly have recounted such a tragic event had it been general knowledge, and Bartholomew had never made any mention of losing a sister.

She turned to the last several pages of the ledger. There were no dates marked in the final entries, but she didn't get to the last one in any event. She was halted by the first paragraph she read, abrupt and shocking.

I intend to stop my scribblings shortly. They no longer serve a purpose. What is the point in being honest to oneself when one's whole life has been a lie? Better surely to live the lie. And that is what I shall do. I tell everyone lies. Why not myself? I lie to my husband and to my son, and even to my grandchildren. It is simpler to tell them what they wish to hear. I believe it is healthier too. Let Jim believe I love the monster that he is, and has always been. Let Stanley believe his grandfather is the hero he presumes him to be. Let Julia believe in the great mythical love shared by her grandparents. My lies protect my family ...

Kate read no further. She closed the book, aghast, a lifetime's illusions shattered in one instant. A sense of panic engulfed her and she glanced about guiltily, fearful that someone might find her with this betrayal of all that her family had held sacred. One of her brothers might appear at any minute, having been sent to fetch her.

Fortunately there was no one in sight, and as she gathered up the ledgers she tried to reason with herself, to make sense of what she had just read. This outburst of cynicism was uncharacteristic, Ellie's 'scribblings' were just random thoughts and feelings, she told herself, these views were the reflection of a passing mood, no more than that ...

But as she carried the armload of books to the car no attempt at logic could stop her mind reeling with unanswerable questions. Had her great-grandfather been a monster to be feared, as Ellie had openly stated? Had Ellie spent her whole life protecting her family from the man she'd married? Had she elevated Big Jim to hero status and created a mythical love in order to do so? Kate was in turmoil. What should she do? Who should she tell?

She piled the ledgers into the boot, and just as she did so she spied Alan walking up the track. He gave her a wave.

'You've been summoned,' he yelled. 'We're all waiting, and we're all starving.'

She slammed the boot shut. 'Yes, sorry, I got a bit carried away,' she called back.

He arrived beside her.

'Come and give me a hand,' she said, leading the way to the storage area, 'there's a pile of Grandmother Ellie's books that I want to take back to Sydney.'

'Right you are.'

He followed her amiably and held out his arms as she loaded him up with the assortment of novels she'd chosen.

'Crikey, they're in good nick, aren't they?'

'Yes, I was pretty surprised, I must say.' She picked up the last several books, 'you should take a look yourself, Al,' she said, closing the trunk, 'see if there's anything in there you want.'

Alan glanced down at the collection clutched to his chest: all were novels and all bore French titles.

'Like a manual on harvesters or something?' he replied.

Kate laughed and they headed back to the car. He halted briefly at the boot, waiting for her to open it, but she didn't, she opened the rear door instead.

'Just dump them on the back seat,' she said, 'I've got other stuff in the boot.'

'Rightio.'

As she drove back to The Big House, Kate was tempted to tell Alan of her find. Despite his youth, she knew that if she were to tell anyone, it would be Alan. She'd always joked that her little brother was the 'strong silent type', but in truth he was. Al's the strongest of the three of us, she thought. He doesn't hurt as easily as Neil and he doesn't lose his temper like me, he just closes off. The truth wouldn't shatter him as it would Neil, and he'd never tell a soul. But then, she asked herself, what is the truth?

Already the secret was a burden that Kate longed to share, but she knew that to shoulder her brother with the same burden at this stage would be unfair. It would be unfair not only to Alan, but also to Ellie and to Big Jim. I must keep an open mind, she told herself. I must make no judgement and draw no conclusion until I've read all of Ellie's writings and know the whole truth. She would take the ledgers to Sydney and study them over the ensuing weeks.

The family luncheon was festive, Hilda having insisted upon the serving of champagne.

'If we are to lose our daughter for close to another whole year,' she'd said to her husband, 'then we must toast her departure in a manner befitting the occasion.'

Kate had told her mother that she would not attempt to return home during the three term breaks allowed. 'We get little more than a week off, Marmee, maybe two at the outside – it would be too disruptive. And I intend to study.'

'Very well, dear.' Hilda, disappointed but stoic, had decided to drown her sorrows. 'What must be, must be,' she'd said, and demanded champagne.

Stan had readily agreed, although he intended to stick to beer himself, and Max had set out on ice two bottles of Dom Perignon. There was an ample supply left over from Christmas and New Year celebrations.

Being a strictly family affair, they dined as they usually did in the pleasantly airy breakfast room, the ceiling fan alleviating the heat of midday, but despite the homely surrounds Cook had gone to some pains to provide a special luncheon. Knowing Kate's penchant for fish, she'd baked an extremely large and extremely fresh barramundi that she'd had Max fetch directly from the fishermen's wharf at Bundaberg Port that very morning. As she sailed stoutly in from the kitchen with the giant platter bearing its giant fish, she was given the customary round of applause. Cook always enjoyed making an entrance.

Kate looked about at her family, at her two brothers dishing themselves hefty portions of the various salads Ivy had set out on the table, at her father pouring her mother a second glass of champagne, at her grandfather studying with avid interest the way Cook was so expertly filleting the baked fish. Such an ordinary, domestic scene, she thought, yet she felt in some way divorced from it. Something comfortable was missing, and she wondered whether perhaps she might live to regret having discovered Ellie's 'scribblings'.

Plates were passed along to Cook, who served the portions of fish, after which she departed with the platter, now bearing the barramundi's denuded backbone and head, its one visible eye glaring malevolently. When she was safely out of sight, Kate leant in to her grandfather.

'Watch you don't cop a bone,' she whispered.

Bartholomew smiled his thanks for the reminder. No one would dare mention such a possibility in Cook's presence, but the occasional bone had been known to make an appearance, so he sifted through his fish with care.

Max's morning trip to the wharfs had resulted in more than a large barramundi: he'd also returned with the mail, which he'd collected from the post office on his way back through town.

'I had a Christmas card from Julia this morning,' Stan announced as he helped himself to the potato salad, 'she obviously didn't realise she'd forgotten the airmail sticker. Typical.' Stan's younger sister, Julia, lived in Canada with her schoolteacher husband and family. 'She sends her love to everyone. Father actually received a letter, didn't you?' he added in a rare address to Bartholomew, who for the most part was invisible to his son.

Bartholomew nodded. He'd been delighted to hear from his daughter. Her letter had been very affectionate and chatty and he'd gained a great deal of pleasure from it. Already, he was halfway through writing a response in his painstaking spidery hand.

'Julia's once-a-year duty,' Stan said dismissively. 'I don't know why she bothers. It's a case of out of sight out of mind on both sides of the Pacific; we all know that.'

Kate found her father's comment shockingly insensitive. The light of pleasure in Bartholomew's eyes at the mention of his daughter's letter had been plainly evident. She glanced at her grandfather, expecting to see hurt, but there was none. Stanley's words had had no effect whatsoever. Impervious to insult, Bartholomew simply continued to sift through his fish. The father was equally capable of ignoring the son, Kate was glad to note.

Stanley Durham had always been dismissive of his sister for deserting Queensland and her roots, which Kate considered most unfair. It was hardly Julia's fault that she'd fallen in love with a Canadian. She had met her aunt on only one occasion, and Julia had seemed to her extremely kind.

'Look after my father for me, Kate,' Julia had said, 'I can tell that he loves you.'

Julia had come back to Elianne three years previously upon the news of her mother's death, her first visit in nearly twenty years. She had been too late for Mary's funeral, but she had stayed for a fortnight, hoping to be of some comfort to her father, whose stroke had quickly followed the death of his wife.

'I only wish I could stay longer,' she'd said, 'but with three children back home, I'm needed. The tyranny of distance, I'm afraid. Australia is so very far away.'

She'd parted with an enigmatic comment, which at the time Kate had presumed was intended to amuse.

'I leave you with Stan the Man, my dear,' Julia had said as she'd hugged her niece warmly, 'or is it Big Jim? Sometimes I have trouble telling the difference.'

Now, with the topic of her aunt raised and Ellie's words still swirling in her brain, Kate recalled Julia's remark and found herself reading more into it than she knew she should. Surely it had been made in jest, with perhaps a touch of sibling archness, but it seemed somehow to take on a deeper significance ...

Stop it! She chastised herself. Stop fantasising: you're being ridiculous. Stop thinking about the ledgers, for God's sake. Put them out of your mind!

But it wasn't that easy. Throughout lunch, Big Jim featured several times in Stanley Durham's conversation, as Big Jim so often did, and on each occasion his name was mentioned,

Kate's mind rebelled. What would you say if I told you your hero was a blackbirder, Dad? Gazing across the table at her father, always so opinionated, his confidence bordering on arrogance, his beliefs inviolable, her mind continued involuntarily to fire questions. Hey Stan the Man, what would you say if I told you Big Jim killed a person in cold blood? What would you say if I told you his wife considered him a monster ...? Stop it, she told herself, stop it!

'You've been rather quiet over lunch, darling.'

They were well into Cook's famous mulberry pie when Hilda voiced her concern to her daughter. Kate hadn't been her usual talkative self. 'Is everything all right?'

'Of course it is, Marmee. I'm sorry, I've been a bit distracted. Just thinking of what lies ahead, lining up new digs, uni and all that.'

'Yes, I sensed you were miles away. Well, I should think that's understandable,' Hilda patted her daughter's hand in a vague gesture of sympathy, 'half of you is probably already in Sydney.'

'That's right.' How she wished she were. Kate couldn't wait. She longed for the distraction of the big city, and of Jeremy and the discovery of sex. She needed to be away from Elianne and all she loved there. She needed to distance herself.

It was a long drive, roughly six hundred and fifty miles, but she loved every minute of it. She took the Pacific Highway, which followed the coast for the most part, breaking her trip with an overnight stay as she had promised her father she would.

'No non-stop driving, do you hear me?' Stan had ordered. 'Regular breaks now and then, and two overnight stays, Brisbane first and then Ballina or Coffs Harbour would probably be your best bet.'

'Yes, Dad.'

She actually made only one overnight stop, Newcastle, far further south only several hours' drive from Sydney, so it was barely lunchtime when she pulled up outside the little two-storey terrace in Glebe.

Jeremy had been looking out for her through the front living-room window of the house, which he shared with two other third-year Arts students. She'd rung him from Newcastle, and as he saw the brand-new gun-metal grey Holden with its gleaming white roof cruising down Cowper Street, he stepped outside.

Picking up the 'witches' hats' he'd placed earlier to reserve a parking spot, he dumped them on the pavement and waved her in ostentatiously like an over-officious traffic policeman. The witches' hats had been stolen from a council road-works crew a year earlier and were put to illegal use on a regular basis.

He watched as she climbed from the car. The day was hot; she was wearing a light cotton dress with narrow straps and she slung her bag over a bare shoulder with easy grace. God she's gorgeous, he thought, and God I've missed her. He'd missed her bold, green-eyed beauty and the way she moved her long, tanned limbs so freely, like a healthy young animal. He'd missed too her fierce intelligence, the heated debates and passionate discussions that could last half the night over glasses of cheap red wine. Jeremy had had any number of girlfriends, he was popular with the opposite sex, but he'd never had anyone quite like Kate. Kate Durham was everything a man could want in a woman. In fact, he thought, if I didn't know myself better I might swear I was falling in love.

'Pretty swish,' he said, running his fingers over the bonnet of the Holden as she circled the car to join him, 'Christmas or birthday present?'

'Eighteenth birthday. I'm a big girl now.'

'How very generous of sugar-cane-king daddy.'

Kate laughed. Jeremy's digs at her wealthy background were simply a part of the nonchalant image he chose to adopt and bore no malice or envy. Jeremy himself hardly came from an impoverished family. His father was a dermatologist. 'Rooms in Macquarie Street,' he would say with humorous disdain, 'so bourgeois – nowhere near the drama of a sugar cane empire.'

As she walked into his arms, Kate was aware of the familiar thrill he aroused in her. Neither tall, nor heavily built, he stood barely an inch or so taller than she did, but he was strong and fit, and through his thin cotton 'Ban the Bomb' T-shirt she could feel the lean muscularity of his body.

They kissed greedily, drinking their fill of each other, uninhibited by the elderly couple passing by, who tut-tutted and muttered something about the indecent behaviour of the young these days.

'University students, I'll bet,' the man said.

'Miss me?' she asked as they parted, both a little breathless.

'Nope. How about you?'

'Didn't spare a thought,' she said, and they kissed again.

Jeremy collected up the witches' hats, which were always stowed in the living room by the front door, available for instant use.

'Leave your gear, we'll get it later,' he said, raking back his unruly sun-bleached hair in a gesture that was typical. 'Come inside and have a coffee. I've got some really great news.' He seemed instantly fired up and excited. 'I can't wait to tell you. You're going to just love it!'

Kate locked the car. His mood change was so characteristic that she felt a rush of affection. Jeremy was such a mercurial mix, boyishly enthusiastic one minute, playing the hardened cynic the next, and the next passionately advocating one of his causes. He was perhaps typical of the 'renegade' Arts student rebelling against a middle-class background, but she respected him for the many stances he took. Some of the more conservative male students considered him pretentious, with his overly long hair and slogan T-shirts, or in winter his signal duffle coat and desert boots, but he wasn't. Jeremy was far too intelligent to be a poseur: Jeremy was making a statement.

Kate followed him inside. Every aspect of Jeremy Venecourt intrigued her, not least of all his sex appeal. He was simply magnetic. In fact she was willing to concede that, like many of the female students, she had the most incredible crush on 'Venner', as he was generally known.

The crush had been more or less instantaneous on both sides. They'd noticed each other around the university campus, both were difficult to ignore, but first- and second-year students rarely mingled. Then they'd met at a party where he'd sought her out, and after a half an hour in each other's company, Venner had made his odd request.

'I want you to call me Jeremy,' he'd said, piercingly blue eyes meeting hers with deadly intent.

'Why? Everyone else calls you Venner.'

'That's why I'd like you to call me Jeremy.'

'But why?' she'd insisted.

'Because you're different.'

She'd smiled. 'All right, Jeremy,' she'd said playfully, calling his bluff. She'd assumed it was a line he'd used in the past, but it was a winning one, she had to admit.

Venner had never once used the line before, and he'd wondered at that moment why the thought had never occurred to him – it was clearly a winner. Then he'd realised. Of course. He'd never *wanted* a girl to call him Jeremy before. He did now.

Jeremy refused to tell Kate his news until he'd made them mugs of instant coffee, after which they adjourned from the kitchen to the front living room to discuss their plans.

The idea from the start had been that Kate would stay for a week or so at the Cowper Street house while she looked for a suitable place within walking distance of the university. Sylvia and Larry, the students with whom Jeremy shared the two-bedroom terrace, were lovers who'd been living together for the past year, and they were perfectly happy for Kate to stay. In fact they'd made her the offer of permanent lodgings.

'Syl and I reckon you should move in,' Larry had said in his customary bald manner. 'We could do with a four-way split in the rent.'

Jeremy's glance to Kate had queried whether she would like him to correct the couple's obvious assumption that they were lovers, but Kate had ignored the offer.

'Thanks, Larry, but I really do want my own place.'

'Suit yourself.'

Larry and Sylvia had presumed Kate was protecting her reputation, which was understandable. The university didn't approve of students 'living in sin', although quite a number did and there was little could be done about it. The couple had naturally assumed, however, that Kate would share Jeremy's bed during her brief stay. They had been wrong.

'You can have my bedroom,' Jeremy had said gallantly before she'd left for Queensland. 'I'll take the sofa in the living room.'

'Don't be silly,' she'd scoffed, 'I couldn't possibly do that. The sofa's mine.'

They'd decided to argue the point upon her return, but the unspoken agreement had been that they would not sleep together until the conditions were right and Kate felt comfortable. She appreciated his understanding, aware that most other young men would not have been so patient.

'I've found you the perfect place!' As they seated themselves on the sofa, coffee mugs in hand, Jeremy made his announcement. 'Single-storey terrace with attic bedroom, fully furnished, up for immediate rental, walking distance from uni,' he said rattling off the sign he'd seen on the university noticeboard and making no attempt to conceal his excitement. 'It's only a few blocks away in Campbell Street. I've given it a good once over and it's the coolest place – you're going to just love it.'

'Sounds ideal,' she said, although she had the vaguest sense of being railroaded. She hadn't wanted everything done for her, she'd looked forward to house hunting, but she didn't want to appear ungrateful, so she smiled. 'I'd better give it a good once over myself then, hadn't I?'

He nodded vigorously. 'And the sooner the better, it's bound to get snapped up. I collected the front-door key from the agent just before you arrived.'

'You what?' She stared at him dumbly.

'I put a twenty-quid deposit down and said we'd call around this arvo.'

'Right.' *I really am being railroaded*, she thought, annoyed by the idea that Jeremy might after all be pressuring her. She had no intention of making a premature decision about where she would live simply in order for them to become lovers.

She swigged back half her coffee, dumped the mug on the side table and took her purse from her shoulder bag. 'There's the deposit.' She put two ten-pound notes on the table and stood. 'Let's go,' she said.

Jeremy was a little taken aback by the speed of events, but he hadn't registered the fact that she might be irritated. 'You don't have to pay me the deposit ...' he started to protest.

'Of course I do. You can't afford twenty quid.'

'Well, yes, there is that.' He took a swig of his own coffee and rose to his feet, pocketing the twenty pounds. 'Come on then, let's check out your new home.'

'Jeremy ...' She halted him before he headed off for the door. 'You do know that if I don't like it, I won't take it, don't you?'

Her eyes signalled a warning, which he either failed to notice or chose to ignore. He grinned. 'Yes of course I know that, silly.'

They walked the four short blocks up Cowper Street and around the corner into Campbell, where Jeremy led the way to a tiny single-storey terrace with an attic window cut into its steep, corrugated iron roof. The house was just one in a line of many, some with attic rooms added, some without, and most with white picket fences in varying states of repair. The only distinguishing factor of this particular house was the gnarled and incongruous gum tree that towered over it, taking up the whole of the front plot that could hardly be called a garden.

'I like the tree,' Kate said.

'I knew you would.' He unlocked the front door and stood to one side as she entered.

Kate had expected the interior of the house to be gloomy, small as it was and conjoined on both sides, but she was surprised to discover quite the opposite. The two poky front rooms that had once led directly from one to another had been gutted to form a comfortably sized living space with a central archway. Another smaller arch led into the kitchen at the rear, where light streamed in through the French windows that opened onto the tiny backyard.

To the right was a mantelpiece, beneath which sat a little open fireplace, its grate attractively framed by burgundy and beige-coloured tiles.

'Cosy in winter,' Jeremy said encouragingly as he watched her take it all in, but Kate made no comment.

She crossed to the rear of the living area where, against the left wall, was a set of steps resembling more a ladder than a staircase.

'Bedroom,' he said unnecessarily, pointing up at the ceiling, but again he received no comment as she sailed through the smaller arch to the kitchen.

Jeremy followed. Her silence was worrying. She seemed dubious and he was beginning to feel unsure of himself. Then the thought occurred. Of course by her Queensland standards the house would appear poky to the extreme, perhaps even claustrophobic.

Kate opened the French windows that led from the sunny little kitchen with its walls of scotched-back clinker bricks directly into the backyard.

She stepped outside. On her left was an addition to the house in modern brick, which she correctly presumed to be the bathroom. The remainder of the yard was taken up by the giant umbrella-like skeleton of a Hills Hoist clothesline and at the far end against the paling fence stood a rickety wooden outhouse.

Jeremy's heart sank even further as he watched her through the French windows surveying her surrounds. Oh bugger, he thought, bugger, bugger, she'd expected a garden.

Stepping outside, he crossed to the bathroom and threw the door open in a gesture supposedly triumphant, but born of desperation.

'Look,' he said over-brightly, 'you won't have to use the dunny down the back.'

She didn't bother examining the modest bathroom with its basic shower, washbasin and lavatory. 'I wouldn't care if I did,' she said, 'I love the dunny down the back.'

She did. She loved both the rickety outhouse and the ridiculous Hills Hoist. To Kate, they signified just one thing – inner-city living. Here I am, in my own little house in the very heart of Sydney, she thought, and looking about at the pocket-sized backyard, she was suddenly imbued with the sense of freedom she'd longed for. This was as far removed from Elianne as it was possible to be.

'I love the house, Jeremy,' she said, 'I love everything about it.'

'I knew you would,' he replied, attempting a nonchalant shrug.

They explored the place thoroughly, Kate listing an inventory of the purchases she would need to make – kitchenware, linen and the like. All the basic furnishings were there, comprising a small round dining table and four chairs, a plain but serviceable sofa with matching armchair, a rather attractive sideboard, and in the attic room, a single bed with a bedside table, a cupboard and a chest of drawers.

'All it needs is a bit of dressing up,' she said as, having climbed the ladder-like stairs, they stood in the little bedroom that was only just above head-height. Had

Jeremy been two inches taller, or indeed had Kate been wearing high heels, they would have had to stoop. 'I'll get in some curtains and coverlets and lampshades and stuff.'

'You could do with a bigger bed,' he suggested.

'Yes.' She didn't even look at the bed as they gravitated into each other's arms. 'You're right,' she said, 'I'll get a bigger bed.'

Their desire was mutual and they could have made love then and there, but they didn't. Jeremy sensed the moment was premature and he didn't try to rush her; he'd waited this long after all. He called a halt to the kiss before it got out of hand and passion took over.

'I wasn't being pushy, Kate,' he said as they parted. 'I didn't find the house just in order to sleep with you.'

'Didn't you?' She smiled and raised a highly suspicious eyebrow. 'Didn't you really?'

'Well, yes, perhaps I did,' he admitted. She was confronting him certainly, but in so good-humoured a fashion that he was willing to be caught out. 'But I knew the house was perfect for you the moment I saw it.'

'And you were right.' She kissed him gratefully. 'Just give me a week, Jeremy. One week, that's all.'

As things turned out, Kate didn't need a week. She invited him around for an official house-christening dinner four days later. It would be just the two of them, she said, and they both knew exactly what that meant.

'Very colourful,' he remarked as he stepped inside, bottle of wine in hand in its bottle-shop, brown-paper bag. Her transistor radio was tuned to the ABC's light musical entertainment hour and 'Zorba the Greek' was playing, which seemed rather appropriate. 'Very colourful indeed,' he said.

The results of Kate's frenzied shopping spree were evident: the house was decked out with curtains and scatter rugs and tiffany lamps, but at first glance it was the shawls that particularly caught the eye. Multi-coloured and fringed, they were draped over the sofa and the armchair, and also over the small circular dining table.

'Yes, the girls I used to flat with were mad about Indian shawls,' Kate said, taking the bottle he handed her. 'Far more interesting than bedspreads and table cloths and much, much cheaper.' She pulled the bottle from its paper bag. 'Chianti, excellent, I plan to have candles all over the place.' Chianti was the popular choice of most students not only because the wine was inexpensive, but because the raffia-encased bottles made attractive candle-holders, and candles were very much in vogue for those trying to create an atmosphere on the cheap.

'You're really getting into the groove of things, aren't you?' he said, although he couldn't for the life of him fathom why she would bother practising frugality when she had money so readily to hand. She'd told him her father regularly deposited cash in her account.

'That's the object of the exercise,' she replied archly, aware of what he was thinking. 'I intend to avail myself of sugar-cane-king daddy's assistance as little as possible. His money will simply sit in my account to be returned to him at the end of the year.'

'I'm sorry, Kate.' Jeremy felt genuinely contrite. 'Was I that readable?'

'Yes.'

'I didn't mean to be critical. Honestly I didn't.' He gave a cheeky grin in order to win her around. 'Hell, if I had a sugar daddy like yours I'd take whatever he offered.'

She couldn't help but smile. 'No you wouldn't, you'd stick to your principles. You always do. You've never accepted assistance from your father.'

'Well, face it, a dermatologist with three kids, two in school and one at university doesn't have much assistance to offer,' he countered.

'That's beside the point,' she insisted, 'you wouldn't accept anything from him even if he did.'

'Oh no?' Jeremy held up his hand, ostentatiously flashing the 21-Jewel Omega wristwatch his father had given him on his eighteenth birthday. 'What about that?!'

'That,' she said, 'keeps perfect time.' The dispute over, they both burst out laughing.

Jeremy Venecourt's expensive Swiss watch had received, and continued to receive, much adverse criticism from his radical friends, who argued the contradictory nature of such a possession. Venner, who professed to despise all things bourgeois, who bought his clothes in op shops and spurned any symbol of capitalism, openly sported an Omega! 'Why?' they demanded.

'Because it keeps perfect time.' Venner's answer was always the same.

'Don't listen to me, Kate,' Jeremy now said, 'I'm a fraud. Nothing will part me from my watch, because quite simply I love it. Change of subject: shall I open the wine?'

'Yes please.' He isn't a fraud at all, she thought as she fetched the glasses. He was as passionate as the next man about his causes, and yet prepared to admit he was human. She respected him for his honesty.

They sat on the sofa and toasted the little house.

'To your new life, Kate,' he raised his glass.

'To my new life,' she said.

They looked into each other's eyes as they drank.

'Something smells good – what's for dinner?'

'Chicken casserole. I can cook, you know. Not very many things, but there's a few dishes I'm quite good at.'

'I don't doubt the fact.'

Their eyes were still locked.

'Chicken casserole, roast beef, and mulberry pie,' she said. 'Those are the three specialities Cook taught me.'

'Good old Cook.'

'Are you hungry?'

'Not yet. Will it spoil?'

'Not if I turn the oven off.'

They didn't bother going upstairs to where her brand-new double bed had been installed that very morning, taking up the entire attic and now draped in a welcoming brightly coloured shawl. They were not impractical, however. They dimmed the lights, ensured the curtains were tightly closed to the outside world and upon his instruction she fetched a towel for them to lie on.

The ABC was playing a medley of songs from *Mary Poppins* as they made love on the sofa. He was gentle, and she was ready. She'd been ready for months. It was a kind initiation.

'I thought the first time was meant to be unpleasant,' she said afterwards as they lay together, Kate revelling in their nakedness and the sharing of bare skin.

He smiled and trailed his fingers lazily over her breast. 'Not if you're a natural.'

'And not if you've been made love to by an expert, I suspect.' She propped on one elbow and studied him accusingly. 'You're very experienced, aren't you?'

'Yes.' There was nothing boastful in his admission. 'You were a virgin, Kate, I needed to be gentle.'

Were, Kate thought, he'd said 'were'. She looked down at the blood on the towel – not all that much, but enough positive evidence. Victory, her mind declared. It had finally happened.

'Next time will be better,' he promised.

She laughed and snuggled herself back into the crook of his arm. The first time had hardly been a disappointment.

Kate had not thought of Ellie since her return to Sydney; the ledgers were stacked away in the bottom drawer of the sideboard to be addressed at a later date. But she couldn't help herself now. She couldn't help recalling Ellie's candid account of her wedding night and Big Jim's violent claiming of her virginity. What a pity, she thought, that Ellie had not had a considerate lover like Jeremy.

They showered together, and then they ate the chicken casserole and drank the wine, after which they went upstairs to the brand-new bed, where they made love again, not so gently this time.

He stayed the night and they made love a third time the following morning, Kate's sexual awakening by now well and truly complete. Indeed so abandoned was she that Jeremy, who prided himself on his prowess and who liked to remain in command until the final moment, found he was fighting to maintain control.

'I've unleashed a monster,' he said as they lay back on the bed, chests heaving. 'You're insatiable, woman.'

'I know,' she panted, 'isn't it wonderful?'

Kate Durham and Jeremy Venecourt were in love. The older and more cynical might perhaps have said 'in lust', but who cared? Kate and Jeremy certainly didn't. They were obsessed with each other in every sense of the word. They excited each other, they stimulated each other both sexually and mentally, and if that wasn't love then what was?

'Let's join the gang on the Freedom Ride,' he said one morning as they lay in the rumpled attic bed recovering from their exertions. They'd been lovers for barely a week and it was still close to a fortnight before the new term was due to start. Jeremy hadn't actually moved into the little Campbell Street house, but he might just as well have; there'd been only two nights when he hadn't stayed there.

'You mean the SAFA bus?' Like most, Kate knew of the Student Action for Aborigines group that had been formed at Sydney University the previous year. SAFA had raised funds and chartered a bus for these last two weeks of vacation, the students' intention being to travel to various country towns on a fact-finding mission.

'Yes.' Jeremy sat bolt upright. The idea had instant appeal and he wondered why it hadn't occurred to him earlier. 'That's what we'll do. We'll join up with Charlie and the Freedom Riders.'

'But how can we? The bus left three days ago.'

'We don't travel in the bus. We follow them in the car.'

Kate was dubious. SAFA's Freedom Ride had been a long time in the planning and would receive a great deal of press. At least that was its aim, so she'd heard.

'Won't we look a bit odd trailing along in a brand-new Holden?' she said doubtfully. 'People might think us frivolous.'

'Who cares what we look like and who cares what people think? We'll be lending our support to the cause, that's all that matters.' Jeremy was clearly excited by the prospect.

'But we're not part of SAFA.'

'I am,' he said, 'or at least I was. Hell, I planned half their fundraisers last year. I worked on the itinerary. I helped line up accommodation in local halls for over thirty bloody people. I was going to be on the bus for God's sake –'

'Then why aren't you?'

Her interruption brought him to an abrupt halt. 'I opted out at the last minute.'

'Why?' He didn't reply, but she'd already guessed the answer. 'Because I was coming back to Sydney, is that it?'

'Yes, that's precisely it.' He gave a rueful shrug. 'So much for commitment, eh?'

She paused only infinitesimally. 'A brand-new Holden Premier Sedan won't be good for your image,' she said, 'you'll be seen as one of the bourgeoisie.'

He grinned, aware that she'd given in. 'The Holden's a bit like the Omega really, isn't it? For a car like that one's willing to run the risk of being misconceived by some.' He jumped out of bed and started pulling on his clothes. 'Actually, Kate, we can do far more than boost the numbers at SAFA's protests,' he said enthusiastically. 'They intend to conduct a survey into Aboriginal housing and health and population: we can help with the questionnaires, we can –'

Once again she interrupted. 'If a specific number of students have had accommodation lined up in advance,' she said, 'albeit in local halls, we can't just barge in unannounced. Where do you propose we stay?'

'We'll book into motels along the way,' he replied as he zipped up his jeans.

'Oh yes, and who pays for that?' He wouldn't have the audacity to suggest such a thing, surely.

'Our sponsor, of course: sugar daddy's funds are about to be put to good use.'

Obviously he would. She stared back in amazement.

He ignored her as he sat on the edge of the bed, hauling on his sandshoes. 'Come along, upsadaisy, time to get going.'

Kate knew she should have taken offence at his peremptory manner, his assumption, the sheer outrageousness of it, but why bother? What was the point in arguing? The madness of his idea held far too much appeal. She opted for dignity instead.

'I am going nowhere until I have had a shower,' she said.

After visiting the bank, they fuelled up the Holden, bought a map and headed out of town with Jeremy at the wheel. As they drove, they discussed SAFA's origins and its aims, Jeremy filling Kate in on anything she didn't know.

Student Action for Aborigines had started out as a general student protest against racial segregation in the United States, but the protest organisers had quickly decided they should look closer to home. A group had been formed in order to expose the racial discrimination that existed in Australia's own backyard, and third-year Arts student, Charles Perkins, himself Aboriginal, had been elected its president. Inspired by the Freedom Riders of the American Civil Rights Movement, SAFA had mounted a fact-finding mission with the intention of broadcasting to complacent city-dwellers the ugly reality of racism in many rural areas.

'It's not only complacency we're dealing with,' Jeremy said, 'it's dead bloody ignorance. A lot of Australians think racism doesn't exist in this country. They see it as belonging to South Africa and the Ku Klux Klan in America. SAFA intends to bring the truth home to the general public. They've got the means to do it, what's more. Darce Cassidy's a part-time reporter for the ABC and he's travelling with his recording equipment, Jim Spigelman's taken his home movie camera, and of course they've got their trump card on board with Charlie. If anyone can wake people up to reality, Charlie can. Charlie Perkins is charismatic.'

Jeremy's excitement was contagious, and Kate was starting to feel a true part of the cause, even though she supposed she would have to class herself as one of the ignorant.

How strange, she thought, that I of all people should have seen so little racism in my life. Discrimination against Aboriginal people was no doubt as rife in Queensland as anywhere else, but the protective cocoon of boarding school and life on the plantation had prevented her from witnessing it. Her father did not employ Aboriginal labourers, considering them unreliable, yet she had grown up with black people, the Kanaka workers of Elianne. There were still many Kanakas, descendants of those first arrivals, who lived in the area, some even on the estate. Yet she had never witnessed anything she could call racism. The Kanakas at Elianne had been well housed, well treated, well respected ...

Her thoughts were interrupted as a quote of Ellie's suddenly flashed through her mind. Something about the colonial use of 'kanaka' and the fact the word simply meant 'man' in the Hawaiian language. *It's ignorant and patronising, and they should know better*, Ellie had written. Oh dear, Kate thought, perhaps I've been a guilty party without even knowing it. Better keep that to myself.

Over the ensuing days any flicker of guilt Kate might have experienced disappeared as she witnessed the true face of racism. She was shocked by what she saw, and she was not alone. The towns visited by SAFA were known to be trouble spots, but the student activists had not expected to encounter such blatant segregation practices. Nor had they expected to be met with such open displays of hostility from the local citizens and police. They were all shocked. The only one who appeared to display little surprise was Charlie.

Kate deeply admired Charles Perkins. A handsome young man with a strong-boned face and an air of command, he confronted the angry hordes with strength and dignity. Charlie was a man with a purpose, and the others followed his lead. They protested and picketed for hours on end at areas where segregation was practised. At swimming pools and parks and pubs, at shops and cafes and clubs, they displayed their SAFA banner with pride and fearlessly stood their ground.

Recordings were made and footage was filmed. The findings of the Freedom Ride were destined to be beamed into the living rooms of Australia, and they were destined to shock.

At Walgett, the vice-president of the Returned Service League Club, was captured on tape saying he would never allow an Aborigine to become a club member. Yet, as the accompanying report would state, Aboriginal servicemen had fought for their country in every major conflict Australia had known.

When a convoy of cars followed the bus out of Walgett and ran it off the road, the drivers and their passengers screaming abuse at the activists, Jim Spigelman filmed the episode with his home movie camera. Darce Cassidy recorded the angry tirade that ensued and then filed a report with the ABC.

At Mooree swimming pool, hostile hordes gathered in protest when the activists arrived with a number of Aboriginal children from the reserve outside town and insisted they be granted the right to enter the baths. In order to prevent a riot, the authorities eventually relented and the children were allowed in. They were even photographed swimming with Charlie Perkins, and the picture was published in *The Australian*. But, as it was later reported, the moment SAFA left town the segregation rules were firmly reinstated.

The Freedom Ride had made headlines even before the bus returned to Sydney. Already the mission had proved a resounding success, and its ongoing effect was to have huge repercussions, raising both public and government awareness and strengthening the campaigns that were to follow.

'I believe I've discovered a new activist in our midst,' Jeremy said as he picked up the bottle and drained the dregs of Chianti into their glasses.

Back home, seated at the little round dining table and scoffing wine, the two had been ardently discussing the highlights of the trip and the purpose it had served, Kate's enthusiasm equalling if not surpassing Jeremy's.

'You have indeed,' she agreed fervently, 'if the cause is one like SAFA anyway. I've never felt such a sense of purpose. We achieved so much, Jeremy! I mean it was so worthwhile!'

'More than an activist, a zealot perhaps ...' He smiled: he'd seen the same heady excitement in many a new recruit. 'Well, good for you, Kate, we need people who are prepared to commit themselves. There's too much apathy about.'

'I don't know how I could have sat on the sidelines until now.'

'All first-year students do – it's expected. Even the most hardened of campaigners don't take up the gauntlet until second year.' Jeremy downed the last of his Chianti and leant in to kiss her.

She was instantly responsive, the taste of their mouths and the red wine mingling erotically.

'Activism inflames the libido,' he whispered. 'I feel the attic beckoning.'

Kate left her own wine.

The following morning, Jeremy broached the subject casually, although he'd been giving it some serious thought.

'Back to school in a few days,' he said as they settled themselves on the sofa with their mugs of instant coffee.

'Yes,' she replied eagerly, 'I'm looking forward to second year.'

'You sound excited.' His tone held a world-weary touch of cynicism.

'Well of course I am. Now that I've got my first-year general science out of the way I'll be starting on the professional Vet course. That's thrilling.'

He contemplated a wry comment, but decided against it. He rather envied Kate her devotion to study and her firm choice of career path. Much as he loved all the extracurricular activities university had to offer, he had no idea where his Arts course would eventually lead him. A rather rudderless existence for an activist, he supposed. But he didn't pursue that avenue of conversation.

'You know, Kate,' he said, 'I've been thinking ...'

'Yes?' He'd left the sentence hanging. 'Thinking what?'

'I've been thinking that as my toothbrush and spare underpants already live here, perhaps I should move in with them.'

Kate was struck speechless. She hadn't expected this.

'What do you say?' Jeremy continued to play things casually. 'It'd halve the rent and I'm here most of the time anyway. Seems practical, don't you think?'

'It's practical, yes,' she agreed, 'but I'm not ready, Jeremy. It's too soon. It's far too soon.'

'Of course,' he backpedalled immediately, 'I expected you to say that.' He had, but it hadn't stopped him hoping otherwise. 'Just thought I'd give it a try.' He didn't even know why he wanted to live with her. He'd never wanted to live with a girl before. 'Probably for the best anyway, a place this size.' He looked around the open-plan living room. 'I'd get in the way of your studies, wouldn't I?'

'Yes you would, I'm afraid.' She smiled. 'You'd be a huge distraction and you know it. In fact when term starts, we're going to have to limit ourselves to weekends.'

'Party-pooper.'

Kate laughed and they dropped the subject. She was glad he wasn't hurt that she'd been so immediately dismissive of the idea, but she needed her own space. She needed her own space for reasons other than study, which wouldn't really be necessary until later in the term anyway. The time had come, she'd decided. She was distanced enough now from her family and Elianne. She must read the ledgers. She must hear Ellie's own words and learn the truth.

Chapter Five

The National Service Scheme, which had been introduced by the Menzies government in November 1964, required all males twenty years of age to register with the Department of Labour and National Service. The young men were then subject to a ballot and if their birth date was drawn and they passed the ensuing medical tests, they were to serve two years in the regular army.

The government's principal concern at this stage was the confrontation between Indonesia and the newly formed Federation of Malaysia, a conflict that could potentially affect the border with Papua New Guinea, for which Australia had defence responsibility. The general population believed, however, that the National Service Scheme had been conceived for the sole purpose of supplying troops for Australia's growing commitment to the war in Vietnam. Conscription was set to become a contentious issue.

'Do you think they'll send you to Vietnam?' Hilda asked.

Neil nodded. 'More than likely.'

'Oh dear.'

The letter addressed to Neil Francis Durham, Elianne Estate, Bundaberg, Queensland had been dated 10 June 1965. It read:

You are hereby called up for national service
training in the Royal Australian Army. You
will present yourself for induction at the
Army Training Depot at Singleton, NSW ...

It went on brusquely to give the date of his departure and the specific details of each train and each connection that would deliver him to the barracks at Singleton, a hundred miles or so north of Sydney.

Neil had been one of those whose number had come up. He'd passed the medical and was now about to join the ranks of Australia's national servicemen.

'Ah well, a couple of years in the army won't do you any harm.' Stanley Durham had decided to take the philosophical approach. 'It could even be a good thing. Military training toughens a man.' He gave his son a hearty punch to the shoulder. 'And you could do with a bit of toughening up, boy.'

The two shared a grin. Neil was strangely ambivalent about being called up. He wasn't sure if he wanted to actually fight in a war, but the world of physical training and weaponry and battle tactics held an allure that was exciting.

'I'm appalled you should treat the matter in so trivial a fashion,' Hilda said frostily. 'Your son –'

'Is about to serve his country,' Stan interrupted. Then he added, 'You can't buck the system, old girl,' as if humouring his wife, though he was in reality shutting her up. Hilda detested being called 'old girl'. 'And it's not as if we haven't been expecting the news. Neil's as fit as a mallee bull – he was bound to pass the physical.'

Upon Max's delivery of the letter, Stan had called the family together in the smaller front sitting room, invading Hilda's solitary morning-tea ritual. With Kate in Sydney and Alan in Brisbane there were just the four of them – indeed had Hilda not insisted upon Bartholomew's inclusion there would have been only three.

'It would be appalling to exclude your father, Stanley,' she'd said. 'Bartholomew is a part of this family. Of course he must join us.'

'Why? He hardly has anything to contribute, has he?'

'That's beside the point. He must be informed of the situation.'

'All right, tell him we're meeting in half an hour.' Stan had shrugged. He didn't really care either way.

'Well, Neil,' he now said, continuing in the same hearty vein, 'it's good to see that you're following in your old man's footsteps. Just make sure you don't cop a bout of typhoid along the way, eh?' He gave a self-deprecating laugh.

Stan was making light of things in order to allay his wife's fears, but he was rightfully proud of his service in North Africa. He'd been a Rat of Tobruk and if he hadn't contracted typhoid during the 9th Division's brief rest period in Palestine, he would have gone on with the others to fight at El Alamein. Typhoid fever had come close to killing him, however, and he'd been repatriated to Australia in early 1942 with a weak heart that prevented him from further military service.

'You'll make a fine soldier, son,' he said. 'The training will stand you in good stead, and it's a minor war when all's said and done: it'll be over before we know it. Mind you,' he added, 'it's a war that could well serve our purpose. We'll be gaining a valuable ally assisting the Americans. But it won't last long in any case. Storm in a teacup.'

Hilda cast a quick glance at Bartholomew. *It won't last long.* Wasn't that what they'd said about the Great War? Bartholomew had lost two brothers at Gallipoli. She wondered what was going through his mind. Very little, it appeared. Bartholomew's eyes were on Stanley, but he appeared quite removed from the proceedings as he methodically sipped his tea.

*

Neil telephoned his brother and sister with the news of his call up. Their reactions were very different.

'Oh shit,' Kate said, 'what a pity you're not at uni – you could defer. Any other way around it, do you think?'

'Nope, mind you I haven't given that aspect much consideration.' He was a little surprised by her automatic assumption that he would do anything to avoid national service. *University is having an effect upon Kate*, he thought. *For starters she never used to swear.*

'Military training camp, wow,' Alan said, when he'd been summoned to the boarders' phone and told the news, 'that could be really interesting. Do you reckon they'll train you to drive tanks?'

'Don't know. We'll soon find out. I'll be home for Christmas. See you then.'

The night before Neil's departure, Stan insisted on an evening at the Burnett Club. Hilda, who had no wish to be deprived of her son's company, would far rather have organised a modest farewell dinner at home, but tradition demanded otherwise.

'It's the done thing, my dear,' Stan was adamant, 'the members will want to wish him well and speed him on his way.'

Objection was futile, Hilda knew. Stanley needed to show off his son. Whenever something of importance required celebration or recognition, the Burnett Club beckoned.

Situated in Quay Street overlooking the river, the Burnett Club with its strictly 'gentlemen only' membership had been the favoured meeting place of Bundaberg's professional and business elite for as long as most could remember. When the son of a prominent citizen came of age he was invariably introduced to the Burnett Club, although in Stan's case things had been a little different. As Bartholomew Durham had had little interest in that kind of socialising, Stan had been introduced to the club by his grandfather, Big Jim. These days, with his own son and heir, Stan adhered to tradition and also to Big Jim's business policy, which he considered of fundamental importance.

'My father never understood the value of cultivating relationships with the more influential members of the community,' Stan said, 'he considered a trip into town for a beer at the club tedious and unnecessary. Big Jim knew better, and Big Jim was right.'

Father and son had deserted the busy bar, which had become stuffy with cigar and cigarette smoke. Crossing through the empty function room that looked directly over the river, they'd stepped out onto the lawn with their beers. The night was still and chill with the bite of winter, but the air was bracing and the river below glistened silver on black in the moonlight. Behind them, even with the doors closed, the babble of men's voices could clearly be heard.

'Good turn up tonight,' Stan said, 'lot of the regulars.'

A healthy cross-section of the town's upper echelon was indeed present, including from the medical profession Dr Len McKeon, prominent physician, and Dr Jack Scott, surgeon. Representative of the business sector was Carl Nielson of Nielson's Musical Store, Stewart Pettigrew of Wypers, Garnet Buss of Buss & Turners and Rob Black of John Black's Drapery and Clothing Emporium. Stanley Durham was on friendly terms with each and every one, and each and every one had shaken his son by the hand. They'd gathered about and toasted the lad, raising their beers and their glasses of 'Special Blend' and 'Governor's Choice', the club's exclusive OP rum blends. 'Godspeed, Neil,' they'd said while Stan had stood by, pretending nonchalance, but bursting with a father's pride.

'The men of the Burnett wish you well, Neil,' he now said as they gazed out at the river and the sprawl of the Bundaberg Foundry on the opposite bank. 'That's a powerful bond forged in there, son, valuable friendships that'll last you the whole of your life.' He downed a large swig of his beer. 'Something my father could never understand,' he added with a touch of derision. 'Just as well I had Big Jim in my life.'

Neil, like Kate, often felt critical of the treatment afforded Bartholomew by his own son. Stan continually ignored or derided his father, which seemed not only unfair but puzzling. Neil himself could clearly remember, in the days before Bartholomew's stroke when he'd accompanied the old man into town, the respect his grandfather had commanded. It had been quite evident that Bartholomew Durham was held in high regard by all those who knew him. Did it make him any less of a man if he chose not to become a member of the Burnett Club?

'Do you know, Neil,' Stan continued, 'I remember all those years ago before I went off to training camp. Big Jim brought me here to the club and his mates all gathered around to wish me Godspeed. Just like tonight.'

'History repeating itself, eh?' Neil said, although his smile was a little forced. He sometimes disliked himself for not taking a stand. I should have spoken up just then, he thought, I should have spoken up for Grandpa: Kate certainly would have. He wondered, as he did on occasions, whether his choice to remain silent was a sign of weakness. Am I a spineless bastard, he wondered, or do I not want to prick Dad's bubble, which is it?

'History repeating itself, exactly.' Stan beamed with pleasure. 'A man's friends are the measure of him, son, and my friends have become yours. I couldn't be more proud, Neil. I swear I couldn't possibly be more proud.' He raised his glass and they clinked and drank to each other.

Neil decided to let himself off lightly this time. Of course I can't prick Dad's bubble, he thought, not a bubble as big as this one anyway. But living in Stan the Man's shadow could be wearing, and living up to his expectations even more so. Neil was plagued by the ever-present fear of disappointing his father.

He drained the last of his beer. 'Come on, Dad, finish her off,' he said, 'my shout. Then I'll beat you at snooker.'

Stan laughed. 'Want to bet?'

The following evening, Stan and Hilda stood on the platform of Bundaberg Railway Station waving farewell to their son who was hanging out the window of the 'Rockhampton Mail', the slow, overnight train that stopped at every station between Bundy and Brisbane. Neil's instructions had been meticulous. Upon his early-morning arrival at Roma Street Station, he was to proceed to South Brisbane Interstate Railway Station, where he was to board the lunchtime train bound for Sydney. He would alight at Singleton in the early hours of the following morning.

'It's only training camp, Hilda,' Stan said unable to disguise a touch of irritation as she ferreted for her handkerchief. 'The boy's hardly going off to war.'

Hilda made no reply. Not yet, she thought, dabbing at her eyes.

The training course at Singleton was tough and deliberately so, the intention being to push the young national servicemen to their absolute limit, even to breaking point if necessary, and then remould them to army requirements. Military experts believed that the new recruits, in taking a dislike to their officers and NCOs, would rely more and more upon each other, thereby forming a bond of mateship that would serve them well in combat. The psychology worked. Over the ensuing weeks, the bond forged between the 'nashos', as they were known, became steadily unbreakable. It was a bond very much embraced by Neil Durham.

After several months of arduous basic training, Neil and his newfound mates were transported to Brisbane where on 5 September they were marched into Enoggera Barracks, home of the newly formed 6RAR. It was here they would embark upon their serious corps training.

The 6th Battalion of the Royal Australian Regiment constituted four companies of approximately one hundred and twenty officers and men, each company consisting of four platoons, numbering around thirty men and one officer. Private Neil Durham was assigned to D Company, 12 Platoon.

Neil loved the routine of army life. He was a fit young man, lean and strong, and, unlike some of the other national servicemen, particularly those from the city, the rigorous physical training presented him with little hardship from the outset. Relentless though it was, he found it exhilarating, liberating even. In fact, Neil embraced everything the military had to offer. He loved the camaraderie of his fellow 'nashos', he loved the precision of weaponry training and the discipline of army drill, and he particularly loved the mindlessness of endless marches to the chant of 'These Boots Were Made for Walking'. The men of the 6th Battalion had claimed Nancy Sinatra's number-one hit as their own and sang it with pride and gusto, always tuneless, but in perfect rhythm, never missing a beat.

Freed from the constant pressure of his father's expectations, Neil Durham loved, above all else, being simply one man in an army of men.

Alan was the first of the Durham siblings to arrive home for Christmas. Unlike Kate, he'd returned to Elianne for each of his term breaks throughout the year, every visit finding him more eager than ever to be reunited with Paola.

The relationship between the two had escalated to the point where it was evident to all and sundry that young Alan Durham and Paola Fiorelli were smitten with each other.

Stan voiced his concern to his wife, and he didn't pull any punches doing so. 'There'd better not be any funny business going on,' he snarled. 'I'll have his bloody guts for garters if he gets the girl pregnant.'

'Don't be coarse, Stanley,' Hilda replied primly. 'Of course there'll be none of that going on – they're only sixteen.'

'Exactly! Just the age when a boy thinks of nothing but sex!'

'A girl, however, does not.' Hilda's response was icy; something in her husband's tone had seemed to add 'you stupid woman'. 'Particularly a girl like Paola, who comes from a very good family.'

She's missed the point entirely, Stan thought. He was surprised, for despite her vague lapses Hilda was usually astute in her observation of others. Dear God, it's the good family that's the worry, he told himself, they're Micks for Christ's sake! He didn't care in the least if Alan bedded the Italian girl, it was time the boy lost his virginity and it might as well be with the Dago. But if something serious were to develop between his son and a Catholic, that would be a different matter altogether.

'I may have made a mistake giving Paola a job here on the estate,' he said thoughtfully. 'Perhaps it would be better all round if she sought work in town.'

Paola had left school the previous year after completing her junior certificate and was now employed as a receptionist at the front desk of Elianne's office, a position which had delighted her father Luigi.

'No, dear, it wouldn't,' Hilda said firmly but gently. 'In fact I believe such an action would be most unwise. If the two are as enamoured as they appear to be, then separating them would only enflame the situation. Better to wait. They will tire of each other in time. Paola will not submit to Alan's advances, if indeed he makes any, and driven by a young man's desire he will move on. Theirs is puppy love, Stanley, and puppy love never lasts.'

Sensing her husband's uncertainty and keen to put him at his ease, she added, 'Besides, were anything serious to develop, Luigi himself would be the first to forbid any form of union.'

Stan nodded. 'You're right,' he said. She was, he thought. Hilda hadn't missed the point at all.

Kate arrived home two weeks after Alan and was immediately embroiled in the situation for no reason other than her car.

'Hey, if I sling on my L plates can I drive the Holden into town tonight, Kate?' Alan said the day after her arrival, which happened to be a Saturday. He'd had his learner's plates for just under a month, and cadged drives into town at every opportunity. 'I want to take Paola to the pictures.'

'What's wrong with the bus?'

A privately operated bus service ran regularly between Elianne and Bundaberg, particularly during the crushing season when shift workers were transported to and fro from dawn until midnight. The service had diminished a little over recent times as cars had become more readily available, but it continued to operate throughout the year, even during the slack season. Employees were delivered to work, children to school, women to shops, and families to picnics at Bargara. And at weekends the bus remained an imperative mode of transport for young people, taking them to and from dances and the Saturday-night pictures.

'The bus was fine for us when we were kids,' Kate said.

'Give us a break,' Alan pulled a face, 'it's hardly as classy as the Holden.'

Ah, she thought, he wants to show off. 'You do know you have to have a licensed driver in the front seat with you, don't you, Al?'

'Course I know that.' He proffered a hopeful smile. 'Do you want to come along?'

'And how do you plan to get home?' she asked, knowing the answer.

'Well we could catch the last bus, I suppose,' he said with a reluctant shrug, then he grinned. 'Or you could come to the pictures with us if you like. *The Sound of Music*'s on,' he added enticingly. 'Everyone's raving about it and Paola's dead keen. What do you reckon?'

'I reckon the sooner you get your licence the better,' she said.

Alan couldn't agree more. It was a source of constant frustration that, expert driver as he was, his legal licence was still a good two months away.

'Is that a yes?' he asked hopefully.

'*The Sound of Music*, how could I possibly refuse?'

The picture theatre was open-air, or rather three-quarters of it was. The majority of the space was given over to canvas deck chairs, where the audience lounged comfortably beneath an open sky, knowing they could make a dash for the covered section at the rear should it happen to rain.

There was no likelihood of rain that night, however. The afternoon's searing heat had gone and the warmth that lingered was sensual as people lolled in deck chairs, bare-legged and sandal-shod, men and boys in shorts, women and girls in light cotton dresses and skirts. Summer nights at the open-air cinema were invariably languid affairs.

'Do, a deer, a female deer …'

As the youngsters on screen joined Julie Andrews in song, Kate glanced at her brother seated beside her. The Von Trapp children had apparently failed to captivate Alan, who was staring up at the stars. The Von Trapps may not have been wholly to blame though: Alan often disappeared into a world of his own.

Kate enjoyed the film more than she'd thought she would, but she was a little distracted by her brother's inattention. Alan's gaze continued for the most part to be directed either up at the stars, which were indeed vivid in a cloudless sky, or at Paola seated on the other side of him. The two held hands throughout, but Paola's own gaze, from the occasional glimpses Kate caught of the girl's profile, remained fixed upon the screen.

'Isn't he terrible?' Paola said during the drive home. 'A film as wonderful as that and he spends the whole time looking up at the sky.'

Or at you, Kate thought. 'Didn't you like it, Al?' she asked.

'Not much,' he said, his eyes on the road as he drove. 'I thought it was a bit soppy.' He smiled apologetically into the rear-vision mirror at Paola, who was seated in the back. 'Not enough action for me, I'm afraid.'

'Not enough action?' She was appalled. 'They get chased by Nazis!'

'Yeah, but only in the last few minutes and nobody's killed.'

'Your brother has no taste at all, Kate,' Paola said. 'Unless it's a gangster film he's not remotely interested.'

'You're lucky. It used to be cowboys and Indians.'

'It still is.' Alan accepted their ragging good-naturedly. 'And if I can't get a dose of either, I'll look at the stars.'

Alan didn't actually care what film he saw. All he could think of was the day when he'd have his licence and be able to drive Paola into town without someone else sitting in the front seat. He was sick of being treated like a child. And more importantly, he was sick of being made to appear a child in Paola's eyes. But he was grateful to Kate.

'It was beaut having the Holden tonight,' he said as they pulled up in the front driveway after dropping Paola home. Kate had no idea whether there'd been a good-night kiss; she'd discreetly looked the other way as he'd walked Paola to the door.

The two of them climbed out of the car and started up the main steps of the Big House.

'Thanks, Kitty-Kat,' he said.

'A pleasure, Al-Pal,' she replied.

They smiled; they hadn't used those nicknames for years.

How different everything is, Kate thought a little later as she lay in her bed, the lamp still on, gazing about at the familiar things that surrounded her; strange how everything can look the same and yet be so different. But then times have changed, she told herself. *Alan's grown up, Neil's off at army camp, I'm at university* ...

But try as she might, she couldn't distract herself from the truth. The changes in her life and her brothers' lives were part of the natural transformation she'd sensed on her trip home the previous Christmas: she could not ignore the difference that now existed. This difference went far deeper than simply growing up and moving on: it was reflected in everything she saw around her. Even the past, now viewed through different eyes, would never be the same. The diaries had made sure of that.

Reaching out her hand, she switched off the bedside lamp. She must not think about Ellie. She'd determined that during this trip home she would put the diaries from her mind. An impossible task, she was aware – their revelations would always be with her – but to dwell upon the unanswerable questions they raised was a pointless invitation to torment. She rolled on her side, willing herself to sleep.

'You and I must visit Elianne House today, Kate.' The following morning over breakfast Hilda made her solemn announcement. 'We must pay our respects.'

'How can we?' Kate replied bluntly. 'It's gone.'

Stan and Bartholomew glanced up from their plates, both mildly surprised by her brusqueness, but Alan stifled a smile as he tucked into his eggs and bacon. He loved his sister's lack of pretension.

Hilda was not amused, however, by what she saw as her daughter's blatant irreverence. 'I am fully aware of that, Kate,' she said, piqued and more than a little hurt, 'but we must pay tribute to the demise of Elianne House. As a measure of respect to Grandmother Ellie if nothing else,' she added tightly.

'Of course.' Kate smiled an apology. She hadn't meant to sound terse; it had not been her intention to offend. As a rule she was happy to indulge her mother's need for drama, but for some reason the words had just popped out that way. 'We'll go straight after breakfast, Marmee, I promise.'

A half an hour later, Kate pulled the Holden up in the front driveway of Elianne House or rather the untidy remains of what had once been the front driveway, for vegetation had steadily claimed the grounds of the old home. As for the house itself, there remained no visible sign that here had once stood an early Queenslander of impressive dimensions and gracious design. Verdant growth had reclaimed the site with a greed that seemed to denounce humanity's right to have ever built here in the first place, vines and bushes and grasses vying for supremacy over the rubble and remnants that lay buried beneath.

The women climbed from the car, Kate circling to stand beside her mother.

'Good God,' she said in amazement, 'it's disappeared completely.'

'Yes,' Hilda replied, 'isn't that terrible? After seventy-five years Elianne House has been wiped from the face of the earth, just like that, gone forever. It's more than terrible,' she said, her face a mask of tragedy, 'it's shameful that such a thing should have been allowed to happen. The past has been stolen from us, Kate.'

Which is probably not a bad thing, a voice in Kate's brain said, but she remained silent as together they stared at the mass of tangled growth that had sprouted to claim its own with such ferocity.

'Big Jim built the house for Grandmother Ellie in 1890,' Hilda said pensively, still seeing in her mind's eye the old home in all its grandeur. 'Elianne House was a gift of love.'

'Yes, I know.' Kate marvelled at the fact that she felt absolutely nothing. Surely this is a healthy sign, she thought, with a vague sense of relief. If only she could put her knowledge of the past behind her with the same ease as she could Elianne House, then perhaps ...

Hilda, having turned to look at her daughter, was now studying her astutely as Kate gazed out at the landscape.

'You've changed, Kate,' she said.

Visited by an unrealistic fear that her mother might somehow have divined her thoughts, Kate started guiltily. 'Changed?' She tried her best to sound casual. 'In what way?'

'You're confident now.'

'Since when have I not been?' What a strange remark, Kate thought.

'I mean that you're at home with your beauty, dear.' Hilda examined her daughter's face, clinically, unashamedly, like a doctor examining a patient for infinitesimal signs of a condition. Yes, she thought, Kate is no longer a virgin. She wears her womanliness like a badge and my goodness how it does suit her.

'Oh my darling,' she said fervently, overcome by a sudden surge of emotion, 'I do hope he loves you. You deserve someone who can offer you true love.' Then in typically mercurial fashion, the feyness vanished to be replaced by maternal practicality, and questions darted like arrows. 'Who is he, dear, tell me? What does he do? Would I like him?'

Relieved though Kate was that no supernatural divination had taken place, she found her mother's perceptiveness confronting. Rather than avoid the issue as she would normally have done, however, she chose to answer in all honesty.

'He's a university student, Marmee,' she said, 'and I don't know if you'd like him. His name is Jeremy, he's just finished his Bachelor of Arts and intends to go on to his Masters, and I'm not sure if either of us knows what "true love" is.' She smiled, not wishing to sound callous. 'To be quite honest, I think it's a strictly fairy tale term.'

'Oh, you modern young career women,' Hilda gave an exasperated wave of her hand, 'I don't understand your cynicism, really I don't.' She wondered briefly whether she should offer a mother's cautionary advice about 'taking care', but it hardly seemed necessary. Kate was far cleverer than she could ever hope to be. Besides, this was the sixties: things had changed. There was the contraceptive pill. Girls knew how to look after themselves these days.

She looked out again to where the old house had once stood. 'Perhaps it is wise after all to be cynical,' she said wistfully. 'Perhaps you're right to keep your expectations to a minimum. Not everyone is destined to experience a great love.'

Kate felt a stab of irritation. Hilda was wandering down some wishful lane to the past again, a past of her own invention.

'Time to go home,' she said briskly. She was no longer prepared to pander to the fantasy.

Any consideration Kate may have once given to the sharing of Ellie's writings, at least in some part, with her mother had gone. She had decided not even to share them with her brother Alan. Not yet anyway. The diaries must remain a secret for the moment, their future uncertain. She had already embarked upon the painstaking exercise of their translation, which she intended to complete in time, but to what end she wasn't sure. Perhaps for posterity – they were documents of historical interest after all – or perhaps to be kept locked away for future generations of Durhams. She might possibly, when she had completed their translation, let Alan read them for himself, thereby gaining a confidant who could help her decide upon a course of action. Right now she was certain of only one thing. She could not expose her parents to the lies and deceit upon which their lives had been based.

Private Neil Durham was granted ten days' leave over Christmas and the New Year, his arrival home completing the family reunion.

'My God, just look at you,' Stan said, holding his son at arm's length, a proprietorial hand on each shoulder. 'Army life suits you, my boy, there's no doubt about that.'

'Dad's right,' Kate said, eyeing her brother up and down admiringly. 'I never realised you were so handsome.'

She was joking, but it was true nonetheless. He had always been good looking, but now Neil's body had filled out, the musculature clearly defined; he was not only fit, he was strong and it showed. But more than that, Kate registered a new self-assurance in her brother, a new manliness.

Neil laughed and hugged her. 'You're not too bad yourself, Sis.'

The Christmas luncheon was a repetition of the previous year with the same intimate gathering of family and friends. The Krantzes were there – Ivan with his wife and son – and the Fiorellis – Luigi, his wife and two children, foregoing their customary extended family gathering for the honour of dining at The Big House. But there was a subtle shift in relationships, or so it seemed to Kate. Surely Ivan is a little less deferential, she thought, his manner a little bolder. It would make sense of course. Ivan was no longer dependent upon Elianne for a living. Elianne was only one in any number of Krantz & Son clients, the most important admittedly, but just one nonetheless. Ivan and his son were doing very well, she'd been told.

'We're branching into some exciting new investment areas, Stan,' Ivan said. 'We'd love to run them by you, wouldn't we, Henry?' Henry nodded. 'These are thrilling times for the sugar industry. Times of expansion, times of change –'

'Yes, yes, we'll talk later,' Stan said dismissively as he reached out and speared another slice of turkey from the platter. 'Now's hardly the time.'

There had been occasions in the past when Kate had felt herself cringe at her father's arrogant treatment of others. She didn't now. She thought it crass of Ivan to talk business over the family Christmas lunch, and she wasn't the only one. Glancing at her mother, she caught Hilda's eye peering over the rim of the champagne glass she'd just lifted to her lips. Poor form, Hilda's eye said, pushy, vulgar. Hilda, too, was pleased to see Ivan put in his place. And put in his place Ivan was. He backed down immediately.

'Of course, Stan, of course,' he said with a bonhomie that denied the insult he'd just been delivered, 'wrong time to talk, I agree.' He beamed at his son. 'We tend to get a bit carried away with the excitement of it all, don't we, Henry?'

Henry nodded again. Neither of them wanted to end up on the wrong side of Stan the Man.

Kate was briefly distracted from the interplay of friction by her grandfather's quiet signal for the hot mustard. She passed him the pot for a second time and watched with amusement as Bartholomew piled another heaped spoonful onto the side of his plate. Then, as she ate her own meal, she looked around at the gathering.

It isn't just Ivan, she thought. The table seemed fraught with undertones, or was it just her imagination working overtime? The glances her father kept darting at Alan and Paola seated together with eyes for none but each other clearly signalled his disapproval, which was hardly surprising. But there was a guardedness also from Luigi, who every now and then scowled in the young couple's direction, he too distracted by the attention they were paying each other.

Maria Fiorelli nudged her husband. Kate was not the only one who'd noticed Luigi's ill humour.

'*Non rovinare le cose*, Luigi,' she whispered.

Luigi re-directed his scowl to his wife. What did Maria mean? How was he spoiling things?

'*Guardo a voi. Non cipiglio. È Natale.*'

'Ah. *Scusa.*' Luigi hadn't even realised he'd been scowling. Maria was quite right, he told himself, he mustn't spoil Christmas. He painted on an obliging smile, which looked rather fake and foolish and Maria smiled gratefully in return.

Maria Fiorelli was not overly concerned about her daughter. She was of the same mind as Hilda Durham, the argument she'd presented to her husband having been very similar to that proffered by Hilda to Stan.

'It is a first love and an innocent one, Luigi,' she'd said when he'd voiced his worry. 'Alan is a good boy. He would not take advantage of Paola. You of all people would know this.'

Luigi did. If there were any one boy in whom he would place his trust it was most certainly Alan Durham. Luigi had been a true friend and mentor to Alan for the whole of the boy's life; he knew the boy better than did the boy's own father. But what if over time the relationship between Alan and Paola developed into something more serious? The two could not marry.

His wife was quick to address his fears. 'And if it were ever to become serious,' she continued, 'you would always have an ally in Mr Stan.' Unlike her husband, Maria was not on first-name terms with Stan the Man. She did not wish to be: respect demanded their employer remain 'Mr Stan' at all times. 'Mr Stan would never allow his son to wed a Catholic,' she said.

'So you do not think I should forbid Paola this friendship?'

'No. That would only make matters worse. And here is something else to think upon, Luigi. Alan's presence will protect Paola from less desirable youths who may come sniffing about. Best we leave things as they are for now. When she is of age we will remind her of the nice Catholic boys she has grown up with. Or we will write home to see if someone there has a son worthy of our Paola.'

'Very well, Maria, I will trust in your wisdom. We will say nothing.' But despite his wife's common sense, Luigi did not stop worrying.

Nor did Stan Durham, and as both families maintained a pained silence, the only two oblivious to the undercurrent of disapproval were Alan and Paola.

Throughout the main course, the customary toasts were made to friends and family, but Stan ensured the principal toast was reserved for Neil and his forthcoming tour of duty in Vietnam.

'To Neil and his military service to this country,' he said solemnly, rising to his feet.

There was a shuffling of chairs as the others quickly followed suit, glasses raised. 'To Neil,' they said.

'So when do you think they'll send you over there?' Ivan asked when they were once again seated.

'None of us knows for sure,' Neil said, 'but not for a while yet. We've got close to another five months of training to go, so I reckon around May some time.'

The general discussion then not unsurprisingly turned to the war in South Vietnam and not unsurprisingly Stan was quick to express his opinion. Stanley Durham was very much in favour of Australia's commitment.

'Communism's spreading like a rampant bloody disease throughout Europe and now Asia,' he said, downing his knife and fork and pushing his plate from him. 'If the Reds take South Vietnam we'll be next in line you can bet on it. They have to be stopped.'

Prior to his son's conscription, Stan had shown little interest in the conflict in Vietnam, which had seemed to him so very far away. A civil war in a remote Asian country couldn't possibly affect us here at Elianne, he'd thought, if indeed he'd given the matter any consideration at all. He was of quite a different mind these days and, never one to dither, his views were as always black and white. Shades of grey rarely entered Stan's arguments.

'But you surely don't believe,' Ivan said, 'that mandatory national service is the answer.' He cast a deferential look to Neil, intending no disrespect. 'I mean Australians said no to conscription twice during the First World War. To introduce it now, and without a referendum, seems a radical move by the government, don't you think?' Ivan Krantz was only too relieved that his son Henry had missed out on the government's national service lottery by a good two years.

'If conscription is what it takes to stem the spread of communism then yes I most certainly do,' Stan declared emphatically. 'Our boys are being called up to serve a noble cause and they should feel proud to be a part of it.'

Ivan didn't agree at all, but he retired from the discussion, knowing argument would be futile; and besides, he had no wish to cross Stan.

Kate felt intensely irritated. Ivan's views obviously differed from her father's and he was an intelligent man – he should have answered back. She wasn't sure which aspect of the exchange irritated her most, her father's belligerence or Ivan's lack of spine, but she found herself diving in.

'What about those who oppose the very principle of war?' she demanded, squaring up to her father across the table. 'What about those who are against the taking of human life? Should they be conscripted? Is it right they should be forced to do what they believe is morally wrong?'

Silence descended. Even the clink of cutlery ceased.

'Yes,' Stan said, glowering darkly at his daughter. 'Sacrifices are made in a war: men kill and are killed. Cowards cannot be tolerated.' He shifted his focus, directing his attention solely to Neil. 'If my son is to answer his country's call, then so must the sons of others.'

Kate had no comeback to that. He'd bested her by personalising the argument and bringing Neil into the equation. She looked at her brother, hoping she hadn't caused offence, and was grateful when his eyes signalled she hadn't, but she knew that to continue the discussion was pointless and in Neil's company tasteless.

Stan smiled a victor's smile. 'Besides,' he said to the table in general, 'the Americans will have this war over in no time, and by joining them we'll have earned the gratitude of a valuable ally. All the more reason to send our boys over there. We have the future to think of when all's said and done.'

Having clinched the argument to his own satisfaction he gestured for Ivy to clear away the plates, even though several guests hadn't quite finished their main courses. Then he turned to his wife. 'Shall we have some more champagne before dessert, my dear?'

'An excellent suggestion,' Hilda replied, relieved that the tension was dispelled.

The exodus that followed lunch found the younger members of the company pondering what to do next.

'I need a swim,' Neil said as the junior Durhams and Fiorellis stood in the baking sun waving goodbye to the Krantzes' Ford Zephyr. 'Let's head for the dam.'

'You're on,' Kate said, but Alan cast a hesitant glance at Paola. The deep dam with its steep banks was a dangerous place for all but the most experienced of swimmers. She was bound to find it alarming, if indeed she dared venture in.

'What about Bargara?' he suggested thinking of The Basin, but the other two shook their heads.

'Too far, can't be bothered,' Neil said.

Alan didn't push the matter further as a better idea occurred. 'Can I borrow the Holden and take Paola for a drive then, Kate?' he asked. 'Only around Elianne,' he added in the moment's pause that followed, 'I promise.' He raised his hand as if swearing an oath.

'Sure,' Kate said. 'I'll grab the car keys while we put on our togs. Won't be a tick.'

As she and Neil set off up the stairs, she heard young Georgio Fiorelli behind her.

'Can I come too, Alan?'

And Alan's good-humoured rejoinder, masking any reluctance he may have felt: 'Course you can mate. The more the merrier.'

Minutes later she and Neil, clad in bathing togs, T-shirts and sandshoes, towels draped around their necks, stood watching as the Holden drove off in the direction of the mill.

'A disaster waiting to happen, those two,' Neil said. 'Did you feel the tension over lunch?'

'Hard not to, surely everyone did.'

'Everyone except Alan and Paola.'

'You're right there.'

The two of them stared thoughtfully out at the trail of dust winding its way up the dirt road.

'Do you reckon one of us should have a word with him?' Kate asked, but even as she did she knew the answer, and turning to each other they shook their heads in unison.

'You know Alan,' Neil said with a shrug.

'Yep, he'd only close off. We'll just have to wait and see what happens, I suppose. Race you.'

She sprinted out of the driveway, her brother hot on her heels, and together they raced along the dirt track that led through the bushland to the Pump Hill railway track, their objective the main dam.

Situated high above the banks of the Burnett River, the main dam was fed with a constant supply of water via the pumping station far below. Here, well upriver, the water was fresh and the main dam was the principal source of irrigation for the cane fields. A further dam up near the mill supplied water to the homes on the estate and the mill itself, but it was the main dam that had always been of greatest significance to the Durham children. Throughout the whole of their lives the main dam had served as a favourite summer playground and, barely a half a mile from the big house, the run there had always proved a gruelling competition, particularly between the two older siblings.

For the past several years, the race had been a neck-and-neck affair, but this time things were vastly different. This time Neil came in the easy winner and by the time Kate reached the dam she discovered him sitting on the small wooden jetty, taking off his sandshoes and barely out of breath.

'Not fair,' she panted collapsing beside him. 'Not fair at all, the army's made a new man of you.'

He grinned. 'I believe that's the general idea.'

She flopped onto her back, chest heaving, feeling the sun-drenched wooden planks warm against her shoulders. 'So I suppose it means I won't get to beat you from now on.'

'S'pose it does.'

'What a bugger.'

They spent the next hour being ten again, racing each other to and fro across the dam – she could equal him in the water – and scrambling up the steep banks to throw bombshells off the jetty, keeping an eye out for snakes all the while. Snakes held little fear for them, accustomed as they were to the many species that abounded, most of which were highly venomous, but like all the locals they were wary of the Brown snake. Browns were not timid. They did not shrink from human contact as other snakes did, you couldn't shoo them away with a stick. Brown snakes were aggressive, and to be carefully avoided.

Exhausted at long last they stretched out on the jetty. They didn't even bother drying themselves off, but just lay on their backs soaking up the sun.

After ten minutes or so, Kate sat up. She hugged her knees and stared out at the distant mill, its tangle of buildings towering gothic-like over the surrounding bushland of the estate and the never-ending cane fields.

'I'm sorry for stirring up that argument over lunch,' she said. The matter had been playing on her mind and she wanted to apologise.

'What argument are you talking about?' he asked dozily, eyes closed.

'Conscription. It was a bit tacky of me, really.'

'Tacky. In what way?' He opened his eyes and squinted up at her. 'Tacky' wasn't a word that featured regularly in his vocabulary, nor in the general lexicon of the Durham household. University speak, he thought.

'Well, pretty tasteless to talk about "the very principle of war" and the taking of human life when your brother's about to go into battle, wouldn't you say?'

'Nup, you were only being you, I'm used to it.'

'It's just that Dad –'

'I know.' Neil stopped squinting up at her and propped on one elbow. 'Dad was on his high horse and you wanted to have a go at him like you always do. Alan and I wonder why you bother.' He smiled. 'I must say I was surprised how quickly you caved in this time. But it was because you didn't want to be tacky, right?'

'Right.'

'You weren't, so don't worry.' He flopped back on the jetty and closed his eyes once more.

Kate rolled onto her stomach and studied him thoughtfully. 'Hey, Neil …?'

'What now?' he said, propping again.

'They give you an option, don't they? I mean, I know you have to serve your time in the army, but when you're called upon for active duty, you don't actually have to go, do you?'

His laugh was affectionate. 'Oh Kate,' he said, as if she was a child who'd asked a truly naïve question, 'a bloke can't opt out just like that, not after training with his mates. Sure, they say it's an option, but we all know it's not.' He could see she was puzzled and he tried to explain. 'Nashos get chucked all sorts of shit at training camp, they really put you through the mill and the blokes form a rock-solid bond. That's the whole aim of the exercise and it works, I can tell you. What are you going to say to your mates when you're all trained up and they ask you to go to war? See you later, fellahs, I think I'll stay behind?'

'I get the picture,' she replied.

'You mustn't worry about me,' he said, keen to put her fears at rest, for he could see that she did worry. 'I love the army, strange as that may seem to you, and I think I'll make a good soldier. Don't worry on my behalf, Kate. Please don't.'

'I won't,' she promised, although she knew she would. What a decent man my brother is, she thought, what a kind man. Kate felt suddenly and inexplicably moved. There was such concern in Neil's eyes. Soft and brown and caring, they reminded her of her grandfather's. Like Bartholomew, Neil was a gentle man. He shouldn't be going to war, she thought. But then of course no one should. She would not voice her anti-war sentiments in the family home again though, she told herself, not even if provoked by her father. To do so would be disloyal to Neil.

She made her vow out loud and emphatically. 'I'm not going to let Dad rile me anymore,' she declared. But her brother only laughed.

'That'll be the day,' he said. 'You won't be able to help yourself, I'd bet my last quid on it. Or should I say dollar,' he corrected himself. 'Either way, I bet you and Dad have at least one big barney before decimal currency comes in.'

'You're on.' Kate held out her hand, 'the fourteenth of February it is.' The government's advertising jingle had been preparing the country for months now. 'Bet you five quid or ten dollars I manage to keep my temper till then,' she said. 'Do you think we'll end up calling dollars "bucks" like the Americans do?' she asked as they shook on the deal.

Neil returned to Enoggera the end of the following week, and Kate came close to losing the bet barely two days later.

So close in fact that she could hear her brother mocking her. See? she could hear Neil say. Told you.

It started out over breakfast with Alan's comment about the ongoing consequences of the Student Action for Aborigines Freedom Ride. He'd read a recent article in *The Australian* newspaper and he knew Kate had been involved.

'The article said that the Freedom Riders attracted publicity overseas as well as throughout Australia,' he said, 'including the *New York Times*.'

'That's right.'

'And that as a direct result of the student action the NSW Aborigines Welfare Board has announced it's going to spend sixty-five thousand pounds on housing in Moree.' Alan was genuinely impressed. 'Wow, Kate, a bunch of students pulling off something like that; you'd have to be pretty proud of yourselves, I reckon.'

'We certainly are.' Gratified by her brother's interest, Kate dived in with an activist's zeal. 'And it's not before time I can tell you. The housing conditions are appalling in New South Wales country towns. So is the state of Aboriginal health and education, not to mention the racism and discrimination that abounds. Aborigines are treated as a sub-human race. It's high time something was done.'

Kate had made a conscious decision not to discuss her activism at home, feeling that it would only antagonise her father and others of his ilk who automatically railed against any action taken by those 'down south'. But now, having gained Alan's undivided attention, she couldn't help herself. Ignoring her barely touched breakfast she continued enthusiastically.

'SAFA's more or less disbanded now, but I've joined another student activist group headed by Charlie Perkins. We intend to campaign for a national referendum. There are other groups pushing the federal government too. We need to right the wrongs perpetrated against Aboriginal people –'

'A national referendum.' There was a snort of derision from the head of the table; Stan had heard quite enough. 'You're talking about New South Wales for God's sake.'

'No, I'm not, Dad,' she countered. 'Queensland's as bad as New South Wales if not worse. Racism's endemic throughout the whole of rural Australia.'

'Not here at Elianne it's not!' Stan snarled. He took instant umbrage at what he perceived to be a personal slur against his character from those interfering bastards down south. 'That's utter bullshit. We've always been good to our blacks here!'

Alan attacked his eggs, regretting the fact that he'd brought up the subject, and Hilda exchanged a glance with Bartholomew that said 'here we go again, another father–daughter slanging match'.

But Kate kept her temper in check. 'How can you possibly say that?' she replied coolly. 'You don't employ any Aboriginal workers, and you never have.'

'Course I don't,' her father snapped, 'why would I? They're a lazy bunch of good-for-nothings. You can't rely on them, Big Jim knew that.' His daughter's expression obviously annoyed him further. 'And don't you look at me like that, missy,' he said knowing how 'missy' infuriated her. 'I'm telling you here and now there's nothing racist about me – I'm just talking plain common sense.'

Nothing racist, Kate thought, you're sailing pretty close to the wind. She was about to comment on the fact when she heard Neil's voice. See? Told you, and knowing any remark she made would invite argument, she maintained her silence.

Stan waved an accusatory finger at Bartholomew. 'Father used to hire a few local blacks now and then, but it always backfired on him. They wouldn't turn up or they'd walk off the job. Isn't that right, Father?'

But Bartholomew continued buttering his toast with meticulous care as if he hadn't heard the question, so Stan re-directed his aggression to Kate.

'I'm not talking about the Abos,' he said scathingly, 'I'm talking about the Kanakas. We've never once had a racism problem here. We've been good to our blacks for generations. Why do you think I still employ a half a dozen or more on the estate? Because they're part of Elianne, that's why. They and their families have been here since the mill first opened.'

Having delivered what he saw as the irrefutable comeback, Stan visibly relaxed. His daughter's continued silence convinced him that the debate was over and that he'd won, and he leant back in his chair embracing his moment of triumph.

'Why I remember Big Jim telling me how he fought to help his Kanakas when so many were sent home in the early part of the century,' he said waxing expansive. '"It wasn't fair, Stan," that's what he used to say to me, "those men and their families had been here for years, they were part of the land. Then the new federal government brings in the White Australia Policy and what happens? They're kicked out of the country. No thanks for the decades of hard work, no thanks for having built this place with the blood and sweat of their labours."'

Stan gazed about at his captive audience. 'Big Jim fought to protect his Kanakas,' he said as his eyes came to rest on his daughter. 'I remember the exact words he said to me. "The Kanakas of Elianne are like family to us, Stan, we owe them our loyalty." That's what he said. And I've honoured that sentiment ever since.'

Having concluded his speech to his eminent satisfaction, Stan looked about once again at his audience as if perhaps expecting applause. He was a little disappointed by the lack of reaction, although his wife obligingly gave a nod and a small smile by way of recognition.

In the ensuing pause, Kate stood. 'May I be excused from the table, please?' she said, addressing her mother.

Hilda was taken aback. 'But you've hardly touched your breakfast.'

'I'm not very hungry this morning. I think I'll go for a walk with the dogs.'

'Oh. Very well, dear.'

Kate left. She couldn't stay in the same room listening to her father rave on about Big Jim a moment longer. Particularly as everything he said was a tissue of lies. It hadn't been that way at all.

Chapter Six

Pavi is coming to Elianne. He and Mela and their baby. Jim surprised me with the news this very afternoon ...

Ellie had been delighted beyond measure when, barely eighteen months after her marriage, she'd learned Pavi Salet was coming to work at the estate.

'You see how determined I am to keep you happy, my dear,' Big Jim said when he returned from his trip to the New Hebrides and informed her of her friend's impending arrival. 'I anticipate that Pavi, together with his wife and baby son, might well be here within the month. As soon as your wastrel of a father has finalised the sale of his property in any event.' He smiled, aware Ellie held little affection for her father.

'Oh Jim, how wonderful.' Ellie jumped from the sofa where she had been resting and in her excitement threw herself at her husband, reaching up to fling her hands about his neck like a boisterous child. 'What a glorious surprise,' she said, her words tripping over each other. 'Is that the reason you went to Efate? I wondered why you would wish to see Papa, but you never said a word ...'

'Gently, now, gently,' he disengaged himself from her embrace and returned her to the sofa, 'you must take care in your condition.' Ellie was four months pregnant with their second child. 'Of course that's why I went to Efate, and of course I didn't say anything,' he continued, towering Goliath-like over her. 'You would have been disappointed had Pavi not wished to be indentured to me upon your father's departure.'

It had taken André Desmarais little more than a year of debauchery to find himself as deeply in debt as he had been when he'd sold his daughter into wedlock. He'd written begging Ellie to appeal to her husband on his behalf and save him from ruination; if she did not, he'd said, he would have no option but to sell up all he had and return to France penniless.

Ellie knew that had she pleaded her father's cause, Big Jim would have come to his assistance, for Big Jim would do anything she asked of him. But Ellie had hardened her heart to her father.

'Let him rot,' she'd said coldly. 'I believe him responsible for the death of my mother through the hardship he caused her over the years. I have no desire to help Papa, nor indeed ever to see him again.'

Jim had agreed with her decision. 'Any monies André received would only be squandered in any event,' he'd said dismissively, which had left her wondering why he had bothered going to Efate. He surely had no wish to see her father, and there was no need for him to make the trip for the purpose of hiring workers. The islanders he employed were contracted through a recruiting agent, government-appointed as required by law, but well-remunerated by Big Jim, who was willing to pay handsomely for the choicest and strongest pick of the catch. She had not queried her husband however, presuming he was conducting some business about which she knew nothing. No one, not even she, ever questioned the actions of Big Jim Durham. She was thrilled now to discover the reason for his trip.

'What employment have you offered Pavi, dearest?' she asked, as if professing a passing interest rather than questioning any choice he may have made. Although undoubtedly the queen of Elianne, she knew better than to attempt any say in the affairs of the estate. She did hope, however, that Jim did not intend Pavi to work as a cane-cutter or field labourer. Pavi was after all an educated man.

Big Jim's laugh was one of eminent satisfaction. He was delighted his wife was so pleased with her gift as had been his intention, but he was pleased too with his acquisition. 'Why, Pavi shall have one of the most important jobs to hand, my dear. A skill in animal husbandry such as he possesses is not to be wasted. Your friend Pavi Salet shall be in charge of the stables.'

Such a position was certainly of major importance. The Clydesdales that hauled the loaded cane wagons to the mill, usually in teams of four, were of inestimable value, and the maintenance of their health and equipment was imperative to the daily operation of the estate throughout the hectic months of the crushing season.

'Ah, how he will love that,' Ellie clapped her hands together delightedly, 'and he will treat the horses with such care. They will become family to him, Jim, just you wait and see.'

'Yes, I do believe they will,' her husband replied drily. 'He said he's looking forward to making their acquaintance and getting to know each one personally. According to Pavi every horse has a distinctly different personality. I must confess I had never thought of working animals in that manner.'

Ellie laughed; she could just hear Pavi's voice. 'Could we give him the title of Stable Master?' she asked, hoping as she did so that such a suggestion would not appear too presumptuous on her part.

It didn't. 'If that will make you happy,' he said.

She looked gratefully up at him. 'You have made me happier than you can imagine, dearest.'

'That is my aim, Ellie.' He lowered his huge frame onto the sofa beside her, taking care not to jar her as he sat. 'It is always my aim to make you happy. You do know that, don't you? I desire only to please you.'

'Yes, I know.' How could she fail to recognise his desire to please her? He was building her a glorious house with the best materials available, all painstakingly transported across the river by barge. He presented her with endless gifts: bonnets and gowns and gloves of fine lace, all imported from Europe and all meaning little to her. All but the books, of course: he imported books for her too, and the books meant the world. And now, clearly aware of her loneliness, he had even imported a friend for her.

'I know you desire to please me, Jim,' she said, and smiled as she delivered the lie, 'and you do please me, dearest, of course you do.'

Does he believe me? she wondered. Of course he did, she could see it in his eyes. He had bought her as he bought everything else and not for one minute did he doubt her gratitude and devotion, which was presumably part of the purchase price. But how could he believe that he pleased her? How could he please her when he was physically incapable of tenderness? I can never be happy while I remain your possession, Jim, she thought, can't you see that? I am a chattel in your bed, and out of your bed I am 'the jewel in your crown' as you so proudly call me. That is not love.

There were times when Ellie felt sorry for her husband. Big Jim loved her certainly, but in the only way of which he was capable – and it was not a love she could return. Not yet, although she lived in hope for the future.

The answer, she had decided, lay in family. Our love will grow through our children, she told herself, and, much as she welcomed the respite from sexual congress her pregnancy granted, she determined to encourage his advances after the birth. She would give him many children and over time the joy of family would lead to a different sort of love, a love they could share. Already Jim was obsessed with his son, who was barely one year old.

As if reading her thoughts Big Jim placed his hand on the small mound of her belly, his outstretched fingers covering its entire circumference. The gesture was made with care, but the sheer size and power of the hand lent an image that was daunting. 'A brother for Edward,' he said. He was overjoyed that she had conceived so remarkably quickly after her first child; it was surely a sign of their sexual compatibility. 'Oh Ellie, what a pair our boys shall be.'

She very much hoped for a girl herself, but she didn't say so.

The reunion between Ellie and Pavi was somewhat restrained at first, at least on Pavi's side. He and his wife Mela were both self-conscious in the presence of Big Jim.

'Hello, Mrs Ellie.' Pavi felt most odd calling Elianne 'Mrs Ellie', but Big Jim had explained that this was the workers' term for the Boss's wife.

'Ellie insists upon it,' he'd said when he'd picked the young family up at the punt landing, where passengers and vehicles were ferried to and from Bundaberg on the southern side of the river. 'She likes to maintain a friendly connection with the workers. But of course you know Ellie,' he'd added with surprising familiarity. 'Beautiful though she is, there are no airs and graces about my wife.'

Pavi had been most surprised to find James Durham waiting with a horse and dray to transport him and Mela and the baby to the plantation. The labour recruitment agent, who had clearly been obeying instructions from some higher source, had accompanied them on the train journey from the port into the township of Bundaberg and had personally seen them aboard the punt, which had been surprising enough, but having crossed the river Pavi expected to be met by a fellow worker. Furthermore, the casual manner of his employer upon greeting them had been astounding – James Durham might well have been greeting an old friend.

Pavi had not been the only one taken aback. Two men who'd travelled with a horse and buggy aboard the punt had tipped their hats to Big Jim upon alighting, but as the horse had taken off at a trot down the road they'd exchanged querying looks. There'd been looks shared too among the small team of Kanaka labourers working on the maintenance of the punt landing, shoring up its sides. It was not customary for workers to be collected by the Boss. The most taken aback of all, however, had been Pavi's young wife, who had stood dumbstruck upon the unexpected sight of James Durham. Mela, a personable young woman and one not in the least timid with those she knew, had always found the huge white man a frightening figure.

'Mela,' Big Jim had said heartily after shaking Pavi by the hand, 'welcome, welcome, and who is this fine little fellow?' He'd gestured at the baby she dandled in her arms, but Mela had said nothing, apparently rendered speechless.

'This is Malou, sir.' Pavi had made the reply on behalf of his wife.

'Now now, Pavi, we'll have none of that "sir" business,' Big Jim had said, 'just "Boss" will do – all my workers call me Boss, we don't stand on ceremony here. Come along, boy, sling your things in the back and I'll show you your new home.'

James Durham's motive in affording Pavi Salet preferential treatment was twofold. Chiefly his aim was to please his wife, who was waiting to greet her old friend at the cottage that had been assigned him near the stables. But there was a further reason for Big Jim's personal show of interest. Pavi's skill with horses and the position of employment he was to undertake at Elianne placed him well above the normal status of Kanaka labourer certainly, but propriety needed to be observed nonetheless, and Big Jim intended to make the situation clear from the outset. He had elected to collect Pavi himself simply in order to have a chat. He had not arrived in a buggy – buggies and coaches were reserved for guests. Drays were sent out to collect workers and supplies.

It was early afternoon and the estate was a two-hour drive away, during which Mela and her baby were to sit in the back with the luggage while Pavi would sit up front beside the Boss, as was appropriate.

Relieved to be distanced from the big white man she feared, Mela leant back against the side of the dray and offered her breast to her hungry baby. She would enjoy this sightseeing trip through the cane fields of her new country.

'My wife is waiting to greet you, Pavi,' Big Jim said as he flicked the reins and the mare moved off. 'Given the friendship the two of you have shared, I decided to collect you myself in order to offer you my personal welcome.'

'Thank you, Boss. That is most kind.' Pavi had by now become distracted by the looks he was receiving from the islander workers, who were openly staring at him.

'They're mine,' Big Jim said, noting the cause of Pavi's distraction, and at a click of his fingers the men immediately returned to their work. 'I hire and lend out my Kanakas during the slack season,' he explained. 'Civic work, neighbour's requests, whatever needs to be done. Have to keep them employed: idleness breeds trouble.'

During the drive, Big Jim outlined Pavi's specific duties. He was to be responsible not only for the grooming and health care of the animals, but for the maintenance of the stables, harnesses and equipment, together with the ordering of supplies and the mixing of the feed.

'Yes, Boss,' Pavi said. He was familiar with such duties, having served in a similar capacity, although on a lesser scale, at André Desmarais's copra plantation.

Big Jim then proceeded to describe life in general at the estate. 'I run a tight ship,' he said. 'I demand discipline, but I'm good to my Kanakas. I'm good to all my workers.

They respect me for it. And of course they love Ellie,' he added, and then he'd gone on to explain his wife's insistence upon being called Mrs Ellie by all.

'My wife is a friend to everyone, and everyone loves her dearly. I sometimes feel we're like parents to our workers,' he said with an indulgent smile, 'I am the strict disciplinarian and Ellie the maternal influence. I think you will be very happy with us here, Pavi. We are a family at Elianne.'

By the time the dray had pulled up outside the little cottage near the stables, Pavi had received the message loud and clear. The warmth of his reception had carried with it distinctly readable undertones. He was being welcomed indeed, for which he was grateful, but he was to know his place at all times. He had expected no less.

Now however, as he stood before his childhood friend, it seemed strange to think that her name belonged to this vast estate. It seemed stranger still to be calling her 'Mrs Ellie'.

Ellie also found it strange, but she too knew the rules. Her husband's authority was never to be undermined and she was respectful of the fact. Big Jim was rightly feared by those who disobeyed him, but he was far more just in the treatment of his workers than her father had ever been.

'Hello, Pavi,' she said and she offered her hand. They shook. Then she turned to Mela. 'Welcome, Mela, it is so lovely to have you here.'

Mela gave a respectful nod. At the Desmarais plantation she had never been shy in Ellie's company, they had been friends, but now, inhibited by the giant presence of her new master, she had no idea how she should respond.

Ellie responded for her. She embraced both Mela and her child, very gently, taking care not to wake the baby, who was by now fast asleep in his mother's arms. 'And this must be Malou,' she whispered as she softly stroked the little brown cheek.

'Yes,' Mela said, 'this is our boy.'

'He's beautiful.' Ellie turned to Pavi. They had exchanged letters; he had written to her of his son. 'He is beautiful, your boy,' she said.

Unable to disguise his pride, Pavi gave the slightest smile and Ellie could resist no longer. She embraced him warmly. 'Oh Pavi, it is so good to see you.'

Pavi did not return the embrace but stood woodenly, frozen to the spot, his eyes darting to the Boss. Mela too glanced at James Durham, fearful of his reaction.

But Big Jim looked benignly on, delighting in his wife's ability to cross all borders while still retaining her regal air. As a true queen should, he thought proudly.

'It is so good to see *all* of you.' Aware of Pavi's discomfort, Ellie shared her affection with the family in general. 'And Malou is so much bigger than I had expected.'

'He is nearly one year of age, Mrs Ellie.' Mela smiled broadly, pleased by her reception and no longer inhibited.

'Indeed? So is my Edward.' Ellie returned the young woman's smile. 'They will be excellent playmates for each other. We must introduce them –'

'Mrs Ellie will show you around the cottage,' Big Jim interrupted; he had no interest in the women's talk of babies, 'and I shall meet you at the stables in one hour, Pavi. This will leave daylight enough for you to become acquainted with your new workplace,' he raised an eyebrow as he glanced at his wife, 'and also with your new equine friends.'

Ellie laughed, feeling a rush of affection; Big Jim rarely made humorous remarks.

'Thank you, Boss.' Pavi didn't get the joke.

The little wooden cottage, with front windows that looked out towards the stables on the opposite side of the dirt road, was simple but attractive. Two steps led up to a verandah, and the front door opened into a narrow central passage with doors either side leading to two small bedrooms on the left and a modest living room on the right. The door at the end of the passage led out the back where, separated by an open walkway in case of fire, was a kitchen with a stove.

Basic though the cottage was, to Mela it seemed a palace. She had never lived in a wooden house before, the sort that white people lived in, and she had never before had her own stove. Both her childhood and married homes had been thatched huts and she had cooked meals out in the open on a campfire. She had worked in a white man's house certainly, André Desmarais's house had been far grander than this, and she had cooked on a white man's stove, but her own home and her own stove? Why even the cottage of her husband's father, which she had often visited before she and Pavi had married and moved into their hut, had been no better than this.

The house was modestly but adequately furnished, and the cupboards well stocked with the fresh food supplies Ellie had ordered in. They would want for nothing over the next several days, she told them, and tomorrow she would show Mela around the estate.

'While Pavi is working, you and I shall go for a walk with our babies, Mela,' she said when, the tour of the house over, they stood chatting in the living room. 'There is a butchery close by where meat is delivered directly from the slaughter yards, and it is barely a fifteen-minute walk to the dairy where milk and cheese may be purchased. There is a sizeable vegetable garden there too, run by Old Willie, a Solomon Islander who works at the dairy. He has set up quite a lucrative business selling his produce, although many workers like to grow their own.'

'We shall grow our own,' Mela announced, and she sat in the small seat by the windows shushing the baby, who had started to cry. A real vegetable garden, she thought, not just taro and yams as she had grown back home, but a proper vegetable garden with beans and corn and tomatoes. She couldn't wait.

'It is very kind of you to look after us so well, Mrs Ellie,' Pavi said.

'Why would I not wish to look after my dearest friend?'

As their eyes met, Pavi nodded acknowledgement of their past friendship, but even in the absence of Big Jim his reticence was evident. The wall is still there, she thought. Perhaps the wall will always be there. The possibility saddened her.

'We both know the rules by which we must abide, Pavi,' she said, 'and it is correct we should do so, but when we are alone, call me Ellie. Please call me Ellie.'

Her voice and her eyes begged him, and for the first time since his arrival Pavi felt himself relax in her presence. He had been unsure how to behave now that she was a great lady. But the answer was clear. Elianne needed a friend.

'Does it feel strange to you that your name now belongs to a vast estate?' he asked. 'It feels very strange to me.'

She smiled, thankful to have broken through the barrier. 'I have grown so accustomed to it that I no longer think of myself as Elianne,' she said. 'The naming of the estate is an honour my husband has bestowed upon me and it would be thankless on my part not to accept such a tribute. Besides,' she added meaningfully, 'you of all people would know that I very much like being called Ellie.'

'Yes,' he said, 'I would know.'

An unspoken moment passed between them as each was visited by the image of Ellie's mother, who had coined the nickname. Pavi too had loved Beatrice Desmarais. She had changed his life. His education was due purely to the intervention of the Englishwoman who had treated him like a son.

They were distracted by the baby's cries, which had now become demanding. Malou was hungry.

Mela slipped her cotton dress from her shoulders and offered the child her breast, Malou grabbing at it greedily as she fed the nipple into his mouth.

Ellie averted her eyes. She was accustomed to seeing native women squatting in the fields or by their huts suckling their young, but here right beside her in a respectable sitting room? She found the sight confronting. Breastfeeding her own child was the most private affair to which no one was witness. It's indecent, she thought. Mela should have retired to the bedroom.

Then, with the image of her mother still freshly in her mind, Ellie heard Beatrice's voice. *She is behaving as nature intended she should, Ellie. Never look down on our native friends, my darling, there is much we can learn from them.* How was it, she wondered, that a middle-class Englishwoman like her mother had come to develop such views? But then how was it that such a woman had chosen to marry a French rogue and run off to the Pacific islands? Beatrice Desmarais had been no ordinary Englishwoman.

Ellie glanced at Pavi, wondering if under the circumstances he too found Mela's conduct unseemly, but far from being embarrassed Pavi was gazing at his wife and son with infinite tenderness.

Looking up, he caught her eye and smiled as if sharing the moment.

'You are with child?' He gestured at the short smock she wore over her gown, beneath which the swelling of her belly was virtually invisible.

Ellie's instinctive reaction was again one of shock. No gentleman would ever ask such a question, if indeed he were to notice or suspect her pregnancy, which most would not. It seems that since his marriage the islander in Pavi has all but obliterated the Frenchman, she thought. Then, once again she heard Beatrice's voice, sharper this time. *Dear me, how very strait-laced you have become, Ellie. Pavi's code of etiquette may differ from yours, but that does not make him wrong. You are behaving like those self-righteous expatriates, French and English both, all of whom you know I abhor.*

Feeling duly chastened, Ellie answered his question with an honesty that surprised her. 'Yes, I am with child,' she said, 'and I am hoping for a girl.' She had never made the admission out loud for fear of annoying Big Jim. 'If it should prove to be so I intend to call her Beatrice.'

'What an excellent idea,' Pavi replied, and they shared a smile.

Ellie blessed her mother for having come to her rescue. She chastised herself also. Had she changed since she'd come to Queensland? If so, this was a timely reminder. I must never lose sight of the example Beatrice set, she told herself.

Over the ensuing months the Salet family embraced their new life at Elianne. Pavi loved his work. The giant Clydesdales became family to him just as Ellie had predicted they would, and if one appeared even slightly off colour he would sleep the night in the stables on a fresh straw bed he'd made up for the purpose. The horses responded in kind. They loved their new friend, and would lower their huge heads to him, snorting and nuzzling their affection.

Mela loved everything about her new life. She loved her house and her stove and her garden, and most particularly she loved the companionship her job as laundry maid offered. Twice a week she would report to the Durham family home, Malou dangling from one hip, and there, hunched over the big tin tubs in the shed out the back, she would happily scrub away at the Boss's work clothes and the household linen. She washed very few of Mrs Ellie's clothes, however, Mrs Ellie preferring to do her own.

'I need to feel useful at something, Mela,' Ellie would say.

The two women would hang the washing out on the clothesline together, Ellie insisting on lending a hand with the linen. They would chat companionably while little Edward and Malou crawled about at their feet.

The presence of Pavi and his family was the salve Ellie had longed for. She enjoyed Mela's company far more than the company of the white women with whom she socialised on her trips into town. Jim had always insisted she accompany him when the occasion included other men's wives.

'It's good for business,' he would say, 'and besides I like being the envy of every man present.' He would invariably add, ostensibly as a joke, 'Of course I would kill any whose envy overstepped the mark,' but they would both know he was not joking at all.

The fact that he was not joking proved socially inhibiting for Ellie. She often longed to join in the men's conversation, which was interesting, but in order to avoid trouble she limited herself to the wives' conversation, which was not. The wives did little else but gossip about others, and she had nothing to contribute even had she wished to. They were the wives of Bundaberg businessmen with whom Big Jim had dealings, and the various subjects of their gossip were for the most part unknown to her. She supposed this was the way the women alleviated the boredom of living in a man's world where little was required of them, but she found them shallow. Did they never read books?

Ellie knew the wives in turn found her aloof, which was hardly surprising. They may even have believed that, as the wife of James Durham and the mistress of Elianne, she considered herself grand, which was certainly not the case. It's a pity, she had thought. She would have liked a female friend.

She now had one in the form of Mela, and Mela's gossip was far more engaging than that of the wives. Mela would chatter on cheerfully about her new friends, the German brothers who worked at the slaughter yards and ran the butchery, and the Kanaka family at the dairy, old Willie who gave her seedlings and cuttings for her garden, and his daughter Molly, one of the dairymaids who was shortly to marry her beau. Ellie found it interesting that Mela herself should adopt the blanket term 'Kanaka'. Clearly the word was in such common usage that its meaning had become bland, even to those who should rightfully find it offensive. She decided as a matter of principle to avoid its use nonetheless.

Ellie was grateful that her pregnancy, now obvious, precluded her from social outings. Jim made his trips to Bundaberg without her these days and she was left to enjoy Mela's company and the rapidly developing bond between their respective sons.

'Edward and Malou will grow up together,' Mela said. She had come out of the laundry hut and caught Ellie fondly watching their babies who, now approaching toddler stage, stood and tottered and fell, each competing to stay up the longest and stagger the farthest distance. 'They will grow up and become best friends, just like you and Pavi, Mrs Ellie.'

'They will, Mela, they will.' The fact that Mela appeared to have read her mind did not surprise Ellie. Despite her carefree, outgoing nature, Mela was a highly perceptive young woman. Our boys will indeed grow up together, Ellie thought, and I shall see that Malou is taught to read and write just as Pavi was. They will be friends for the whole of their lives.

Ellie had come to accept that her friendship with Pavi could never be as it once had been. Despite her request, he never called her Ellie. She remained Mrs Ellie always, even on the odd occasion when they found themselves alone. Perhaps he was fearful he might be overheard, or perhaps wary that the familiar use of her name might become a habit that could catch him out, although he appeared to her neither fearful nor wary. She never queried his reasons and she never pushed him further, accepting the decision as his. But the bond of the past was still there, resting unspoken between them. It surfaced most strongly when she visited the stables.

To Pavi and Ellie stables had always been special places. On her father's plantation they had shared their love of horses and stables both. Ellie had grown to love even the smell of a stable, the pungent mix of dung and hay and harness leather, and now here at Elianne, during the height of the crushing season, she loved the very busyness of the place. She would stand quietly watching Pavi and his stablehand as they mixed the general feed, and then as they made up the endless feed bags to be taken out into the field at dawn for the following day's harvest. Or at the end of the work day she would watch as they watered the returning horses and brushed them down meticulously, Pavi inspecting each one for any possible injury. The stables, like the mill itself and like the cane fields, was an essential link in the chain during the hectic months of the crushing season.

From time to time Pavi would look up from his work to meet her eyes and the silence between them would say everything. Their silence was enough. They had no need of words. Such moments were precious.

In November, when Ellie's time came, there was a doctor on hand as there had been for Edward's delivery and also a woman with nursing experience to assist. Ingrid Kearn was a local farmer's wife and lived on the estate, but the doctor had been transported from Bundaberg several days earlier and accommodated at the Durham family home while they awaited the event.

Alfred Benson, general practitioner, had delivered baby Edward and he couldn't help feeling guilty at once again so deserting his other patients, but James Durham had made him such a generous offer that once again it had been impossible to refuse. Indeed, had the good doctor been forced to hold up at the Durham home for a full two weeks' wait, the daily rate of his incarceration would have been five times more than he would have earned in town. As it turned out, he was only required to be there three days, which was a blessing, or perhaps a disappointment.

James Durham, as before, had spared no expense. He intended to take no chances with the birth of this his second son. His expectations, however, were thwarted. The child was a girl.

Big Jim returned from his morning's work at the mill around midday to discover his wife had given birth. He had rather expected that she might for she'd been suffering some discomfort when he'd left the house at dawn, but he'd had no wish to be around during the process. The messy business of childbirth was the realm of women and doctors.

The doctor met him at the front door. 'Your wife gave birth two hours ago,' he said, 'and Mrs Kearn is tending to her. She and the child are both well.'

Two hours ago, Jim thought. How strange. Why didn't they send news to the mill?

The doctor followed him inside. 'You are the father of a baby girl, Mr Durham,' he announced.

Jim stopped mid-stride in the sitting room, the doctor all but colliding with him. A girl ... That's why they didn't send a messenger, he thought, they didn't wish to be the purveyor of such ill tidings. He cursed his own stupidity. How unrealistic he'd been. He'd had his heart so set on another son that somehow he had never considered the child might be a girl. The outcome was hardly Ellie's fault, however. He must do his best to disguise his disappointment. She was young and healthy: there would be other sons.

He strode out of the sitting room and down the hall towards the master bedroom, the doctor following hastily, trying to keep up.

'The child is healthy, Mr Durham,' Alfred Benson said, doing his best not to appear as if he were scuttling, 'although there is one complication ...'

'Ellie, my darling.' Upon entering the room to discover his wife propped up against the pillows of the four-poster bed, Ingrid Kearn standing capably by, Jim ignored the doctor. A lace bedjacket was about Ellie's shoulders, her hair was freshly brushed from her face and, though wan and exhausted, she was as beautiful as he had ever seen her. Their child, wrapped in a baby blanket, lay asleep in her arms. What matter that it is a girl? he thought. She will be a beauty like her mother, a princess to bear the Durham name.

'A girl, Doctor Benson tells me,' he said, sitting carefully on the side of the bed, wary of disturbing mother and child. 'I have a feeling you will not be too disappointed with the outcome,' he added wryly.

'Oh Jim, I must admit that I am not.' Ellie was deeply relieved to discover that he was not angry. 'I have so longed for a daughter. The next child will be a son, I promise,' she added, hoping her admission was not cause for annoyance.

'Of course.' He smiled. 'And in the meantime, Elianne has a new little princess.'

He reached out his hand in order to peel back the blanket and see his daughter's face, at which point the doctor tried once again to offer a cautionary word.

'As I said, Mr Durham, there is a complication –'

Too late. 'What's wrong with her mouth?' Jim barked. His expression was a mixture of horror and disgust as he gazed at the puckered hole where the baby's upper lip should have been. 'Good God, what's happened to her mouth? She's deformed.'

Alfred Benson and Ingrid Kearn exchanged uneasy glances. They themselves had been startled by the sight upon the child's delivery.

'It is known as a hare lip, Mr Durham,' Alfred explained, maintaining a strictly professional tone while trying to mask a growing nervousness. 'The child has suffered a birth defect that is not altogether uncommon. She also has a cleft palate, which as I have explained to your wife will inhibit her feeding, given that the sucking and breathing mechanism is altered, but in the long term ...'

Jim stood to tower threateningly over the doctor. 'You said she was healthy.'

'She is, Mr Durham, she is.' Professional ethics forced Alfred to stand his ground although he longed to back away. 'The abnormality of cleft palate and harelip is not life threatening. As I said, the condition will inhibit feeding initially, and later there will be speech impairment, but your daughter can be expected to live a normal life –'

'My daughter is deformed.' Big Jim's voice was cold and his rage contained, which if anything made him even more frightening. 'You said "abnormality" Doctor. *Abnormality* is not *healthy*. You said she would live a "normal life". A life with physical disfigurement and speech impairment is not *normal*, my friend –'

'Stop it, Jim,' Ellie interrupted, 'stop it, I beg you. Doctor Benson is hardly responsible for the defect that has been inflicted upon poor little Beatrice.'

Beatrice. So the child already had a name. 'And how do you feel about this *defect* that has been inflicted upon your daughter, Ellie?'

Ellie looked down at the baby in her arms. She had had two hours to adjust to the sight of the deformity, two hours during which she had examined every perfect little finger and every perfect little toe and had felt the fierce clasp of her daughter's tiny hand. 'I shall love her all the more for it,' she said.

'I see.' Jim nodded briskly to the woman standing by the bedside. 'Well, I shall leave you in the good hands of Mrs Kearn,' he said, then to Alfred Benson, 'I will arrange a driver and buggy to take you to the punt, Doctor, and you will invoice me as agreed, yes?'

'Of course, Mr Durham. Mrs Kearn will visit daily over the next week or so to check on the child's progress, and should there appear any problems, do send word.'

'Yes, yes.'

'Where are you going?' Ellie asked as he turned to leave.

'To have lunch, my dear,' he replied, 'after which I shall return to the mill. As I'm sure you're aware, Doctor,' he said, turning to Alfred, 'with a further month of the crushing season ahead of us, we are extremely busy.'

'Yes indeed,' Alfred replied, relieved to no longer be the focus of the man's fury.

For the remainder of the crushing season, Big Jim successfully avoided the sight of his latest offspring. He distracted himself by toiling long hours at the mill, and by roaming the plantation, checking on the teams of cane cutters and field workers, although the overseers appointed to the task were more than competent. Over-work and fatigue and the gnawing knowledge of exactly what it was he was avoiding found him constantly irritable. Workers lived in fear of the Boss's unexpected appearance.

'Get up, you lazy bastards,' he screamed on one occasion when he came upon a team of six Kanaka cane cutters taking a well-earned break. 'What do you think I pay you for?' Grasping a man by the collar of his heavy work shirt with one hand and his belt with the other, Big Jim picked him up bodily, lifted him above his head, and hurled him into the wall of uncut cane a full five yards away. The man fell to the ground with an ominous crack of bone. 'Work, you black bastards, work,' Big Jim yelled, whirling on the others who'd already jumped to their feet. He stormed off, leaving the team thrashing away with their cane knives in a frenzy of labour until, assured he was gone, they could tend to their friend's broken arm. Word quickly got about after that. 'Watch out for the Boss,' they warned each other.

The delaying tactics did not ultimately work in Big Jim's favour, however. With the crushing over, the slack season followed and he could no longer avoid his home and the baby his wife so doted upon.

Ellie appeared to have no idea that the sight of her precious daughter was repulsive to him. She has become inured to her child's deformity, he thought. He found it disgusting that a woman of Ellie's beauty should dote on something so grotesque. The fact bewildered him. Why nurture such a creature? he thought. The child will grow to look ugly, she will grow to sound ugly, what value will she have to herself or anyone else? What value does any woman have without at least some shred of comeliness?

It was early one morning in mid-December that Ellie discovered little Beatrice dead in her cot. Through habit, she awoke at dawn and rose to feed the child, wondering why Beatrice herself was not already awake and demanding to be fed. At first the baby appeared to be sleeping peacefully, but the moment Ellie picked her up she knew. Her demented wail echoed throughout the house.

Big Jim appeared instantly from the bedroom across the hall. They slept in separate rooms while she was breastfeeding.

'What is it?' he asked, concerned to see his wife on her knees on the floor, the child cradled in her arms, frantically rocking it from side to side. 'What's happened?' he demanded.

'She's not breathing,' Ellie screamed hysterically, 'she's not breathing, she's not breathing,' and she rocked the baby's body back and forth ever more fiercely as if the sheer force of movement might put breath back into its lifeless form.

As Big Jim knelt beside her, another figure appeared at the open door, the housekeeper, awakened by her mistress's screams, tying the cord of her dressing gown and watching with horror.

Jim clasped his wife firmly by the shoulders. 'Stop it, Ellie,' he ordered, 'stop it,' and obediently she halted her frenzied rocking. He took the baby from her, Ellie relinquishing it freely.

'Bring her back, Jim! Bring her back,' she said frantically, desperately, over and over. 'Bring her back. Bring her back.'

He looked at the child, who was quite clearly dead. 'I can't Ellie. She's gone.'

Taking her arm, Jim tried to assist her to her feet, but Ellie would have none of it. 'No, no,' she said, 'no, no,' and reaching out she snatched the baby from him, hugging the body close, sobbing now, hysteria replaced by anguish as her mind was forced to acknowledge the inescapable truth.

Jim stood. He signalled the housekeeper, who came forward and gently coaxed her mistress to rise.

'Come along, Mrs Ellie,' Bertha said, 'come along and sit down.'

Ellie stood, allowing herself to be led to a chair, where she sat cradling little Beatrice.

'What happened?' she asked. 'What went wrong?' She looked up at her husband and the housekeeper, her eyes begging answers. 'I fed her only three hours ago. She was all right then. What happened? What did I do wrong?'

'You did nothing wrong, Ellie,' Jim said comfortingly, 'she just died in her sleep. It's not your fault.'

'Oh yes, it is. It *is* my fault, it has to be.' She kissed the baby's cold little face. 'Oh my poor darling, how did this happen, what have I done?'

The housekeeper, too, tried to comfort her distraught mistress. 'It's a tragedy, Mrs Ellie,' Bertha said, 'but you mustn't hold yourself to blame.'

'But I do,' Ellie wept, 'I do, I do.'

Nothing either could say would convince her she was blameless, and eventually Big Jim sent a man to fetch the doctor.

'It is not healthy you should lay blame upon yourself in this manner, Ellie,' he said stringently, as if he were speaking to a wayward child. 'The doctor will inform you I'm sure that there was nothing you could have done to save the baby.'

Alfred Benson arrived six hours later and in some trepidation. He'd been told the news en route and was unsure of what treatment he might expect from James Durham. He was relieved by the cordiality of his reception.

'Thank you for coming, Doctor Benson,' Big Jim said, 'I'm most grateful. Do please forgive me for calling you away with such urgency, but my wife is convinced she is responsible for the child's death and is driving herself to distraction. I am hoping you can help.'

'Of course, Mr Durham.'

Jim ushered the doctor through to where Ellie lay curled up on the bed, her dead baby still cuddled to her breast. She would allow no one to take Beatrice from her – no one until Alfred Benson that is.

'I should like to examine little Beatrice, if I may,' Alfred said, and Ellie finally relinquished her child.

She watched as the doctor made his examination. At first she was quiet, but the silence seemed more than she could bear and she soon became agitated.

'I fed her twice during the night,' she said. 'I didn't think there was anything wrong. She was making snuffling noises, but she always did that. She was swallowing all right; she didn't choke or gag. I don't know what I did wrong, Doctor. I don't know what I did wrong.'

'You did nothing wrong, Mrs Durham,' Alfred Benson assured her. 'There is no obstruction in the baby's windpipe, no undue swelling in the throat, nothing that would present a possible cause for asphyxiation.'

'Then what happened?'

'Sadly we will never know. Such events have occurred in the past and they appear inexplicable. For no apparent reason, a baby can simply stop breathing and suffocate in its sleep. This would appear to be the case with little Beatrice, I'm afraid. Under no circumstances must you feel in any way responsible.'

Jim was delighted that the doctor's report had proved

him correct. 'You see, my dear, I was right,' he said, 'the baby died in her sleep. There was nothing you could have done.' Good, he thought, Ellie was absolved of guilt. They could get on with their lives now.

But Ellie could not get on with her life. She no longer blamed herself, it was true, but she was inconsolable in her grief. Little Beatrice was laid to rest in Bundaberg Cemetery and, in the weeks that followed, Ellie remained listless, distracted. Sometimes she was maudlin, sometimes moody and irritable; at no time was she the Ellie of old.

Big Jim found it all very tiresome. He tried cheering her up with reports of the new house, which was nearing completion, but she showed no interest, and when he attempted to play the nurturing husband he was rebuffed.

'You have a lot to be thankful for, Ellie,' he would say, 'you have a healthy son –'

Her reply would bounce back as an accusation. 'If Beatrice had been a boy you'd be grieving her loss,' she'd say.

After several such responses Jim ceased his nurturing attempts.

Christmas came and went, and then the whole of January, by which time he'd had enough. The planters' conference in Townsville was the perfect excuse, he decided. After the conference he'd stay up north for a month or so and allow her to grieve on her own. When he got back she'd hopefully be over the worst of it.

'I regret having to leave you at this crucial time, my dear,' he said, 'but I'm afraid my trip north is unavoidable: the planters' conference in Townsville is of great importance to us all.' Her indifference irritated him. She might at least have had the courtesy to show some interest in his business concerns.

'You are possibly not aware, Ellie,' he said, 'indeed it is hardly a woman's place to be so informed, but the government passed legislation some time ago to stop the importation of Kanaka labour by 1890. A year, which I might point out,' he added drily, 'is currently upon us. The same government also denies planters the right to import Indian coolies for fear of upsetting the British Colonial Government. The position is untenable.'

She remained staring into space, which annoyed him even further.

'Do you not realise the significance of what I am saying?' he continued testily. 'Some sugar growers in the north are actually contemplating removing their mills to the Northern Territory if a supply of coolie labour can be guaranteed them there. These rulings will have an immense impact upon our entire industry. It is imperative we fight for the continuation of the Kanaka labour system.'

He had finally gained her attention, what little she afforded him anyway, and for what little it was worth.

'Then fight,' she said, 'go to your conference. But I know the real reason you're leaving: you want to get away from me, you're tired of my grief.'

What could he say? In essence she was right, although her petulance was irksome. 'I can assure you,' he said stiffly, 'that the conference is of vast importance ...'

But she wasn't listening. Staring once again into space, she'd become maudlin. 'What would you know of grief?' she said. 'You never loved Beatrice. You never held her in your arms. You don't even care that she's dead.'

What a stupid remark, he thought. Of course he didn't care. He'd felt no remorse at all as he'd smothered the child. His only fear had been Ellie herself as he'd watched her through the mosquito netting that shrouded the four-poster. He'd had his lie at the ready. If she were to awaken he would pretend he'd heard the baby cry and had come to its assistance. But she hadn't awakened.

'If Beatrice had been a boy you'd care,' Ellie said. 'If Beatrice had been a boy you'd –'

'You're wrong, I would not.' He looked at her, wallowing

in her world of self-pity, and all he could feel was contempt. 'I would care nothing for a boy with a deformity like that,' he said coldly. 'Any child with such a deformity is better off dead.'

Ellie was shocked from her torpor. His chilling words broke through the grief that had consumed her for weeks and, like pieces of a jigsaw puzzle thoughts and images flooded through her mind to make a hideous connection. She remembered his reaction upon first seeing the baby, the way he'd avoided the house, how he'd ignored little Beatrice's presence as if willing her not to be there. Never once had he held her. Never once, she now realised, had he even uttered her name.

'What have you done?' she said her voice barely a whisper. Why, she wondered in horror, had such a possibility not occurred to her? She'd been so absorbed in her baby that she'd failed to read the signs. 'In God's name what have you done?'

'What have I done?' Big Jim asked in all innocence. He was grateful that he'd garnered her attention at long last. What have I *done*? Why, an act of kindness. I've put a maimed creature out of its misery. The child should have been destroyed at birth, before the mother was allowed to form an attachment. 'I don't understand you, Ellie. What is it exactly that you're asking?' He rather enjoyed making her say it out loud.

'You killed her.' She could not believe the words even as she said them. 'You killed my baby.'

His smile was indulgent. 'Now, now, you're being silly, silly and fanciful – your imagination is working overtime. You heard what the doctor said. Sad though it is, such deaths are not uncommon.'

Ellie felt confused. What was she to think? What was she to believe? He didn't appear in the least confronted by her accusation and yet …

'You're glad Beatrice is dead, aren't you?' she said.

'Yes,' he replied matter-of-factly, 'yes I am.'

His eyes were cold now. Remote, emotionless; she had seen such a look before, but never once had it been directed at her.

'Things have turned out for the best, Ellie,' he said. 'It is time you realised that.' Then he turned abruptly and left the room.

They did not speak of the matter again. He left the following day, and his parting words were a direct order.

'You must rid yourself of your melancholy, my dear. You have a son to look after.'

Once again his expression was detached, his eyes the eyes of a stranger. He did not smile, he did not kiss her farewell, he did not even wave goodbye as the horse and buggy set off for the train station.

Ellie was left in a state of utter distraction. Had her husband killed her baby? No, no it was not possible. No one was capable of such an atrocity. But he had willed the event. He was glad the child was dead. How was she to live with a man like this? How was she to live at all? She could end her life, drown herself in the dam perhaps. But Big Jim had been right about one thing. She had a son. There was Edward to consider.

In her grief and despair, she turned to the only friends she had: Mela and Pavi Salet.

Chapter seven

Mela and Pavi have been my salvation. I cannot write of what happened, not yet, perhaps never. But I owe them both if not my life, then my sanity.

Upon his return, Big Jim was relieved to find his wife in a stronger frame of mind than when he'd left. Indeed despite a certain reserve, which he supposed was to be expected, she was very nearly the Ellie of old. He was pleased that his approach had proved the right one and that she'd come to her senses. He'd been a little callous with her, certainly, but she'd needed to be shocked out of her melancholic state and it had obviously worked. He could be kind to her now.

'Oh my darling girl, how I've missed you,' he said. Engulfing her in his giant embrace, he lifted her from her feet to whirl her about the living room. The sight of her beauty and the sound of her voice as she'd welcomed him home had filled him with joy: his Ellie was back.

Little Edward, now nearly eighteen months old and ever-eager to exercise his newfound mobility, joined in the game, scampering about, grabbing a fistful of his mother's skirts as she swirled past, falling over as she swirled on, then picking himself up to repeat the exercise.

'Yes, yes,' Jim laughed at the boy's antics, 'I've missed

you too, Edward. Oh it's so good to be home with my dearest ones.'

He finally released her, breathless and dishevelled, and they sat down to talk while Bertha arrived with the afternoon tea.

'Was the conference successful?' she asked, still panting a little.

'Extremely so,' he replied. 'There was a great show of strength, powerful men all, our cause is strongly supported. The Queensland sugar growers are not prepared to lose their Kanakas. We are quite confident the government will be forced to repeal its legislation, or if not, at least to grant a ten-year extension before its enactment.'

'That will be a relief for many, I should imagine.'

'It most certainly will.'

'Thank you, Bertha. I'll pour.' Ellie nodded to the housekeeper, who left.

She poured her husband's tea, added sugar, stirred it and handed him the cup. How strange, she thought, to be serving him tea and having a normal conversation as if everything was as it had once been, as if Beatrice had not died. No, no, rather as if Beatrice had never existed. That is how Jim sees things, she thought. To Jim, Beatrice was no more than a brief, unwelcome visitor who has now ceased to exist. I wonder, had she lived, what his treatment of her would have been. He surely could not have ignored his daughter for the whole of her life. Perhaps they may even have grown close over time ...

Ellie forced her mind back to the present. She must not torture herself with thoughts of Beatrice and what might have been. She focused instead upon her husband as he forecast the dire consequences that would ensue should Queensland be deprived of Kanaka labour.

That night, when Big Jim came to her bed, Ellie welcomed their union. She would give him children just as she had planned, as many children as she was physically capable of producing. But the children she bore him would not be the salvation of her marriage as she had intended. They would be the salvation of her life. She knew now that there was no form of love she could share with James Durham, even that of common parenthood. She would dissemble though. For the sake of her children she would dissemble even to herself.

Children were already proving a great source of comfort to Ellie. Edward and Malou had become inseparable. The two little boys delighted in each other's company, and she regularly visited the Salets' cottage in order that they might play together. Big Jim commented on the fact not long after his return.

'I am glad to see, Ellie,' he said, 'that in my absence you have had the friendship of the Salets to help you through your difficult time.'

'Yes.' It was the first reference he'd made to Beatrice's death, and although Ellie found his attempt to sound sympathetic the height of hypocrisy, she was indeed grateful for the provision of Mela and Pavi in her life. 'I am thankful to have such friends,' she said.

Big Jim rightfully took her remark as the personal vote of thanks it was intended to be and was delighted. Their relationship once again on harmonious ground, he would do anything and everything to please his wife.

'I should like to visit Beatrice's grave on our trip into town tomorrow,' she said.

'Of course,' he replied after only the briefest hesitation.

It was April and this was to be Ellie's first social outing since the death of her baby four months previously. They were to attend a garden party at the home of Cedric Tatham, a wealthy entrepreneur with whom Big Jim had had a number of business dealings.

'The directors of the rum distillery will be present with their wives,' Jim had told her, 'and as I am about to invest in the company, I would very much like you by my side. That is, if you feel up to it,' he'd added as a hasty afterthought.

He'd sensed that she did not at all welcome the prospect, but she'd agreed dutifully and with good grace, so he now supposed that a visit to the child's grave was a fair exchange. He would not allow such visits to become regular though: they were not healthy and could evoke maudlin bouts. He hoped tomorrow's wouldn't. She hadn't been to the cemetery since the burial.

He stood ten yards or so from the grave and watched her. She presented an attractive but forlorn picture, lace parasol in one hand, posy of flowers in the other as she gazed down at the little headstone. He had physically distanced himself in the pretence that he had no wish to intrude, but he hoped more to serve as a reminder that a pressing engagement awaited them and her visit must be kept brief.

As she bent to place the flowers on the grave, he saw her lips move. It seemed she was saying goodbye. Then after a further moment's contemplation she turned away. The entire exercise had lasted barely five minutes.

'Thank you,' she said, taking his arm as she joined him, and together they walked back to where the horse and buggy was waiting.

Her show of restraint pleased him immensely. And she looked so lovely in her pretty lavender dress. Her choice of lavender, he knew, was evidence she was still in mourning, but no matter – at least she hadn't insisted upon black. And her hair, pinned up beneath the little straw boater as it was, displayed the elegant line of her neck to perfection. What an asset she is, Big Jim thought proudly, she will certainly serve me well today.

After leaving the cemetery, they drove down the wide thoroughfare of Bourbon Street towards the Tathams' house, past the Royal Hotel with its majestic balconies, past Buss & Turner's ever-busy department store and past other businesses that Ellie could swear had not been there on her last trip to town. Bundaberg seemed to grow by the day.

The Tathams' house, like many, was of Queenslander design, but a little grander than most as befitted Cedric's status. Broad verandahs overlooked spacious grounds that were perfectly designed for garden parties. Tables with umbrellas and wicker chairs dotted the lawns and there was ample room for the erection of a marquee that comfortably housed twenty to table. The Tathams, a stylish middle-aged English couple, held their annual garden party always in autumn, never spring, which would clash with the crushing season, and despite an air of social occasion the event unashamedly lent itself to the business of the day.

In only several decades Bundaberg had blossomed from little more than a logging camp into a thriving timber town, and had then gone on to become, barely overnight it would seem in historical terms, the prosperous centre of a major sugar-producing region. A number of entrepreneurs had emerged during this massive boom, clever men who recognised and seized the opportunities that abounded. One such was Cedric Tatham. A prominent citizen and member of the Bundaberg Municipal Council, there was very little local commerce in which Cedric was not involved and very few major businesses that had not benefited from his investment, silent or otherwise.

Cedric's garden parties were therefore specifically designed for the purposes of mixing and mingling. Along with wishing to consolidate his place in the town's hierarchy, Cedric Tatham firmly believed that business conducted on a social level was expedient for all concerned. Besides, his wife very much enjoyed playing hostess.

Contrary to Ellie's expectations, the garden party did not prove a gruelling affair, although in its early stages, it augured to be all that she had feared.

'My goodness gracious, just look at them,' Margaret Tatham said with a flippant wave of her hand, 'you'd swear, would you not, that our husbands are solving the gravest problems the world has to offer.'

Margaret Tatham was considered by many the social doyen of Bundaberg; the several women with her at the table on the verandah laughed as they followed her gaze. Across the expanse of landscaped lawn and garden, their husbands were gathered with a number of others having pre-luncheon drinks and the conversation was clearly of the most intense nature.

Seated beside Margaret, Ellie dredged up a smile, but she couldn't bring herself to laugh. What, she wondered, would Jim think if he could hear himself so belittled by these empty-headed women? Jim of course would not care in the least, but somehow she did. She thought it disloyal of women to deride their husbands. She wished as always that she could join in the men's conversation, which was bound to be interesting. Particularly today, for she knew of the business involved.

While the wives chatted on, Ellie continued to watch their men. Jim and Cedric Tatham were in discussion with Frederic Buss, the sugar producer and highly successful entrepreneur who had helped initiate, among his many other enterprises, the Bundaberg Distilling Company. With them were several of the major mill owners who also served as directors of the company. Jim had confessed to her his lost opportunity in not joining forces with the well-established sugar-mill owners who had formed the company five years previously. He'd agreed with them at the time that a distillery could well prove profitable and that it would certainly solve the problem of what to do with the volume of molasses waste left after the sugar's extraction, but his own mill had been in a younger stage of development and he'd not had the finance available for further investment. Things were very different these days. A great deal had changed over the past five years. Elianne was now a highly productive mill and the Bundaberg Distillery, after only two years of rum production, was showing a profit. Expansion was the word on everyone's lips. Expansion was the reason behind Cedric Tatham's garden party.

As Ellie distractedly watched the men, she didn't realise that she herself was being watched, and at close quarters.

Margaret Tatham leant in to her. 'We're prattling on rather, aren't we?' she murmured in Ellie's ear.

Ellie gave a guilty start. Had she seemed rude? She must have. 'I'm so sorry –' she started to reply, but Margaret continued, her voice still a murmur.

'We're all pretending to be jolly because we don't know what to say to you.'

Ellie looked into the matronly face of her hostess. It was a face whose expression she had always seen as superficial, yet now in the woman's eyes was such compassion and depth of understanding she found she could not look away.

'I hope you will forgive my intrusion, Ellie,' the older woman said quietly, 'but I wish to offer you my deepest sympathy. Oh my dear, how my heart does go out to you.' Margaret Tatham had suffered the loss of two children in the earlier years of her marriage, one at birth and the other at three years of age. She remembered the dreadful months afterwards and was very sad to see another woman in the throes of that grief.

Ellie couldn't help herself. Confronted by such naked sincerity, she could not stop tears springing to her eyes. She blinked them back fiercely: she must not cry here.

The chatter around the table had gradually died down. Margaret's words had not been audible to the others, but her communication had been quite clear and the women were now looking at Ellie, each of them kindly, each concerned.

'We were so saddened to hear the news, Ellie,' one said. She was younger than her companions. Her name was Elizabeth. She had given birth to a stillborn three years previously.

'If there is anything we can do ...' said another.

The tears suddenly flowed freely, Ellie stemming them as best she could with the linen handkerchief Margaret handed her.

'Thank you,' she said, 'you're very kind, thank you.' Caring though the women were, she wished they would stop; she wished the subject of Beatrice had not arisen. 'Oh dear, I'm making a spectacle of myself,' she said with a nervous glance in her husband's direction. Jim would certainly not approve of her weeping in public. She made as if to rise from the table, but Margaret took her hand preventing her.

'You're not making a spectacle of yourself at all, my dear.' Margaret had noticed the apprehensive look Ellie had cast at her husband. 'You are among friends.' Another nervous look, she now noted: Big Jim Durham was clearly insensitive to the extent of his wife's suffering. *The poor girl has been marooned out there on that remote plantation with no one to turn to*, Margaret thought.

'Sometimes men are best ignored, Ellie,' she said firmly. 'Sometimes women need the support of other women. A number of us have been through similar tragedies, my dear, and it does one good to talk.'

Ellie found the next five or ten minutes difficult to believe. With the women's encouragement she openly spoke of Beatrice and her grief, even recounting the shocking morning when she discovered her daughter's body. She did not weep as she talked, but felt rather a great sense of relief. She was no longer alone. These women understood.

Margaret was glad that she'd brought up the topic. She'd wondered whether she should, but it pleased her now to see young Ellie Durham unburden herself so freely. 'You have a little boy, do you not?' she asked when she sensed the time was right to move on.

'Yes, Edward.' Ellie was amazed to hear herself laugh. 'He is over eighteen months old now, extremely active, extremely tiring and a huge distraction, I must say.'

The conversation then turned to children in general, the women comparing notes about their various offspring. Husbands came into play also, as they talked about the ordeal of having brought up a family while their men forged careers in an often hostile new world. The women told funny stories, making light of their past adversity, laughing together, and as they did, Ellie wondered how she could have so misjudged them. These were pioneer women, women who had experienced hardships she had never known. She felt guilty, and chastised herself for having presumed them superficial. It was I who was superficial, she thought. The fault was in me, not them.

A male voice broke through the women's chatter. 'It would seem, my dear, that members of the staff are getting restless.' Margaret looked up from the table to find her husband standing opposite her, Big Jim Durham by his side. 'And I for one,' Cedric said, 'am starving.'

'Oh my goodness,' Margaret turned to peer at the verandah's open doors, where the housemaid stood awaiting the order that luncheon be served. 'How remiss of me,' she said merrily, once more in her social role of hostess. 'We were having such a lovely chat I quite forgot the time. Do please call people to table, Cedric dear.' She gave a wave to the housemaid, who disappeared to alert the kitchen staff.

'Women and their gossip,' Cedric muttered in an audible aside to Big Jim before obediently setting off to carry out his wife's instructions.

But this had not been gossip at all, Ellie thought as she rose and accepted her husband's arm. This had been support of the finest kind.

'I noticed you in deep conversation with Margaret,' Big Jim said approvingly as they sauntered across the lawn towards the marquee. 'You appear to have struck up quite a friendship with her.'

'Yes, I believe I have.'

'Excellent, I'm delighted. Surprised also, I must admit. I had the feeling that you considered her shallow.'

'I did. I was wrong.'

'How very perceptive of you, Ellie,' Big Jim halted to look at her with newfound respect, 'an excellent observation on your part, my dear.' He checked that no one was within hearing distance and lowered his voice. 'For all her social airs and affectation, Margaret is a highly astute businesswoman. She is in actuality the power behind the throne. The fact is little known, but Cedric doesn't make a move without her.' Big Jim secretly despised Cedric Tatham for his weakness in allowing his wife so much say in his affairs, but there was no denying the woman's acumen.

'A personal relationship between the two of you will work well in our favour,' he said as they continued on their way to the marquee. 'Margaret Tatham is a powerful woman.'

Ellie made no response. She felt no need to do so. But she thought how generous and how loyal it was of Margaret to play the giddy hostess while her husband received the credit for astute business decisions that were actually hers. What a great deal I have learnt today, Ellie thought.

Several hours later, when the garden party had come to an end and they were taking their leave, Big Jim was delighted to witness further evidence of the bond that appeared to have developed between his wife and Margaret Tatham.

'I have a small gift for you, Ellie,' Margaret said as they stood on the front verandah looking down on the main drive, waiting for the stablehand to arrive with the horse and buggy.

Upon her signal, a housemaid who was standing nearby came forwards and presented Ellie with a loosely wrapped brown paper parcel.

Ellie pulled the paper aside to reveal a mantel clock. It was an extremely attractive piece made of cherry wood with a brass-fitted face and a separate dial that counted seconds.

'How lovely,' she said, overwhelmed and more than a little mystified. Why would Margaret Tatham wish to present her with a gift?

'It's an Ansonia, made in New York,' Margaret said. 'I had it set aside when the delivery arrived two months ago.' Among his many and varied business undertakings Cedric Tatham imported a line of fine goods and furnishings. 'I was hoping I would see you before too long,' she said meaningfully, 'and I am so glad that I have.'

A gift to welcome me back into society, Ellie realised. 'How very kind of you, Margaret,' she said.

'It will go perfectly with the rosewood mantel Jim has bought for your new home.' Margaret gave a light laugh. 'I visited the warehouse myself just to be sure and the match is superb.' Big Jim had purchased a number of furnishings, which were currently in storage awaiting delivery to the new house that was his pride and joy. 'Cedric tells me the house is nearing completion, Jim,' she said turning to him. 'You will be making the move shortly, I take it?'

'We will indeed. I hope to move us into Elianne House within the month.'

'Excellent.' She turned back to Ellie. 'A new clock to mark time in a new home and a new life,' she said gaily. 'How apt.'

As the stable hand arrived with the horse and buggy, Margaret kissed Ellie goodbye. 'Always remember, my dear,' she said quietly enough for the others not to catch her words above the clatter of hooves and the rattle of harness, 'we women can be a source of great strength to each other. I am here should you ever be in need.'

'I will remember,' Ellie replied. Then as they parted she said, 'Thank you, Margaret. Thank you so much for a lovely afternoon and for my beautiful gift.' Her eyes spoke of a great deal more. 'Thank you for everything.'

Big Jim was immensely pleased, but also bewildered. 'I don't know what you've done to so impress the woman,' he said as they drove out of the main gates and into the street, 'but she's certainly taken a liking to you. What in heaven's name possessed her to give you the clock?'

'She's kind, that's all. It's a housewarming present.'

The garden party signalled a turning point for Ellie. Less than one month later they moved into Elianne House and not long after that she discovered she was pregnant. She had suspected she might be, but had hardly dared hope and had said not a word for fear of being proven wrong. Now, overjoyed by the doctor's confirmation of her condition, the clock that sat on the rosewood mantel acquired an even greater significance. 'A new clock to mark time in a new home and a new life,' Margaret had said. The words were prophetic. To Ellie the clock now marked time with the new life growing inside her.

She gave birth in November. The child was a boy and they called him Bartholomew.

'Bartholomew James Durham,' Big Jim said. He held the tiny bundle of his son in his massive hands and offered him up like a toast to the gods, admiring the flawless features that peered from the blanket. The child was perfect in every way. He leant down to kiss his wife on the forehead. 'Oh my dearest love, you have made me so happy, so happy and so proud.'

Ellie was glad. She had hoped, more perhaps to spite him than anything, that the child might be a girl, but she was glad now to have given birth to a boy. No child should be born of spite. Her next baby would be a girl, she told herself, and if not, then the one after that, or the one after that. She planned to have many babies.

As it turned out, however, such plans were not meant to be. Following the delivery of her third son two years later,

Ellie haemorrhaged badly. George William Durham was born healthy, but his birth very nearly cost the life of his mother. During her slow recuperation Ellie learnt the dreadful news.

'The severe haemorrhage you suffered has had repercussions, Mrs Durham,' Alfred Benson explained. 'You are on the road to recovery, I am happy to report, but you will be unable to breastfeed for some time.' Then after a pause he added, 'And the long-term prognosis is bleak, I must warn you. We are unsure of the reasons for it, but after haemorrhaging such as yours a woman invariably ceases to ovulate. I am sorry to inform you, but I fear your child-bearing days are likely to be over.'

Ellie was devastated. If the doctor proved right, not only was she to be denied the large family she had planned, but even more heartbreaking, she was to be deprived of the little girl she had always longed for.

Big Jim comforted her as best he could and in the only way he knew how.

'You have three healthy sons, my dear,' he said time and again. 'Who could ask for more?' He was perfectly happy.

But her husband's happiness was not enough for Ellie. Memories of Beatrice and her sweet little damaged face surfaced bringing with them the reflection upon what might have been. Ellie knew that for the sake of her children, and most particularly her newborn, she must fight back the thoughts that plagued her, but in her still-weakened physical state it was difficult.

'We can share little Sera, Mrs Ellie,' Mela said. 'You can be number two mother to my Sera as she grows; she will like very much to have two mothers.'

Mela had given birth to a daughter the previous year. She and Pavi had named the child Sera after his mother.

'That is very kind of you, Mela,' Ellie said, wondering as she always did at Mela's intuitive powers. She had said nothing at all of her thoughts, yet her friend had sensed the deep-seated source of her unhappiness.

'In my village children grow up with many parents,' Mela said, 'aunties and uncles and grandparents who look after them when their mother and father are working. It is good for the children. It is good for the parents too.'

'Yes, I'm sure it is.' Ellie smiled. 'Thank you, Mela.'

Over time, little Sera did very much fill a place in Ellie's heart. All of the children did. They gave meaning to her very existence. As the years passed and her monthly cycles failed to return she resigned herself to the fact that the doctor's prognosis had been correct, but she refused to feel defeated. She was after all surrounded by children, her own and the Salets'. Edward and Malou had been inseparable from the outset, as close as brothers. Now her two younger sons and Sera grew together like siblings completing a rowdy gang of five, Sera, needless to say, an incorrigible tomboy.

Ellie encouraged the children to socialise from a very early age; a potpourri of races co-existed at Elianne and she considered it healthy they should mingle and learn from others. She and Mela and the children attended the community gatherings at the hall that Big Jim had built for his workers. The concerts, the kiddies' parties, the church services on Sundays – they joined in everything, becoming a genuine part of the family that was Elianne. Indeed Mrs Ellie and her mixed brood were much loved by both the workers and their families. As they wandered the estate, passing the rows of married men's cottages and the wooden tin-roofed barracks of the white workers and the thatched huts of the Kanakas, they were enthusiastically greeted by all.

When the children had grown to a manageable age, Ellie decided to further broaden their horizons and, with Margaret Tatham's encouragement, she decided also to make a bid for her own independence.

'You would like to do what?' Big Jim was flabbergasted by his wife's request.

'I should like to drive into town,' she repeated firmly. 'I am extremely capable with a horse and buggy, as you well know.'

'It's unthinkable. I will not allow it.'

'But I have seen other women on occasions driving their children into town.'

'The wives of farmers,' he said dismissively. 'The mistress of Elianne does no such thing.'

'Please Jim.' Her eyes beseeched him. 'Please grant me this one favour – it is important to me.'

He could see she was begging, but he couldn't comprehend why. 'Is it so important, my dear?' he asked. 'I am quite happy to drive you into town. What purpose is served by your driving yourself?'

'The purpose of independence ...' She took his hand in a further bid for understanding. 'I want to be more self-sufficient, dearest. A little less cosseted perhaps,' she said, struggling to express herself, 'a little less reliant –'

'I see.' It appeared she had not expressed herself at all well. 'I was not aware that you felt *cosseted*,' he said stiffly.

'Oh Jim,' she smiled, exasperated, 'do not take offence. Of course I am cosseted. You know full well that you spoil and indulge me shamelessly. All I ask is that you grant me a little independence now and then.'

He relaxed, no longer offended, but still confused. 'I would be happy to oblige if I could, Ellie, but you must surely see that it would be most irresponsible of me to allow you to drive into town unaccompanied.'

'I would not be unaccompanied, dear,' she was quick to reassure him, 'that was never my intention. Mela would be with me. The children too,' she added, 'all five of them.'

He was once again flabbergasted. 'The children?'

'Of course, that is the very purpose for my visit to town.' She went on patiently to explain. 'Edward and Malou are seven now, Bartholomew is five, Sera four, baby George three: I believe it is time for them to travel further afield. It will do them good to see how the townspeople live.'

'Oh it will, will it?' Jim wasn't sure whether to be amused or outraged. 'And what exactly will you do in town?'

'We shall visit Margaret Tatham.'

'Really?'

'Yes, it was her suggestion we do so the last time I saw her. You remember the occasion? I took afternoon tea with her while you attended the meeting at the distillery.'

'I see. And does she know that you will be arriving with a veritable tribe?'

'Indeed yes. As I said it was her suggestion.'

Jim wondered briefly whether Margaret realised that several of the company about to descend upon her were Kanakas. He very much doubted the fact, but decided to forego any comment. Ellie's relationship with the Salet children continued to dumbfound him. She didn't seem to see they were black and treated them like family, even teaching young Malou to read and write alongside her own son. But then, Jim thought, that was the way she and Pavi were brought up, so it possibly does not seem unnatural to her. He had raised no objection to her tutoring of the boy, wishing as always to keep her happy. Besides, being perceived as a benevolent boss served his purpose. The fact that Mrs Ellie tutored the son of a worker lent credence to his boast of an extended Elianne family.

Now, despite the fact that he considered his wife's request bordering on ludicrous, Big Jim decided to further indulge her. She would after all be travelling with a black maid in the form of Mela, so appearances were somewhat served.

'If I were to grant you permission, you will of course go directly to the Tathams' house. You will avoid Saltwater Creek and the disorderly blacks in Kanakatown.'

'Yes of course,' Ellie said. She would obey whatever restrictions he chose to place upon her, although secretly she disagreed that it was the blacks who were at fault in Kanakatown. Pavi had told her that the fault lay with the whites who had set up liquor stores and brothels and gambling dens specifically targeted at the workers. The peaceable islanders had been enticed into a way of life previously unknown to them. It seemed unfair, she thought, to now blame them for their unruly behaviour.

Big Jim's smile was wry. 'How extremely generous of Margaret to extend her invitation to the entire clan,' he said. He found the thought of Margaret Tatham's reaction most amusing. 'I shall look forward to hearing all about it upon your return.'

'Oh thank you, Jim, thank you.' Ellie flung her arms around him.

'Happy to oblige, my dear,' he said as he returned her embrace.

No matter of the outcome in any event, he thought. If Margaret chooses to disown us, it will be of little consequence. Cedric still hasn't recovered from the bank crash. The Tathams are no longer of any great value.

Cedric Tatham, unlike many other colonial entrepreneurs, had not been wiped out by the Great Banking Crisis of the early nineties, but he had come very close to ruin as across the country businesses had suspended trading and companies had ceased to exist during the worst financial depression Australia had ever known.

Big Jim Durham had weathered the storm with minimal damage. In fact the turbulent years of '91 to '93 had carried with them some benefits for Big Jim and others in the sugar industry. The planters had finally won their battle with the Queensland government. In 1892 adjustments had been made to the Polynesian Labourers' Amendment Act, which had called for a halt to the importation of Kanaka workers. Given the pressure brought to bear by the Planters' Association, Premier Samuel Griffiths had been forced to grant a ten-year extension to the use of coloured labour. For those like Jim Durham the victory had helped sweeten the bitter taste of the depression that held the country in its grip.

To Big Jim's utter surprise, Margaret Tatham proved not in the least outraged by the intrusion of Ellie's Kanaka companions. Ellie returned from town with glowing reports.

'Margaret was so welcoming,' she said effusively, 'so extraordinarily generous.' Ellie herself was exhilarated; the day had been immensely liberating. She felt a sense of freedom she'd not known for years. 'We had afternoon tea, scones with jam, and the children made absolute pigs of themselves.' She laughed. 'Margaret adored them all the more for it of course – she really is the most good-hearted woman. We sat outside in the little back garden. Do you know, Jim, I find the cottage that she and Cedric now have, although modest in comparison to their previous home, extremely attractive …'

Jim let his wife babble on. He found her excitement most engaging. He wasn't sure who he admired most or for what: Margaret for her tolerance in embracing a situation that would surely meet with the disapproval of her peers; or Ellie for her spirit in asserting her independence and flaunting convention.

Over the following year, however, as Ellie continued to assert her independence and as the trips to town with Mela and the children became steadily more frequent, Big Jim started to find the situation less amusing.

Has my company become so wearisome, he thought, that she need seek out Margaret Tatham with such relentless regularity?

'Again?' he queried with an edge of irritation. 'You're going into town again. Tomorrow? Why so soon? You saw Margaret only recently.'

'No, dearest. It has been nearly two months since I last visited Bundaberg with the children.'

'Very well, very well,' he said tetchily. 'I shall arrange for your buggy to be brought around mid-morning.'

But what had at first been a source of irritation to Big Jim steadily became a threat as his mind started to wander down dangerous paths. For a long time now, he had sensed his wife's reluctance in bed. Never once had she denied him his conjugal rights, it was true, but she was not as receptive as she had once been. He had presumed this was because she was no longer able to bear children. He'd told himself that, conception no longer being the purpose of their coupling, it was only natural she should be less eager to receive him. Now other possibilities and other scenarios started to plague his mind. What if she really was tiring of him? What if she was seeking distraction in these visits to Margaret Tatham? Certainly, she had the children and Mela with her, but it was not implausible that someone in town could have attracted her. The financial depression was long over ... Cedric was well on the way to re-establishing himself ... God alone knew who she might meet at the Tathams' house ...

'I would prefer you curtailed your trips into town,' he said one day, and from his icy tone Ellie instantly knew it was not a request, but an order.

'Very well, if that is what you wish.' The frightening coldness in his eyes warned her not to ask why.

'That is what I wish.'

Ellie reluctantly obeyed.

But Big Jim continued to torment himself, his paranoia turning closer to home as he studied his wife for visible signs. There were aspects of her behaviour that he now perceived as evidence of a cooling in her feelings towards him. She does not pay me the attention she once did, he thought. She prefers the company of others. Her Kanaka friends are more important to her than I ... Big Jim Durham was driving himself insane.

'Where have you been?' He confronted her late one afternoon when she arrived home only moments after he'd returned himself. She'd not been there when he'd come back from the mill at lunchtime – she'd been gone from the house for half the entire day. 'Where have you been and who have you been with?' he demanded. He already knew the answer of course.

She wondered why he would ask such a question: he would surely know. 'I've been with the Salets dear. Mela and I took the children to the stables and Pavi taught them ...'

'You spend far too much time with your Kanaka friends,' he growled. 'Look to your own family, woman. Your place is here. Here with me.'

Ellie recognised the signs. She had seen them before. Always possessive, he wished to share her with no one. But his jealousy of late puzzled her. He'd been jealous of her relationship with Margaret Tatham. Why? And now he resented the very friendship he himself had gifted her. He was jealous of Mela and Pavi.

Ellie did not ask the reasons. His rage was brewing and she dared not trigger its release. There was madness in her husband.

She ceased to visit the Salets for fear he would vent his anger upon them. She should have been more careful, she told herself. She should have concealed the importance of Pavi and Mela in her life. Nothing must threaten their existence here at Elianne, nothing.

But Ellie could not have known about a final reckoning that was to come with the birth of Federation. The first legislation to be passed by the new Commonwealth Parliament in October 1901 was to have vast repercussions for them all.

'The Immigration Restriction Bill,' Big Jim said derisively. 'Already they're calling it the White Australia policy.'

'Well the colonies have been working towards a White Australia for years, haven't they?' Cedric replied mildly.

'Ever since the inundation of Chinese during the gold rushes of the fifties. Hardly surprising the federal government should consider the matter its top priority, old chap.'

They were taking afternoon tea in the front sitting room of the Tathams' new house, which was rather grand, just the four of them at table: Cedric, Margaret, Big Jim and Ellie. It was a social call. Having long since deprived his wife of her unaccompanied trips into town, Big Jim felt it only right he should offer her the opportunity to socialise now and then. Besides, the Tathams had successfully re-established themselves and were once again a most worthy connection.

'Hardly surprising indeed,' Jim replied archly. He found Cedric's complacency annoying. All very well for you *old chap*, he thought, you're not a sugar grower. 'But it's one thing to keep out the Chinese and another thing altogether to deprive the Queensland planters of their Kanaka labour. The endorsement of the *Pacific Island Labourers Act* as part of the White Australia policy is a typical show of arrogance and ignorance from those down south,' he said heatedly. 'They're creating laws that shouldn't apply to this state – the Southerners don't understand Queensland, never have.'

Cedric refused to be rattled by Big Jim's belligerence. 'Well their argument that the importation of cheap indentured labour lowers wages and conditions for Australian workers is hardly unreasonable,' he said.

'Of course it is!' Jim gave the arm of the sofa he was seated on a resounding thump with his fist. 'It's more than unreasonable – it's unrealistic! If we were to rely solely on white labour in the cane fields, we'd be ruined. White workers can't handle tropical conditions like the Kanakas; that's one of the principal arguments we've been putting forward for years.'

Cedric didn't comment upon the fact that the semitropical region from Bundaberg to the south of the state was far less extreme than its northern counterpart, a detail which Big Jim and his ilk continually and deliberately left out of their equation. The man is touchy enough already, he decided.

Margaret intervened, steering the conversation into a more general area. 'I do believe the formation of the Commonwealth has imbued in us all a sense of nationalism,' she said. 'There is a strong awareness these days of the need to preserve our British heritage and character. Australians desire to be one people, one race, with a common identity in which we can take pride as a nation. This is surely a good thing, would you not agree?'

In the brief silence that followed, Big Jim glared at her. What in God's name did nationalism have to do with Kanaka labour? The woman should keep her views to herself and limit her conversation to bonnets and children like other women.

'Well put, my dear,' Cedric chimed in. He was quite accustomed to his wife expressing her opinions. 'Jolly well put. Now, Jim,' he said turning to his guest, 'would you like a tot of rum to go with your tea? I intend to have one myself.'

'No, thank you.'

As Cedric rose to fetch the bottle, Big Jim directed his scowl out the window, ignoring the women.

Ellie and Margaret exchanged looks. Ellie's was one of admiration – she knew no other woman who spoke out on politics. Margaret returned a smile that was tinged with regret, for she very much missed Ellie's visits. What a pity, she thought. Travel was easier than ever now with the grand new traffic bridge across the Burnett River, yet still Ellie was not permitted to journey alone. Big Jim Durham had found his wife's freedom threatening. What a very great pity.

The *Pacific Island Labourers Act of 1901* was not only designed to put an end to the system of Kanaka labour, but in accordance with the White Australia policy, to return workers to their islands of origin. A time lapse had been agreed upon, the Act giving the Federal authorities power to deport any Kanaka found in Australia after December 1906.

'But this cannot affect Pavi and his family, Jim, surely,' Ellie said in a panic, when she learned the facts. 'Pavi is not a labourer: he is a valuable employee. He has been in Queensland for thirteen years, this is his home, his daughter was born here –'

'We'll see, we'll see, time will tell,' her husband said brusquely. 'There are protests being made and petitions being signed to keep the Kanakas in the country. We're doing all we can to quash this Act, Ellie. You must remain calm.'

But Ellie could not remain calm. The thought continued to weigh upon her as she awaited the verdict.

The general outcry did have repercussions, but not in granting the planters continued island labour. Following a Royal Commission inquiring into Islander repatriation, it was decided exemptions needed to be granted, and the *Pacific Island Labourers Act of 1906* was passed listing those allowed to remain in the country.

Ellie breathed a sigh of relief. It seemed like a last-minute stay of execution. Pavi is bound to qualify for exemption, she thought.

But it appeared he wasn't, or so her husband informed her.

'They must leave, I'm afraid, your friends the Salets.'

At first Ellie didn't believe him. Jim had assisted many of his workers in their applications, and she had made her own enquiries among the islanders she had come to know so well at Elianne. Quite a number had received their certificates of exemption.

'That cannot be true,' she said. 'Old Willie who works at the dairy has been granted permission to stay.'

'All Kanakas who arrived prior to 1879 are permitted to stay, my dear,' Big Jim replied. 'Willie, I believe, arrived in the region around 1870.'

'But Pavi has a family, a daughter who was born here –'
'As do many. It makes no difference –'
'Namou,' she interjected triumphantly, quite sure that she'd caught him out. 'Namou is a family man like Pavi, but he has been in the country for only six years, less than half the length of time Pavi has been here. Namou has received his certificate of exemption.'

'Namou's wife is an Aborigine,' Big Jim said. 'He married a Bunda woman, Pavi's wife is a Kanaka, therein lies the difference.'

'Then for goodness' sake what *are* the requisites?' Ellie demanded as panic once again started to set in. Her husband's apparent indifference to the situation was frightening her. 'Pavi and his family must surely qualify somehow.'

'Sadly no.' Jim said and he rattled off the list of necessary qualifications. 'He is not infirm, he has not been here the required length of time, he is not married to a local woman, his life would not be threatened by repatriation and he does not own freehold land. So there you are, my dear.' He shrugged, indicating a *fait accompli*. 'I'm afraid there is nothing we can do.'

'Of course there is. There must be. You can declare his services essential to Elianne – you're an important man in the community, Jim, a man of authority, they would listen to you ...' Already he was shaking his head. 'Then we can give him acreage,' she said desperately, 'we can make him a freehold landowner.'

But the more frantic she became the less impact she made.

'As you have remarked, Ellie, I am a man of some standing in the community,' he said, 'and as such I cannot be seen to flaunt the new government's regulations. Men such as I must set an example to others.'

His tone was cold, his eyes expressionless, and Ellie knew that any further protestation on her part was useless. Big Jim Durham had no intention of helping Pavi Salet and his family, despite the fact that it would most certainly be within his power to do so. Keeping her emotions in check, she attempted to reason with him, to present the one logical argument that surely he must recognise.

'You will not find another with the natural skills of Pavi,' she said, 'and your horses remain among your most valuable assets.' It was true. Since the purchase of the steam locomotive, the mill had seen a huge increase in production and the horses were essential for transporting the cane to the train's pick-up points. 'Malou as you know has inherited his father's talent with animals,' she said fighting to keep her voice steady, 'and he is now a strong young man. You will be losing two valuable workers.' She would have gone on to mention Mela, who was also a hard worker, and fifteen-year-old Sera – he would be losing a whole family of workers, surely he must see that ...

But he interrupted. 'Yes,' he said, 'it is regrettable to lose my most valued Kanakas, particularly one such as Pavi. Ah well, we must blame the government for that.'

They said their goodbyes outside the Salets' cottage on the dusty dirt track with the driver and the horse and dray standing by.

They were self-conscious, all of them, for also standing by was Big Jim, his presence casting an added pall over the proceedings.

Ellie and Pavi shook hands.

'Goodbye, Pavi,' she said.

'Goodbye, Mrs Ellie.'

They both knew they would never see each other again.

The families shook hands in a solemn ritual, starting with eighteen-year-old Edward and Malou. Then Bartholomew and George shook with each of the Salets and finally Sera, fighting back tears but determined to be as stoic as the boys, shook hands with her three white brothers and the woman who had been her second mother.

No one addressed Big Jim and Big Jim addressed no one. He stood silently by like a giant referee.

'Goodbye, Mrs Ellie.' Mela waited for her handshake.

But Ellie did not offer her hand. 'Goodbye, Mela.' Surely one hug is permitted, Ellie thought; and as she embraced Mela, she embraced the entire family.

The women looked into each other's eyes as they parted. 'Thank you,' Ellie said.

Mela nodded, remembering that time long ago after the baby had died and the Boss had gone away, how Mrs Ellie had come to her distraught. She'd comforted her and said all the right things. The Boss didn't mean to be cruel, she'd said, he just didn't understand women's feelings – some men were like that. But Mela had secretly believed the Boss had killed his baby daughter. She still did. Such things happened. In her village an uncle of hers had killed a deformed baby his wife had borne him. Others before him had done the same thing. They were poor. They could not afford to feed a child who would grow up incapable of work or unable to be sold into marriage. But the Boss was not poor. And Mrs Ellie had so loved her baby girl. The Boss is a bad man, Mela thought. She felt sorry for Mrs Ellie, being robbed of her daughter like that.

'Your sons will be a comfort to you, Mrs Ellie,' she said, looking at the Durham brothers, her eyes resting briefly on each one. 'They are fine boys.'

Ellie stood and watched as the dray drove off down the track, its wheels kicking up the midsummer dust, the family waving their last goodbyes. Shielding her eyes from the glare, she waved back. My friendship has cost them dear, she thought. Then she glanced at her husband. Standing beside her, steely-eyed and emotionless, Big Jim too was watching the dray. Perhaps it is best after all they leave Elianne, she thought. When Jim's jealousy is aroused, there is no telling where his madness might lead him.

I have learnt a lesson, she told herself. Never must I appear to neglect Big Jim. Never must I give him cause to believe I may favour others over him, even my own children. Dear God, she thought, least of all the children. For the safety of her family, Big Jim must always appear the very centre of her existence.

Chapter eight

During her Christmas holidays at Elianne, Kate had done some sleuthing. Eager to discover someone who might know what had happened to Pavi and Mela Salet, she'd asked around among the several islanders who worked on the estate. It was the proud boast of one farm labourer that his ancestors had been in the region since 1870 and that members of his family had worked at Elianne from the mill's first days in the early eighties. As he was a Solomon Islander Kate presumed he may well be a descendant of Old Willie and she proved right, but neither he nor others of his family had any knowledge of the Salets. Nobody did.

Bartholomew would of course remember Pavi and Mela, Kate thought, he'd have been around sixteen years of age when they'd left Elianne. But she was not prepared to reveal her knowledge of the past to her grandfather. Besides, Bartholomew would have no idea what had happened to the Salets. Ellie had written in her final ledger that there had been no further communication of any kind between the families.

Kate's other attempt at sleuthing had also proved fruitless. Bundaberg Cemetery on the outskirts of town had been in its present site since 1879 and she had hoped to find Beatrice's grave. But search as she might, she had discovered nothing. The headstone appeared to have crumbled into dust, obliterating any sign of poor little Beatrice's existence.

Clearly the grave had not been tended – a further poignant comment, Kate thought, on a sad story. Ellie had said in her diaries that Big Jim had forbidden her to continue visiting the grave for fear it would upset her. How unjust that after suffering the pain of her baby's inexplicable death Ellie had received neither sympathy nor support from her tyrant of a husband.

Kate returned to Sydney in mid-February, once again with a sense of relief. In the city she would continue her laborious translation of the diaries, writing everything out by hand, one ledger after another, then typing the pages up on her faithful Olivetti. But there, in the living room of her little Glebe house, the exercise would become academic. Here at Elianne, the diaries and their revelations were an obsession that threatened to engulf her.

She drove over the bridge and into town, but before setting off on the long trek south, she called in at the post office.

Neil Durham found a quiet spot in the canteen, or rather a spot that was a little less noisy than elsewhere, and sat down to read his mail. He ripped open the first envelope, recognising his sister's handwriting. As always, Kate's letter was chatty and amusing. He smiled when he got to the end.

By the way, you owe me ten dollars. Dad and I didn't have a barney. Peace was maintained, but I have to admit with the greatest of difficulty. As a matter of fact I nearly lost the bet two days after you left. I shall expect ten dollars or five quid, whichever is most convenient during this period of dual currency, by return mail.

In the meantime, stay safe, and I mean really safe. Keep me posted won't you, Neil. I want to know when I need to start worrying.

Lots of love,
Kate

Less than three months later, a letter arrived from Neil, who closed with the news Kate dreaded, although he made light of it.

We're off to Vietnam shortly. But don't start worrying yet. I've heard the task at hand is to build a military base before leaping into battle. Do you reckon I should tell them I failed carpentry at school? Anyway I don't think we'll be seeing any action for a while.
  Love always,
  Neil

The chosen site for Nui Dat, the Australian Task Force Base in Phuoc Tuy Province, was ten miles north of the coastal township of Vûng Tàu. Built from scratch, mainly by men of the 5th and 6th Battalions, Royal Australian Regiment, the base was completed by July 1966 and was to serve as the principal headquarters for all Australian operations.

During the building of Nui Dat, the nearby port town of Vûng Tàu, attractively situated at the tip of a small peninsular and flanked by beautiful beaches, became a favourite haunt for the Australians, as it was for the American support units that had arrived the previous year. The locals, who had been quick to embrace the Americans, now embraced the new arrivals with equal fervour. Australian soldiers roaming the town's streets and exploring the roadside markets were eagerly welcomed by hawkers and shopkeepers plying their trade, and at night bargirls enticed them to enter the open doors of clubs and bars where prostitution abounded. New clubs and bars were already springing into existence to accommodate the men's needs, and many more would follow as the war ground relentlessly on and Vûng Tàu became the favoured in-country R & R centre. Soldiers were known to spend up big. For the Vietnamese, there was money to be made in Vûng Tàu.

'G'day, girls, can we buy you a drink?'

Neil's mate Bobbo was an out-and-out larrikin with an insatiable lust for women, and his other mate Phil although less obvious wasn't much better. Like Neil they were 'nashos'. Bobbo was a fellow Queenslander, from Rockhampton, loud and sometimes vulgar, but eminently likeable, and Phil was a Sydneysider with a veneer of style, but a recently discovered predilection for the seamier side of life. The two frequented brothels with alarming regularity and thought nothing of picking up street prostitutes. Neil, although happy to get drunk with his mates, baulked at the idea of indiscriminate sex – the thought of disease frightened him off. At least it had so far: he wasn't sure how much longer he'd last. He was starting to feel toey, and it only got worse when Bobbo raved on as Bobbo was wont to do.

'Seriously, mate,' Bobbo would urge, 'you should give it a burl. You've never had sex like this, I'm telling you. These girls offer a whole new ball game, pun intended.'

Neil didn't doubt for one minute that Bobbo was right. His own sexual experiences had been limited to the back seats of cars and once a hay barn, but he nonetheless managed to resist temptation.

Bobbo teased him mercilessly about his celibate state.

'Don't be a wowser, mate,' he'd say when Neil refused to negotiate with a bargirl or do a deal with a mama-san. 'What are you, a bloody virgin?'

'Give it a rest, Bobbo.' Phil would invariably come to Neil's defence. 'He's smart, that's what he is. At least there's one of us who won't get the clap.'

Neil didn't actually need defending. Bobbo's teasing didn't bother him in the least, although there was the odd occasion, he had to admit, when Bobbo's crassness made him cringe. Today was one such occasion. It was late afternoon and they'd been wandering the downtown markets when out of the blue Bobbo had accosted the girls. He was leering at them as he offered to buy them a drink, clearly implying he wanted to buy a great deal more. But these girls weren't prostitutes. No more than eighteen or nineteen, pretty all three, they'd been innocently browsing the markets' wares. Neil felt embarrassed; he hoped they weren't insulted.

Phil to the rescue, playing it with his customary debonair style. 'We're going to the Sand Bar to watch the light fade over the ocean, ladies. We'd be delighted if you'd join us for a beer.' He gave a slight bow and offered his arm to one of the girls, on the presumption that if she didn't speak any English the body language would suffice. She would certainly have understood the reference to the Sand Bar. Everyone knew the Sand Bar. Built primarily of bamboo, thatch-roofed and with a verandah fronting onto the beach, it was a colourful and popular meeting place.

'OK.' The girl put a hand to her face and gave a light giggle. 'Sand Bar nice,' she said and returning his bow she took his arm.

'Excellent,' Phil beamed at his friends, 'you speak English. And what's your name?' he asked.

'Kim,' she said, 'my name, Kim.'

'I'm Phil. This is Bobbo and this is Neil.'

As the girls introduced themselves, Neil silently blessed Phil's intervention. He didn't doubt for one minute that Phil was hoping to see some action, but at least he hadn't treated the girls like whores.

He offered his arm to the third girl, who said her name was Yen. She was extremely pretty, but seemed a little shyer than the others. Perhaps she didn't speak English.

Upon arriving at the Sand Bar, they crammed themselves into the corner of the verandah at the last remaining table, which looked out across the beach to where the light would shortly fade over the South China Sea. More soldiers, some with girls, were pouring in to prop themselves at the bar. The Sand Bar was crowded at any time of day, but particularly at dusk.

Bobbo bought a round of beers for them all and he and Phil launched into conversation with Kim and her friend Mai, both of whom it turned out could communicate quite well in their broken English. But Yen said nothing. She sat in silence, looking rather grave and giving the occasional nod as if she understood, but Neil had the feeling that perhaps she didn't. He felt self-conscious, unsure how to include her in the conversation.

'I am sorry,' he said in Vietnamese, the only phrase he had yet learned apart from hello and thank you, 'I do not speak Vietnamese.'

'Is no matter,' she replied, 'I speak some English. A little. Not well.'

He was surprised. Even from the few words she'd said, it was clear her command of the language was superior to that of her friends.

'Whatever English you speak is a great deal more and a great deal better than any Vietnamese I shall ever master,' he said.

She smiled, her serious little face suddenly transforming, and Neil was enchanted. He thought how extraordinarily attractive she was. All Vietnamese girls were attractive, it was true, petite, delicate, their hair a glossy jet-black, but Yen seemed to him flawless. Her features were perfectly formed, like those of a porcelain doll. And that smile!

'You live here,' he asked, pointing rather foolishly at the floorboards of the verandah, 'Vûng Tàu?' He was probably stating the obvious and felt a bit silly, but he wasn't sure how else to continue the conversation. He only knew that he wanted to retain her interest. The others were downing their beers and chatting away animatedly and at any moment her attention would be drawn to them.

'Vûng Tàu, no,' she said, and she waved a finger to the north, 'my village two mile away.'

'Oh, so you've come in from your village to Vûng Tàu,' he repeated unnecessarily.

'Yes.' As she smiled again he noticed the dimple that flashed disarmingly in her left cheek. 'Family have stall in market,' she explained.

'I see.' Perhaps it was the dancing dimple that made her smile so infectious. Something did anyway: he found her mesmerising. 'But you don't work at your family's stall, do you?' She wasn't dressed like the peasant girls who sold vegetables in the market. Perhaps she worked in an office.

'No, no,' she appeared surprised he should ask such a question, 'my two sister work stall. They more young than me.'

'Right.' The comment confused him a little, but for simplicity's sake he decided not to pursue it. 'Where did you learn to speak such excellent English?' he asked.

'My priest, he teach me,' she said proudly. 'My priest is Irish man, teach many English.'

'So you're a Catholic?' He found the fact interesting. Despite the predominance of Buddhism throughout Vietnam he had heard there was a strong Roman Catholic minority.

'Oh yes,' she said, 'my family all Catholic.'

Their conversation was suddenly interrupted by Bobbo.

'We're heading off with the girls now, Neil,' he said, 'you coming?'

Bobbo stood, Mai with him, their arms around each other, Bobbo's hand already straying to her breast. Phil and Kim also stood, similarly linked; it was clear an arrangement had been struck.

Neil looked dumbly up at them, feeling all of a sudden incredibly stupid. The girls were street prostitutes. But how could he possibly have known? They'd not been advertising the fact, they wore pretty little cotton dresses, they'd been wandering the markets ...

'You coming or not mate?' Bobbo urged with a jerk of the head towards Yen, indicating he should do a quick deal with his girl.

Neil was confronted and embarrassed. Yen couldn't be, surely, and yet surely she must be. He glanced at her, but she made no movement, as if awaiting instruction.

'Um, no thanks, Bobbo,' he said, hiding his confusion by pretending to consider the matter briefly, 'I reckon I might give it a miss. Heck,' he said holding up his virtually untouched beer, 'can't leave a full glass, mate.'

'Suit yourself.' Bobbo glanced at Phil. 'Wowser,' he said with a good-natured grin. 'Come on, girls.'

A glance was also exchanged between the three girls, and as Kim and Mai turned to go Yen quietly rose from the table.

Neil was further confused. He felt a rush of concern for Yen. Had he insulted her? In saying no had he humiliated her in front of her friends? In any event, he didn't want her to go.

'Would you like another beer?' he asked. The invitation was vaguely ridiculous as her glass sat untouched on the table, but he took out his wallet, indicating he was willing to pay for her time. 'I would very much enjoy your company.'

'OK.' Grateful to be saved a loss of face, Yen smiled her pretty smile and resumed her seat.

'Bye bye,' Kim and Mai called, waving as they left.

The seats they'd vacated were quickly grabbed up by a bunch of new arrivals and Neil edged his chair closer to Yen's to make room.

'If I had gone with you and your friends,' he asked, getting straight to the point, 'how much would it have cost me?'

'Ten Australian dollar, short time,' she said. 'I do only short time.' Once again his question seemed to surprise her. 'You never go with girl here in Vûng Tàu?'

'No.' He placed the money on the table.

'Ah.' The fact was clearly of interest as she folded the notes and slipped them into the pocket of her dress. The pocket had a flap, which she carefully buttoned. 'You want go with me now?'

She made as if to rise but stopped as he shook his head.

'No,' he said, 'no, I just want to talk.'

'Oh.' She appeared concerned and put a hand to her chest. 'You not like me?'

'I like you very much,' he said. 'That's why I want to talk to you.'

'But you not want to sleep with me?'

'Not yet.' Of course he wanted to sleep with her. He wanted to sleep with her very much, but he didn't want to be one in a queue and then out the door minutes later. 'Not right now. I want to get to know you a little first.' She probably considered him downright stupid, or at least naïve, which no doubt he was, but he didn't care. She intrigued him too much.

'OK.' She shrugged: he'd paid her, it made no difference either way. 'What you want to know?'

He indicated her untouched glass. 'You don't like beer, right?'

'No.' She shook her head vigorously. 'Mai and Kim and other girl, they drink beer because men like. Me, no,' she wrinkled her nose in an expression of disgust, 'beer make me sick.'

He laughed. 'So what do you like?'

'I like sweet drink.'

He bought her a sickly concoction of pineapple juice and coconut milk, which she very much enjoyed while they admired the shimmer of light across the ocean's surface.

'How long have you been doing your sort of work?' he asked, avoiding the term 'prostitute' more for his own sake than hers – he had the feeling she wouldn't have been remotely offended.

'Two month only. Mai and Kim, they go with American soldier one whole year, make lot of money.' Far from being offended, Yen was more than happy to talk about her work. She liked the Australian. He was very polite. 'Mai and Kim have place in town with many other girl.

We have deal, is good. I teach Mai and Kim speak English, they teach me way to get soldier.'

'Oh? And what way's that?'

'They teach me not look cheap like bargirl. And they right,' she said eagerly. 'Bargirl show too much, you know? Here. Here.' The way she heaved up her bosom with one hand and slapped her thigh with the other was comical and instinctively he wanted to laugh, but he didn't, aware that she was intent upon getting her message across. 'They teach me how look at soldier in street nice way, friendly, you know?' She offered a demonstration, bobbing her head a little, putting a hand to her face and smiling in a way that was at once demure, provocative and flirtatious. There was no mistaking the signal, and Neil realised yet again how absurdly naïve he'd been. Bobbo's behaviour in the marketplace hadn't been crass at all. One of the girls had obviously flashed him the sign and he'd known in an instant the three were prostitutes; so had Phil.

'Yes, I see,' he said, 'very effective indeed.'

'Yes, yes, is correct way.' Yen was pleased that she'd made her point so succinctly, and that he agreed she was right. 'And make more money,' she said with an efficient nod. 'No need for pay barman, no need for pay mama-san,' she counted the benefits off meticulously on her fingers, 'and soldier no have to buy girl Saigon tea,' she added, referring to the non-alcoholic drinks posing as hard liquor that the bars sold to the servicemen for exorbitant prices. 'You see? Is good for soldier too.'

'What a very astute businesswoman you are, Yen.'

She was gratified by the compliment, but felt compelled to give credit where it was due. 'Mai and Kim teach me,' she said. 'They teach me lot.' She ran her hand affectionately over her pretty, peach-coloured dress, the fabric of which was far finer than the coarse peasant garb she was accustomed to. 'They teach me wear nice dress like this. They teach me be nice girl. Soldier like to go with nice girl.'

'But they didn't need to teach you that. You are a nice girl.'

No comment he could possibly have come up with could have pleased her more. 'Thank you,' she said.

They smiled, the moment resting between them. Then he asked the question he was unable to resist, even though he suspected it was further evidence of his naïveté.

'Do you like your work?'

'Is OK.' Another shrug. 'My family poor, I make lot more money from soldier than market stall.'

'So your family know what you do?'

That was when he realised he may have overstepped the mark. Her face lost its eagerness to communicate and went blank as she focused upon a nearby cormorant perched on a piece of driftwood, wings outstretched, feathers drying in the last heat of the day.

'I'm sorry,' he said quickly, 'I didn't mean to pry. It was rude of me, I'm sorry.'

'Is OK.' The cormorant took off, but she appeared not to notice as she continued to look out at the fading light. 'I must go now.'

'Please don't be cross, Yen. I really am sorry.'

She shook her head. She wasn't at all cross. 'Market close soon, I go home with sisters. I work only daytime.'

'Can I see you tomorrow?' He had a full three days' leave. 'Not just to talk,' he added and, feeling strangely self-conscious, he patted his wallet to ensure there would be no misunderstanding.

'OK.' Although barely eighteen, Yen felt far older than the Australian. He is very young, she thought. Then she corrected herself. No, no, he is very innocent. She wondered if he was a virgin. She'd had the occasional virgin soldier in the past. 'What time you want?'

It was Neil's turn to shrug – any time that suited her, he didn't care.

She chose noon. 'The market, where we meet,' she said.

She would not take him to Kim and Mai's place, she decided, where often many girls serviced soldiers in the same room. She would take him to her other place. The Australian was nice.

The following day they walked a half a mile to the outskirts of town where wooden huts and tin shanties dotted the countryside.

'I take you nice place,' she had said as they'd set off, 'quiet, you like.'

He enjoyed the walk, although it was no leisurely stroll: Yen strode along at a brisk, business-like pace. They spoke little as they went, but glancing at her from time to time he did not feel uncomfortable or self-conscious as he'd suspected he might. She looks so pretty, he thought, in her blue sleeveless shift, her arms swinging healthily in time with her bare legs and sandal-shod feet as she marched. He found it difficult to encompass the purpose of their assignation, that she was a prostitute and that they'd done a deal, that his ten-dollar note was already folded and tucked away in the pocket of her dress. The situation was somehow bizarre.

It became even more so as the town petered out and they were suddenly among rice paddies where peasant workers and farmers were going about their daily business and where the odd water buffalo stood motionless in the fields, baleful eyes staring fixedly at them as they passed.

By now the purpose of their trek seemed quite unreal, lost as he was in the splendour of the surrounding countryside. 'How beautiful it is,' he said, gazing across the rice paddies to the distant mountains, but she either didn't hear or wasn't listening.

'There auntie's place,' she said, pointing to the tin-roofed hut that stood twenty yards or so from the side of the road. They had arrived at their destination.

Auntie had seen them coming, as auntie always did, she kept a regular lookout for Yen, and as the young couple entered the hut, which was virtually one room, she nodded to her niece and gave a quick bow of recognition to the soldier.

Neil returned a respectful bow to the weathered peasant woman before him and waited for an introduction, but there was none. Before he knew it, auntie had grabbed one of the many bundles of raffia that hung from pegs about the walls and disappeared wordlessly out the back door.

Yen took a dollar coin from the pocket of her dress. It made a tinkling noise as she dropped it into the empty jar on the table.

'Is nice place, yes?' She started to undress. 'Quiet, more nice than town.'

'Yes, very nice,' he said. Looking around at the poky little hut where two wooden boxes served as seats and where the bed was a hessian-covered pallet in the corner, he wondered what the alternative would have been.

Following her lead, he sat on one of the boxes and removed his boots. When he'd done so, he rose to discover her standing already naked before him, but he had barely time to admire the pertness of her breasts and the flawless satin of her skin before she embarked upon the ritual that was to follow. Her own disrobing had been quick and efficient, requiring seconds only. Her disrobing of him was to take much longer. As his hands went to the belt of his shorts she stopped him.

He stood motionless, watching her as she undressed him in silence, her eyes not meeting his but focusing rather on each tiny detail. Even the undoing of a button was a daintily performed process. She might have been undressing an emperor. And as she slipped the shirt from his shoulders, her fingers trailed across his naked skin with the same reverence, as if she were serving a lord and master. Neil found the whole process intensely erotic.

Given Bobbo's reports, he had anticipated a sexual awakening, and he was not disappointed: she served him with her mouth and her body in ways he had never envisaged let alone experienced. But it was her final pleasure in the act that took him completely by surprise. When she sensed he was nearing his climax, she gave herself up to her own release with a spontaneity, unrestrained and abandoned, that excited him beyond measure.

When it was over, she recovered herself remarkably quickly and, as he lay on the pallet still gasping for breath, she rose to wash herself. He watched, somewhat dazed, as she crossed to the bucket of fresh water that sat by the back door of the hut. He'd expected the sexual ministrations of an expert certainly, but the sheer uninhibited pleasure? Did other women behave like that? Had it been an act on her part, had she been faking her pleasure? She couldn't have surely. It hadn't felt that way to him.

She returned with the wet rag and bathed his penis, chatting happily as she did so.

'Nice, yes?' She smiled. 'Good for me too.' Yen preferred to orgasm whenever possible, it made work so much more pleasurable, and the soldiers always liked it. 'You have good time?'

'Yes,' she might have been asking if he'd enjoyed a meal. 'Very good, thank you.'

'I think you virgin,' she said and gave a light laugh, 'but you not virgin, hey?'

'No not virgin. But not very experienced,' he admitted wryly.

'No, I think that too.' She rose and returned the rag to the bucket. 'That why I bring you here,' she said as she started to dress, 'special place.'

He hurriedly stood and also started to dress. 'You don't bring many men here?'

'Only nice soldier,' she said. Yen very much preferred the privacy of auntie's place to Mai and Kim's, but when a soldier was overly drunk or aggressive she needed the back-up on offer at the girls' rooms. There was a practical aspect too that further complicated things. 'Cheaper here,' she said, 'pay Auntie one dollar, pay Mai and Kim half money, but take more time bring soldier here from town, so ...' She shrugged. The financial issue was indeed a complex one. 'Still, I like better here.'

'I'm glad I'm one of the nice soldiers,' he said. He wasn't sure why or how he qualified, but the thought somehow pleased him.

'Oh yes, you very nice. You very, very nice soldier.' She smiled as if he was something special, and Neil's heart seemed to foolishly skip a beat. 'You first *uc dai loi* I bring here,' she said. 'Other nice soldier come here all American.'

Uc dai loi, literally meaning people from the south, was the local term applied to Australian soldiers, and Neil supposed he should be complimented that he was the first Australian she'd brought to auntie's place, but he felt vaguely disappointed.

'We go now,' she said.

'Yen.' He halted her at the door and she looked up at him questioningly. 'Would it be all right,' he said feeling extraordinarily gauche but unable to resist asking, 'I mean would you mind awfully if I kissed you?' He wondered if it was true what they said, that prostitutes didn't kiss – he had no idea, having never been with a prostitute. He only knew that he desperately wanted to kiss her.

She gave the matter a moment's consideration. 'OK,' she said, and closing her eyes she leant her head back, lips dutifully pursed.

He cupped her face in his hands and bending down gently kissed her. 'Thank you,' he said as they parted.

His tenderness impressed her. 'You are gentleman,' she said.

'Neil.' He wasn't sure if she remembered his name. 'My name's Neil,' he said.

'Yes. You are gentleman, Neil.'

*

Over the next several weeks, every single day's leave Neil could scrounge saw a trip to auntie's place. He discovered a great deal about Nguyen Thi Yen. As the oldest of three sisters and with no brother in the family, she had taken it upon herself to be the principal breadwinner. Each morning she and her sisters would wheel the big wooden barrow the two miles from their village into the marketplace, stopping off regularly at their widowed auntie's hut on the outskirts of town to collect the raffia craftwork she made for sale.

Once in town, Yen would change into one of the pretty dresses she kept at Kim and Mai's and while she worked the streets with her friends, her sisters would sell the vegetables their father grew, together with the sandals and mats and bags woven by their auntie. At dusk, Yen would change again into her work clothes and the three girls would trundle the barrow back to their village.

Yen's auntie and sisters knew of her double life, but apparently her parents did not. Or so Yen said. Neil found it odd they shouldn't question the radical improvement in their market sales; more probable, he thought, that they suspected the truth, but would not admit it even to themselves. He never questioned Yen on the subject, however, as she clearly wished to believe in her parents' ignorance.

The more he grew to know her, the more Neil came to realise that he genuinely loved Yen. At first he'd tried to convince himself that his obsession with her was due to no more than a newly awakened lust. Bobbo had been quick to warn him of such a danger.

'Geez, mate, you're mad to get involved with the first hooker you sleep with,' Bobbo had said, not unreasonably. 'Try another one. They're as sexy as all get out, the whole lot of them.'

But Neil didn't want to 'try another one', and before long he was forced to admit the fact that he was in love. That he'd quite possibly been in love from the first day he'd met her.

'I want to look after you, Yen,' he said one afternoon. They'd had sex and she was bathing him in her ritual manner. *How many other cocks does she bathe like this?* he wondered as he watched her efficient ministrations. He was plagued by such images lately and had been for some time. Unrealistic though he knew he was being, he loathed the thought of her with other men.

He took the cloth from her and eased her down beside him on the pallet, propping on his elbow to talk to her. 'I don't know what you earn and I'm sure I couldn't match it, but I could help you support your family. I could do that if you would let me.'

'You want look after me?' No one had ever looked after Yen before. As the oldest in a family of three girls, she had always been the one to do the looking after. No soldier had ever treated her like Neil did either. Neil treated her in an honourable way, with respect. And now he wanted to look after her? She was overwhelmed.

Neil's love was possibly predictable, perhaps even inevitable, but the far less predictable had happened. Yen too was in love, in her own way, a way that would prove fiercely loyal.

Everything changed from that moment on. As evidence of her fidelity, Yen gave her pretty dresses to Mai and Kim, proof of the fact that she had no wish to attract the attention of other men. She worked in her peasant garb at the market alongside her sisters, and when Neil was granted leave they spent the day together.

'You want I keep pretty dress just for you?' she asked the next time they went to auntie's place.

'I like you exactly as you are,' he said. When he'd arrived at the marketplace to find her in her work clothes he'd been deeply touched, realising in an instant the statement she was making. 'You are beautiful, Yen, in whatever you wear.'

It had seemed a more or less routine patrol – at least that's what the men had first thought. For some time the

Australians had been aware through radio intercepts and sightings that a sizeable enemy strength was operating not far from Nui Dat, but patrols sent out in search of the Viet Cong had not encountered the force. Then a barrage of enemy mortar was fired upon the base, and in the mid-afternoon of 18 August, D Company, 6RAR was sent on patrol into the rubber plantation of Long Tan to discover where the shells had been fired from.

At quarter past three, 11 Platoon encountered a small group of Viet Cong and a skirmish ensued, leaving one enemy dead and the others fleeing. Clearly the enemy was in the area, but as the Australians continued their patrol they still believed themselves the numerically superior force. They were soon to learn otherwise. 11 Platoon was unaware it had encountered the forward troops of a full-force regiment.

Shortly after four o'clock, the men of D Company, 6RAR were met by the main body of the Viet Cong 275th Regiment.

The battle conditions were horrendous. Heavy monsoon rain broke out, reducing visibility to barely fifty yards and breathing became difficult as men literally sucked in water. All about them, the ground turned to a boggy mess, but 10 and 11 Platoons fought valiantly on, still ignorant of the full force they had encountered.

The advancing battalions of Viet Cong attacked with mortars, rifle and machine-gun fire in an attempt to encircle and destroy the Australians. As assault followed assault it became evident that the enemy force was far stronger than had at first been envisaged and 12 Platoon was ordered through from the rear to support 11 Platoon, which was by now all but surrounded.

Neil and Bobbo fought side by side. Blinded by rain and dragged down by mud, the men of 12 Platoon faced a barrage from all directions, forcing a path through the fire to defend their comrades. The noise was horrific. The explosion of enemy mortars joined the boom of heavy artillery support that was now being fired from Nui Dat, several miles to the west, and all about was the constant *rat-tat* of machine guns, the whistle of bullets and the unnerving bugle calls of the Viet Cong.

Despite the cacophony, Neil heard the murderous screams begin nearby. So did Bobbo. Through the blanket of rain they saw them appear from out of the rubber trees barely twenty yards away: three Viet Cong charging directly at them, firing at random and screaming like madmen.

The Australians raised their rifles and fired. Neil's bullet found its mark. A headshot. One of the Viet Cong dropped instantly and Neil turned his sights on the next.

Rattled by the surrounding mayhem, Bobbo's aim had been erratic and wildly off target. He fired again frantically. The soldiers were by now virtually upon them. His second bullet proved successful, as did Neil's, and the two Viet Cong all but collided with them as they fell, each shot through the chest. But Bobbo had paid a price for his inaccuracy. He lay on the ground beside the enemy soldiers, also felled by a shot to the chest.

Neil halted momentarily, presuming his friend dead. The Viet Cong certainly appeared to be. But then he saw that Bobbo was not dead. His mate's eyes were alive, fearful and bewildered, but signalling him nonetheless. Go on, Bobbo was saying, go on. Neil knew there was no alternative. Others of 12 Platoon were surging ahead through the chaos. He had no way of carrying him to safety. There was no safety zone anyway.

'Hang in there, mate,' he said, 'you'll be right. They'll come and get you later.'

He left his friend and ploughed on through the mud and the rain and the bullets. He didn't believe for one moment they'd come and get Bobbo. How could the wounded be evacuated from this bedlam? If anyone was to get Bobbo it would be the Viet Cong. But Bobbo would probably be dead by then. At least Neil hoped so.

By six o'clock, the Australian troops had successfully manoeuvred themselves into an all-round defensive position, but it was now nearly two hours since the battle had begun and still the enemy kept up its assault, their numbers seemingly inexhaustible. They came in lines of twenty or more, wave after wave of them, deathly black shapes hurtling out of the rubber trees in relentless response to the awful call of their bugles. No sooner had one line succumbed to the barrage of Australian artillery and gunfire than another line rose up from behind the mangled bodies of the fallen like spectres, indestructible and never-ending.

To the beleaguered men of D Company 6RAR the outcome appeared inevitable. Indeed they would already have been wiped out had the two RAAF Hueys not managed to deliver them their sorely needed ammunition. Despite horrendous conditions, the aerial drop had been made miraculously on target, the pilots led in by the red smoke from the flares that had been released. D Company had had a new lease of life there for a while, but they now knew to a man they couldn't go on much longer.

Then at seven, as darkness descended and all seemed lost, the relief force appeared from out of the gloom. 6RAR's A Company arrived mounted in the armoured personnel carriers of 1st APC Squadron and as they thundered through the plantation the enemy forces melted away into the gathering night. The Battle of Long Tan was finally over.

The facts were revealed during the days that followed. D Company, 6RAR, a force of one hundred and eight, had encountered a full regimental strength of approximately two and a half thousand Viet Cong and North Vietnamese Regular Army, engaging them in battle for close on three hours. Eighteen Australians had been killed and twenty-four wounded. Enemy casualties were far more difficult to ascertain. Two hundred and forty-five bodies were found in the battle area, but it was estimated up to a further three hundred and fifty dead had been collected during the night, together with an unknown number buried along the evacuation route. The true statistics would never be known.

The Battle of Long Tan proved a decisive victory for the Australians. It also proved a major local setback for the Viet Cong, forestalling any imminent action against Nui Dat and challenging their previous domination of Phuoc Tuy Province.

'You'll be off home soon, mate, something to look forward to, eh?'

Neil visited Bobbo at the base hospital just before he was shipped back to Australia. Bobbo hadn't died after all. The bullet had hit him high in the chest, smashing through his upper ribs and out his left shoulder blade: a nasty wound, but resulting in no damage to vital organs.

'Yeah, aren't I the lucky one.' Bobbo gave a wink that looked somehow odd, somehow lacking his customary larrikin flair. 'I'll miss the girls though.'

Neil pretended a bit of a laugh, knowing the act was sheer bravado.

'Just as well you're a better shot than me, mate.' Keeping up the pretence, Bobbo chatted away, trying to cover his twitchiness. 'I wouldn't be here at all otherwise, and that's a fact.'

'Luck, Bobbo, that's all.'

'Balls. You're the best marksman we've got. Bloody good bloke to have on side when there are three of them coming at you ... Geez, mate, if it hadn't been for you ...'

Bobbo's manner was suddenly urgent. He seemed to want to talk about it, so Neil let him rave on, giving a nod from time to time. Bobbo had the jitters: he could see that. Little wonder, he thought. The battle alone had been enough, but Bobbo had gone through a whole other form of hell.

The Australians, after consolidating their position, had evacuated a number of wounded during the night using the lights from their APCs to guide in the helicopters. But some of those less fortunate who had fallen in a peripheral area of battle had been forced to lie there throughout the whole terrifying night while all about them the Viet Cong had crept, whispering as they gathered their dead. Bobbo, like the others, had lain doggo.

'I just did my best to look dead, mate, nothing else for it,' he said, unable to stop talking, the words coming out in bursts as images flashed through his mind like a speeded-up film. 'Geez, Neil, they collected the three blokes we shot. I could hear them. I could see them even though my eyes were closed. What do you reckon those bastards would have done to me if they'd known I was alive?' Another shaky grin. 'I tell you mate, I'm fucking lucky to be here.'

Bobbo was a different man. His nerves were shattered. Already Neil had seen others like him, and there would no doubt be many more. A tiny element in Neil wondered why he wasn't that way himself. But he had weathered the storm of battle, and he knew he would again. Perhaps he was tougher than he'd thought.

Chapter nine

The conflict in Vietnam had become suddenly real. It was already dubbed 'The Television War', and those back home did not have to wait for news from the battlefront as they had in past conflicts. As though it were a soap opera, disturbing images were beamed into households across the world, and for Australians the first great shock in this television saga was the Battle of Long Tan. Eighteen dead and twenty-four wounded in just one afternoon! Over the ensuing weeks, the anti-war movement gained momentum as the voice of activism became more readily heard.

'The VAC's planning a demonstration for Johnson's visit,' Jeremy announced to Kate and the other students gathered at the Empress in Redfern, a pub favoured by university activists. 'They're going to mass at Hyde Park corner for the start of the motorcade procession and they're calling on all protest groups to join them – it's going to be massive. We'll show bloody Holt that we're not all the way with LB bloody J,' he scoffed. 'Christ alive, not content with selling us down the river the sycophantic bastard can't even come up with something original.'

'Go Venner!' Larry punched the air with closed fist and grinned at his girlfriend Sylvia as he urged his mate on. They both knew Venner couldn't stand Harold Holt, and Larry so loved to stir.

Jeremy Venecourt had joined the Vietnam Action Campaign and true to form was deeply passionate about the new cause he'd embraced. He was enraged that Prime Minister Harold Holt, upon taking over the leadership after Robert Menzies's retirement, had strengthened American ties with the declaration that Australia would go 'all the way with LBJ' – Lyndon Baines Johnson's US presidential campaign slogan.

Kate watched in silence as Jeremy and the half dozen or so set about discussing their strategy. It was decided to call a meeting with fellow radical students at the university's Wallace Hall during lunchtime the following Tuesday. They would inform the others, a plan of action would be adopted and word spread about the campus. Then a day or so before the American President's arrival a full demonstration would be mounted on the front lawn to rally the troops in preparation.

As the group moved on to the subject of placards, avidly jotting down in notebooks the most effective protest slogans they could come up with, Kate remained silent. She was as much against the war as the rest of them, but she felt she had little to offer. Jeremy had chastised her on a number of occasions for not lending her voice to the anti-war campaign.

'Why aren't you more vocal, Kate?' he'd demanded. 'You're a fighter, why aren't you making yourself heard? We need people to speak out.'

She'd tried to explain. 'My brother's in Vietnam,' she'd said. 'It doesn't seem right. I feel disloyal ...'

But he hadn't listened. Or rather he'd chosen not to hear her, which to Kate was subtly different, so she hadn't attempted to explain further. 'All the more reason to speak up,' he'd insisted. 'All the more reason to pull out of Vietnam, to bring our boys home. This is not our war, they shouldn't be there ...'

She'd let him rave on, knowing he wouldn't understand. How can I expect him to understand anyway, she'd thought, when I don't understand myself?

Living in constant fear as she did for her brother's safety, Kate had become uncharacteristically superstitious. Neil had survived the Battle of Long Tan, but for how much longer would he be spared? She loathed and detested the Vietnam War, just as she loathed and detested all wars, but her brother, like so many others, was risking his life upon the orders of his government. It seemed disloyal and disrespectful not to acknowledge that fact, but of far greater importance it seemed somehow to court disaster. She was prepared to demonstrate against the war itself, but she could not bring herself to condemn the troops by saying they shouldn't be there.

'No, no,' Larry interrupted Jeremy's flow, disagreeing with the suggestion they should include the conscription issue. 'We must keep the protest aimed solely at LBJ and America's involvement in Vietnam. Make it a direct attack on American policy; conscription's a local concern. Don't you agree, Syl?' He looked to his girlfriend for back-up.

'Absolutely,' she said, 'and besides the SOS is bound to be there – they'll make their presence felt.' Formed by the mothers of young conscripted soldiers, the Save Our Sons campaign, now steadily growing in numbers, called for the immediate abolition of conscription.

'All right, I take your point.' The rest of the group was clearly in agreement and Jeremy was forced to defer to majority opinion, although he did so reluctantly. 'But in rallying the troops it's imperative we push the moral issue of conscription,' he insisted. 'Bill White was arrested for refusing to kill people for God's sake! That's a powerful message to students. Conscientious objectors are destined to become a major symbol in the anti-war campaign. The voice of youth! We can't afford to ignore that.'

As always his argument was persuasive and the others were quickly convinced. The drive of the demonstration on the front lawn at university must strongly incorporate the wrong perpetrated upon William White for his moral stance. It would rouse the students into action.

Kate watched Jeremy, again feeling a sense of disloyalty, but this time to him. She knew him very well: Jeremy would love to have been Bill White. The newspaper image of the young man dragged from his home by three burly policemen had become the potent symbol of youthful revolt. How Jeremy wished that image could have been his. And the moral reasons Bill White had given for refusing to report to an army induction centre had been stirring, erudite – how Jeremy longed to have written those words.

Young Sydney schoolteacher, William White, in rebelling against his government's orders, had become the country's first conscientious objector, setting the example for others to follow. And there'll no doubt be many who will, Kate thought. But sadly Jeremy would not be one of them as he so yearned to be. The bizarre truth was, Jeremy Venecourt regretted having been one year too old to qualify for the conscription lottery. He'd told her so in no uncertain terms.

'I'd have shown those bastards,' he'd said. 'I'd have gone to gaol at the drop of a hat rather than agree to fight in this filthy bloody war that's none of our concern. Every conscript should have stood up to the government as Bill White has. The National Service Act is morally wrong …'

He'd ranted on at some length, several of his quotes sounding suspiciously like William White's, although Kate supposed it was a little unjust of her to be critical, for his views were the same as White's. But she couldn't help feeling, as she had on occasion lately, that the radical way Jeremy switched causes and with such passion denoted more a craving for personal excitement than the achievement of change so fiercely fought for by other activists. He'd all but forgotten the campaign for a referendum on Aboriginal rights, a cause that had been of great concern to them both and one to which Kate remained intensely committed. These days Jeremy seemed to revel more in the drama that attended the anti-Vietnam war campaign, particularly since the arrest of William White, and although he remained as charismatic as ever an awful suspicion was dawning on Kate. Over the year and a half of their affair, had lust blinded her to the fact that Jeremy Venecourt was perhaps a little shallow?

> *The stars at night – are big and bright*
> *Deep in the heart of Texas.*
> *The prairie sky – is wide and high*
> *Deep in the heart of Texas ...*

Aided by a powerful amplification system, the voices of the Mormon Tabernacle Choir rang out across the park offering a robust and friendly greeting to the Texan president. As yet the motorcade was nowhere in sight, but the idea was to create atmosphere and whip up excitement amongst the massive crowd gathered at Hyde Park Corner. Here the motorcade, having travelled from the airport, would come to a brief halt for an official welcome before starting on its slow procession through the maze of cordoned-off city streets to the Art Gallery of New South Wales, where a state reception would be held in the president's honour.

The whirlwind three-day, five-city Australian tour by Lyndon Baines Johnson and his wife, Lady Bird, was a 'thank you' for Australia's ardent support of the US-led war in Vietnam. The official visit had been warmly embraced by Prime Minister Holt, who was only too keen to host an occasion of such historic significance as the first presidential trip to Australia, and the general public had been urged to show its appreciation of the honour bestowed upon the nation.

The big day had now arrived and all was in readiness. Countless thousands of specially designed 'Welcome LBJ' flags had been distributed for the populace to wave at the passing motorcade; schoolchildren had been marshalled from their classrooms to line the streets; the young, the old, and family groups had taken up their places alongside the multitudes whose employers had been harangued into giving their workers time off, and now, as the final minutes ticked by, close to a million people thronged the pavements of the procession route, jostling for position, eager to witness the momentous event.

The sage in bloom – is like perfume
Deep in the heart of Texas.
Reminds me of – the one I love ...

At Hyde Park Corner, where media had massed to capture the precious moment of the motorcade's arrival, excitement mounted. But there was a sudden hitch. The Mormon Tabernacle Choir's full-voiced rendition petered out to almost nothing. The singers continued, but 'Deep in the Heart of Texas' had dropped so drastically in volume it could barely be heard over the noise of the crowd. Activists had cut the power line to the amplifier and it was now the cries of the protestors that could be heard above all else.

Word of the demonstration had spread throughout the entire city and a total of around ten thousand protestors of all ages and from all walks of life had congregated at Hyde Park Corner. Militant Vietnam Action Campaigners together with left-wing student activists, trade unionists, women from Save Our Sons, and ordinary suburban middle-class citizens affiliated with no particular action group at all had gathered with the intention of making their presence felt in whatever way they could. There was even a bunch of elderly female pensioners, organised by the Communist Party of Australia, who had arrived at the site early enough to take possession of a number of the seats that had been officially laid out for groups welcoming the president.

*There's a yellow rose in Texas that I am gonna see,
Nobody else could miss her not half as much as me ...*

The resilient members of the Mormon Tabernacle Choir, having managed to repair their power line, were now giving hearty and defiant voice to the ever-popular Mitch Miller version of another of LBJ's favourites.

'The Yellow Rose of Texas' did not last long, however, the activists cutting the power line at another point and once again taking up their chant. Even before the appearance of the motorcade, Hyde Park Corner was becoming the scene of a battle for vocal supremacy.

*She's the sweetest little rose bud that Texas ever knew,
Her eyes are bright as diamonds they sparkle like the dew ...*

The choir refused to admit defeat. Five minutes later they'd repaired the line and were again singing out in full amplified force.

Having rounded the corner at Taylor Square, the presidential motorcade finally came into view, making its way down Oxford Street towards the park, presenting even from some distance a splendid sight. Limousines with Australian and American national flags fluttering were flanked on all sides by a police motorcycle escort, while bringing up the rear were further police mounted on horseback. A buzz of excitement ran through the crowd. Children were hoisted onto shoulders and myriad flags started frantically waving as the procession drew nearer.

The stars at night – are big and bright ...

The choir had segued back to 'Deep in the Heart of Texas', deeming it the appropriate choice for the official welcome, but their triumph was short-lived as an activist went to work for the third time with a set of pliers. At the crucial moment, just as the motorcade approached Hyde Park all that could be heard above the general noise of the crowd was the angry chant of anti-war protestors.

'Johnson – murderer! Johnson – murderer! Johnson – murderer!'

The mood was contagious and others took up the chant. Even those who'd intended to demonstrate in relative silence, to wave their placards demanding an end to the Vietnam War, were compelled to join the activists in voicing their anger.

'Hey, hey, LBJ. How many kids did you kill today?'

A further chant rang out and again it was picked up by the masses to be repeated over and over like a mantra.

'Hey, hey, LBJ. How many kids did you kill today?'

Then the scene ignited as hundreds of protestors surged forwards in an attempt to break through the barrier and the cordon of police. They were held back, but not for long, the sheer force of their numbers proving too powerful. Suddenly the barriers were broken and a number of university students raced out into the street, throwing themselves down in front of the president's car, forcing the motorcade to a halt.

Chaos ensued. American Secret Service men rushed to form a wall around the car; horses following the vehicle reared, their riders struggling to maintain control; police raced forwards and dragged the students bodily across the asphalt, clearing a path for the motorcade to continue. The activists did not fight back, choosing to employ a different delay tactic that was less dangerous and far more effective than resistance. As each student was dragged away another simply took his or her place, egged on by the constant chant of fellow protestors.

'Hey, hey, LBJ. How many kids did you kill today?'

'Johnson – murderer! Johnson – murderer!'

Before long before the police and security teams had the situation under control and the motorcade was able to continue on its way, but the plan for a brief welcoming halt at Hyde Park and a leisurely procession through the city streets had now been well and truly abandoned. The president, the prime minister, the premier and the rest of the official party were to be transported along the planned route to the Art Gallery with as much haste as was humanly possible.

'Come on, Kate,' Jeremy urged, 'we've got to beat them to it.'

He started racing off through the park and Kate joined him, matching his pace. Jeremy had been among the first to fling himself down in front of the president's car, Kate quickly following suit, but both had easily escaped the clutches of the police who'd dragged them out of the way, as had most of the other protestors. Amidst the bedlam the police had been frantically intent upon clearing the roadway to allow access for the motorcade. There'd been no time to make on-the-spot arrests.

From the outset, the students' idea had been to cut through the park and arrive at the Art Gallery before the official party, thereby allowing opportunity for a further concerted protest, and already demonstrators were racing on ahead.

Kate and Jeremy, sprinting at top speed, overtook many and were with the first dozen or so to arrive. Others soon joined them. They too had moved fast and were well ahead of the motorcade, despite its speedy journey through the city streets.

American flags had been hoisted from the many flagpoles of the New South Wales Art Gallery, and a cheer went up as the demonstrators managed, one by one, to haul them down. By the time the motorcade arrived, a single flag only remained.

Accompanied by the chants and jeers of protestors,

the members of the official party were hastily whisked from their limousines and into the art gallery. The entire exercise had been a public relations disaster. This was not at all the warm welcome intended by the Holt government; nor was it the reception the Americans had expected from their staunch ally. The demonstration had proved an immense success.

The full measure of its success became evident in the media coverage that followed. Some of the local reportage was condemnatory, accusing the demonstrators of ruining the day for schoolchildren who hadn't even noticed the president speed by. How heartless, they said. But the true impact resonated far and wide, the message broadcast on television screens and splashed across the front pages of newspapers around the globe. There were clearly many Australians who were not 'all the way with LBJ'.

'I think we made our point,' Jeremy said smugly and in a huge understatement. 'Well done, everybody.'

The students assembled at the Empress raised their glasses and cheered, Kate as loudly as any present. Despite her recent reservations about Jeremy, she supported the protest action on every possible level. If a demonstration of such magnitude could help put a stop to Australia's involvement in the Vietnam War then she was proud to have played her part. Besides, the sooner her brother came home the better.

Kate missed Neil that Christmas when she returned to Elianne. The two had always been close, as had all three of the Durham siblings, but the letters she'd received from her older brother over the past several months had introduced a new level of intimacy.

There's so much I'd like to share with you, Kate, he'd written on one occasion. As a rule, he wrote chattily and often with humour, avoiding any talk of the war, but this time he'd closed on a distinctly serious note.

... so much I long to talk about and can't with my mates over here. Don't get me wrong, they're a really beaut bunch of blokes – you couldn't get better – but in this particular instance they don't understand. I suppose I feel the need to unburden myself to a woman, which of course makes me the 'softie of the family' that you always said I was, but I don't care. I'd love to pour a whole lot of things out to you, but I'm unable to in a letter, the army being the way it is. I know I sound enigmatic – sorry, don't mean to, but the simple fact is I miss you ...

Several other letters had contained similarly veiled references to something he couldn't write about and Kate started to suspect that it might be a woman. Is he having an affair? she wondered, on active duty, in the middle of a war? If so, how extraordinary.

The latest letter, addressed to her at Elianne and arriving in mid-January, had concluded even more enigmatically. After regaling her with the raucous Christmas Eve he and his mates had spent in Vûng Tàu and the endless toasts to family and friends back home, which he vaguely recalled had reduced them all to drunken tears, he'd once again ended on a serious note.

I have a secret I need to entrust you with, Kate, and a favour I need to ask of you. As before I can't write of it, and I'm sure by now these cryptic references to 'something afoot' have become thoroughly irritating, but my tour of duty will be over in July and I promise all will become known then. I won't go home to Elianne on my return to Australia: I'll come directly to Sydney and we'll talk.

In the meantime, a Happy New Year to you, Sis. I hope 1967 proves everything you wish it to be, particularly the outcome of the referendum. I know how strongly you've been fighting for Aboriginal rights and I admire your devotion to the cause, just as I admire everything about you.

My love always,
Neil

Far from finding the mystery her brother hinted at irritating, Kate was intrigued. If anything his cryptic references were helpful, distracting her as they did, just a little, from the daily worry for his safety.

'I get the feeling you're not too happy about Tech, Al. Am I right?'

'My oath you are, but Dad's dug his heels in so there's not much I can do about it. I wish he'd just let me get on with my apprenticeship – I don't need a bloody diploma!'

Kate smiled sympathetically. Such vehemence was rare in Alan, and she was aware of his frustration. 'You probably know as much as the teachers do anyway,' she said, but it appeared there was no humouring him. He just scowled darkly and gazed out at The Basin, where Paola and Georgio were splashing about in the shallows alongside the families and their children.

It was a hot Saturday afternoon and the four had driven to Bargara, Alan at the wheel – he'd had his licence for a long time now and revelled in the freedom it afforded him. This would be their last opportunity to spend time at the beach together before Alan's departure in two days. Having matriculated the previous year, he was to take up his apprenticeship in Brisbane as a fitter and turner, but his father had insisted he simultaneously undertake a Diploma course in mechanical engineering at the Technical College. Stan the Man considered it only proper that as a Durham his youngest son should have a qualification that set him above the average mechanic. Alan himself couldn't have cared less.

'Look at them dog-paddling, will you? Georgio's nearly as lousy a swimmer as Paola,' he now said in a bid to make amends, aware that his manner had been unnecessarily surly. 'Mind you the kid makes up for it at footie: by crikey, he can kick!'

Kate followed the direction of her brother's gaze, but Alan was not looking at Georgio. His eyes were unashamedly fixed upon Paola, which was hardly a surprise. Kate had sensed from the moment she'd arrived home that their relationship was stronger than ever.

'You'll miss her, won't you?' She expected the directness of her question to be met with a careless shrug or some attempt at nonchalance, but as he turned back to her the candour of his reply took her completely by surprise.

'Of course I will. I always do. But we're used to it now, both of us. And I'll be back.'

How incredibly assured he is, she thought. He's become a man and a confident one at that. Her brother's body had broadened certainly, and his face had lost its boyishness to take on the brooding Durham look, but it was his manner that most impressed. Alan was mature far beyond his seventeen years.

'I love her, Kate,' he said. 'You're the only one I'll tell, because I know I can trust you. I love her and she loves me.' Although he hadn't planned upon making any form of declaration, Alan found that he enjoyed saying the words out loud. 'Mum and Dad ... Luigi and Maria ... they all think that my going to Tech will somehow change things, or that Paola will meet someone else while I'm away. But nothing will change. We've made our plans. We're going to wait until we're eighteen and then we're going to tell them we want to get engaged. We won't marry until after I've finished my apprenticeship and gained my Diploma, but Paola and I will be together. Nothing will stop us.'

For Alan it was quite a speech, but as usual he was succinct and to the point. Alan never minced words. He awaited her response.

Kate could have stated the obvious. She could have warned him that all hell was bound to break loose, but she didn't. Why bother? He already knew. 'I'm happy for you Al,' she said. 'I'm happy for you both.' She smiled. 'And I have to admit, just a little envious.' She was, she realised.

She'd never experienced the depth of feeling these two shared. She didn't love Jeremy; she never had.

'It's good to have an ally, I must say.' He grinned, his face reverting to its former boyishness, and she resisted the urge to hug him, jumping to her feet instead.

'Come on,' she said, 'I'm boiling. Let's join the dog-paddlers.'

Before her trip home for Christmas, Kate had again contemplated sharing the secret of Ellie's diaries with Alan. After almost two years, she had nearly finished translating the ledgers, there was just one more to go, and throughout the entire process she had relived every moment of their revelations. She welcomed the prospect of sharing the burden. But the timing was wrong, she'd decided. Alan's life was about to undergo a radical change; he didn't need the added pressure.

Perhaps she'd tell Neil when his tour of duty was over and he returned in July. She always said 'when' not 'if' to herself, by way of affirmation that Neil really would come home. Yes, that's the best plan, she thought. By then she'd have finished the translation and he could read the diaries for himself. And he was now capable of handling the truth. Far from being the family 'softie' as she'd jokingly accused him it was quite clear the army had strengthened him immeasurably.

The following day a farewell luncheon had been planned for Alan along traditional family lines, complete with champagne, at Hilda's insistence. 'I refuse to toast my son's future with a glass of beer,' she'd announced when Stan had said he'd prefer to stick to Four X.

Ivan's son, Henry, was to be present as representative of the Krantz family. 'Mum and Dad are in Melbourne,' he'd told Hilda when she'd rung to invite them, 'Dad has a series of meetings with investors and Mum likes to head south whenever she can during the summer.'

Stan had harrumphed at the news and the fact that no

apology had been offered. There had been a time when Ivan Krantz would have jumped to any required height upon the merest click of his good friend Stanley Durham's fingers, but those days were clearly over. Stan felt like telling young Henry not to bother turning up, but he didn't. Ivan remained a close friend, and far too much investment was at stake to risk a parting of the ways. Elianne was reliant upon Krantz & Son.

Alan had wanted to invite the Fiorellis as well, but his mother and father had suggested they keep the lunch strictly a family affair.

'It's easier on Cook, darling,' Hilda had said mildly. 'Four more guests entails a great deal of extra work.'

He didn't bother countering with a query about the Krantzes' invitation. And since when had the number of guests worried Cook, whose favourite saying had always been 'the more the merrier'? The reason behind the Fiorellis' exclusion was all too pathetically obvious, but it didn't matter anyway: he'd already arranged to take Paola for a drive in the late afternoon. They'd make their own farewells in private, which was vastly preferable.

With only six to table they dined casually in the breakfast room, although Cook and Ivy had gone to great pains to create a celebratory atmosphere, laying out one of the heavier lace tablecloths, the best silverware and the cut crystal champagne flutes.

'You're at the other end, son,' Stan said peremptorily as he seated himself in his customary chair at the head of the table.

Alan dutifully took up his position while Hilda and Kate sat either side of Stan as was expected, leaving the other two chairs for Bartholomew and Henry. Being a sign of pecking order, seating was always important to Stanley Durham, and most particularly today. Under no circumstances would he have young Henry Krantz placed at the foot of the table, a position that would have been reserved for his father had Ivan been present. Henry was an uppity little prick with tickets on himself.

Henry Krantz did indeed give the impression of arrogance, possibly because he tried too hard. Like his father he was a dapper dresser, believing as his father did that in business appearances were all-important, but at twenty-five, his body already tending to the fleshy, the image he wished to portray was sadly beyond him. What should have been style and panache came across as pomposity and self-importance. Young Henry had certainly inherited his father's head for business, but he'd missed out altogether on Ivan's intrinsic elegance.

Despite Cook's lavish baked dinner and Ivy's attention to the re-filling of beer tumblers and champagne flutes, the luncheon was not a successful affair. Henry insisted upon talking business from the outset, launching into a detailed account of a further enterprise that could well be to Elianne's advantage.

'With the mechanisation of the sugar industry galloping ahead as it is, there are huge profits to be made for forward-thinking investors ...'

He went on at some length, Stan the Man studiously ignoring him, and when he finally got the message that he wasn't being listened to, he turned his attention undeterred to Durham the younger.

'You of all people, Alan, with your expert knowledge of things mechanical would be well aware that –'

By now Stan had had quite enough. 'Shut up, Henry,' he growled, and Henry did, stopping mid-sentence, jaw agape. 'This is not a bloody boardroom, boy. Give it a rest, for Christ's sake.'

Hilda did her best to compensate, filling in the awkwardness with pleasant chit-chat. What a pity, she said, that Henry's mother and father couldn't be here, she did so hope Ivan and Gerda were enjoying Melbourne. 'Such an elegant city, don't you think? I vastly prefer it to the raucousness of Sydney myself, although in the winter of course it's so unbearably cold, I really don't know how people can suffer such weather ...'

But Hilda's social graces did little to ease the general discomfort. Henry remained sullen in the face of such an unmitigated insult. He would complain to his father, although he knew it would do no good – his father would simply say he'd asked for it trying to talk business at a Durham family luncheon. Stan ignored the table altogether, concentrating on his roast lamb, and so did Alan. Even during the height of midsummer, a baked dinner preferably lamb was always Alan's favourite, a fact well known by Cook, but much as he was enjoying his food, Alan was wishing the luncheon was over. Even Hilda, having finally run out of chat, decided it was a lost cause and forsaking the niceties signalled Ivy to fetch a fresh bottle of champagne.

Kate looked about the table. The only person present who appeared oblivious to the tension was her grandfather. Seated beside her, Bartholomew had picked up the fine-bone china sauce jug and was clasping it gently in both hands, examining its contents, breathing in the aroma of Cook's home-made mint sauce, which obviously evoked some pleasurable memory. He's off in a world of his own, Kate thought. She'd seen him do it before, usually when unpleasantness threatened. Her grandfather had the enviable talent of disappearing somewhere else altogether.

Watching him, Kate wondered, as she had many times over the past two years, how much Bartholomew might know. Ellie had said in her diaries that she'd lived a lie in order to protect her children from the threat of Big Jim, but was it possible Bartholomew knew the truth, or at least part of it? Had he been aware that the great love shared by his parents was a sham, that his mother had actually considered her husband a monster?

If only Grandpa could speak, Kate thought. But then what difference would that make? He didn't need to, did he? His mind was unimpaired, he could hear and understand. I could ask him questions, she thought. I could ask him questions and he could write down the answers. But she knew she would take no such course of action. Prior to the death of his wife and his ensuing stroke, Bartholomew had spoken often of his brothers and of his mother and father, but there had been no mention, no apparent knowledge at all of a sister who had died as a baby. Wasn't that something of a giveaway? Most families shared such a history. Surely the omission of baby Beatrice's existence was indicative of Ellie's secrecy about so much more.

Kate watched her grandfather place the sauce jug back on the table with infinitesimal care as if it was something quite precious, and she thought how frail he looked, much more so than last year. He's old and he's suffered quite enough tragedy, she told herself, he doesn't need to be confronted with harsh truths at the end of his life.

She switched her brain back to the present, and her voice cut through the oppressive silence. 'Hey, Dad,' she said, 'isn't it time for the toast?'

Stan Durham stopped attacking his second serve of lamb and rose to his feet.

'Of course it is, how remiss of me,' he said. 'Thank you, Kate. Glasses charged, everyone.' How could he have allowed himself to be so distracted from the true purpose of the lunch by that dumb prick Henry, he thought as Ivy scuttled about replenishing everyone's drinks.

'I propose a toast to our son ...' Stan shared a smile with Hilda, who breathed a sigh of relief that some form of normalcy had returned to the gathering. 'After achieving a fine matriculation Alan is about to embark upon his Diploma of Engineering and I know he will do us all proud.' He raised his glass in true patriarchal fashion. 'To my son,' he said, 'to Alan,' and they all followed suit.

'To Alan,' they chanted.

When the seemingly interminable lunch was over, Henry took his departure with a stilted thank you to his hosts. He hesitated for a moment, uncertain whether Stan would offer the customary handshake.

Stan did. 'Give my best to your parents,' he said amiably enough. He could tell Henry was desperately nervous. Good, he thought, insufferable little prick.

'I will indeed, they're bound to phone tonight.' Henry winced at the bone-crushing clasp, which he could swear was even more brutal than usual.

When Henry had gone, the family went their separate ways, Bartholomew returning to his quarters and his latest book, Hilda weaving her way off for 'a bit of a lie down' and Stan retiring to his study and his paperwork, leaving the younger members to fill in the remainder of the day as they wished.

'Well the lamb was good,' Alan drily remarked.

'Poor Henry,' Kate said, 'he's so terrified of Dad.'

'For once I'm on the old man's side. Henry's a pompous bore.'

She couldn't disagree with that. 'Want to go for a swim in the dam?'

He checked his watch. 'Not enough time. I'm picking Paola up at half past four.'

'Ah, of course.' She should have known. 'Do you want to borrow the Holden?'

'No thanks.' He registered her surprise. 'Too conspicuous,' he explained. 'I always use a Land Rover from the mill. Ted signs one out to me and half the time no one even knows who's driving the thing, let alone who the passenger is.'

'That's smart.'

'Yes, I suppose it is, but I don't want to be smart.' He frowned. 'I don't want to sneak around, it's bloody annoying. I'd much rather be open about everything.'

'Of course you would.' She smiled brazenly as she threw out the challenge. 'Well the offer's there, Al, if you want to flaunt it on your last day you're welcome to swan around in the Holden.'

The smile he returned her was wry. 'Crikey, Kate, I'd be in it like a shot if the choice was mine – I couldn't give a damn what turn Dad put on – but I'd only be making trouble for Paola. She's playing a cat and mouse game at home. Luigi doesn't say anything to her face, but she knows he disapproves. Better we keep things as low-key as possible – for now anyway.'

'Fair enough.'

Forty minutes later, Alan drove out of the massive garage that housed the pool of work vehicles: the Land Rovers, the Holden utilities, the Blitz trucks and more. He circled around the rear of the towering mill and pulled up behind the nearby sugar shed, where Paola stood waiting in the shadows. It was their customary rendezvous point during the slack season. When he was home on holiday during the crushing the mill and its surrounds was a hive of human activity and finding time alone was far more difficult. They were forced then to meet down near the pumping station and make do with a walk along the track that, during childhood days, had been forged through the tumble of growth beside the river.

She climbed hastily into the passenger side, sinking low in the seat so that she was not visible to anyone they might pass. She would remain that way until they had left the property and were on the Bundaberg–Gin Gin road heading into town.

Like Alan, the need for subterfuge annoyed Paola. She was tired of the game being played out between her and her parents. Whenever she returned home, her father would glower suspiciously at her, while the glances her mother darted him halted any challenge about where she'd been or with whom. If he'd asked, she would have told him – it was clear he knew anyway – but her parents had obviously agreed to avoid confrontation on the assumption that she and Alan would get over their childhood crush now that he was joining the work force and the adult world. Well they're wrong, Paola thought. They're very, very wrong.

Pretty little Paola Fiorelli was no longer the shy, insecure girl she'd once been. She'd developed a steely side. Paola was a young woman in love, prepared to defy her parents, her religion and her entire upbringing.

'How was the farewell lunch?' she asked, looking up at him from the depths of the passenger seat.

'The roast lamb was good.'

She laughed. 'That bad.'

'Yep, that bad. Henry Krantz talked business, Dad told him to shut up and after that everything went downhill.'

'Just as well we weren't invited then.'

'Yep.' He drove on a little further and they turned into the main road. 'Safe now,' he said.

She sat up and wound down the window, the warm afternoon wind streaming through, whipping her hair into a fierce black frenzy. Scraping the unruly mess back from her face, she reached behind her head, deftly twisted a pony tail and locked her hair at the base of her neck in a knot of its own making.

Alan just loved the way she did that.

They drove over the bridge and upon reaching Bourbong Street turned right, away from the town centre, heading for Queens Park, the favoured haunt of many a young courting couple.

Alan pulled the Land Rover up in the rear grounds of the Hospital and when they'd alighted they took each other's hand to wander the narrow paths that meandered through the park. They were comfortably silent, words unnecessary, although the ache of their imminent parting rested between them.

Upon reaching their favourite spot beside the river's steep banks, away from the paths and the eyes of others, they came to a halt and wordlessly gravitated into each other's arms.

Their kiss was tender, but full of the longing they both felt. Passion was never far away. Alan fought a constant battle to keep himself in check, and he wondered sometimes if Paola knew just how sexual a creature she had become. The fullness of her breasts against his chest, the softness of her lips, the inviting moistness of her mouth ... God it drove him mad. But inevitably it was he who was the one forced to call a halt – Paola didn't seem to recognise when enough was enough.

Paola in her innocence may have been unaware of the extent to which she aroused him, but she was not unaware of her own longing. Just turned seventeen, she was undeniably beautiful, but it was love that lent her the confidence she'd always lacked. Far from feeling self-conscious about her Italian looks as she once had, she now revelled in her appearance. Alan loved the way she looked, and if Alan found her beautiful, then she felt beautiful. She was his, her beauty belonged to him, and she yearned to please.

Paola's desire to please was a continual test of Alan's powers of restraint and today was no exception. Despite the passion mounting on both sides, he broke away, as he always did, in order to create some physical space between them. She must surely have been aware of his erection.

They stood, a little breathless, looking down the steep banks to the river far below, where the late afternoon light played prettily across the water's surface.

'I'll miss you,' she said after a minute or so. He nodded; he'd miss her too. 'It'll hardly be the same as boarding school, will it?' she added lightly. 'You won't be locked away with hundreds of other boys. I suppose I should worry.'

She'd tried to sound as though she was making a joke, but he sensed her concern.

'No need,' he said simply. 'Why would I look at anyone else? I love you.' Alan, as always, was a man of few words.

'I love you too.'

They kissed again, very gently. Then they sat on the grassy riverbank, his arm about her, her head resting upon his shoulder, and gazed down at the glistening water.

A half an hour or so later, as the light faded and the day began its transition to dusk they left the park and drove back to Elianne.

Two weeks after Alan's departure, Kate returned to Sydney. She was relishing the prospect of fourth year. There were some who found the veterinary science course gruelling, but to Kate, who was academically gifted, it presented little hardship: she enjoyed her studies.

University and the multi-faceted existence she led in Sydney continued to stimulate Kate on every level, but it was her commitment to the fight for human rights that added true purpose to her life, and this year promised a major breakthrough in the campaign most dear to her.

'They've set a date for the referendum,' she said as she unlocked the front door. She'd arrived home late Saturday afternoon to discover Jeremy sitting on the doorstep of the little cottage in Campbell Street. He'd been waiting for nearly an hour he'd said, disgruntled, but she hadn't listened, she was too excited. 'They told us at the meeting this arvo: 27th of May. It'll be announced to the media on Monday.'

'Great,' he said in a manner she found rather lacking in interest.

They stepped inside and he closed the door behind them.

'You don't sound very enthusiastic,' she said critically. 'Charlie Perkins and the gang have been working day and night, Aboriginal rights groups have been campaigning all over the country – you could at least sound pleased that the date's finally been set.'

'I am, Kate, I am, I'm very happy for you, honestly.' His patronising tone annoyed her. 'But come on now, you have to admit,' he added, aware she was piqued, which in turn annoyed him, 'it's not a really big deal in the scheme of things. Even if the yes vote wins, the referendum's hardly going to change the face of the nation.'

'I beg to disagree,' she said, aware she sounded prim. 'In my personal opinion amending the Australian constitution is a very big deal indeed.'

'You know what I mean,' he said, trying to remain patient when all he wanted to do was take her upstairs to bed, 'it's not as if you're giving Aborigines the vote, for God's sake – they've had that for ages.'

'Aboriginal people were not granted the right to vote in Western Australia until 1962,' she replied icily, 'and Queensland gave them the vote less than two years ago. You call that ages, do you?'

'All right, all right, WA and Queensland were late coming to the party.' Bed would have to wait, he realised. She was angry now. 'I know the facts as well as you do, I worked on the campaign, remember?'

'Yes I do. What happened?'

'I believe in the referendum, Kate, truly I do,' he said, trying to appear earnest as she clearly needed placating. 'I'm just questioning its importance, that's all. I mean voting rights were given to all British male citizens including Aborigines in the nineteenth century – there were Aborigines who voted in the first Federal election.' He reeled off the statistics in his customarily superior fashion, which most found impressive, but which to Kate was now intensely irritating. 'The Chifley government gave the federal vote to those who'd been granted a state vote in '49, and the Menzies government gave the vote to all Aborigines –'

'Yes, yes, in 1962,' she interrupted impatiently, 'I know all that. Where the hell is this leading, Jeremy? What exactly is it you're trying to say?'

God, she's belligerent, he thought. 'In bringing up the vote issue, I'm just putting a perspective on the referendum's historic significance,' he said with a saintly patience that to Kate sounded more patronising than ever, 'the suggested amendments to the constitution will hardly alter the Aboriginal condition –'

'Of course they will,' she burst out angrily, 'they'll change perceptions across the nation. It's called awareness, Jeremy, *awareness*! People, both white and black, live in ignorance. Most Aborigines don't even know they're allowed to vote. They're not counted in the census, they're not treated as equal citizens, the white population is encouraged to think of them as inferior, the referendum will open people's eyes ...'

Jeremy watched with admiration as she blazed away, angered by the injustice that surrounded her. She's magnificent, he thought. How amazing that someone so enraged can look so beautiful. Kate, when impassioned, was terribly sexy.

'This is the sixties, for God's sake!' There was no stopping her. 'Look at what's happening in America! Look at what's happening in South Africa! How can we let that happen here in Australia? There should be no colour, no race issue in this country. We're a new nation, we should be learning from the mistakes of others, not following in their path!'

'OK, OK.' He held his hands up in surrender. 'You've won me. Calm down, now, calm down.'

She came to an abrupt halt. 'Sorry,' she said, 'I got carried away.'

'Yes, you did a bit.' He grinned amiably. 'We're on the same side, you know. It's hardly as if I need converting.'

'I know. I'm sorry.'

'Don't be. I was impressed, truly I was.' He took her in his arms and she didn't resist. 'You really did win me, Kate,' he murmured. 'Now can I win you?' He kissed her, his hand straying to her breast, and Kate, obeying the dictates of her body, couldn't help but respond.

They retired to the attic, where their lovemaking was as mutually satisfying as ever, but she knew the affair was over. The affair's been over for some time, she thought, it's only been lust keeping us together. Well she could live without sex, she decided.

He stayed the night and they made love again in the morning as they always did. Then, over toast and coffee at the little table, she told him.

'You're joking.' Jeremy didn't believe for one moment she could possibly be serious. 'After two years, it's over,' he snapped his fingers, 'just like that.'

'Yes, I'm afraid so,' she said apologetically.

'Oh, I get it.' He gave a knowing nod. 'It's because I wasn't as passionate about the referendum as I should have been – that's it, isn't it?' he said. 'I'm sorry, Kate, I should have –'

'It has nothing whatsoever to do with the referendum, Jeremy. It's over, that's all.'

He stared at her in stunned amazement. Good God, he thought, I'm being dumped, I'm actually being dumped. He'd never been dumped before. He was always the one who did the dumping, and usually after three months, six at the outside. He'd never had a relationship that had lasted a whole two years. What on earth had gone wrong?

'Is there someone else?' There has to be, he thought. But how come he hadn't read the signs? How come he hadn't guessed?

'Of course there's no one else.' Kate couldn't help but smile. His reaction was one of amazement, not heartbreak, and his disbelief was verging on comical. 'You're special to me, Jeremy,' she said in all sincerity, 'you always will be. It's only the affair that's over, not the friendship. I'm grateful for everything we've shared and I hope we'll remain friends.'

'Oh we will, Kate, we will, no doubt about that.' He stood, still dazed and somewhat in a state of shock. 'Well I'll just gather up a few things, shall I?'

'Would you like another cup of coffee?'

'No, no, best to get it over and done with I think.'

She fetched him a carry bag and, five minutes later, when he'd gathered together his toothbrush and toiletries and spare underpants, they said their goodbyes at the front door.

'I feel rather pathetic,' he said forlornly.

'You don't look it. You look as gorgeous as ever.' She kissed him fondly. 'Thank you for being my first love. I consider myself very lucky, and I really do mean that.'

'My pleasure,' he said with his customary panache. 'So I'll see you around the campus then.'

'Yes. See you around, Venner.'

He smiled, and Kate saw in his eyes a regret that she found surprisingly touching. Then he turned away and she closed the door.

Chapter ten

Alan was finding his new life in Brisbane frustrating. He was not an impatient young man as a rule, nor was he afraid of hard work, but it seemed to him that he was slogging away for extraordinarily long hours and for very little purpose.

It's a bit like being on a treadmill, he wrote to Paola, *where one walks and walks but never actually gets anywhere.* They exchanged letters at least once a week, he forwarding his to the Bundaberg post office in order to avoid the eagle eyes of her parents. *Of course Dad would say the whole point of the exercise is to gain my qualification as a mechanic and to achieve my Engineering Diploma, but surely I should be learning something along the way.*

His education did appear to have reached a stalemate. The apprenticeship he was serving at Evans Deakin & Company's machine shop in South Brisbane involved endless hard work that he found extremely mundane, and his first-year studies at Technical College were teaching him nothing he didn't already know. He resigned himself to the fact that the course was bound to pick up over time and made the college library his salve, borrowing manuals and textbooks designed for final-year students and devouring them on Sunday afternoons.

He lived in Woollangabba, a suburb on the south side of the river, in a pleasant boarding house run by a pleasant middle-aged widow who provided most of his meals, including an excellent hearty breakfast, which was just as well for his day was long and tedious. First thing in the morning, he would catch a tram to Evans Deakin, where he would work a solid eight hours, the lunch break provided allowing time only for a quick visit to the nearby sandwich shop. Then upon returning to the boarding house, he would scrub away the grime of the day and, if he had time, gobble down the tea prepared by the kindly widow – if time did not allow, it would be put aside and reserved for his supper – after which he would catch the cross-river ferry from Kangaroo Point to the Alice Street jetty. He would make his way from there to Central Technical College at the Botanical Garden end of George Street to attend his Diploma Course lectures, which lasted most nights from six until nine.

The relentlessness of Alan's existence lent particular joy to Saturdays, the one day of the week reserved for social activity, when he'd go out on the town with a couple of friends from his boarding-school days. Barry and Dave were now in their second year at university and although they were two years Alan's senior the three shared a great love of jazz. They would visit a pub or a club that had a live band playing on a Saturday night, while the afternoons were more often than not spent in the beer garden of the Breakfast Creek Hotel.

Known simply as Brekky Creek, the magnificent French Renaissance-style hotel nestled at the mouth of an estuary of the Brisbane River was not only the city's most popular watering hole, but possibly the most famous in the entire state of Queensland. Here people from all walks of life gathered and had for generations past – dockside labourers, members of the racing fraternity, politicians, middle-class workers, tourists and students alike. It seemed everyone congregated at the Brekky Creek pub, particularly on a Saturday afternoon.

Seated in the crowded beer garden, the boys had finished their meal and Barry had just left for the bar to fetch yet another round. They were drinking schooners and, as they'd already shouted a round each, Alan was beginning to feel the effects despite the gargantuan steak he'd devoured – Brekky Creek was famous for the size of its steaks.

Although under the legal drinking age, Alan looked considerably older than his years and was never asked for identification. But then things were different throughout the country these days. Since the introduction of national service attitudes had become more liberal and fewer questions were asked. It seemed immoral, most tacitly agreed, that a man could be conscripted at nineteen to fight for his country, yet was unable to legally buy a beer.

Alan watched Barry disappear into the bar. Crikey, he thought, I'll be drunk as a skunk after another three rounds. He wasn't a heavy drinker – he never had been; he couldn't handle his beer the way Barry and Dave did – but what the heck, the four-piece cover band that was playing had put them all in a party mood and the day was unseasonably hot for late March: it just cried out for beer. He skolled the remaining dregs from his glass. Alan loved Saturdays.

'Don't go away, folks,' the lead guitarist announced, 'we'll be back with some more Beatles in about fifteen minutes. We're just going to grab a quick beer.'

The band had finished its bracket with 'Love Me Do' and was taking a break.

'They're good, aren't they?' a female voice said.

Alan and Dave looked up at the young woman who'd arrived to stand by their table, glass of wine in hand. To Alan she appeared vaguely familiar, but he couldn't recall from where.

'I'm Jane,' she said, 'Jane Campbell, I've seen you around at Tech.' She offered him her hand.

'Oh yes, of course.' At the Gardens Tuck Shop several days earlier, he recalled, she'd literally bumped into him on his way out with a coffee, but he hadn't stopped to introduce himself as he'd been running late. 'Alan Durham,' he said as they shook, 'and this is Dave Johnson.'

'Hello Dave.' She shook hands with Dave too, but rather perfunctorily, her attention remaining focused on Alan. 'Mind if I join you?'

'Sure, why not?' Alan was a little nonplussed: she was extraordinarily forthright and he wasn't accustomed to pushy girls. He looked around for a spare vacant chair that he could pull up to the table for her, but there wasn't one.

She plonked herself in the seat that Barry had vacated. 'Just while the band takes a break,' she said, 'then I'll go back to my friends.' The boys followed her eye line as she waved to a nearby table where her two girlfriends were waving back. 'You're doing an engineering course, aren't you?' she said, turning back to Alan.

'That's right.' He wondered how on earth she could know that.

'I've seen you going into A Block,' she explained in response to his puzzled expression. It was true that the Engineering Diploma Course was run out of A Block, but Jane had actually made her own enquiries to be sure. 'I've had my eye on you, Alan Durham,' she added with a cheeky wink.

He laughed as if he'd enjoyed the joke, although he felt a bit self-conscious. He found the way she was ignoring Dave rather rude.

Dave, however, was far from offended. To the contrary, Dave was signalling a look that was distinctly envious. *She's after you, mate,* Dave's eyes were saying. *You lucky bastard!*

Jane was without doubt attractive. Slim, fair-haired and oozing self-confidence, she was the sort most would call 'sexy'. Alan judged her to be around twenty or so.

'What are you studying at Tech, Jane?' he asked.

'Certificate in Business,' she said with a dismissive shrug, 'book-keeping, secretarial stuff and all that, but only as a back-up. I intend to go to NIDA next year.'

'Oh, really?' Seemingly riveted by the announcement, Dave cast a meaningful glance at Alan.

'NIDA?' Alan asked blankly, ignoring the prompt that he should appear impressed even if he didn't know what the hell she was talking about, which Dave clearly didn't.

'The National Institute of Dramatic Art,' Jane said, 'it's in Sydney. I'm going to be an actress.'

'Wow, that's impressive.' He obliged with the response that was obviously required.

'It sure is,' Dave echoed.

'Thank you.' The smile she flashed them both was suddenly genuine and devastatingly attractive. 'Of course I have to pass the audition first,' she admitted with disarming candour, 'and only a handful out of the thousands who audition ever manages to get in. But what the hell? I intend to give it my best shot.'

'You'll get in, I bet,' Alan said. Heck, someone as good looking as her is bound to, he thought.

'I bet you do too.' What a stunner, Dave thought, bloody pity it's Alan she's after.

'Hello, hello.' Barry had arrived juggling three schooners. 'Who do we have here?' he said as he placed them on the table with care and only minimal spillage.

Introductions were made and Jane rose to her feet. 'Sorry, Barry, I've stolen your chair.'

'No worries, I'll get another one.' What a stunner, he thought.

'I don't think there are any,' Alan said.

'No, no, it's all right,' she insisted, 'I'll go back to my friends.'

'Why don't we join up the tables?' The suggestion was Dave's.

'What a good idea,' she replied as if the thought had not already occurred. 'I'm sure Sal and Wendy won't mind.'

Sal and Wendy didn't mind in the least, and after the boys had dragged the tables together, the afternoon became quite a party. The band returned and opened with another Beatles bracket, which led to the inevitable discussion about which Beatle was whose favourite and which Beatles song was the best, and before long it was time for another round of beers. Alan insisted upon the shout being his although it was actually Dave's; he wanted to sit the following round out – the mix of sun and beer was going to his head.

'How about you girls?' he asked as he stood. 'Another carafe?' The girls were drinking the house white, which was sold by the glass or the carafe.

Jane stood also. 'Yes, absolutely, but we'll buy our own, thanks.' She smiled, again disarmingly, and Alan thought that, despite her pushy introduction, she really was nice. 'We're liberated women, after all,' she said and, collecting money from the kitty she and her friends had placed on their table, she accompanied Alan to the bar.

As they waited in the queue she pressed herself intimately up against him, so intimately in fact that at first he thought it was a mistake, that she'd been jostled by the crowd. He edged away to give her a little space, but she edged with him, her left breast continuing to make contact with his right bicep, which was bare as he was wearing a short-sleeved shirt. She even manoeuvred her body slightly so that he could swear he felt a nipple. She's not wearing a bra, he thought. The realisation was both shocking and tantalising. To think that through the thin fabric of her dress, he could feel so distinctly the shape and the very texture of her breast against his skin. With Paola he'd always been aware of the brassiere forming a barrier between them, a barrier he had never abused, much as he'd longed to.

'After we've had another drink, do you want to go for a drive?' she murmured seductively, her lips all but caressing his ear. She was obviously unaware of his self-consciousness.

'I don't have a car.'

'I do.'

'Where would we drive to?'

'My place. It's not far.'

The answer didn't surprise him. Alan had finally got the message and a series of overwhelming responses physical and mental were coursing through his being. His pulse had quickened, he was aware of a growing erection, and the prospect of sex with Jane was so intensely arousing that his mind had become a veritable battlefield. It's just the beer, he told himself, but he knew it wasn't. I can't be unfaithful to Paola, his mind said, we're promised to each other. Yes, you can, a voice from somewhere else countered. You ought to gain some experience before you get engaged. A man should have a degree of expertise before bedding a virgin wife, that's what they say. Who the hell are 'they'? his mind demanded.

Stop it, he told himself, stop it!

'Let's see how we feel after another drink, shall we?' he said calmly, playing it cool, buying time. They'd arrived at the counter and were next in line to be served.

Jane smiled, in her book that was a definite yes. 'Another drink it is,' she said confidently, oblivious to the internal battle that had just raged.

'What'll it be, mate?' the bartender asked.

'Three schooners and a carafe of white, thanks.'

They returned to the others, but they didn't bother carrying through with the pretence of 'another drink'.

'Alan and I are going for a drive,' Jane announced after barely five minutes.

They stood together, Alan equally eager to be on his way. The gentle friction of her thigh against his beneath the table had erased any agony of indecision. All he could think of now was the fact that he was about to lose his virginity.

'Aren't you going to finish your beer?' Dave eyed Alan's virtually untouched glass: leaving a full schooner was nothing short of a crime.

'Nup. I've had enough. Bit of a drive and some fresh air, that's what I need.'

'Right.' Dave gave a nod and cast a knowing look at Barry that said he's in there, lucky bastard.

'OK, Alan,' Barry chose to ignore Dave's overt signal for fear of offending the girls – he very much hoped to score with Wendy, who'd already agreed to go on with him to the club. 'Might see you a bit later then at The Downstairs. We're heading off there in an hour or so.'

'Rightio. Probably see you there then.' The Downstairs was a jazz club they often frequented on a Saturday.

As Sal and Wendy fluttered fingers in goodbye, they exchanged their own knowing glances. Neither was surprised that Jane had made her intended conquest: she'd offered a bet when they'd first arrived, the moment she'd seen Alan there with his mates.

'God I find him sexy,' she'd said. 'He goes to Tech, I bump into him all the time, but he never even notices me.' Going unnoticed to Jane was not only a novelty, it was an absolute turn-on. She couldn't resist a challenge. 'Well, he'll notice me today all right. Bet you ten bucks I get him back to the house.'

The girls hadn't taken her up on the bet.

'Your carriage,' Jane announced with jokey dramatic flair as they arrived beside her shabby second-hand Volkswagen. 'Hardly a thing of beauty, but she goes.'

'They're good cars, VWs,' Alan said climbing into the passenger seat, 'good and reliable. Engine needs a bit of a tune up though,' he added when she turned on the ignition.

She wondered why he didn't have a car of his own. He was always well dressed, he'd hardly be short of money. She whacked the gearstick into first and took off. Besides, she'd learnt through enquiry that he came from a wealthy country family, a sugar plantation no less. No car, that's strange, she thought.

Alan tried not to wince. She was a truly terrible driver.

The house that Jane shared with Wendy and Sal and two other girls was a short drive away in Fortitude Valley, an inner-city suburb to the north-east of Brisbane's business centre. Known affectionately as 'The Valley', the once fashionable hub of shops and restaurants was starting to wane as outer-suburban shopping centres came into existence. The Valley, although still popular, was showing a slightly seedier side of late and in some of its surrounding backstreets were homes that had known better days. The ramshackle two-storey, five-bedroom house rented by Jane and her friends was one such, having been in its time the family home of a well-to-do retail merchant. Here the girls lived a buzzy, bohemian existence. They loved The Valley.

'Come on in,' Jane said, unlocking the front door, and he followed her through a very messy open-plan living and dining room, complete with overflowing ashtrays, into an even messier kitchen. 'Anyone home?' she yelled as they went, and Alan was visited by a sudden sense of misgiving. Eroticism having momentarily deserted him, he wondered what he'd let himself in for.

'Sorry about the mess,' she said, oblivious to his unease, 'Sunday's clean-up day.' She smiled happily. 'But at least we have the place to ourselves, it's usually deserted on Saturday afternoons. Do you want a beer?'

'Sure.' A beer was the last thing he wanted. 'Thanks.'

She lifted two stubbies from the refrigerator, opened them and handed him one. 'Come on up to the less mucky part of the house,' she said, and he followed her once again as she led the way upstairs to her bedroom.

He discovered to his relief that she was right. Upstairs was certainly less mucky, at least Jane's bedroom was. In fact Jane's bedroom was something altogether different.

He gazed around at the posters that adorned the walls, mostly reproductions of Lautrec and Degas. There were several lamps with ornately painted French lampshades, the bedspread was of plush red velvet, the corner table and two small chairs were covered with lace cloths and on the dresser was a collection of porcelain pots and vases together with a pair of candelabras that appeared antique. The overall effect was cluttered but attractive.

'Wow,' he said, 'you've done a great job.'

'Thanks. I like it.' She sat at the small table and took off her sandals. 'I haunt second-hand shops as you can see. My aim is to create a Parisian look.'

'I'd say you've certainly succeeded there,' he said, 'not that I'd know of course, I've never been to Paris, but it looks pretty authentic to me.' He sat on the other chair, wondering whether he should follow her example and take off his shoes.

'Well, when you live with four girls you need a world of your own to disappear into and this is mine. Aren't you going to take your shoes off?'

'Sure.' He was feeling more relaxed by the minute: she was very easy company.

She downed a swig of her beer and studied him as he took off his shoes. 'Why don't you have a car, Alan?'

'I will in July.'

'Oh? Why wait till then? Why not get one now?'

'It's a family thing, same with my brother and sister, Dad gives us a new car when we turn eighteen.' He failed to notice her reaction. 'What I'd really love to do is buy a vintage vehicle and restore it, even an old jalopy would do, but Dad'd be furious if I didn't wait for the big presentation.'

'Are you telling me you're only seventeen?'

Uh oh, he thought, I've stuffed things up. 'That's right. But not for long,' he added hopefully, 'I'll be eighteen in July.'

'Good God, I thought you were at least twenty.'

'Yes, most people do. I'm sorry, Jane. I didn't intend to mislead you.'

'Of course you didn't. How could you? I was the one who made a line for you, remember?'

He remembered all right. 'Does that mean you don't want to …?' he left the rest unsaid, which he thought was tasteful.

She was intrigued. How can a seventeen-year-old be so mature? she wondered. Her brother was seventeen and he was an absolute dill.

Her hesitation seemed answer enough to Alan. 'Would you like me to leave?'

'Don't you dare.' And how can a seventeen-year-old be so damn sexy? she asked herself. Putting down her beer, she circled the little table to sit on his lap. 'I am feeling so randy, don't you dare leave,' she murmured, draping her arms around his neck and kissing him, her breasts nuzzling enticingly against his chest.

The response was immediate. Alan's body leapt to attention, there was no disguising his arousal, and she laughed. 'Shall we get undressed first?' she suggested.

He stripped as hastily as he could, and when he'd dumped his clothes on the chair he looked up to find her stark naked, carefully folding back the plush velvet bedspread. He was momentarily awestruck. He'd never seen a naked woman before – well not in the flesh anyway: he'd seen plenty of centrefold pictures in the magazines furtively handed around at boarding school.

She removed the coverlet altogether, placed it on the floor and lay down, propping on an elbow, not even bothering to cover herself with the sheet.

'You're beautiful,' he said, hoping he didn't sound gauche and feeling self-conscious about his rampant erection. He needn't have.

'So are you,' she said approvingly, and patted the bed.

He joined her, the mere touch of flesh upon flesh setting them both aquiver; she too was ready, and as they kissed, his hands explored the exquisite contours of her body. He was becoming excited beyond measure, but even as she parted her thighs to allow him access, he realised there was something he'd overlooked.

'Oh hell ...' He broke away from her, calling a breathless halt to the proceedings. 'I'm terribly sorry, Jane,' he said cursing himself for not having stopped off at a chemist's shop.

'What is it, what's wrong?'

'I don't have a condom.'

She looked at him quizzically as if he might be joking, then when she realised he wasn't she burst out laughing. 'Good grief, Alan, this is the sixties, where have you been?'

His response was blank.

'I'm on the pill, of course.'

'Oh yes, of course. Sorry.' He cursed himself again – how could he have sounded so dumb? He supposed these days most girls were on the pill.

'You really are a country boy, aren't you?' She didn't sound in any way disparaging, just amused.

'Yes, I suppose I am,' he admitted.

'I like country boys,' she said, wantonly reaching her hand down to him, and as they kissed again she parted her thighs and guided him into her.

Alan tried desperately to retain control, but the sensation that engulfed him was overwhelming. The inside of a woman was more sensual by far than his wildest imaginings, and before long he realised he was fighting a losing battle.

For a novice he acquitted himself admirably nonetheless, indeed perhaps a little too admirably. Jane was teetering on the brink of orgasm when he finally exploded.

Bugger it, she thought as they lay on their backs gasping for breath like a couple of hundred-metre sprinters, couldn't he have lasted just thirty seconds longer?

Despite his inexperience, Alan was aware of his failure to satisfy. 'I was a bit quick, wasn't I?' he panted.

Something of an understatement, she thought. 'Yes, just a bit.'

'I'm sorry, Jane, really I am. It's just that was my first time, so I suppose ...' he tailed off apologetically.

'Oh God, don't tell me ...' She rolled on her side to face him. 'You're not only seventeen, you're a virgin?'

He grinned, he couldn't help himself. 'Not anymore.'

'Why didn't you say anything?'

'Why would I? No bloke would, surely.'

Jane returned a wry smile: he was right of course. 'Well I have to admit for a beginner you're not bad. Shall we finish our beers and give it another burl? That is if you think you'll be up to it,' she added suggestively.

'Oh, I'll be up to it all right. But I can do without the beer.'

'Me too. A cup of tea then.' She sprang from the bed. 'You wait here, I won't be a tick.' She slipped on her dress, but ignored the undies. 'Stay in the mood,' she said with a wink and then she was out the door.

After their cup of tea, Alan was more than in the mood, he was raring to go, but this time he was determined to practise restraint. He'd come to a decision while she'd been downstairs. He must learn from his experience today. He must learn how to give a woman pleasure.

He took his time as best he could, matching his pace to hers, and when finally he sensed her approaching orgasm, he held himself in check, allowing the movement to be hers alone, careful not to thrust, knowing that if he did he was gone. She was uninhibited in her pleasure, which he found intensely erotic, and it took every ounce of willpower he could muster not to let go, but he managed. Only when he was sure she was completely satisfied did he give in to his own climax.

Jane flopped back on the pillow, sweaty and sated. 'Well that was a whole heap better,' she said when she'd regained her breath, 'you're a quick learner, I'll give you that much.'

'Thanks.' He was pleased. It was exactly what he wanted to hear.

During the days that followed, Alan mulled over the event of his sexual awakening. He had enjoyed the act. Indeed he'd found sex as exciting as his friends had boasted that it was. But Alan Durham was not like his friends. To Alan, the casualness of the act and its supreme lack of meaning made sex in itself a shallow, empty thing. Sex was not making love. Making love would be something entirely different. He would not have sex again until it was with Paola, he decided. No matter that their marriage was some years away, he would wait.

He didn't agonise at all about whether or not he should tell Paola of his sexual encounter: of course he would tell her, they'd agreed they were never to have secrets from one another. But should he feel guilty for having so unashamedly used Jane? He wasn't sure about that one. Jane seemed liberated, certainly, but would she presume there was some form of ongoing relationship? Girls usually did when they'd been to bed with someone, didn't they?

'Hello, Alan.'

'G'day, Jane.'

It was during a break between lectures and he was sitting in the Gardens Tuck Shop eating a pie with peas and mashed potato, his favourite of the daily specials when he hadn't had time to scoff down his landlady's tea. Seated by the door as he was, he saw her the moment she walked in and, the chair opposite him being vacant, he expected her to join him. He rather hoped she would so they could clear up any possible misunderstanding.

She didn't join him, however. In fact she paid him scant attention. She appeared to be looking for someone. Then her eyes lighted upon the young man at the counter who'd just been served a cup of take-away coffee.

The young man turned from the counter and Alan watched as Jane stepped directly into his path.

'Oops,' she said when they bumped into each other. 'I'm most terribly sorry.'

Alan smiled at the familiarity of the scene. He smiled even more when the young man introduced himself. She's home and hosed, he thought.

The referendum of 27 May 1967 sought approval for two amendments to the Australian constitution that were considered discriminatory to the Aboriginal people. The first clause related to the government's power to produce laws with respect to *the people of any race, other than the aboriginal race in any State, for whom it is deemed necessary to make special laws*. The second related to the government census. *In reckoning the numbers of the people of the Commonwealth, or of a State or other part of the Commonwealth, aboriginal natives shall not be counted.*

It was recommended the reference to 'the aboriginal race' be removed from the first clause, and that the second clause be removed altogether.

The two simple questions put to the Australian people were, should Aborigines be counted in the census, and should Aborigines be subject to Australian Federal law. The public voted overwhelmingly 'yes' on both issues.

'Well done, Kate.'

Jeremy had turned up at the celebratory party that was held on a fine, but chill, Saturday afternoon in the rear courtyard of the Bondi Pavilion. The once-grand bathing pavilion overlooking Bondi Beach had gone to seed over the past decade, but its main hall, rarely put to community use of late, had served as a convenient meeting place for the campaigners, particularly the younger members, who during the summer months liked to finish the day's business with a swim.

'Thanks, Venner.' Kate returned his effusive handshake. She was surprised to see him. He hadn't been particularly committed to the campaign. But then Jeremy liked to maintain an interest in all major causes whether as an active participant or not, seeming to know every single statistic and every single person involved in every single campaign. 'Knowledge is power, Kate,' he'd repeatedly told her in those early days when, Svengali-like, he'd groomed her for a future in social activism.

'I felt compelled to come and offer my personal congratulations,' he now said in all earnest. 'Truly Kate, you've every right to feel proud. Good God an almost ninety-one per cent affirmative vote! That's got to be the most successful campaign for change this country's ever seen. Well done!'

He embraced her and she returned the hug, although she was conscious of the wary look from Isobel, his new girlfriend, whom she knew vaguely from university. Isobel was aware of their previous relationship.

'It was hardly a solo effort,' she said with a laugh. 'Hello, Isobel.'

'Hello, Kate. Congratulations. Venner's told me how hard you worked on the campaign.'

'So did everyone here,' she said looking around at the crowded courtyard, 'and so did hundreds of others all over the country. I don't think I can take any personal credit,' she added with a smile.

'Bullshit,' Jeremy protested, 'you gave it your heart and soul.' He could see several other people out to attract her attention. 'Don't let us hold you up, Kate, go and mingle. It's your night.'

'All right, I'll circulate for a while. I think I'm meant to. There'll be a few speeches soon. Not long ones, I promise,' she hastily added, 'we've all agreed there's been enough haranguing at rallies to last us a lifetime. I'll see you a bit later on.'

Jeremy watched as she melted into the gathering. God how he missed her. He took his girlfriend's hand. 'Come on, Izz, let's grab a drink,' he said and they headed for the white-clothed trestle tables that served as a bar, where glasses of beer and champagne were being doled out.

Charles Perkins introduced the short round of speeches. After graduating from Sydney University in 1965, the first Aboriginal student to do so, Charlie had become manager of the Foundation for Aboriginal Affairs, an organisation that had played a key role in advocating the referendum's 'yes' vote. His opening speech was brief and succinct, but as always impressive.

One of the principal actions that had led to this referendum and its successful outcome, he informed the assembled gathering, was the Freedom Ride of 1965, which had raised public awareness about racism. Student Action For Aborigines no longer existed as an organisation, he said, but student activists continued to play an immensely important role in the campaign for Aboriginal rights. He then introduced one of the leaders of the student movement, Kate Durham.

Kate joined Charlie up on the small makeshift stage and, looking out at the hundred or so gathered, she thanked all those who had worked on the campaign, individually naming a number with whom she'd been closely associated.

'As a friend of mine remarked just a short while ago,' she said in conclusion, 'a yes vote exceeding ninety per cent makes this referendum one of the greatest victories Australia is ever likely to see in a campaign for change.' There was a resounding cheer and as she caught Jeremy's eye he nodded and gave her the thumbs up. 'I'd like to congratulate everyone involved,' she said, 'most particularly Charlie Perkins, without whose dedication none of this would have happened.' She shook Charlie's hand, they'd become good friends over the past year or so, and a round of applause followed as she left the stage.

Charlie then introduced the special guest speaker who'd just flown up from Melbourne. Frank Madigan had joined the cause less than a year ago, he said, but during that time he'd become one of their most valuable speakers and co-ordinators who, for the past two months, had been tirelessly campaigning across the country.

'Over to you, Frank,' he announced and he left the stage.

Frank Madigan was a good-looking young man in his mid to late twenties. Lanky, casually dressed, with unruly dark hair and a lazy smile, he appeared something of a larrikin at first glance, but he wasn't. As he loped up onto the stage, his manner was not cocky, but rather laidback and assured. Frank was not a man who felt the need to prove himself, a fact that became evident the moment he spoke.

'You're quite right, Kate,' he said, looking down at her where she stood beside Charlie and smiling his easy smile, 'this is certainly the greatest victory a campaign could hope for.' His eyes, grey-blue and fiercely intelligent, scanned the gathering. 'And I too would like to congratulate all those involved.'

In addressing the crowd, he didn't appear to raise his voice, nor did he attempt to project his personality: the simple power of his presence seemed enough. 'But the outcome of this referendum is far more than a victory for our campaign,' he said, 'it's a victory for Australia. It's more than a "yes" for change, more than an agreement to make a couple of amendments to the constitution, it's proof of the enlightened attitudes of the general population. This referendum has been far more important than most Australians realise. In travelling the country as I recently have, I can tell you here and now we have a long, long way to go, but I can also tell you here and now that this is a momentous step for Australia. People are actually talking out there. They're communicating. And they're communicating about a problem that many have been blind to, that some hadn't even known existed ...'

Frank Madigan spoke for barely ten minutes, but Kate found him riveting. She was not alone. His audience was captivated. He could have gone on for a further half hour if he'd wished. He chose not to.

'Thanks for your attention, everyone, and thanks for a tremendous effort.'

He gave a wave and stepped down from the stage to a huge round of applause and pats on the back from eager admirers.

Kate was surprised she'd not met him before through the campaign. She knew all of the principal organisers in Sydney and many others who'd travelled from interstate over the past year. His was certainly a commanding presence, he's probably a lawyer, she thought, a lawyer with political aspirations ...

'Hello, Kate, I'm Frank.'

He was suddenly there by her side, his hand outstretched, not waiting for Charlie's introduction, although Charlie offered one anyway.

'Kate Durham, Frank Madigan,' Charlie said.

'Hello, Frank.' They shook. 'I thought your speech was great.'

'Thanks. I'm hanging out for a beer, do you want one?'

'I'll go a champagne.'

'Goodo. What about you, Charlie?'

But Charlie was already being claimed by others. Now that the speeches were over, people nearby were vying for his attention as people always did and Charlie, as always, good-naturedly obliged.

'No thanks, mate. I'll mingle.'

Kate accompanied Frank to the trestle tables where two volunteer barkeepers were frantically refilling glasses and doling out fresh ones. He handed her a champagne, grabbed a beer for himself and they edged their way out of the melee to sit at one of the tables that had been set up around the periphery of the courtyard.

'Good turnout,' he said lowering his lanky frame into the chair and gazing about at the crowd. Few had availed themselves of the tables and chairs, most milling in groups and avidly chatting. 'You know all these people, I suppose?'

'Not all,' she replied, 'but I've seen most of them around at rallies and meetings.'

'They're strangers to me,' he said, 'apart from Charlie and a few others. I've been working solely out of Melbourne.'

Well that explains why I hadn't met him, Kate thought.

'We've built up a strong movement there too, I'm proud to say.'

'Charlie said you've been campaigning all across the country.'

'Yeah, the timing was spot on. I'd just given up my job so I was able to travel around and co-ordinate regional action groups.'

'What actually was your job?' she asked with characteristic directness. He probably found her impertinent, but she couldn't resist.

He didn't find her in the least impertinent. 'I'm a plumber.'

So much for a lawyer with political aspirations, she thought.

'What are you studying at uni, Kate?'

'Vet science.'

'Really?' He appeared quite astounded. 'Strange. I automatically presumed you'd be doing law or something that'd lead to a political career.'

In the face of her own presumption she couldn't help but laugh. 'Makes us an unlikely pair of activists doesn't it, a vet and a plumber?'

'Yes I suppose so.' He was intrigued. 'Why vet science?'

'I've never wanted to do anything else for as long as I can remember.' She shrugged, end of story, it was that simple.

But his focus was now solely upon her, the crowd seeming to vanish as his eyes urged her to go on. So Kate did. She was not to know that Frank Madigan had a rare talent for drawing information out of anyone who interested him.

'I come from the country,' she explained, 'a property in Queensland. My brothers and I grew up with horses and livestock. I remember helping birth calves and foals when I was ten. I loved anything to do with animals. And as for being a vet,' she rolled her eyes in mock adulation, 'well, where I come from, the vet's more important than the doctor, the lawyer and the judge all rolled into one.' She smiled self-deprecatingly – she seemed to be talking a lot. 'So perhaps all I really wanted was to be somebody very important.'

'Did your brothers want to be vets too?'

'Oh good heavens no. My younger brother's obsessed with all things mechanical and has been from the age of six, and my older brother's being groomed to take over the management of the property. Eventually, anyway,' she added, her face clouding a little. 'At the moment he's in Vietnam.'

'Oh.' He'd noted her concern and didn't enquire further, but she volunteered the information anyway.

'Neil was conscripted,' she said. 'His tour of duty's nearly over though; he'll be home next month.'

'That's good news.'

'Yes it is.' She sat back and sipped her champagne. 'Your turn.'

'For what?'

'To talk. What about your background, Frank?'

'Nothing to tell,' he said with a wry smile, 'I doubt you'd find plumbing of interest.'

'Try me.' Whether plumbing was of interest or not was immaterial to Kate. It's the man himself who's interesting, she thought.

His father was a plumber, he told her, or rather had been, semi-retired now after a recent stroke. 'Usual scenario,' he said, 'kid follows in old man's footsteps. I didn't have any other ambition at the time, apart from kicking a footie around, so why not?'

He was going to leave it at that. Frank was obviously a man who preferred to hear the stories of others rather than tell his own, but upon further badgering she learnt that he was actually a master plumber with a degree in education. For the past two years, he'd been teaching an apprenticeship course in plumbing and gas-fitting at Technical College in Melbourne, he said, but since his father's stroke it had been agreed he'd come home and take over the family business in Redfern.

'Don't tell me,' she said in triumphant recognition, 'Madigan's Plumbing Services, Chalmers Street, opposite Prince Alfred Park!'

'That's the one. How come you know us?'

'I walk in the park at least once a week. I'm always passing your shop – it's most impressive.'

Having intended no more than a routine compliment, Kate was surprised by the eagerness of his response.

'Oh it is, believe me. My father's done an amazing job. The shop's far more than a retail outlet. Dad has three vans that service the city and eastern suburbs and he employs two other plumbers full-time, together with two office staff. That's not half bad,' he said boastfully, 'for a bog-ignorant Irishman with no formal education.'

The change is amazing, she thought, noting how the reticence to talk of himself had disappeared the moment his father came up for discussion. She found his enthusiasm utterly engaging.

'How's your dad's health since the stroke?' she asked tentatively, hoping not to appear intrusive, but keen to further the conversation.

'He's made a good recovery. Not allowed to do the physical stuff these days, doctor's orders, but he looks after the shop and that keeps him happy enough.' Frank studied the glass of beer on the table before him; his father's stroke had radically changed his own life and the plans he'd had to pursue his teaching career. 'He'll be even happier with me around to run things though,' he said thoughtfully. 'A Christmas visit is somehow never enough.' He glanced at her, adding hastily as if to correct any possible misunderstanding, 'Not that he ever complains, but I know how much he's missed me these past three years.'

'Do you have any siblings, Frank?'

'Nope.' He picked up the glass, 'I'm all Dad has, all he's ever had. But then he was all I had throughout my childhood – mother, father, best mate, you name it.' He swigged back half his beer in one go, wondering why he'd spoken so openly to this girl he'd just met – he rarely did such a thing – but he refused to feel self-conscious. She was a nice girl, he liked her. 'My father worked his guts out to put me through school and give me the life he'd never had, it's only right I come home now.'

Kate longed to ask him what had happened to his mother, but she had a feeling this was as far as the interrogation was permitted to go. She was right.

'Why don't you introduce me to some of these people?' he suggested, looking about at the crowd as if it had suddenly and magically re-appeared.

'Of course.' She stood with her glass of champagne, 'bring your beer and we'll do the rounds.'

They circulated among the gathering, which had turned into quite a party as glasses were re-filled and finger food handed about on trays. Most of those present were eager to meet Frank, whose speech had impressed them, and he and Kate joined in the discussions and arguments that became steadily rowdier and more animated as the day wore on.

By late afternoon things were winding down. Those with families and Saturday-night commitments left, and the several volunteer workers, of whom Kate was one, embarked on the cleaning-up process. But as dusk crept in a hard-core mob remained, volunteers and members of the student brigade for the most part, still in passionate debate. With them, not competing for attention as most were, but observing with avid interest and offering the occasional astute comment, was Frank Madigan.

Finally, at Venner's suggestion, they adjourned to Bates Milk Bar. 'I'm bloody starving,' he loudly declared to the bunch of fifteen or so, 'and it's getting bloody freezing.'

Venner was stating the obvious, they all agreed. The finger food having long since been demolished they were hungry, and with the sun gone the night ahead promised to be a bitterly cold one.

'Not by Melbourne standards,' Frank commented to Kate as they followed the troops out of the courtyard and across the main road.

Bates Milk Bar on the corner of Campbell Parade and Hall Street was famous. Established in 1951 by hard-working Greek brothers George and Nick Bagiatis, who'd anglicised their name, it operated seven days a week, often late into the night, and was renowned for the best milk-shakes and the biggest 'mixed grills' in town.

With Venner leading the way, the rowdy group arrived to find they had the place fairly much to themselves. Being the first week in June, there were no beachgoers vying for the wooden booths with their pink Laminex-topped tables and, as it was barely six o'clock, there were not yet many evening diners, just a few diehard regulars who lived in the area.

Jeremy bagged a booth for himself and Isobel at the far end where he had a good view of the main doors. He hoped to catch Kate's eye as she entered and wave her over, although he was aware that for Isobel's sake he must keep any invitation to join them as casual and impromptu as possible. His plan was thwarted, however. Leading the troops, as he always did, had proved his downfall. Larry and Sylvia, ever eager to be in the charismatic presence of Venner, slithered in beside him and were quickly joined by others who claimed every available booth nearby.

Damn, Jeremy thought as he watched the place fill up and saw Kate and Frank, the last to arrive, claim the only remaining empty booth down near the main doors. Damn, he should have dawdled and brought up the rear.

Mary and Chris Bates, the Greek brothers' wives, who were just as hard working as their husbands, scuttled about taking orders and doling out the milk bar's ever popular 'choc-malts' in metal milkshake containers.

'Are you up for the mixed grill?' Kate asked. 'I have to warn you, it's absolutely enormous.'

'Then I'm absolutely up for it, I'm ravenous.'

'Me too.'

They ordered the mixed grill.

Frank checked his watch. 'I'll have to eat and run though,' he said apologetically; he was catching a taxi direct to the airport for his night flight back to Melbourne. 'Wouldn't it be better if you joined your friends?'

'They're in for the long haul, they'll still be here when you leave,' she said. 'Believe me, I'll have plenty of people to talk to.' She smiled. 'I'm glad for a bit of a breather actually. I'm sure you've noticed that as a mob we can be quite exhausting.'

'Stimulating too: I've enjoyed the afternoon's conversations. You're a lively bunch all right.'

'When do you settle back in Sydney, Frank?'

'About a month I'd say. I've been pretty well established in Melbourne for the past three years and with everything put on hold for the last couple of months' campaigning there's a lot to tie up. I'll take my time with the move, but there's no rush – the old man has a good manager who can hold the fort.'

'I'll bet your dad's counting the days,' she said.

'Yeah, I'd put money on that all right.'

As he smiled his easy smile, Kate felt a vague sense of relief that her affair with Jeremy was over. Frank had shown no particular sign of interest, he'd made no suggestion they meet upon his return, but it pleased her now to be unattached. She was not seeking a relationship, on the contrary she was revelling in her current single state, but she would like to get to know this man. Just as a friend.

From where he sat at the rear of the milk bar, Jeremy could see Kate's reflection in one of the mirrors that lined the walls. The mirrors, with scenes of the beach and of bathers etched into the glass, were a feature at Bates of which the brothers were justifiably proud. He was unable to see Frank, who was masked by the booth in which the two were sitting, but Kate, facing towards him, was clearly visible and he couldn't help but note the avid attention she was paying to her companion.

She's not interested in the bloke, surely, he thought with a stab of jealousy. She can't be! Doesn't she know about Frank Madigan? Isn't she aware of the man's background?

Jeremy knew he was being unreasonable, that he had no hold over Kate and that their affair was over, but he couldn't help wanting her back, and he couldn't help hating the thought of someone else having her. Frank Madigan in particular was quite out of the question. I'll tell her about him, he decided. Yes easily solved, that'll put the kybosh on things ...

'Four mixed grills.'

His attention was diverted as huge plates of food were plonked one by one onto the Laminex-topped table. The kitchen was churning out mixed grills at an alarming rate.

'My God,' Frank said, gazing down at his own chop, steak, bacon, sausage and lambs fry topped with a fried egg, 'you were right.'

'I did warn you.'

He ate every skerrick and Kate, who'd always possessed a healthy appetite, very nearly matched him.

'I don't suppose you want my sausage,' she asked, finally forced to admit defeat, but he shook his head.

'Sorry, you're on your own there.'

A half an hour later, Frank bade her goodbye and having paid his bill was about to steal quietly away, but Kate decided his departure should not go unnoticed.

'Frank's leaving everyone,' she announced crossing to the booths where the others were sitting, 'he has to fly back to Melbourne tonight.'

Venner immediately rose to his feet, those with him also standing to make way as he edged out of the crowded booth. He strode forwards and shook Frank's hand. 'Good on you for coming, Frank,' he said, 'it was a bloody great speech,' and as he initiated a round of applause the others readily joined in.

'Yeah, well done ...'

'Good to meet you, Frank ...'

'All the best mate ...'

The several regular elderly diners, who'd anticipated a peaceful early meal, traded dark looks. By now they'd had quite enough of this youthful gang that had invaded their territory.

Frank gave a wave to everyone and sloped out into the evening. So much for a quiet exit.

Jeremy returned to his seat, watching as Kate joined two other students in a booth that was half empty. So Frank's going back to Melbourne, he thought, relieved. Good, that was that, problem averted.

Chapter eleven

'We're married.'

Seated at the little round dining table in the little house in Campbell Street, Kate froze, coffee mug mid-air, and stared disbelievingly at her brother. 'You're what?' she said, knowing she sounded stupid, but too dumbfounded to react otherwise.

'It was a very respectable ceremony,' he assured her, 'at the Catholic Church in Gia Long Boulevard right in the heart of town, a most reputable –'

'But you're not a Catholic.' Again she knew her comment was inane.

Neil laughed – an involuntary reaction: he didn't intend to trivialise the moment – but he'd never seen his sister at such a loss for words. It's to be expected, he supposed. She'd listened with infinite patience and understanding as he'd told her all about Nguyen Thi Yen and their love affair.

'Yes,' she'd said apparently unsurprised by the news, 'I gathered from the hints in your letters that there was a girl involved.'

The bombshell of his marriage was a different matter altogether.

'How can you be married in a Catholic church if you're not a Catholic?' Kate asked, feeling utterly foolish. There were a dozen or more questions of far greater importance she could have offered up, but in her state of stupefaction it was the first thing that came out.

'The priest who married us was Vietnamese,' Neil explained, 'he's a friend of Yen's family. He asked me if I was a Catholic, I said yes and he believed me, or rather he pretended to. The fact that I donated a sizeable sum to the church probably expedited matters. Although to give the man credit, I don't think the transaction was purely mercenary. I think he agreed to marry us so that Yen would have a marriage certificate, allowing me to bring her back to Australia and a better life. With three daughters and no son to help support the family her father's pretty poor.'

'But ... but ...' Kate was astounded by her brother's calm, matter-of-fact delivery and found herself stammering as she sought answers to the myriad questions that assailed her. The ramifications of Neil's action were huge, the obstacles surely insurmountable. 'But what about the war, Neil? You won't be able to bring her home, they won't let you.'

'I don't intend to bring her home, not yet anyway. Not until the war's over.'

'So you'll live apart until then?'

'No. I'm going back to Vietnam.'

'But you've served your tour. They won't let you go back.'

'They will if I'm in the regular army.' Another bombshell, she realised. 'I'm joining up.'

She stared wordlessly at him. You're volunteering to fight in this hideous war, a voice in her brain screamed, you're risking your life to return to a battle zone, and all because of a girl?!

'I don't like war any more than you do, Kate,' he said reasonably. God how he adored his sister. Her face was a page with every thought readable, but of course it always had been to him. It's what I love most about you, Kate, he thought, your lack of duplicity, your utter inability to hide your true feelings; you are the most honest person I know.

'Please don't blame Yen,' he said.

Feeling caught out, Kate wondered whether she should defend herself – the girl was his wife after all – but if he returned to Vietnam and was killed she knew she would never forgive this person called Yen. She said nothing, but again her face spoke multitudes.

'I would have joined the army with or without Yen,' Neil continued, 'it's where I belong, or rather where I feel I belong.'

The statement made no sense at all to her, and with nothing to contribute she waited for him to go on.

'I like being in the army,' he said. 'I liked it right from the start, even at training camp. It was a way to be free of Dad's expectations. I liked being one of the boys.' Her face was clearly saying 'so what?'. 'But things have gone much further than that, Kate,' he went on to explain. 'The fact is I'm a good soldier. I've seen men fall apart in battle, I've seen them wrecked in its aftermath, and understandably so, but somehow I've survived the experience. I know I can do it again, and I will if it's required of me. That will be my job.'

She remained staring at him, still confused, still unable to fathom his reasoning, and Neil knew he must dig far deeper into his own psyche in order for her to understand. Her honesty deserved honesty in return.

'I've been living a lie for years,' he admitted. He'd never spoken like this before, never even dared think like this before. 'I can be a good soldier, Kate, I know that much. The one thing I know I cannot be is my father. I can never live up to what Dad wants of me. It seems from birth I've been groomed to be someone I'm not. I can't repeat the cycle. I can't be Stan the Man. I can't be Big Jim.'

Of course you can't, the voice in her head said, nor should you ever want to be. Big Jim is a myth. It's your father who's been unwittingly living the lie. She wanted to say the words out loud, but she knew she didn't dare.

'I'm joining the army because that's who I am now, Kate, that's the person I've become. And I'm going to Vietnam to be with Yen because I love her more than I love life itself. She means everything to me, as I do to her. My decision is really that simple.'

'I see.' She'd finally found her voice although she had no idea what to say. 'And what does the army think of your marriage?' Again a banality, she didn't give a damn what the army thought.

'Oh Good God, the army doesn't know,' he said as if the mere notion was preposterous. 'We were married in secret; the military would never have allowed it. I told a couple of close mates who acted as witnesses, but they're sworn to secrecy. And no one else must know, Kate, until I'm able to bring Yen home. I'm only telling you now as a safeguard.' He took an envelope from the breast pocket of his jacket. 'You remember I wrote that I had a favour to ask of you?'

She nodded. Words once again seeming to fail her, she felt utterly helpless.

He placed the envelope on the table. 'This is a copy of the marriage certificate,' he said. 'Yen has the original. If anything happens to me, you must send money to support her. The bank details are all there in the envelope. And when the war is over you must bring her home to Elianne.'

Kate stared down at the envelope, thinking how horribly finalised everything sounded, wishing there was some way she could dissuade him from this path, yet knowing she couldn't.

'Will you do that for me, Kate? Will you promise?'

'Yes.' She looked up and met her brother's eyes. 'Yes, I promise.'

Neil stayed that night. They bought take-away food and sat up talking until well after midnight. He spoke openly about the war, the way he never did in his letters. 'What would be the point,' he said bluntly. 'What can you say? You're there, you're living it, you just have to get through each day. Besides,' he added, 'you're not allowed to write about burnt-out men.'

He told her of Bobbo and the others he'd seen fall by the wayside. 'It's not the physical wounds, Kate,' he said, 'it's the mental scarring. They're changed for life, fragile or angry, but fractured somehow, different. And there are so many, particularly among the nashos.' Aware of her concern, he gave a reassuring smile. 'Don't worry,' he said, 'I don't intend to be one of them.'

He caught the train north the following morning.

'Good that I'll be home in time for Alan's birthday,' he said as they parted at the front door; he'd refused to allow her to drive him to Central Station. 'I will not be responsible for you missing a lecture,' he'd said, slinging his kit bag over his shoulder, 'besides, there's nothing I like better than a good brisk march.'

He grinned now at the thought of his young brother. 'With the crushing in full swing it won't be a massive eighteenth, in fact Dad will probably put us both straight to work, but I reckon a new car will more than make up for that.'

They hugged each other.

'Give Al my love,' she said, 'I feel guilty not being there myself, but he told me over the phone he didn't mind in the least.'

'Well he wouldn't; you know Alan. He's only going home himself for the car.'

They laughed, but Kate secretly thought oh no he's not. Alan had taken a whole week off from his work and studies in order to return to Elianne for his eighteenth birthday, but neither the birthday nor the promised car were the real attraction, Kate was sure, rather they were the excuse. It was Paola who beckoned.

'I won't tell Dad about my decision to join up until the birthday's out of the way and Alan's gone back to Brisbane,' Neil assured her. 'I wouldn't want to spoil things: it's bound to cause a stir.'

A stir, Kate thought, that was surely the understatement of all time. Her father would be apoplectic with rage. She was only thankful that she wouldn't be there to witness his fury. And what on earth would Stan the Man say she wondered if he knew that his favoured son, the heir to his throne, had married a Vietnamese girl?

'See you at Christmas,' Neil called as he closed the gate of the little white picket fence. He'd told her he would not be returning to Vietnam for some time and that he'd be home for the family Christmas.

'Yep, see you at Christmas,' she called back with a wave, thinking how unbelievably normal they sounded when the world all about them had just been turned upside down. 'But you will ring me and let me know how it all goes, won't you?'

'Course I will.'

'Good luck.'

It was only as she closed the door that she realised she'd said nothing of the diaries as she'd originally intended. How could she? Her brother's life had taken a whole new direction. The burden of the truth remained hers, for the moment anyway, hers and hers alone.

Alan's car turned out to be a brand-new HR Holden Premier sedan. With green body, white roof and tan bucket seats, it was hot off the assembly line.

'Happy birthday, son,' Stan said handing over the keys with his customary flourish. Despite the friction that existed from time to time between father and younger son, Stanley Durham had a great love of family ritual and this was indeed a proud moment to be relished by all.

'Thanks, Dad.' Alan didn't disappoint, running his

fingers lovingly over the gleaming chrome signature 186-fender badge. 'She's a beauty all right.'

After the traditional family lunch, Stan returned to his work at the mill, where the crushing continued its relentless twenty-four-hour cycle, but Alan and Neil, having been allowed the rest of the day off, followed up the birthday proceedings with a tradition of their own.

The Holden was driven into town, Alan revving the engine up to top speed along the Bundaberg–Gin Gin road. All about them the cane fields were flowering, ready for harvest; a beautiful sight, particularly from afar, the sea of green blanketed in a haze of soft, silvery-lilac. But the brothers didn't notice. They were intent upon more important things.

Once in town, the Holden was paraded up and down Bundy's main streets, Alan at the wheel, Neil waving out the open window at everyone they passed, most of whom he knew and most of whom were familiar with the Durham family ritual. Young Alan must have turned eighteen, a number remarked.

'Hey, Neil,' Alan said as they rounded the block to drive up Bourbong Street for the fourth and final time, the window now wound up against the wintry nip in the late afternoon breeze, 'will you do me a big favour?'

'Whatever you want, mate, it's your birthday.'

'Will you stay in town and lie low for a bit? Only an hour I promise.'

'What the hell for?'

'I want to take Paola for a drive. I'll pick her up secretly and people will think it's still you and me lairing around.'

'A drive ...?' There was no innuendo to Neil's query, more an element of disquiet.

'Yes, a drive,' Alan replied firmly. Registering his brother's genuine concern, he was not offended. 'Just a drive. I'm meeting her down near the pumping station after five when her office shift's over. We usually go for a walk along the river track, but I want to show off the new car.'

'Sure, birthday boy,' Neil agreed. 'Drop me at the Commercial, I'll down a few beers.'

Outside the Commercial Hotel, as Neil gave his brother a wave and watched the car drive away, he was relieved that his query hadn't offended. Worrying though the outcome may prove, it was after all none of his business if his brother was having an affair with young Paola Fiorelli.

As it was a weekday and still during working hours, the pub was not yet busy. One girl tended the bar, a small group of hippies was gathered at a table and the publican was upstairs in his office. Neil bought a schooner and settled himself on a bar stool well away from the hippies. There were five of them, obvious out-of-towners, three long-haired young men and two women, the men wearing headbands and the girls flowing headscarves each with a badge pinned prominently on the front bearing the Campaign for Nuclear Disarmament symbol.

No points for guessing who owns the Kombi, Neil thought wryly as he looked through the window at the van parked outside. It was crudely scrawled with slogans, *Ban the Bomb*, *Viva Che*, *Make Love Not War*, and clumsy drawings of a smiley face, a two-finger peace sign and the CND symbol. Bit of an overstatement in his opinion.

City hippies posing as activists were not Neil's style; he found them pretentious, and he was glad when the group left ten minutes later. But a further ten minutes and they were back, re-instating themselves at their table. Ah well, live and let live.

He ordered another schooner, his nostrils assailed by the smell of marijuana – they'd been out to share a quick joint, he realised, their clothes stank of it.

'Thanks,' he said, paying the young barmaid and as he took a sip he heard loud and clear behind him, 'Love a country boy in cowboy boots,' from one of the girls. She was stoned and blatantly flirting, goading her boyfriend, the one she was draped over in the orange Che Guevara T-shirt.

Che Guevara Orange, the taller and more muscular of the men, didn't find his girlfriend's remark at all funny, but the others considered it hilarious and fell about laughing.

Neil tried to ignore them by reading the labels on the spirits bottles that sat on the shelves behind the bar, but annoyance flared in him. Bugger the lot of them, he thought. Out of work by choice I'll bet, smoking dope and getting pissed, probably on dole money and all shagging each other under the bullshit Free Love banner.

When he'd finished his schooner, he checked his watch and was contemplating whether or not to order another. Still fifteen minutes or so to go, he thought, why not? And he stood and signalled the barmaid for one more beer.

At that moment, the door opened and two of the regulars walked in, older men both of whom knew Neil and his family. They greeted him warmly.

'Well I'll be blowed,' Bill Farraday said. 'G'day Neil, good to see you back from Vietnam and in one piece, all's the better.'

'Yeah,' his mate Maurie agreed, 'good to have you home safe, son.'

The word 'Vietnam' had caught the ear of Che Guevara Orange and he nudged his mates. There followed a brief muttering among all five and they turned to stare at Neil.

'Thanks Bill, thanks Maurie,' Neil said as the men shook his hand and patted him heartily on the shoulder. 'Good to see you too.'

'Can we buy you a beer?'

'Nah,' he picked up the beer the barmaid had placed before him, 'I've got to go soon, so this'll be my last.'

'Give our best to your old man.'

'Sure will.'

As Bill and Maurie wandered over to the cigarette machine, Neil decided to down the beer and get out of the place. The hippies were glaring at him now, openly hostile, nudging each other and muttering a little louder.

'Go on …' He heard the insistent urging from the girl who'd made the cowboy boots comment '… go on, say something.' They were out to stir and Neil didn't want a bar of it. He crossed to the door and opened it, about to step outside. He'd walk in the direction of the bridge and meet Alan on the way, he decided.

But Che, in response to his girlfriend's urging, had sauntered over beer glass in hand and was suddenly right behind him, hissing in his ear.

'Where are you off to, baby killer?'

Then another hippy, the skinnier and more weasel-like of the three men, joined his mate. 'Trying to get away from us are you, man?'

Neil's fuse suddenly ignited. Why would I need to get away from you, you little runt? Whoa, Neil, he told himself, keep your cool, there's nothing but trouble for you here.

The girls were right behind their men, egging them on.

'Kiddie killer,' Cowboy Boots said.

'Yeah, yeah, kiddie killer,' her less imaginative mate echoed.

Neil let go of the handle and the door swung shut. Why should I be the one forced to get out of the place, his mind reasoned. It's you bunch of smartarses who should piss off.

He glared at Cowboy Boots. 'Why don't you go and get fucked, you moll.'

Pretending offence Cowboy Boots appealed to her man. 'Geoff …?' She saw herself as a rebel with a cause and made a habit of confronting returned soldiers. This one had taken the bait, hook, line and sinker. 'Geoff, are you going to let him get away with that?'

Neil glared at Che, now obviously Geoff. 'Of course he's going to let me get away with it, aren't you, Geoffrey?' he sneered. 'Because Geoffrey hasn't got the guts to do anything else, have you, Geoffrey.'

'Don't bet on it, soldier boy!' Incensed by the slur upon his masculinity, Che smashed his beer glass on a table and waved it about threateningly. 'Think killing innocent civilians is fun, do you, psycho,' he jeered. 'Do you, eh? Do you?'

'Yeah, gives you a kick killing civilians, does it man,' Weasel taunted, egged on by the boldness of his leader.

Something snapped in Neil. 'You bet it does,' he said dangerously, 'and from where I'm standing, you look like civilians.' It happened in an instant. He grasped the wrist that held the broken beer glass and punched Che hard in the temple, knocking him unconscious. Then he grabbed a fistful of Weasel's hair and slammed his face into the brick wall.

'Hey, there's no call for violence, man.' The third hippy quailed at the sight. 'We're only trying to make a point here ...' But he didn't get any further. Neil's fist slammed into his jaw and he reeled backwards, crashing into a table and chairs and falling to the floor stunned.

The two hippy girls were by now screaming. Cowboy Boots dropped to her knees to tend Che's unconscious form while her friend wailed like a banshee.

Bev the young barmaid was frantically dialling the police when Bernie Hall, the middle-aged publican, came galloping down from upstairs to discover the cause of the commotion.

Neil remained motionless, appalled by what he'd done.

'What the hell's going on here?' Bernie demanded, taking it all in. Young Durham over there by the door, he'd heard he'd just got back from Vietnam, the hippies on the floor bleeding like stuck pigs, what the hell had gone on?

He looked to Bill and Maurie seated at the far end of the bar and received meaningful glances from both that indicated the hippies and clearly said it's not the kid's fault, it's the out-of-towners.

'I've rung the police,' Bev told her boss as she hung up the receiver, 'they're on their way.'

'Good girl,' Bernie said. Bev had done the right thing, obeying instructions – 'Any trouble, you ring the cops,' he'd told her – but she was a new girl to Bundy and couldn't be expected to understand that this situation was a little different. She didn't know who Neil was. She didn't know the Durham family. In this instance Bernie would have preferred to have been informed before the cops were called.

He crossed to where young Durham stood. The lad seemed a little stunned by what had happened. 'I suggest you go home,' he said, very quietly so the others couldn't hear. 'Go home, for your own good, son.'

'I'm sorry.' Neil snapped out of his semi-dazed state. 'I'm really sorry, Bernie ...'

'Go home, son,' Bernie repeated firmly, but gently. 'Go on home.'

Neil nodded and as he stepped out into the street Bernie glanced at the hippy, who'd regained consciousness and who, with his girlfriend's help, was struggling to his feet and into the nearest chair. Then he crossed to Bill and Maurie to get a quiet report on what had actually happened.

Outside, Neil started walking in the direction of the bridge, keeping a lookout for the Holden that would be driving towards him on the other side of the street. He was overcome with guilt: how could he have allowed that to happen? He'd seriously risked his re-enlistment should word get out. And of even greater importance he'd risked damaging the reputation of his regiment. He'd been lectured on social protocols by senior officers so many times. He'd disgraced himself and felt thoroughly ashamed.

After collecting Paola at Elianne, Alan had headed for Queens Park as usual, Paola squirming down low in the seat as she always did during the drive through the estate, although it was more difficult to conceal herself in the Holden than it had been in the Land Rover.

When they'd parked and walked to their favourite spot high on the riverbanks, she'd taken a small gift-wrapped box from the pocket of her cardigan.

'Happy birthday, Alan,' she said handing it to him.

He unwrapped it and opened the box to reveal a shiny silver medallion with a magnet on the back.

'It's for your dashboard,' she explained, 'that's Saint Christopher. He's the patron saint of travellers.'

Alan knew exactly what it was. A number of his friends had similar such medallions, some even had miniature magnetised statues in their cars, Saint Christopher having become a form of talisman and dashboard accessory among young drivers. Paola, however, was unaware of this fact.

'I don't mean it to be anything religious,' she hastily added. 'I know you're not a Catholic and that Saint Christopher has no special meaning for you, but he'll look after you on your travels ...' Visited by a sudden doubt, she petered off lamely, fearing he might have interpreted the gesture as some clumsy attempt to convert him. 'You know, during those long drives to Brisbane and back ...' Her voice tailed away altogether and she looked down at the medallion wishing now that she hadn't bought it.

'Of course he'll look after me,' Alan assured her, 'this is the perfect present, Paola, I love it.' He gathered her in his arms and she responded to his kiss. 'And I love you,' he said as they parted. 'I love you more than ever. You do know that, don't you?'

'Yes, I do.' She believed him, she could read the depth of his love in his eyes, but it didn't stop the insecurity that gnawed away at her.

Alan sensed a difference in Paola since he'd told her about his sexual encounter in Brisbane. He'd blurted out the truth two days previously, the moment they'd met down at the pumping station upon his return to Elianne. He'd been longing to purge himself of his guilt.

'I had sex two months ago,' he'd said as they strolled along the track beside the river.

Her response had been unexpectedly enigmatic. She hadn't stopped walking. She hadn't even looked at him.

'An affair,' she'd queried, 'or a one-night stand?'

The term and its worldliness had sounded odd coming from Paola, and he'd found the remoteness of her tone worrying.

'A one-night stand of course,' he said. 'Well a one-afternoon stand actually,' he corrected himself and taking her hand he brought her to a halt, forcing her to look at him. 'I'm sorry, Paola, truly sorry. It meant nothing, I can promise you, and it will never happen again I swear. I love you. I will always love you and no one but you.'

She'd not resisted his kiss, but her reaction to it had been altogether different. She'd been withdrawn, guarded even. She's angry, he thought, angry and hurt, which given the circumstances he found quite justifiable.

'Please don't be angry,' he said, 'and please forgive me, Paola, I promise it will never –'

'I'm not angry,' she'd interrupted coolly, looking out across the river, 'and I forgive you.'

Once again he turned her to him, forcing her to meet his eyes. 'We said that we'd never have secrets from each other, remember? Was it wrong of me to tell you?'

'No, Alan, no it wasn't wrong. I respect your honesty.' She'd smiled and added with a worldly shrug that once again seemed a little out of character, 'Besides it's only natural, isn't it? Men are supposed to experience sex before marriage.'

Alan had been left confused. He couldn't have lived with the secret of his infidelity, which he considered a betrayal on his part, but he sensed that his admission had subtly changed things. He wasn't sure how and he didn't really know why. To him the situation seemed quite simple, but obviously to Paola it was not.

Paola was not in the least confused. Paola lived in fear. The unreasonable wave of doubt that had just now overcome her as she'd given him the Saint Christopher medallion was symptomatic of a deep-seated insecurity.

She could not rid herself of the sickening sensation upon hearing those three simple words *I had sex* ... Endless connotations had tumbled through her mind at the time, all her worst fears appearing to have come to fruition. Of course you've had sex, she'd thought, and of course you will again, you're a healthy young man with a healthy young man's appetite. What will happen when you fall in love with one of these girls you sleep with ...? Such thoughts had continued to torment her for the past two days.

Now, as they held each other close, Alan was again aware of the difference in Paola. She was not as uninhibited as she had been. When they kissed, he no longer had to call a halt to their passion. Was this a deliberate act on her part? Was she perhaps punishing him for his indiscretion?

'It will never happen again, Paola, I swear,' he said. 'I'll sleep with no one until the day we marry.' He made the declaration with all solemnity. 'You do believe me, don't you?'

She didn't. 'I believe you mean what you say.'

'You don't trust me, is that it?'

'That's not what I said.'

'Perhaps you don't know me as well as you think you do.'

His smile was intended to reassure her, and she smiled in return.

'I know that I love you. That's enough.'

'You'll be eighteen in five months,' he said, 'and we'll deliver the ultimatum at Christmas just as we planned: we'll get engaged with or without their permission. You know what that means,' he continued eagerly, 'it means there'll be no more sneaking around like this. It means we'll go to the pictures and we'll go dancing at the Palais and at the Surf Club at Bargara – we'll be a courting couple.'

His enthusiasm was so disarming that she laughed in spite of herself. 'We will,' she said with a positivity she didn't possess, 'we most certainly will.' She was helpless. There was nothing she could do but wait and see what happened. The mere thought of losing him terrified her.

They left the park and Alan drove back to the pub to collect Neil, but to his surprise, he discovered him walking along the street.

The brothers gave each other a wave of acknowledgement and when Alan had circled and pulled the car into the kerbside he suggested Paola hop in the back.

'When we get home to Elianne, stay down low,' he instructed, 'and Neil and I'll make a show of lairing around.'

Paola obligingly hopped in the back. 'Hello, Neil,' she said, but Neil simply gave her a nod as he climbed into the front passenger seat.

The car took off and Alan glanced at his brother, sensing something was wrong. 'What's up?' he asked.

Neil sat quietly nursing his bruised knuckles. 'Nothing,' he said dismissively, 'bit of a blue, that's all,' and Alan knew better than to enquire any further.

Back at the pub, the cops had arrived, fifty-year-old Sergeant Buchanan and young Constable Riley.

'Been a blue, I take it,' Clive Buchanan said, glancing at the weasel hippie with the busted nose.

Bernie Hall nodded. 'Yep,' he knew the sergeant well, 'the bloke who did it shot through though, don't know who he was.'

'He was a baby killer, that's who he was,' Cowboy Boots burst out aggressively.

Clive turned to her with an icy stare. 'A baby killer,' he said, 'by that I take it you mean a returned soldier?' How he detested bolshie little pseudo-activist bitches like this. He could tell at a glance she was no more than white trash.

'That's right.' Cowboy Boots was undeterred by the copper's obvious displeasure. 'And they knew him what's more,' she said pointing an accusing finger at Bill and Maurie. 'They knew him all right, those old bastards. "Good to see you home from Vietnam," that's what they said.' She included Bernie in her accusation. 'They all knew him, all three of those bastards, they're lying if they say they don't –'

'Well, well, are they now? Constable, would you be so kind as to take down these young people's details, while I get to the bottom of this.'

Leaving young Sam Riley in charge of the hippies, Clive joined the three men at the bar.

'This bloke wouldn't have been from Elianne by any chance?' he asked quietly.

'No way, Sergeant, no way,' Bill Farraday said, 'he was a blow-in from the south. Murwillumbah, I think, from memory.'

'Yeah,' Maurie nodded, 'definitely a Southerner from over the border, Mittagong, I thought he said, or was it Merimbula?'

'Merimbula?' Clive Buchanan raised an incredulous eyebrow. Mittagong he could accept, just, but Merimbula? Merimbula was practically in Victoria. 'Don't try too hard, Maurie.'

The four laughed at the joke, Clive the loudest of the lot, and then he turned back to the hippies.

'When you've finished taking down those details, Constable,' he instructed, 'you might like to point our young friends in the direction of the hospital.' He looked at the bolshie troublemaking bitch as if he actually cared. 'Your boyfriends really should be seen by a doctor, specially that one with the busted nose.'

'Aren't you going to find the bastard and charge him?'

'Well, that'd mean you'd all have to come down to the station and make statements,' he said pointedly, 'and that'd mean I'd have to search your Kombi van,' he took another brief pause, 'because I don't like the smell in here.' He looked Che in the eye, 'if you get my drift.' He'd probably find more than dope in the van, he thought. Stolen goods wouldn't surprise him. These weren't your harmless, layabout hippies. This lot was scum, out to cause trouble.

'No worries, Sergeant,' Che quickly responded, 'it was all just a bit of a misunderstanding.' He grabbed Cowboy Boots by the arm. 'We'll get going if it's all right with you.'

'Nothing would suit me better,' Clive Buchanan winked, 'and it'd be a real smart move on your part.'

The following day, just as Neil had predicted, he and Alan were put to work by their father. Alan's one-week holiday and Neil's recent return from Vietnam were no excuse for idleness during the crushing season, when all hands were needed.

The weather forecast was ideal for the burning that was planned that evening, the most important factor being the wind, which was expected to be consistent, and in the late afternoon Neil and Alan joined Luigi Fiorelli and the several field workers who were preparing the portion of block 31 that was to be ignited. The plantation was divided into large numbered blocks separated by six-metre-wide grassy 'headlands' or carriage ways. The thousand tonnes to be burned that evening, an area of approximately ten hectares, constituted roughly half of block 31 and preparation called for the forcing of a path through the cane to form a separate block and create a firebreak.

Luigi, as field boss, selected the particular path they would follow through the rows of cane, which were distanced one and a half metres apart. Then he led the way in a tractor fitted with a break row pusher that separated the cane, flattening it back against the adjacent rows on either side, Neil, Alan and the others following behind raking away the 'trash', or dry dead leaf of the stalk, which was highly flammable. Burning was a complex process carried out by those with experience and the Durham brothers had been trained in the practice from the age of fifteen, but it was Luigi, one of the plantation's most senior and experienced workers, who would lead the team that night.

Stanley Durham himself would be watching from the lookout tower at the mill, which had been designed specifically to monitor burnings. Stan the Man loved the spectacle and all that it represented. My grandfather stood right here in this very spot, he would think. Big Jim had surveyed his realm in just the way he was now doing as he'd looked out at the mighty fires of yesteryear. Even more than the spectacle, Stanley Durham loved the sense of history that burnings evoked.

The burning of cane prior to harvesting had been introduced in the thirties as a preventative measure against Weil's disease and was now standard procedure. In the days when cane had been cut green the horrendous effects of Weil's disease, which was spread by the urine of rats that at times reached plague proportions, had presented an often-fatal threat to cane cutters.

In earlier times, vast expanses of cane had been burnt, but during recent years more contained burns had been introduced upon the discovery that a higher-quality sugar resulted if the cut cane was delivered to the mill as quickly as possible, preferably within twenty-four hours. Smaller burns allowed for easier and therefore speedier pick-up and delivery.

Whether larger or smaller areas, however, the burning of sugar cane was, as it had been for the past thirty years, a spectacular affair. Word would get around among locals, and kids would be piled into the back of utes and driven to watch the show.

Tonight proved no exception. By seven o'clock, as the ten-man team made its final preparations, twenty or more children of workers who lived on the estate were waiting expectantly, together with several carloads of families who'd driven from nearby South Kolan.

Paola and her brother, upon their father's instruction, had been elected to oversee the younger unaccompanied local children whose parents were working their shifts in the mill or the cookhouse or out in the field. Fully versed in the procedure after much past experience, Paola and fifteen-year-old Georgio kept their young charges well back in the safety zone and waited for the spectacle to unfold.

Clad in combination overalls and hats, the crew watched as Luigi lit a small trash fire on the headland to check the wind direction, which as predicted was a moderate and steady south-easterly. He'd outlined the plan to his men, and Neil and Alan, who would be doing the firing, stood at the ready with trickle burners fuelled by four parts diesel to one part petrol. The other members of the crew carried shovels in order to pitch dirt on outbreaks of fire caused by cinders from burning trash. They would protect the surrounding cane, particularly block 30 to the north, and in doing so control the course of the blaze.

Working their way south against the direction of the prevailing wind towards the cane-break prepared earlier in the day, the team's all-important opening strategy was to create a back burn of around twenty metres at the top of block 31. They would then circle the selected section, Neil firing from the eastern perimeter and Alan from the west, the back-up team carefully guarding against any flash fires, and the final firing would be made from the cane break to the south. By that time the intensity of the blaze would have created its own updraft, which, being greater than the prevailing wind, would result in a contained combustion.

The team was now in position awaiting Luigi's order to commence firing and Alan, closest to the Italian, caught his eye as Luigi checked everything was in readiness. Once again he couldn't help but register the man's animosity. Luigi Fiorelli, normally good-natured, had been surly all afternoon and his surliness had been plainly directed at Alan.

Alan knew why, or rather he could guess: it seemed only too obvious. Someone had seen Paola in the Holden. Someone must have seen us driving off together yesterday, he thought, and whoever it was told her father.

He'd waited throughout the afternoon for Luigi to take him aside and say something, but Luigi hadn't. Luigi had done nothing but glower.

Alan had wondered also whether Paola had been challenged by her father, but upon seeing her ten minutes previously gathering her young brood together to watch the burning she'd displayed no sign as she'd given him a cheerful wave. Ah well, he thought philosophically, I'll just have to wait for the big confrontation. Luigi won't be able to resist. He's hardly one to keep things to himself.

Luigi Fiorelli gave the command and the Durham brothers commenced firing, the burning was now under way.

When the twenty-metre back burn had been successfully completed and the fire was slowly and steadily burning against the wind, Neil and Alan commenced their way down the block's eastern and western perimeters. Two crew members remained at the northern headland to protect block 30, while the others split into teams following Alan and Neil. Luigi, working with a shovel alongside his men, remained with the team on the western side, which, given the wind's direction, was more likely to produce flash fires.

All was going according to plan. The blaze was magnificent, and the onlookers were already ooh-ing and ah-ing by the time Alan and his team reached the cane break where they were to make their way through to the eastern side.

By now the heat was intense, and upon entering the break men held up their shovels to guard their faces, Alan continuing to forge ahead firing while his back-up crew carefully monitored the potential for the wrong side of the break to ignite.

They were halfway through. The blaze was about to reach its spectacular finale when the fires from the back burn and the cane break would meet, but things took a sudden unexpected turn. The wind changed. As if by wilful and deliberate design, it suddenly veered to bear down from the north-east, forcing the flames towards Alan where he was in the unlit portion of the cane break. Behind him, the men were able to make their escape through the already burnt section, but overcome by the heat and the lack of oxygen, Alan found himself losing focus. The world started to spin hazily around him and before he knew it he was falling to the ground as if in slow motion.

He was barely conscious when he landed. The last thing he remembered was the strength of the man who picked him up bodily. He felt himself slung like a bag of chaff over a powerful pair of shoulders. Then everything went black.

By now the intensity of the fire and its gases had created an updraft of such strength that despite the wind change all went according to plan. The fires from the back burn and cane break met in one final magnificent crescendo. Here was the show that the onlookers had come for, a great wall of fire, envelopes of flame exploding twenty metres above the cane, a pyrotechnic display of spectacular proportions.

Then, like magic, the fire devoured itself. As if exhausted by its own power, it suddenly became nothing. The cacophony of explosions abruptly halted and darkness descended upon block 31. All that remained was a huge pall of smoke spiralling ever upwards.

The onlookers enthusiastically applauded another magnificent show, and up in his lookout tower Stan the Man gave a nod of satisfaction, unaware that he had nearly lost his younger son. But then, with the exception of one man, no one knew that Alan Durham had been on the verge of asphyxiation. His own team members, in making their escape, had assumed he was right behind them. Only Luigi Fiorelli had seen him fall.

Alan had quickly regained consciousness after being carried from the cane break. Now he stood in the semi-darkness, Luigi beside him, watching the fire's dying moments.

He turned to the Italian. 'Thank you,' he said, but he could see in the eyes that glinted back at him the direst of anger.

'You will respect my daughter,' Luigi said. He'd retained his silence all afternoon, having made a promise to his wife when Maria had once again fought Alan's case. 'He took her for a drive, Luigi,' Maria had said, 'nothing more, he is a good boy.' But Luigi could contain himself no longer. Alan was not a 'boy', Alan was a man and Luigi would trust no man with his daughter, even this man who had been like a second son to him. 'You will respect my daughter,' he repeated threateningly, 'or I will kill you.'

'I have always respected your daughter, Luigi,' Alan met the Italian's gaze unflinchingly, 'and I always will.'

Luigi believed him. The anger left his eyes. 'Good,' he said simply and he looked away at the cane field.

Alan wanted to declare his love for Paola there and then. He wanted at that very moment to beg Luigi's permission to marry his daughter. But he knew that he must honour the pact he'd made with Paola and so he said nothing. Instead he stood beside her father, this man who had just saved his life, and together they stared silently out at the smouldering cane.

In deference to Luigi, Alan did not invite Paola for another drive in the Holden. Not through fear of the Italian, for he knew Luigi believed he would not take advantage of his daughter, but it would be disrespectful, he decided, to flaunt their relationship until they were ready to declare themselves.

For the remaining four days of Alan's stay at Elianne the young couple's trysts were kept to a walk along the river track from the pumping station to the weir at the end of their daily work shifts. Then Alan returned to Brisbane.

Neil's announcement over breakfast three days after his brother's departure resulted in the volatile reaction he had expected, although at first his father had refused to believe him.

'Don't be bloody stupid, boy,' Stanley Durham had growled. 'Join the army? How absurd, your career's right here, you belong to Elianne.'

'Not any more, Dad, I belong to the army, or rather I intend to. I'm driving down to Brisbane today to join up at Enoggera Barracks. I'll be back tomorrow to work through the rest of my service leave, though,' he quickly added – he felt guilty deserting them during the busy crushing season. Mind you, he was hardly indispensable. They'd been managing perfectly well without him for the past two years.

During the stunned silence that followed, Hilda managed to stammer, 'But if you join the army, they'll send you back to Vietnam, Neil.'

'Yes they will, Mum. There's a war on.'

The seriousness of the situation had finally registered with Stan and his son's glib response annoyed him even further. Jumping to his feet, he roared and ranted about the breakfast room, smashing his fist on the table and the sideboard, rattling cutlery and crockery, mouthing oaths and casting threats at his son while Hilda tried to stop things from breaking and Neil watched in silence. There were only the three of them present. Bartholomew was unwell and had taken to his bed. Ivy was delivering his breakfast to his quarters.

'Damn you, boy! If you leave now, you don't come back, you hear me? I'll disown you! I'll bloody well disown you for the ingrate you are! Christ Almighty, you have the world handed to you on a plate and you turn your nose up at it? You deny your own family? You're no son of mine, you hear me! You're no son of mine! I'll disown you!'

Neil sat quietly throughout the entire performance, seeing nothing but bluster and knowing that deep down his father was suffering hurt more than anger. He wondered how he could have allowed himself to be so intimidated for so long by this man who loved him so fiercely.

His son's continued silence was driving Stan to distraction. 'Haven't you got a bloody word to say for yourself?' he roared. 'Cat got your tongue, boy? Speak, for Christ's sake!'

'I'm sorry to let you down.'

A pause. 'That's it? That's all!'

Neil nodded.

'Right. Right. Well that's that then. Go and sign up, but don't come back here when you have.' Stan returned to his seat and abruptly sat. He stared down at his congealed eggs and gave a peremptory wave of his hand. 'That's that. You're disinherited as of now.'

Neil stood. 'I'll be home for Christmas, Dad,' he said, 'I'll see you then.'

Hilda rose and fluttered about ineffectually trying to restore peace. 'Of course you will dear, of course you will.'

Stan ignored them both as he attacked his eggs, but his hands were shaking.

'Bloody hell!' Alan rarely swore, but he was too agog with amazement to do anything else. Neil had telephoned to say he was in Brisbane and wanted to meet up. He had some news, he'd said.

They'd decided upon a steak and a beer at Brekky Creek that Saturday. The pub as usual was crowded, but it was a blustery winter's day and most drinkers were inside so they had the beer garden pretty much to themselves.

Alan shook his head in disbelief. 'Bloody hell,' he said again, 'you've actually gone and done it, have you?'

'Yep, joined up two days ago, it's what I really want to do.'

'Wow.' Alan looked at his brother with newfound respect. Much as he loved Neil, he'd never once seen him stand up to their father. Indeed it was a sight he'd never expected that he *would* see. 'Good for you, mate,' he said. 'What was Dad's reaction?'

'The full histrionics, as you can imagine. I've been disowned, disinherited and am never again to darken the doors of Elianne.'

'Crikey, what'll you do?'

'I'll go home for Christmas,' Neil said with a grin, and they both laughed.

But even as they laughed, Alan wondered how his father would cope when the time came. Disowned elder son returns to the fold and younger son announces his engagement to a Catholic, he thought. It's going to be a rocky old Christmas all right.

When Neil rang Kate, as he'd promised he would in order to keep her abreast of the news, her reaction was much the same. What a heck of a Christmas it promises to be, she thought. She'd decided to bring the ledgers back to Elianne this year, together with her completed translation. She would at long last share them with Alan, as she had originally intended. Then if and when he deemed the time right they would present them to their father. The decision to reveal the secrets of the past would no longer be hers alone.

Having made her plan, Kate felt a strange sense of freedom. She hadn't realised what a continual distraction the diaries had become. Busy as she'd been with her studies and her causes, they were somehow always there in the dim recesses of her mind. Was it nearly three years since she'd first discovered them? Had it really been that long, she now thought as she strode through Prince Alfred Park on her regular Saturday morning work-out, wishing as she always did that Cobber and Ben were trotting along beside her.

She stepped into Chalmers Street and continued briskly towards Cleveland, where the bridge would take her over the railway tracks and back in the direction of Glebe. I can put Ellie and the past aside for a while, she thought thankfully, until Christmas anyway.

On the opposite side of the road up ahead she saw the sign that said *Madigan's Plumbing Services* and slowed a little, wondering vaguely whether Frank was back from Melbourne. She looked across at the shopfront and even contemplated popping inside to enquire, but decided against it.

'G'day, Kate.'

As she'd set off at speed once again she'd all but collided with him. He was on his way to work.

'Oh hello, Frank,' she said, 'I was just wondering if you were back.'

'Been back for over a fortnight now,' he said, 'I bought a little terrace in Surry Hills. Want to come into the shop and have a coffee? I'll show you around.'

'I'd love to so long as I'm not in the way.'

'No, no, I'm not booked out on a job until ten. Just paperwork in the meantime and I'll grab any excuse to avoid that.'

'Good. Consider me your excuse.'

They crossed the road and entered the shop.

'G'day, Dad.' Frank greeted the man sitting behind the counter hunched over a book of crossword puzzles. 'This is Kate Durham. My dad, Pete,' he said to Kate.

'Hello, Mr Madigan.'

The man rose and circled the counter to offer his hand. He's every bit the older version of Frank, Kate thought, a little less lanky in frame and sandy-haired rather than dark, but with the same grey-blue eyes, even the same lazy smile, although it was a little lop-sided, she noted, probably the result of his stroke.

'Pete, please,' he insisted as they shook, 'no one ever calls me Mister.' The brogue was distinctly Irish, despite the fact that Pete Madigan had been in the country for thirty-five years.

'Hello, Pete,' she said with a smile.

Frank introduced her to the young girl, Alice, no more than sixteen, who was working on the window display.

'Would you rustle us up a couple of coffees, thanks Alice?' he said.

'Sure, Frank.'

'I'll leave you to the hard yakka, Dad,' he said, and Pete returned to his book of crossword puzzles. 'The man's addicted,' Frank added loudly for his father's benefit, 'they're not even cryptic – designed for simpletons,' but Pete chose to ignore the jibe.

As Frank gave her a brief guided tour, Kate was surprised to find the place far bigger than she'd expected.

'I won't show you upstairs,' he said, 'that's Dad's private domain and he's a messy old bugger.' Pete lived in the rooms above the shop and had done for years. There were two offices downstairs, one where a motherly, middle-aged woman called Rose was typing away furiously.

'Rose runs the whole business,' Frank said upon introduction. 'We'd be lost without her.'

'Bullshit,' Rose replied good-naturedly, which rather surprised Kate.

He showed her his own office, and then they retired to the tea room, where Alice was making the coffee.

'There's a store room out the back and a small workshop,' he said, 'but I don't reckon they'd be of much interest to you. We've got our own car park though, with rear access via the back lane, where Dad houses the vans. Having off-street inner-city parking's a huge bonus.'

'The place is so much bigger than it appears,' she said as they sat and he poured the coffee from the jug Alice placed on the table before them.

'Yeah, like I told you, the old man's done really well for himself.'

They sat talking for nearly three quarters of an hour, the conversation not flagging for one moment.

He asked after her brother, who he presumed had by now returned from Vietnam, and was astonished to hear that Neil had signed up to join the regular army.

'How remarkable,' he said.

'Yes,' she admitted, 'I was absolutely gobsmacked to be quite honest and I still am, but he has his own reasons, so ...' She shrugged.

Frank tastefully made no further enquiries, but their discussion turned to the reception Vietnam veterans were receiving upon return from active service.

'Whatever your feelings are about the war,' he said, 'it's a shocking thing not to show respect for these men and what they've been through. Do you know, there are reports that some soldiers have had their uniforms spat on as they walk down the street?'

Kate agreed with a passion. 'Exactly,' she said. 'Neil told me that he'd heard stories of returned nashos being reviled even in RSL clubs. Good God, the Returned Servicemen's League!' she exclaimed, outraged at the thought. 'If they can't support the nashos, who can? What have these men been doing if not serving their country? It's absolutely disgusting ...'

On and on they went, and it was only when they'd drunk the entire jug of coffee and eaten half the plate of shortbread biscuits Alice had set out that Kate looked at her watch to discover it was a quarter to ten.

'Good grief,' she said, jumping to her feet, 'you have to be out on a job at ten.'

'You're quite right, I do.' He stood. 'What a pity. I could have gone on chatting all day.'

She smiled. 'Ah well, another time.'

'Indeed.'

But strangely enough, he didn't nominate another time.

'Goodbye, Pete, goodbye, Alice, thanks for the coffee,' she said as they walked through the shop.

'See you, Kate,' Pete called.

'No trouble,' Alice said and, after bidding a farewell to Frank, Kate stepped outside and continued on her way down Chalmers Street.

She was intrigued and more than a little mystified. There was no vanity at all in Kate Durham, but she was accustomed to repelling men's advances not wondering why they had offered none. She and Frank were like-minded people with a passion for justice and an enjoyment of conversation and the sharing of views. They had a great deal in common and she sensed that he found her attractive. Why had he made no specific offer to meet again? Why had he left the possibility simply to chance?

She could create the chance herself if need be. But she would find out. The man was clearly not shy. There had to be a reason.

Chapter twelve

Neil's return to Elianne the day before Christmas Eve did not result in the high drama that might have been expected. Stanley Durham had given a great deal of thought to the subject of his elder son and he'd come to the conclusion that Neil had developed a lust for battle. The boy had joined the army because he wanted to return to war, Stan had decided. Stan had known men like that. Hell he'd been one himself. But the war won't last forever, he thought. When it's over, Neil will leave the army and come home to take up his rightful position at Elianne.

Stan had it all neatly worked out. The only worrying element was his son's survival. That part he tried to put from his mind.

'Welcome home, son.'

'G'day, Dad.' Neil dumped his kit bag on the front verandah and returned his father's hearty hug, surprised by the warmth of his welcome. He'd not feared being thrown out upon arrival at the family home, aware as he was that Stan's previous tirade had been principally bluster, but he had certainly expected to be met with a frostier reception than this.

He cast a querying look at Kate. She'd been home for a week now and had driven into town to collect him at the station, Cobber and Ben in the back seat – the dogs had adopted the Holden. She answered his query with a shrug and a smile that said your guess is as good as mine and went inside leaving father and son to themselves.

'We parted under a bit of a cloud a few months back,' Stan said. 'That was wrong of me.'

Another surprise, Neil thought. This was surely the closest thing to an apology he'd ever heard from his father. Stan the Man never apologised.

'The truth is I'm proud of you, son, and I know exactly how you feel.'

'You do?' Impossible, Neil's brain said.

'I most certainly do. I felt exactly the same way after Tobruk, when they repatriated me from Palestine because of that bout of typhoid. I felt I'd deserted my mates. God I can't tell you how I longed to be fighting by their side at El Alamein! There's an unbreakable bond between men who've been in battle together, Neil, I understand that, believe me.' Stan clapped an enthusiastic hand on his son's shoulder; the boy really was a chip off the old block when all was said and done. 'I fully understand your need to be back there with your mates.'

'Goodo, Dad.' Neil left it at that. Things were easier that way.

Alan arrived home late the following afternoon. The family was now reunited for the ritual of Christmas Day, which in Hilda's case always started with the special nine o'clock Christmas morning service at Christ Church Anglican Church in Bundaberg.

When the children had been little, the morning church service had been a mandatory part of the Christmas tradition, following the dictates of Grandmother Ellie herself. The Durhams had always been seen out in strength at Christ Church on Christmas morning, indeed it was the one day of the year they attended church, apart from family weddings, funerals and christenings.

In the years following Big Jim's death, Stan had continued his grandparents' tradition for appearances' sake, but when the children got older he'd lost interest. In truth the church service had bored him witless, as he'd suspected it had Big Jim, so he'd left the responsibility in his father's hands. It had become Bartholomew's job to drive the family to church on Christmas morning.

Bartholomew had willingly embraced the task until the death of his beloved wife Mary and the ensuing stroke that had rendered him incapable. Things had rather fallen apart after that. To Hilda the church service had remained of vast importance, more as a matter of form than faith, but Stan couldn't be bothered taking up the reins once again so Max had been appointed to drive his employer's wife into town along with any other family member who might be interested.

Young Kate had always accompanied her mother, mainly because she knew Hilda wished her to, and when Bartholomew had become well enough he'd joined them. Unlike the rest of the family Bartholomew's faith, admittedly in God rather than the church itself, remained resolute. During the Christmas service, he would disassociate himself from the pomp and ceremony and within the confines of God's house feel particularly close to Mary, whose spirit was with him always and with whom he believed he would be reunited after death.

Neil and Alan had been quick to follow their father's example and made a point of opting out of the Christmas church service altogether.

'I think you should come with us this morning,' Kate said meaningfully to her brothers over the breakfast table. For the past several years, since she'd had her license, it had been Kate who had driven her mother and grandfather to church.

'Why?' Neil demanded.

'I don't know.' She shrugged. 'Because we're a family and because we're going our separate ways, and because …' she tailed off. Kate really wasn't at all sure why. Perhaps it was superstition rearing its head again.

'Because I'm going back to Vietnam, you mean.'

'Maybe.'

'Bit hypocritical, don't you think?' Neil glanced at Alan for back-up.

'Yep.' Alan was in complete agreement. 'I don't reckon God's going to sit up and take much notice after we've ignored him all this time.'

'Fine, forget it, just a suggestion that's all.'

Kate and Hilda attended church on their own that morning. The journey to town and back, the very action of getting in and out of the car, would have been too much for Bartholomew in his weakened state. He joined them for the ritual Christmas lunch, but even that was a surprise for his appearances were rare these days. He remained for the most part in his quarters, waited upon by Ivy.

'Glad you could make it, Grandpa,' Kate said. God he looked frail. She pushed the hot mustard in his direction. 'Christmas dinner wouldn't be the same without you.'

Something in his smile told Kate that he was there especially for her.

The numbers had dwindled even more this year. The Krantzes had not been invited, and it was a strictly family affair, with just five seated to table, but the champagne and beer flowed and Cook had gone to the extraordinary lengths she always did.

Roast turkey with vegetables, a baked leg of ham and even a Christmas pudding with brandy sauce to follow, the full catastrophe, Kate thought, on a thirty-five-degree afternoon with the ceiling fans whirring. It seemed somehow ridiculous, yet somehow wonderful. Time had stood still, and she rather wished it could remain that way.

'This is the ninth day now,' Alan said. 'They've given up on him, haven't they?'

'Yep,' Neil replied through a mouthful of turkey, 'called off the search. Presumed drowned, the reports say.'

'Terrible thing,' Hilda shook her head tragically, 'terrible, terrible thing. Poor Zara, one always feels for those left behind.'

The conversation, as was happening at family tables throughout the country and indeed across the world, had turned inevitably to the disappearance of the Australian Prime Minister. Harold Holt had vanished on 17 December while swimming at Cheviot Beach near Portsea in Victoria and now, over a week later, despite extensive sea and coastal search, his body had not been recovered.

'Bit of a mystery,' Alan said. 'He was a really strong swimmer and he knew that beach well – why would he drown? Conspiracy theories are cropping up already, at least they are at Tech. Some reckon he defected and that the Russians collected him in a submarine.'

'Bullshit,' Neil said dismissively, 'nothing mysterious at all. The weather conditions were shocking, the man was showing off and he drowned, simple as that.'

'How come there's no sign of a body then?' Alan demanded. 'Crikey, did you see the size of those searches on the telly? They were huge, an army of choppers scouring the coast.'

'So? He's either still out there wedged under a rock somewhere, or else a shark got him.'

'Oh, poor Zara,' Hilda said once again, and she took several frantic sips of champagne in order to calm herself. 'Oh dear oh dear, that poor, poor woman.'

Stan loudly harrumphed to make clear his feelings on the subject. He could not have cared less about Harold and Zara Holt, but he always liked to play a leading part in the Christmas table chat, so he turned to his daughter.

'I bet you're pleased to see the end of the bloke, aren't you,' he said provocatively.

Oh God, Kate thought, here we go. 'In what way, Dad?'

she asked as if she didn't know the direction her father was heading.

'Well given he was "All the Way with LBJ",' Stan said with a pseudo-jocular emphasis that invited battle, 'and given your commitment to the anti-war movement borders on the zealous,' he added a bit of a wink to the table in general, 'you'd hardly have had much time for Holt, would you? You'd find him something of a warmonger, surely.'

Kate refused to take up the specific bait her father offered, not just in deference to Neil's military service, but because in this instance there was a far easier way to best Stan the Man.

'Holt's LBJ quote and war policy haven't gone down too well with many, I agree, Dad,' she calmly admitted, 'but the man's done a lot for this country in other areas. The *Migration Act 1966* introduced immigration reform that's all but dismantled the White Australia Policy. I consider that a splendid achievement on the Holt Liberal Government's part.'

Stan was momentarily caught out. He hadn't expected the debate to take this direction and in the brief pause that followed Neil and Alan exchanged a quiet smile that said here they go again.

'And the decision to increase access to non-European migrants will include refugees fleeing the Vietnam War,' Kate continued. 'I hardly call that the action of a warmonger. Rather one of a humanitarian, wouldn't you say?'

Stan glared at his daughter. He was fiercely proud of Kate and would boast of her achievements to all and sundry, but when she turned her intellect upon him, and particularly in this superior manner, it infuriated him. Smartarse little bitch, he thought.

Kate knew exactly how infuriating she was being and was thoroughly enjoying herself. 'Under the new law, applications for non-European migration will be accepted from those considered of value to the country,' she said, 'and

I believe a certain number of "temporary resident" non-Europeans will be eligible to apply for permanent residency and citizenship after just five years. That's exactly the same rule that applies to Europeans,' she concluded. Then she sat back and waited for the inevitable reaction.

'We don't need any more bloody Asians in this country,' Stan snarled, 'and we sure as hell don't need them to become citizens. They're not Australians, for Christ's sake, they never will be! Look at the trouble we had in the old days – there was no keeping the bastards out! They overran the bloody place and they'll do it again.' Stan the Man was becoming more worked up by the second. 'You should have heard Big Jim on the subject and he was damn well right. It was because of the bloody Chinese that they brought in the White Australia Policy in the first place. And what happened to us then, eh? You tell me that, girl. What happened to us then? We lost our Kanaka labour, that's what happened.'

'All right, Dad, all right.' Kate had made her point and was quite prepared to call a truce. 'I'm just saying times have changed, that's all.'

But Stan didn't want a truce; Stan wanted a fight to the finish. 'And what about the Japs, eh, we're supposed to welcome them in with open arms now too, are we? The yellow bloody peril! Over my dead body, girl, I'm telling you, over my dead body!' His explosion was final, and he glared at his daughter, defying her to offer a retaliatory response. She did not.

'Hey, Grandpa, do you want some more ham?' Alan slid the platter across to his grandfather, who as usual appeared to have disappeared into some other place altogether.

'May I have another drop of champagne, Stanley dear?' Hilda also came to the rescue and, although Stan glowered as he poured his wife's wine, any further discussion on the subject was dropped.

It was evident to all that Stan, despite his tirade, had come off second best, but Kate didn't feel particularly victorious and the smile she tendered her father, while not apologetic, was a peace offering. She had not intended to arouse his personal ire to such a degree. Stan the Man was a product of his time and a Second World War veteran. His views were understandable. Many of his era felt the same way.

Friction between father and daughter had been predictably volatile and conversation was quick to revert to the mundane as it usually did, but Kate didn't join in. She found herself reflecting instead on circumstances that now appeared to her rather surreal. She recalled how she'd arrived home at Elianne on 17 December, the very day the prime minister had disappeared. And how just the previous week in Sydney, only several days before that fateful Saturday, she'd discussed Harold Holt at great length with Frank Madigan, whom she'd not seen for months. Their conversation had been vigorous. They'd sat out in the back tea room of Frank's shop, just the two of them, talking about the Migration Act and the changes it had brought to bear upon the White Australia Policy. She remembered how fervently they'd agreed that the Act would usher in a new age for a nation built upon ignorance and fear, and how they'd been so congratulatory of Holt and his foresight. It seemed strangely unreal now to think that the leader of their country, the very man about whom she and Frank had spoken with such passion, had disappeared without a trace from the face of the Earth ...

'Would you like some more champagne, dear?'

She was jolted back to the present by Hilda's offer, which was really a discreet reminder that she should join in the social chat now things were back on an even keel before her state of distraction, which was obvious, proved an annoyance to her father.

'Yes please.' Even as she took her mother's hint Kate couldn't help but wonder briefly whether she'd been more distracted by her thoughts of Harold Holt or of Frank Madigan. 'That would be lovely, thank you, Marmee.'

The day progressed as Christmas Days always did at Elianne. The elder Durhams retired to their various areas of the house while the younger members, when sufficiently recovered from the feast, donned bathing costumes and sandshoes and raced each other to the main dam. Neil being the undisputed leader from the outset, the true race proved now to be between Kate and Alan, with Ben belting along the track beside them and Cobber arriving a good half hour later, footsore and weary, but determined not to be left behind.

'We'll call it a draw,' Alan graciously conceded as he and his sister flopped onto the jetty in a state of exhaustion.

'No,' Kate gasped, 'you won.' He had, but only just. 'I've turned into a girl. Isn't that sad?' she added with a mock-tragic air. 'After all those years as one of the boys.'

They played together like the ten-year-olds they felt themselves to be, revisited by the freedom of their childhood, then as late afternoon crept towards dusk Alan went off to meet Paola down by the pumping station. He donned the shorts and shirt he'd worn over his swimming togs, which were now dry, and made a casual announcement just before he left.

'I'm telling Mum and Dad tomorrow morning,' he said as he sat to haul on his sandshoes, Neil and Kate sprawled out beside him on the jetty.

'Telling Mum and Dad what?' Neil asked.

'Oh shit.' Kate sat bolt upright. Of course, how could she have forgotten?

Alan stood, buttoning his shirt. 'Then I'm going to the Fiorellis,' he said, 'and Paola and I are going to tell Luigi and Maria.'

'About what?' Neil asked.

'She'll fill you in.' Alan gave a jerk of his head towards Kate. 'See you back at the house,' he said and left.

'Tell Mum and Dad what?' Neil demanded.

'Alan and Paola want to get engaged.'

'Oh shit.'

'Exactly.'

The following day, Alan arranged a meeting with his parents in the smaller downstairs drawing room where his mother took her ritual morning tea.

Stan was in an excellent mood. He always loved Boxing Day, the test cricket on the telly and the cold turkey and ham lunches Cook dished up with her special potato salad.

'So what is it, boy?' he said with fond joviality when the maid, having served the tea, had departed. 'A special meeting, eh, must be something important.'

In typical fashion, Alan did not mince words. 'Paola and I are going to get engaged.'

Hilda very nearly dropped her teacup, but upon managing to rescue it, gracefully and without spilling a drop, she remained frozen awaiting her husband's outburst.

Stan did not rant and rave as she might have expected however. His face lost its good humour, certainly. In fact he studied his son as one would a creature beneath contempt.

'Got it all worked out, have you boy,' he said, and Hilda noted that 'boy' was no longer fond or jovial: 'boy' was an insult, delivered with something bordering on loathing.

It was true at that moment Stan loathed his younger son. Not for the boy's temerity in suggesting such a ludicrous match, but for the fact that he wasn't asking permission, he was making a statement. How dare the little prick show such lack of respect! How dare he front up and just spit the words out! But that was Alan, always had been.

'You've got everything planned, I take it,' Stan said mockingly.

'Yes, I have actually, Dad.' Alan knew his father was intensely irritated, and he knew the reason why, but he didn't see any purpose in pussyfooting about, trying to reason or rationalise. The man never recognised any point of view but his own.

'Paola and I are prepared to wait,' he said. 'We won't marry until we're twenty-one, but we intend to get engaged now.' Alan then turned for the first time to his mother and there was an air of apology in his tone and a plea in his eyes as he added, 'We would of course like it to be with your blessing.'

Stan didn't allow his wife the right of reply, considering it wasn't her place. 'I bet you bloody well would,' he sneered, but he kept his voice down: no point in blowing a gasket over a stupid adolescent fantasy. Christ alive, they'd all had romantic crushes in their time and on the most improbable girls who didn't remotely qualify as marriage material. You got them into bed if you could and then you moved on. Why couldn't the boy just grow up?

'Now listen, Alan,' he said, doing his best to sound patient. 'You must realise that your suggestion is hardly a logical one. You haven't thought things through, son. You're being unrealistic, you must know that.'

'Why?'

'Why? The girl's Italian, that's why.' He's a moron, Stan thought, the boy's a bloody moron. 'The Durhams are royalty in these parts; we don't marry beneath ourselves, never have and never will. She's an Italian, she's a Catholic and she's an Elianne employee,' he said. Surely he didn't need to spell things out any more clearly than that.

'Yes I know, and I'm going to marry her.'

'Right,' Stan had had quite enough. He'd had enough of the boy's idiocy and more than enough of his impertinence. 'Now you listen to me, you disrespectful little prick,' he stabbed a forefinger at Alan's forehead, 'and you get this through that moronic skull of yours. Bed the Dago if you haven't already, which you probably have – sleep with her as often as you like, I don't give a damn. But don't you dare get her pregnant, and don't for one minute think you're ever going to marry her because that won't happen, I can tell you here and now.'

Stan didn't bother slamming the door behind him, the matter wasn't worth getting riled up about, but he was annoyed nonetheless. What a bugger of a way to start Boxing Day.

'Well that went pretty much as expected,' Alan said to his mother. Then he bent and kissed her on the cheek. 'Just to let you know, Mum, I really am serious,' he said quietly, 'and I really am sorry if it causes problems for you down the track.'

'Wish me luck,' he called as he crossed to the door, 'I'm off to the Fiorellis now. Bye.'

And Hilda was left speechless, bone china teacup and saucer in hand, untouched orange sponge cake on the table before her. She hadn't said a word throughout the entire proceedings.

Luigi and Maria Fiorelli were far more prepared than the Durhams. Young Georgio was conspicuously absent, having been sent off to play footie with his cousins, which would have been his Boxing Day preference in any event, and the Fiorellis senior were waiting with Paola in the sitting room of their cottage in South Mill Row. The sitting room looked out over the verandah and the pretty little garden and was especially reserved for the receiving of guests. Family and friends always gathered in the huge kitchen out the back where a wall had been demolished and two rooms formed one giant space that was the heart and soul of the house.

'Paola she tell her mother you have something to ask of me,' Luigi said.

'Yes.' Alan found the Italian, whose moods were normally so transparent, difficult to read. Luigi was not his jovial self, which was to be expected, but nor did he seem angry. If anything he was solemn, a most unusual state for Luigi Fiorelli.

Alan glanced at Paola, who was sitting beside her mother, both of them on little hardback chairs that looked as uncomfortable as the one upon which he was seated – and Luigi's carver appeared much the same. The room was not designed for comfort. Paola gave him a smile and an encouraging nod.

'I wish permission to marry your daughter,' Alan said boldly. In the silence that followed he was painfully aware of the ticking of the clock that hung on the wall above Luigi's head. Didn't they realise how loud it was? And the mesmerising swing of its pendulum was unbearably distracting. In fact the whole room was distracting. More than distracting, it was intimidating. As he kept his focus trained upon Luigi, he couldn't help noticing the china cabinet to one side displaying pieces that were plainly never used, but just for show. Everything surrounding him seemed so out of keeping with the Fiorellis.

Alan had never before sat in the front room. In fact he couldn't remember ever having seen the front room. The approach to the Fiorelli house had always been via the back door and straight into the kitchen. There, on many a weekend throughout their childhood prior to boarding school days, he and his brother and sister had been welcomed into the fold. The entire extended Fiorelli family would be gathered in that kitchen during the slack season, a birthday, an anniversary, a baptism – any excuse, and sometimes for no specific reason at all. Luigi's three brothers would arrive with their wives and children. Alfonso, the oldest of the brothers, would play his harmonica and everyone would sing Italian songs and gorge themselves on the food served up by Maria and the cakes and the delicacies brought along by the wives.

Now, somewhere beyond the interminable ticking of the clock, Alan could hear the raucousness of those early days. He could smell the garlic and the herbs and he could taste the richness of the sauces and pastas and cheeses, flavours and textures exotic and unknown to most Australian boys of his age. He remembered how he'd wished that he lived in a cottage like the Fiorellis' instead of The Big House, and how he'd wished that Luigi was his father instead of Stan the Man ...

'You love her?'

Awaiting Luigi's reaction, Alan had felt his life in the balance. His father's approval had meant nothing because he knew he would never receive it, so informing his father of his intention had been a mere courtesy. But for all the bravado of his declaration to Paola that they would defy both their parents Alan desperately desired Luigi's blessing. As he'd waited for the man to speak, his childhood and his future had hovered side by side for what seemed an eternity. In actual fact it had been only seconds.

'Yes, I love your daughter. *Lo amo tua figlia*,' Alan repeated, his pronunciation perfect. Paola had been teaching him Italian for some time now.

Luigi nodded. He'd known the answer, he'd had no need to ask, but he'd wanted to hear the boy say the words, and was particularly pleased to hear them in Italian. Paola had spoken to her mother the previous evening and Maria had prepared him for this formal visit: it was the proper way. Luigi did not doubt that Alan Durham loved his daughter, and he knew Alan Durham to be an honourable young man, but he'd voiced his concerns to his wife. There were complications, he'd said, there were many, many complications ...

'Beware, Luigi,' Maria had warned. 'You must tread a very careful path. Paola loves him more than her life.'

'You are not of the Roman Catholic faith,' Luigi now said. This to Luigi Fiorelli was the greatest complication of all.

'I intend to convert.' For Alan, the matter of faith was simple. He'd been honest with Paola right from the start, when she'd considered his offer to be one of immense sacrifice.

'How can it be a sacrifice when I have no particular faith?' he'd argued. 'I don't mean to trivialise the church and all it stands for, Paola, please don't be insulted, but my conversion would be more for show than anything. Although I promise,' he'd added earnestly, 'that I'd make a good job of it to please your parents.'

Paola had not been insulted. She'd laughed. She would have been prepared to abandon the church, thereby risking eternal damnation and breaking her parents' hearts, all for Alan Durham.

Luigi was impressed beyond words. 'You would do such a thing for my daughter?'

The man's amazement at the enormity of his offer made Alan feel like a fraud, but his answer was nonetheless honest.

'I would do anything for your daughter, Luigi. I would do anything humanly possible.'

Maria had been following the exchange closely, her understanding of English was excellent, but she'd always lacked confidence in speaking the language. She now interrupted the conversation with a quick suggestion to Luigi in Italian, which brought an instant smile to her daughter's face.

Alan looked from one to the other.

Luigi stood. 'Maria she say let us talk in the kitchen.'

Paola took Alan's hand as they walked out the back to the kitchen where seats and stools and a communal wooden bench lined the walls ready to be pulled up to the huge table that dominated the room. Pots and pans hung from hooks in the ceiling beams alongside bundles of dried herbs and strings of garlic, and nestled in the corners of workbenches were baskets of vegetables. Alan had the strangest feeling that he'd come home.

Paola brewed coffee and Maria served slices of the treacly cake Alan so strongly remembered while he and Luigi sat at the table and talked. They talked of many things. Luigi enquired of Stanley Durham's reaction – he'd been told Alan had planned to tell his parents. Alan naturally did not repeat his father's words.

'Dad didn't take me seriously,' he said, 'in fact he dismissed the idea altogether.'

Luigi nodded; he'd have guessed that Stan the Man's reaction would be along such lines. 'You will defy your father?'

'I am prepared to do so, yes.'

'There will be much anger.'

'Yes, there will be.'

It was Alan who then brought up the subject of Luigi's position at Elianne. What if his father chose to become vindictive? But Luigi shrugged off any concern. Ego did not dictate his complacency, as Alan himself well knew. There was not a mill owner in the entire region who would not beg for the services of Luigi Fiorelli. And when Alan queried the position of his brothers, so reliant upon Elianne for the crushing of their cane, the answer to that also was simple. The brothers were highly successful growers. They needed the mill certainly, but the mill needed their cane.

'The mill, she is a monster, she need constant feeding,' Luigi said.

The more they talked the more Alan's hopes soared. Luigi was prepared for the consequences – come what may, he was clearly not going to contest the match.

And the more they talked the more Luigi thought of all it was that Alan was prepared to sacrifice. Stanley Durham was a hard man who might well disinherit his son, Alan would surely know that. Luigi did not worry for Paola's future should this happen, of course. Alan Durham was gifted. He did not need his father's wealth. This young man is prepared to forego his wealth and his religion, Luigi thought. My daughter has done well to win such a love.

'You have my blessing,' he said. The two stood and embraced. 'Welcome to my family.'

Hugs were shared all round and Alan presented Paola with the ring that he'd bought her. It seemed right to do so formally in the presence of her parents.

'It's beautiful,' she whispered as he slipped it on her finger. The gemstone was her favourite, as he had well known, a deep violet amethyst that was set simply in a ring of white gold. She had not wanted a diamond.

They agreed they would not flaunt their engagement, that for now she would keep the ring out of sight. She would thread it beside the crucifix that she wore at all times on a chain about her neck. She didn't mind in the least.

'It'll be closer to my heart there anyway,' she said with a laugh and she kissed him. Paola finally felt safe.

In the Durham household over the remaining week or so of Alan's holiday, no further mention was made of the suggested engagement. Stan had forbidden any discussion on the subject. While Alan openly courted Paola, taking her to the pictures and dancing at the Palais, Stan, steely-faced and determined, ignored the entire issue.

'He's either turning a ridiculously blind eye to the fact that I'm serious,' Alan said to Kate and Neil, 'or he's assuming we're sleeping together and that I'll get her out of my system.' Alan had confided in his brother and sister, but he'd said nothing to his mother of his acceptance by the Fiorellis for fear of the trouble it might cause her. 'God, he's a cantankerous bastard!'

The general exodus started in early January. Neil was the first to leave and over breakfast on the morning of his departure he made an announcement that took the others by surprise.

'I've been transferred to 4RAR at Lieutenant Colonel Greville's request,' he said, which wasn't exactly truthful. In trying to return to Vietnam as soon as possible he'd had to pull strings, in fact he'd had virtually to beg. Greville had finally accepted him into the battalion because he was a veteran of the Battle of Long Tan and his presence would prove invaluable among the new national servicemen.

'So what's that mean?' Alan asked.

'It means I leave for Vietnam in the middle of the year and I'd like to get the family farewells over and done with now while we're all here together,' he said. 'I won't come home before I'm posted, it's tidier this way.' They all looked at him in astonishment. 'It's no big deal,' he said, aware that he'd shocked them. 'I'll be seeing you in Brisbane, Alan, and Dad, you'd be busy as hell here anyway with the start of the crushing, and Mum, I'll ring regularly, I promise. And I'll ring you too, Kate, like I always do. It's better this way, don't you reckon?'

'If that's what you want, son.' Stan cleared his throat, a little caught out. 'Your decision of course. If that's what you want.'

'That's what I want.'

An hour or so later farewells were made on the front verandah, Hilda bravely refusing to cry or even reach for her handkerchief, but her feelings so evident she might as well have been sobbing, while Stan, gruffer than ever, fought with little success to disguise the depth of his emotion.

'Stay safe, son,' he said, clapping Neil heavy-handedly on the back as they embraced.

'Sure, Dad.' Neil then hugged his mother. 'I'll ring you next week, Mum, I promise. See you in Brisbane, Alan,' he said with a wave and then he was down the front steps and into the passenger seat of the Holden, where Kate was waiting behind the wheel, Cobber and Ben in the back.

'Christ I hate goodbyes,' he said as they drove off, his parents waving from the front verandah as they always did.

Kate kept herself in check when they arrived at the station.

'Don't get out,' he said as he lifted his kitbag from the boot.

She wanted to. She wanted to get out and say 'Where's my hug?' but she didn't. 'You will give me a ring from time to time, won't you,' she said instead.

'Course I will, regular as clockwork.' He put his hand through the open window and tousled her hair the way he used to when they were kids in order to annoy her. It didn't annoy her now. She loved it. 'Thanks for the lift, Sis.' Then he walked off into the station. She waited, ready to give a wave if he looked back, but he didn't.

Alan was the next to leave. He received a pleasant enough farewell from his father, a perfunctory hug and a slap on the shoulder.

'Look after yourself, son,' Stan said. Stan was prepared to forgive and forget. There'd been no further mention of that silly engagement business and while the boy was squiring the Fiorelli girl around town they were presumably sleeping together. Let him have his fun, Stan thought, so long as he's careful. Surprising Luigi hasn't put his foot down though.

Stan and Hilda remained on the front verandah ready to wave as the car drove off while Kate and the dogs accompanied Alan to the Holden, Cobber and Ben waiting expectantly, eager to be invited into the back.

'Sit,' Kate ordered, and they did, obedient but dejected, aware they were not to be included on this trip. 'Take all the time you want, Al,' she said quietly. 'Go through each of them slowly: there's a lot of material to absorb.'

The boot of Alan's car was stacked with the ledgers and a matching folder for each containing the pages of Kate's meticulously typed translation. She and Alan had transferred the lot from the boot of her Holden to his just the previous day. Although he would be unable to read the original ledgers, Kate had decided to include them by way of authentication.

'I found them under the house three years ago,' she'd explained, 'Grandmother Ellie's diaries, or rather her scribblings, as she called them. They're in French, the translations have taken me over two years, and I want you to read them. I need your opinion.'

He'd registered her seriousness. 'My opinion about what?' he'd asked.

'About whether or not we should show them to Dad,' she'd said. 'Or any other member of the family for that matter.'

'But surely we should.' Alan had been mystified. 'Hell, Grandmother Ellie's diaries! Mum'll be over the moon!'

'No she won't.' Kate had decided to give her brother no preconceptions of what to expect, apart from a warning. 'You're in for some shocks, Al.'

'Call me when you've finished them,' she now said as he climbed into the Holden. 'I'll come up to Brisbane during a term break and we'll discuss what to do.'

'Right you are.'

Kate joined her parents on the verandah and they all waved at the Holden as it pulled out of the main drive and set off along the dirt track towards the Bundaberg–Gin Gin Road, Alan's hand waving back at them through the open window.

It was in the last week of January that Kate left for Sydney. She could have stayed for at least another fortnight, but she wanted to do some preparation before the start of first term, she told her parents. This was to be the fifth and final year of her Vet Science course, although if everything went according to plan she intended to continue to a PhD.

In truth, Kate didn't need to prepare for first term, but she was ready to return to Sydney. Elianne seemed empty without her brothers. When Neil and Alan were there she could return to her childhood. All three of them could. But without her brothers things weren't quite the same.

So much has changed, she thought as she watched her grandfather asleep, remembering the capable man she'd known throughout her early years. Bartholomew had been the backbone of Elianne. Not loud and showy like his son, but quiet, hardworking and diligent, a man of great dignity.

Kate had popped in to her grandfather's quarters to say goodbye, but she was loath to wake him, he looked so peaceful sleeping in his armchair. Will he still be here on my next trip home? she wondered. Or is this possibly the last time I'll see him?

Bartholomew's fragility was such these days that the family had discussed whether or not they should send word to his daughter in Canada, but when they'd suggested the idea to Bartholomew himself, he'd been adamantly against it. He'd even written a note to his son, his spidery hand delivering an unequivocal command.

Julia lives on the other side of the world, he'd written. *She has a family of her own. Under no circumstances is she to be given cause to worry or feel duty-bound to rush to my bedside.*

Stan had found the note irritating. 'God almighty, Dad, if you cark it Julia'll come over for your funeral anyway,' he'd bluntly stated, but Bartholomew's response had been a shrug that said what will be will be, and the subject had been discussed no further.

Kate studied her grandfather now, so serene in his sleep. She wanted to kiss him, but she didn't. Instead, she walked quietly away, turning back at the door.

'Goodbye, Grandpa,' she whispered, just in case it might be for the last time.

To her surprise, his eyes opened. He smiled to see her standing there, and raising a frail hand to his lips he blew her a kiss. Then he closed his eyes once again and went back to sleep. Kate left feeling inexplicably happy.

'Hello, Kate. What an amazing coincidence.' Venner was propped against the partition of the alcove when she returned carrying the armload of books she'd ferreted from the library's shelves. 'Fancy bumping into you like this,' he said in wide-eyed innocence.

Kate couldn't help but smile. Sydney University's newly completed Fisher Library was a well-known assignation point. Students would leave their recognisable belongings in the one-person alcove they'd chosen for their study time in order that the intended person of interest would know where to find them. This had not been Kate's aim at all, but Venner had clearly sought out her voluminous trademark worn-leather shoulder bag and had been lying in wait for her return.

'What do you want, Venner?' She kept her voice down, respectful of the several other students who were studying in similar open cubicles nearby.

'I was wondering if you're going to tomorrow's SRC meeting,' he said.

'Of course I am. I always do. You know that.' She dumped the armload of books onto the desk.

'Just thought I'd check to be sure because we're going to be bringing up the subject of union amalgamation and I know how important that is to you.'

The Students' Representative Council consisted of male and female members, but the student unions were gender based. The women's union held little sway, all things pertaining to union issues being virtually run by the male students, a fact which the feminists naturally considered the height of inequality. There had for some time now been attempts to amalgamate the two unions, but as yet to no avail.

'Yes, I know we're going to be discussing the possibility of amalgamation,' Kate said, studying him suspiciously. Of course she would know such a thing, and of course he would know that she would know: she was one of the prime advocates. What was Venner after?

'I intend to offer you my full support, Kate.'

'Excellent, that's great.' She was pleased – quite a number of the male union members were coming on board lately. Good, she thought, it'll be only a matter of time. 'I'll see you at the meeting then,' she said and she sat, opening one of the library books.

'You're not going to study now, surely.'

'Why not?'

Venner checked his Omega wristwatch, as always so out of keeping with his tattered T-shirt, which Kate suddenly noticed bore the slogan *Equal Rights for Women*.

'Because it's one o'clock and it's lunchtime,' he said, 'and I think we should discuss a plan of action over fish and chips at the refectory.'

He's making a play, Kate thought. How typical of Venner and how silly of me not to have realised. The whole thing's a line. The SRC meeting, the union amalgamation, and above all the T-shirt. He doesn't give a damn about women's rights.

'I take it Isobel's no longer on the scene,' she said drily, recalling that she hadn't seen the two of them together for some time.

'That's right. She's a lovely person, Izz, really lovely, but not quite the right sort of girl for me, I'm afraid.' He'd dumped Izz way back in early October and there'd been another girl since then, but he'd dumped her also. No one matched up to Kate Durham. 'So is it lunch and a plan of attack?' He gave the charismatic smile that had once caused Kate's heart to skip a beat, as it still did many a female heart.

But Jeremy Venecourt's charisma no longer worked on Kate. You're such a phoney, Venner, she thought, not without a touch of affection for the old days, but with no interest at all in rekindling the passion. She was about to say a simple 'no thanks' and return to her studies when an idea crossed her mind. Venner had always made a point of knowing everything about everyone connected with every imaginable cause. He would surely know something about the mystery surrounding Frank Madigan.

Kate continued to find Frank baffling. Twice in the latter half of the previous year she'd created 'chance meetings', both of which she'd sensed Frank had found as pleasurable and stimulating as she had. Upon the first meeting he'd again invited her into his shop where Alice had served coffee and they'd talked. The second time, she'd boldly suggested they save Alice the trouble and go to a nearby coffee shop, which they'd done, again very much enjoying each other's company. But on neither occasion as they'd parted had he suggested another meeting. She'd decided to stop being pushy: it wasn't dignified. The man was not interested and was obviously just being polite. She should leave him alone.

But then there'd been the meeting that really had happened by chance, the week before she'd left on her Christmas holidays. He'd invited her back to the shop, clearly eager to talk, and that was when they'd had their passionate discussion about Harold Holt and the Migration Policy and she'd been left intrigued all over again. Why was Frank Madigan, who obviously found her interesting, keeping his distance in such a manner? Was he married? Was that it?

Kate had never been one to choose the devious path, but the thought now occurred that perhaps two could play at Venner's game.

'Lunch and a plan of attack it is then,' she said, and they left the study area together, each with a different agenda in mind.

Kate signed the library books out at the front counter, piling them into the large leather shoulder bag, which Venner gallantly insisted upon carrying.

'Are you sure?' she queried as they stepped outside into the courtyard, where on the opposite side of the car park huge Moreton Bay figs faced off the impressive jacaranda that stood beside the library. 'I have to warn you, you're bound to be noticed. That bag may not be a thing of beauty, but it's distinctly female.'

He tapped his chest. 'I'd say given the T-shirt it's rather apt,' he said.

They crossed the broad lawn that fronted the grand sandstone edifice where lion statues guarded entrances, and once inside the portals they cut through the main Quadrangle with its grassy central square, its towers and paved walkways and surrounding stone buildings. So much of Sydney University was so very beautiful.

Taking a short cut through the Vice Chancellor's Quad, they headed for the sprawl of buildings known simply as 'The Union', one of the major student venues that housed several eateries. They decided against the refectory, however. The refectory and the buttery, both popular dining places, were crowded, so they opted to eat outside in the courtyard instead, greeting and being greeted by others they knew, but refusing offers to join them. Venner quickly seized upon a table for two and they settled with their choices of fare, his being fish and chips and Kate's a pie with tomato sauce. At home she dined for the most part on salads and fruit to make up for all the rubbish she ate at Uni.

Venner dropped the pretence of a discussion about student union amalgamation. There was no particular 'plan of attack' they could follow anyway, as both well knew, and he presumed her agreement to join him for lunch was a definite display of interest on her part.

'So tell me, Kate,' he said casually enough, but with obvious intent, 'any particular person in your life?'

'Nope,' she replied, concentrating on her pie, 'not interested.'

'Right.' He noted the briskness of her tone and took it as a warning. Don't come on too strong too soon, Venner, he told himself. 'All work as usual, I see.' He gave her a friendly smile and tucked into his fish and chips.

They chomped away in comfortable silence for a minute or so before he made further conversation. 'This is your final year, isn't it?' he said. 'What are your plans when you leave? Join a veterinary practice?' He grinned cheekily. 'Open one of your own with a little help from sugar-cane-king daddy?' The remark was not a dig, but rather a reminder of their familiarity.

Kate was not in the least offended, but familiarity was not a path she wished to pursue. 'No, I'll go on to a PhD. I want to specialise in livestock. How about you, Venner? What are your plans when you finish your Masters this year?'

He shrugged. 'I don't know.' He really wasn't sure. He seemed to live in a constant state of marking time, waiting for something to happen. 'Do a post-graduate tutor course maybe. I wouldn't mind teaching, preferably here, I like Uni life.'

'Yes.' Kate smiled. The answer was so typically Venner. 'It suits you.'

He found her response most encouraging, and pushing aside the fish and chips that no longer held appeal, he leant towards her, elbows on the table, eyes gleaming with the old intensity. 'Tell me what's going on, Kate – what are you up to? I didn't see you at the anti-war rally in the Domain.' Venner himself was still a committed member of the Vietnam Action Campaign. 'Apart from the feminist student union movement, which particular cause claims you these days?'

Here was the opening she'd been waiting for, Kate thought and she followed his lead, pushing her plate with the half-eaten pie to one side. 'I'm still involved with Charlie Perkins's fight for Aboriginal Rights,' she said.

Oh that tired theme, Venner thought. Since the referendum there was really little mileage to be had from the Aboriginal question, but he maintained an appearance of avid interest.

'As a matter of fact, there's something I wanted to ask you,' she continued.

'Fire away.'

'Charlie is manager of the Foundation for Aboriginal Affairs, as you know ...'

'Absolutely,' Venner gave an enthusiastic nod, 'a great organisation. Without them I doubt the referendum would have had such an amazing result.'

'Well I went to a meeting they held in Redfern a week or so before Christmas and Frank Madigan was there.'

'Oh yes?' At the mention of Frank Madigan, Venner was on instant alert.

'Yes, he moved up from Melbourne about six months ago.'

'That's right. I'd heard that he'd shifted back to Sydney.' She's trying to sound casual, he thought. Why? 'Don't tell me you're interested in the bloke, Kate,' he said teasingly.

She found the comment and its innuendo annoying. 'I'm not interested in the way you're inferring, Venner, no, but I do like him as a friend ...'

What a load of bullshit, he thought, recalling the night in Bondi when she'd been hanging on Madigan's every word, but he didn't say anything, merely raising a facetious eyebrow.

'We have a great deal in common,' she added icily, the eyebrow irritating her further.

Venner gave an abrupt bark of laughter. 'I hardly think so.' She obviously doesn't know the truth, he thought triumphantly. 'Frank Madigan's not exactly your type, Kate, believe me.'

The comment this time was more than annoying, it was downright insulting. 'How the hell would you know what my type is?' Angry though she was, Kate hissed the words, keeping her voice down, aware of those seated nearby. 'Frank's a man with a genuine commitment, Venner, unlike some I could name,' she added scathingly. 'He believes in the fight for Aboriginal rights —'

'Of course he would. He's black.'

Brought to an instant halt, she stared at him in wordless amazement.

Well that's shut her up, he thought. 'Or his mother was black,' he said, 'black or half black, I really can't remember, but whether he looks it or not Frank's a blackfella all right.'

Kate's mind was reeling. Little wonder indeed that Frank was passionate about the Aboriginal cause. Little wonder too that their conversation about the Migration Act and its effect upon the White Australia Policy should have been so vigorous. Everything was starting to fall into place.

'Sorry to be the bearer of bad tidings.' Venner gathered by her continued silence that he'd successfully frightened her off. 'Although you really should have known,' he added gently. A well-meaning word of advice wouldn't go astray, he decided. 'That's the trouble with you, Kate,' he said, 'you're always so carried away with the cause you don't bother getting to know those involved.'

Kate stood. 'And that's the trouble with you, Venner. You're so busy gathering data on people that you lose sight of the cause altogether.'

'What's that supposed to mean?'

'It's supposed to mean that you're shallow. You always have been.'

She heaved her bag over her shoulder and marched off, leaving him wondering how things had gone so very wrong.

As she walked along Science Road towards the Vet Science Centre at the far end of the campus, Kate pondered this surprising new discovery. It certainly explains Frank's passion about many things, she thought, but does it explain his reticence in asking me out? She had a distinct feeling it did. Well she'd have to do something about that, she decided.

Chapter thirteen

Kate called into Madigan's Plumbing Services mid-morning on Saturday, but Frank wasn't there.
'He's out on a job,' Pete said. 'Shouldn't be all that long, he left pretty early. I'd say he'll be back by midday.'
'Thanks, Pete.'
She returned on the dot of twelve.
'G'day, Kate.' He was pleased to see her. 'Dad said you'd called around. Want a coffee?'
'Why don't we grab a sandwich and go to the park? It's lunchtime. I'm starving, aren't you?'
'Yeah, sure, good idea.'
After buying ham and salad rolls and takeaway coffees from the milk bar on the corner, Kate insisting upon paying for hers, they walked into Prince Alfred Park, where they sat on a bench looking at the view of the city skyline.
They talked pleasantly as they ate, exchanging notes about their respective Christmas and New Year experiences, then Kate rather abruptly changed the conversation. 'Do you like the theatre, Frank?'
'Um ... yes, yes, I do.' He was a little taken aback by the non sequitur – he'd been telling her about the New Year's Eve party he'd spent aboard a builder mate's boat on Sydney Harbour. 'I don't go all that often,' he admitted,

'in fact I haven't been once since I shifted back to Sydney, but in Melbourne –'

'I'm particularly fond of the Old Tote Theatre,' she said, 'their productions are excellent. Not that I'm an aficionado on the subject,' she added. 'Anyway, I was wondering whether you might like to come along with me one evening.'

Her eyes didn't waver as they met his, defying him to offer any valid reason why he shouldn't take her up on the offer.

'Which particular evening did you have in mind?' he asked.

You're hedging, Frank. 'No particular evening,' she said. You're not getting out of it that easily. 'Any that would suit you. Just name the day.'

As he hesitated she continued to study him unwaveringly. You're cornered aren't you? You're trying to figure a way out. 'Are you married, Frank?' she asked.

The baldness of her question startled him. 'No. No I'm not, why do you ask?'

'I'm interested to know why you never suggest we go out somewhere together,' she shrugged, 'the theatre, a jazz band, a pub, whatever.' Kate was aware she was being extremely confronting, but she was determined to force an answer from him. 'When we meet up by chance we get on very well, so why is it that you don't want to further our friendship?'

Her tactic worked, he stopped being evasive and answered her directly. 'I don't believe you're aware of my background, Kate.' She offered no hint either way, but waited for him to go on, so he did. 'My mother was Aboriginal,' he said. 'Or rather she was what they used to call "half-caste",' he added dryly. 'Her mother, my grandmother, was a Wiradjuri woman and my grandfather was the foreman on a farm near Wagga Wagga.'

Frank waited for the reaction he was accustomed to receiving upon the revelation that he was black. Surprise and disbelief to start with, then shock and amazement followed by a distinct change in attitude, but once again, she stumped him.

'I see. And that means we can't be friends, does it?'

'Of course it doesn't,' he protested. 'I know that working with Charlie as you do you have many Aboriginal friends. It's just that ...' He started to waver.

'Frank.' Kate decided to cut to the chase. 'I'm not seeking an affair, if that's what's worrying you. The last thing I want at this stage in my life is a full-on relationship and I really mean that. But good friends are rare and I like you. I'd like to get to know you. Won't you let me?'

Frank relaxed and smiled his lazy smile. 'Of course I will; how could I refuse such an offer?' I would very much enjoy being friends with you, he thought, frustrating though it may prove. He'd found Kate Durham hugely attractive from the moment he'd first met her, what man wouldn't, but he'd deliberately kept his distance, knowing they couldn't have an affair. For all her dedication to the cause, she came from a different world. 'Friends it is, then,' he said. 'So what do you want to know about me? Fire away.'

'I'd like to know about your mother for starters. What was she like?'

'No idea, I never knew her, but very beautiful I'm told. At least that's what Dad says, and from the odd photograph I've seen, he's not lying. They were together for three years. She was ten years younger, and he was madly in love with her, but she wouldn't marry him.' Frank grinned. 'Which makes me a bastard into the bargain,' he said. But the grin quickly faded as he added, 'She shot through on the old man when I was eighteen months old and I grew up spending the whole of my life hating her for it, at least until a couple of years ago.'

'What changed your mind?'

'Charlie Perkins. Meeting Charlie, getting involved in the fight for Aboriginal rights, learning about my mother's people, finding out who I was. Charlie changed my life.'

Kate nodded. 'Charlie's changed the lives of a lot of people,' she said.

'He certainly has. But strangely enough he didn't tell me anything my father hadn't already told me. It's just that I refused to believe Dad until I met Charlie.'

Intrigued, she waited for him to continue.

'My old man did things hard in those early years, bringing up a child on his own,' Frank explained, 'but he wouldn't hear a word against my mother. Not one word. I remember him sitting me down and giving me a lecture when I was about ten and an angry kid. "You mustn't blame your mum," he said, "she was restless. She wanted to go back to the bush." He told me she would never have stayed in the city at all if it hadn't been for him. "She felt trapped in Sydney," he said. Dad reckons if he'd gone back to the bush with her they'd still be together, but he'd wanted to start a business, so they stayed. Then one morning he woke up to find her gone. He blamed himself, still does, says he did a bad thing. "I deprived her of her freedom," he told me. "Your mother's people they're a different breed altogether, son, you've got to understand that." But I couldn't understand it; I refused to understand it. I spent most of my life in denial, living as a white man, not interested in anything to do with the blackfella part of me. That is until Charlie came along.'

Frank laughed fondly at the memory. 'When we first met I told Charlie about Dad and what he'd told me and Charlie simply said, "Your old man's spot on, mate." Then he told me to go and find out for myself. So I did.'

'You went in search of your mother?'

'That's right.'

'Did you find her?'

He shook his head. 'She'd been dead for eight years – usual blackfella causes, diabetes, renal failure. Barely made it to fifty. But I met a lot of her mob. Some of them sadly were lost souls, probably like my mother since she hooked up with the wrong bloke, and some were living full and happy lives. They welcomed me into their extended family once they knew I was Wiradjuri. I learned such a lot, Kate, more than I could possibly tell you. I have only one regret. I should have learned it sooner. I should have learned it much, much sooner.'

'Forgive the cliché, but better late than never, wouldn't you say?'

'I most certainly would.' He drained the last of his coffee. 'So now that you know all about me, when do we go to the theatre?'

'Next Friday.'

'What's on?'

'I have no idea,' she said collecting up the refuse that sat beside her on the bench. 'I'll have to check it out.'

They put their rubbish in a nearby bin and left the park.

It was late March when Alan finally rang his sister. He'd had the diaries for almost three months. He'd read through Kate's translations twice, very slowly, and he'd compared the dates in the ledgers and read the bits and pieces here and there that his schoolboy French could grasp, hearing as Kate had the voice of his great-grandmother. Then he'd thought for a further fortnight about the diaries' revelations and the havoc they would wreak upon the family before making the phone call.

'Bloody hell,' were the first words he said. 'You weren't wrong.'

'Yep.' No need to ask what he was talking about. 'You can see why I've been in such a quandary. We have to talk, Al. I'll come up to Brisbane during the one-week term break in May and we'll discuss what to do.'

'Don't bother coming up,' he said, 'there's no point.'

'No point!' She was taken aback. 'But we have to make a decision about whether we tell the family. We have to –'

'There's only one decision we can make, Kate,' he said.

'I've given the matter a lot of thought, believe me. They have to know the truth whether they like it or not, every single sordid detail. They have to read the diaries for themselves.'

'Oh God, do you really think so?' Even as she voiced the question, Kate knew he was right.

'I don't think so, I know so,' he said. 'They can't keep living this lie the way they do, it's ridiculous. Dad's modelled himself on Big Jim the hero and Mum lives out the past like it's a romance novel – the whole thing's wrong.'

'Poor Marmee,' Kate said, 'the truth'll probably kill her.'

'No it won't,' the reply came briskly down the line. 'Mum'll invent some other romantic slant, Ellie the martyr or whatever. The truth's far more likely to kill Dad.'

'Yes,' she replied, 'I know.'

'We might as well leave it until Christmas, when we can front them together. They've been living in ignorance the whole of their lives, can't do any harm to leave things a bit longer.'

'Good idea,' Kate said, grateful for her brother's support. 'We don't need to tell Grandpa though, do we? That is,' she added regretfully, 'if he's still with us at Christmas.'

'Not if you don't want to. Although it's quite possible Grandpa might know, Kate. Ever think about that?'

'Yes, I've thought about it a lot, but something tells me he doesn't, and if that's the case, I don't want to disillusion him at the end of his life.'

'Fair enough.'

Much as she dreaded the prospect of confronting her parents with the truth Kate felt immensely relieved that the decision had at last been taken out of her hands.

'Thanks, Al,' she said. 'I don't know what I'd do without you.'

Several months later, Neil rang to say goodbye.

'I'm off in a couple of weeks, Kate,' he said as if he was leaving on holiday, 'just called to say cheerio.' He'd been telephoning her regularly as he'd promised he would and they'd always spoken in their customary light-hearted vein. This time was to prove no different. There was no acknowledgement of the danger he faced, and Kate played things his way, aware that he wanted no drama.

'Keep working hard,' he said just before he hung up, 'we're all very proud of you, Kate. I expect no less than a pass with honours in this final year.'

'And I expect you to write regularly,' she said, deliberately sounding like a schoolmistress, 'if not each week, then at least on a fortnightly basis.'

'Don't I always?' he replied, and she could hear the smile in his voice. Then she could hear the seriousness as he added, 'You're the one person I really do write to, Kate, the one person who doesn't get the duty letters. I find it a great comfort, confiding in you the way I know I can.'

Glad that the conversation was ending on a serious note, Kate took the plunge. 'I love you, Neil,' she said.

'Love you too, Sis, always have, always will. Bye.'

No one was sure exactly how the rumour started, although in actual fact it had been young Beth, the typist at Elianne's office, where Paola served as receptionist behind the front desk. Beth had seen the ring on the chain about Paola's neck one day in the ladies' toilet. The ring and its crucifix companion had inadvertently swung into view through the open neck of Paola's blouse as she'd leant over the washbasin.

Beth had ooh-ed and ah-ed and Paola had blushed and denied any special significance as she'd tucked the ring away out of sight, but Beth wasn't stupid. Beth could add up two and two. Beth knew Paola was going out with Alan Durham, and she couldn't wait to tell her friends.

At first it had been no more than supposition and girlish gossip passed around among young women who shared a penchant for romance. But as rumours tend to do, it swiftly took on more substantial proportions, until one day ...

'G'day, Stan. I believe congratulations are in order.'

Stan had been on his way up to the mill when he'd bumped into Garry Gregg coming out of the mess hall near the cookhouse. Garry was Elianne's Sugar Boiler and an expert at his trade, as was essential. It was Garry's job to tend the giant vats, maintaining the correct pressure and temperature. He would taste the sugar in its liquid state, testing it for purity, and then make adjustments where necessary. Responsible as he was for the very quality of the product, Garry Gregg was without doubt one of the mill's most important employees and therefore on easy terms with Stan.

'Congratulations about what?' Stan asked as the two men walked on together towards the mill where, from the chimney, smoke belched unrelentingly into the air. Garry was returning to work after his brief morning-tea break.

'Young Alan's engagement of course. I've heard it's now official with a ring and all the trimmings.' Like many, Garry had been surprised to hear that Stanley Durham was allowing his son to marry the daughter of an employee and a Catholic one at that, but he was nonetheless pleased. 'And keeping it in the Elianne family, Stan, that's really good news. She's a lovely girl, Paola, I'm sure they'll be very happy.'

'Yes, yes,' Stan growled, he couldn't trust himself to say anything more, 'yes, yes.' If Garry Gregg knew then the whole damn mill knew. It would appear he was the only one who'd been kept in the dark. What the bloody hell was Luigi up to, allowing this nonsense?

He left Garry without another word and stormed off across the railway track towards the office fifty metres or so from the mill, halting briefly as he passed the sugar shed.

'Get Luigi Fiorelli,' he barked at one of the workers. 'Tell him I want to see him in my office, and tell him I mean right now!'

'Yes, Boss.' Young Andy sprinted for the mill; you jumped to it quick smart when the Boss was in one of his moods.

Inside the massive steel maze the noise was overwhelming, as Goliath-like machines went about their tasks chopping and crushing and mashing with demonic persistence. Giant wheels and rollers and presses seemed set in perpetual motion, rhythmic and relentless like the inside workings of a colossal watch.

Luigi was on one of the upper levels, overseeing the activity below.

'Hey, Luigi!' Andy screamed at the top of his lungs in an attempt to be heard above the din. 'Hey, Luigi!' He waved as he screamed, 'The Boss wants you!'

Luigi saw rather than heard young Andy. What on earth was the boy doing without a tin hat? The wearing of tin hats was mandatory at all times in the mill – Luigi himself had made it a rule. He climbed down the steep steps, bent on admonishing Andy.

'Why you have no tin hat?' he demanded at the top of his voice, stabbing a finger repeatedly at the boy's head. During the crushing season, Luigi communicated a great deal by mime; he found gestures most effective.

'The Boss wants to see you,' Andy yelled. 'And he said right now!'

They left the mill together.

'He didn't seem in a very good mood,' Andy warned when they were outside and the noise had abated to a dull roar.

'Next time you have tin hat,' Luigi ordered once again pointing to Andy's bare head.

'But the Boss –'

'I don' care, tin hat in mill.'

Waving the boy away, Luigi started towards the office and as he did he saw Paola step out of the main doors. They walked towards each other, meeting halfway in the dust fifty metres between the office and the mill.

'Why you leave work?' he asked. She looks worried, he thought.

'Mr Durham told me to go to lunch,' she said.

'But is not lunchtime.'

'He was angry, Papa. He knows, I can tell.'

'*Non ti preoccupari*, Paola,' he took her hand in both of his reassuringly, '*andrà tutto bene. Prometto.*'

Paola smiled tremulously. Her father's promise that everything would be all right was of some comfort, but it did not stop her worrying. Stanley Durham frightened her.

Stanley Durham did not, however, frighten Luigi.

'What the hell do you think you're up to?' Stan demanded the moment the Italian had closed the office door behind him. He did not invite Luigi to sit, nor did he sit himself, instead the two faced each other squarely across the large office desk. 'What's possessed you, man! Are you mad? The whole idea's preposterous!' Stan was in one of his ranting moods. 'Why in God's name would you grant permission for your daughter to marry my son! Give me one good reason. Why the hell would you do that!'

'They are in love.'

Stan was flabbergasted. 'In love, you have to be joking. You think it's that simple.'

'*Si.*'

'Oh for Christ's sake, Luigi, don't take me for a fool. You're telling me you'd allow your daughter to marry a Protestant, you of all people!'

Luigi paused, uncertain how to respond. Stanley Durham did not know that his son planned to convert. But then Alan had said his father had not taken the situation seriously, that he'd dismissed the idea altogether. Stan the Man obviously underestimated the scale of his son's intent. *But it is not my place to tell him this*, Luigi thought. *Alan will do so when the time is right.*

'I think,' he said with great care, 'is best I allow my daughter to decide.'

Stan had noted the Italian's hesitance and now studied him shrewdly. What was Luigi after? He appeared to have a plan. Was he misguided enough to think that a union between his daughter and the Boss's son might gain him wealth and elevate his family to a position of power? Such self-interest seemed out of keeping with the Italian, but of course greed altered every man's perspective.

'What do you hope to profit from this, Luigi?' he asked. 'You must realise that I am quite prepared to disinherit my son should he insist upon following such a path. You and your daughter and family would not benefit.'

Luigi found Stanley Durham's suggestion not only surprising, but deeply insulting. There had been a time when he and Stan had been on the friendliest of terms. Their children had grown up together. Always they had maintained the distance dictated by their status, but never once had they been disrespectful to one another.

'I seek nothing,' he said coldly.

'Good. Because there will be nothing. There will be nothing for you or your daughter or your brothers and their wives, there will be nothing for any of you, I hope you understand that.'

'You would insult the Fiorelli family?' Luigi's eyes flashed dangerously, but he contained his anger. 'You are a brave man to do such a thing, Mr Stan.'

Stan suddenly realised that he'd gone too far, and in no insignificant way. Luigi's response carried an inherent threat that even he in his position would be foolish to ignore. Luigi Fiorelli was a proud man. So were his brothers. And his brothers' sons, now men, were also proud. One did not insult a powerful clan like the Fiorellis.

'I intend no insult to your family, Luigi,' he said stiffly, 'I simply wish to make myself clear.'

'You make yourself clear, I understand. Now I make myself clear. Alan and Paola, they have my blessing. They have the blessing of my family. What you do ...' Luigi gave a dismissive shrug; his flash of anger had passed '... what you do, it is your business.'

'Very well.' Stan was not prepared for one minute to leave the confrontation on an equal footing, certainly not when he held the trump card. 'But I suggest you warn Paola this union will never take place,' he said, 'I will forbid my son to marry your daughter.'

'If that is what you wish.' Luigi felt sorry for Stanley Durham. How little you know your son, he thought. You are about to lose him.

'That is what I wish. And with regard to your daughter's position here, I think it would be more comfortable for all concerned if –'

'Paola will get a job in town,' Luigi interrupted. 'I will arrange this. Is not good she work here, she will be unhappy.'

'Good, we understand each other.' Stan sat. 'You may go now, Luigi.'

Neil had continued to write to his sister every fortnight, sometimes even weekly when he felt the desire to confide. He would tell her as much as was possible while guarding his secret and avoiding army censorship. Kate had no trouble at all reading between the lines.

I have come to know these people, Kate, he wrote, *those with whom I work and others I have met personally on trips into town.* She knew instantly that he was referring to Yen. *They are a modest hard-working people with a love of family. They respect their elders and lend support to one another, sharing the responsibility of children and the burden of poverty.* He's telling me about his wife and her family, Kate thought, he's painting a picture for me. *It is a great shame this war is tearing apart such a peaceful community.*

Neil continued to paint pictures in his letters, describing huts and villages, never giving place names that would be censored, but creating what appeared to be a sort of general travelogue, which Kate knew was intensely personal. This is Yen's village, she would think, this is the hut where her family lives.

They are a physically beautiful people, particularly the women, he wrote, *but of course like most men I would be biased in that direction. The women are petite and delicately featured with the finest of skin and the blackest of hair that often seems tinged with a blue-ish sheen.* As she read his words, Kate could see Yen, just as Neil intended she should. *They are sometimes shy, sometimes bold, sometimes funny, but unlike their Australian counterparts always the essence of femininity. Oh dear*, he added with wry humour, *what have I done? I don't mean to insult Australian womanhood, Sis, really I don't, but Vietnamese women, even while suffering the severest of hardship maintain a grace that I find quite extraordinary.*

Kate smiled as she read on, knowing that her brother was not really referring to Vietnamese women in general, but rather talking specifically about his wife, and with such love. She was touched that he should so wish to share his feelings with her, but as always she kept her reply frivolous.

Dear Neil,
I promise I shall endeavour to achieve the grace that is gifted to Vietnamese women having now been informed that we clumsy Australians are so sadly lacking. I have of course passed your letter on to my feminist friends who I am sure will follow suit ...

Not all of Neil's letters were veiled accounts of his wife and her family, however, and not always was Kate able to respond frivolously. There were times when he wrote of the war, times when he felt the need to unburden himself.

This is a terrible war, Kate. As if there is ever any war that isn't, of course, but in past wars men have at least known their enemy. That's not the case here. Friend and foe are so often indistinguishable ...

Kate received the most revealing of Neil's letters in mid-November. She'd completed her exam in the Great Hall that morning and upon collecting her mail at the university post office was surprised to find only one letter from him. She hadn't received word for over three weeks and when such was the case, given the sporadic nature of army delivery, usually two or even three letters would arrive at the same time. But upon opening the envelope where she stood in the street and upon reading her brother's first words, she understood why. The strain of battle had been taking its toll and, unable to write in the chatty fashion he preferred, Neil had refrained from writing at all. But he needed to talk now, as he had on past occasions. He needed to relieve the pressure, and she was his outlet.

She returned the letter unread to its envelope and walked on as planned to the Fisher Library where, outside, the huge jacaranda was ablaze with purple blossom. The blossoming of the jacaranda had a frightening significance for most students, coinciding as it always did with the end-of-year examinations that could determine their very future.

Inside the library, a number of cubicles were occupied by those desperately bent on last-minute cramming, but Kate found an empty one and took up possession, spreading her study books out before her. She had no further examination that afternoon and, well-prepared as she was, no need for last-minute cramming, but she preferred the quiet of the library to the tension and lunchtime chatter that abounded at the Union or at Manning House where students were sure to be comparing notes about the horror of final exams. She would do some refresher reading and jot down some reminders for her next exam, but first, Neil's letter. She took it from its envelope and proceeded to read, hearing her brother's voice as he unburdened himself to her.

If we were fighting the North Vietnamese army alone, things would be a great deal simpler, but the Viet Cong guerrilla forces make it impossible to discern who's who, and their methods are ruthless ...

The platoon of forty or so men approached the village with caution. Viet Cong activity had increased around Nui Dat since the battalion's return from Operation Hawkesbury on the Long Khanh–Bien Hoa border.

It was an unseasonably warm day for late November, with a light drizzle that did nothing to relieve the humidity, difficult to believe in this heat that winter was just around the corner.

They spread out as they entered the village where, among the tangle of tin shanties and thatched huts, bodies lay sprawled on the ground – men, women and children. The Viet Cong had not discriminated.

'Don't touch anything,' the sergeant yelled, 'they're bound to have left booby traps,' and the troops split into units of two, working their way through the village, exploring each hut and shanty in turn.

Life means nothing to them. The Viet Cong will happily sacrifice their own people. They'll destroy whole villages, and plant booby traps on dead bodies ...

The village appeared completely deserted – deserted of the living, anyway: the bodies were numerous; and here and there even dogs lay dead – but the men practised extreme caution as they went from hut to hut. The possibility of ambush was unlikely, although their eyes scanned every nook and cranny for movement just in case: far more dangerous was the threat of explosives planted by the departing enemy.

'Jesus Christ,' young Sam Brennan muttered as he and Neil entered the hut.

'Don't touch anything, private.' Corporal Neil Durham

barked a repetition of the Sergeant's order. Sam was a nasho and this was his first taste of the real thing. He's rattled, Neil thought, and why the hell wouldn't he be.

Neil felt sickened himself as he looked about at the scene, which told a story in explicit detail, a scene and a story all too familiar to him. A man lay dead outside the door of the hut, they'd had to skirt around his body to enter, and inside the hut the family he had tried to defend had been systematically slaughtered. The woman still held her dead baby to her breast and on either side of her lay the bodies of two small children. Upturned bowls were beside them, rice was scattered everywhere, and a dish of stewed vegetables sat undamaged in the centre of the matting that served as table and floor in one. The family had clearly been sharing a meal.

> *The people who suffer most are the innocent villagers. Not only those whom the Viet Cong so brutally annihilate, but those who are forced to live in a state of abject terror. Many villagers fear for their own lives and for the lives of their family.*
>
> *These are good people, Kate, as I have told you before, but when we enter a village that is presumed friendly we don't know who we might confront. We don't know who might be housing the Viet Cong out of sheer terror, or who might have been used to plant a trap ...*

Neil and the young private left the dead family as they were and once outside continued silently on to another hut. All about them other soldiers were doing the same, moving with stealth through the drizzle that had turned the dirt beneath their boots to mud, carefully skirting bodies, exchanging only the barest muttered comment one to another, eyes searching keenly for any sign of a trap.

Nearby, a dog barked, shattering the eerie silence, and to a man they jumped, startled by the noise. Then from behind a tin shanty, the animal appeared. A lean and bedraggled mongrel, the only sign of life in the village, the dog stood its ground and gave another bold bark, as if ordering the soldiers to leave. Wry smiles were shared all round and the men continued their search.

Then, as Neil and young Sam approached a hut, another noise from within, barely discernible: the muffled whimper of a human baby. They both heard it.

The two exchanged a glance. Neil gave a nod and, rifles at the ready, they entered.

Seated on the ground, her back against the hut's rear wall, was a young woman, a baby in her arms. She held the child's head tucked tightly into her chest in an attempt to stifle its whimpers and her eyes were wide with fear. When she saw the soldiers she started to tremble, her body visibly shaking.

Neil could see the beads of sweat on her brow. He could hear her laboured breathing. Something's wrong, he thought.

'Don't be afraid,' Sam said, 'we're not going to hurt you.' He extended his hand in a calming gesture, but the young woman became even more terrified and started to scream hysterically.

'You're safe with us,' Sam assured her, 'you're safe,' and he took a step forwards.

Neil spoke Vietnamese, so he knew full well what the woman was saying. She was screaming, 'Stay away, don't come near, don't touch me,' but had he not known the words, he would have registered their meaning. He had seen her eyes flicker to the trip wire.

'Stop,' he yelled, 'it's a trap!'

Too late. Sam had already embarked upon a second step, a step that proved fatal. The hut exploded, instantly killing those inside and wounding several troops nearby.

I'm sorry to write this way, Kate, I don't mean to upset you. But it does me good to let off steam. You're the only one I'll

turn to as you well know, which is bad luck for you because it means you cop the whole brunt. Sorry about that. I'll write in a happier vein next time, or at least I'll try to.
  Love Neil

But there was no next time. He didn't write again, and two weeks after Kate had received the letter that so eerily echoed the circumstances of her brother's death, the Durham family was informed that Neil had been killed in action.

His body was flown home to Bundaberg, where a funeral service was conducted at Christ Church. There was standing room only. It seemed the entire community had turned up, along with many others, including a military detail of six uniformed soldiers, who formed a guard of honour outside the church. There were eulogies from family and friends and former national service buddies and also an address delivered by a brigadier from Canberra on behalf of the army, paying tribute to Neil and the ultimate sacrifice he had made in the course of his duty.

Kate and Alan, representing the family, both spoke very movingly of their brother. But Stan did not speak of his son. Stan couldn't. Stanley Durham sat grey-faced and silent throughout the entire service. He was flanked either side by his wife, who was quietly weeping, and his fragile father, also visibly moved, but Stan himself appeared incapable of displaying any form of emotion. Ten days after being informed of his son's death, Stan remained in a numb state to all about him.

Following the service, Neil was buried in the military section of Bundaberg Cemetery, after which thirty or so guests were invited back to Elianne for the wake. Hilda had taken charge of all the arrangements, considering it only right and proper. 'One must have a wake,' she'd said to Kate, 'as a show of respect, a select number only of course.'

When the family returned to the house, Kate and Alan helped their grandfather up the front stairs and into his quarters, all but carrying him in the process. Bartholomew could barely walk these days, but had insisted upon attending the service. Then they prepared themselves for the ordeal of the wake, which nobody wanted, including Hilda herself, but propriety must be observed.

Stan seemed barely to notice there were guests in his house. He sat in an armchair at the far end of the main drawing room, glass of Scotch in hand, sipping occasionally, but oblivious to those milling about, to Max topping up glasses, to Ivy serving finger food on silver trays, to his wife pouring tea while bravely shouldering the burden of social niceties.

When people filed up to him respectfully, as each of them did one by one, offering their condolences, he gave them a nod, but didn't even look at them. After a while they stopped attempting to make contact and left him to himself.

Thankfully the guests did not overstay their welcome and within an hour and a half the last were taking their leave.

Ivan Krantz decided upon one final attempt to break through the impenetrable wall of Stan's grief, or his shock or whatever it was that was rendering the man's mind so incapable of making any form of connection. How terrible, he thought, to see Stanley Durham in such a condition.

He left his wife and son chatting to Hilda at the drawing room door – they were the last of the guests to depart – and returned to where Stan sat in his armchair.

'Just want to let you know that I understand what you're going through, Stan,' he said sympathetically. 'You and I go back a long way and I know how hard it must be. I know the plans you had for Neil and for Elianne. Well, of course I do,' he said a little over-heartily, 'we were a team, the three of us, you and Neil and me.'

Stan's eyes slowly focused upon Ivan. He didn't seem to particularly comprehend what was being said, but Ivan was nonetheless pleased to have made some sort of impact. How he'd done so he wasn't really sure. He thought he'd sounded rather clumsy himself, but his desire being to buoy the man's spirits, he continued as he'd intended.

'We'll pursue those plans, Stan,' he said with a positivity he hoped was finding some connection. 'When you feel up to it, we'll throw ourselves into the business. That's what you need, distraction. With fresh investors, ready capital is no problem – Elianne is booming. We'll accomplish everything we intended. It'll be a tribute to Neil. And Alan will join us. We'll be a team just like we've always been, the Durhams and the Krantzes.'

Ivan glanced to the doorway where his wife and son, Henry, were chatting to Hilda, and when he looked back he saw that Stan had followed his gaze. Another healthy sign, he thought.

'Well, that's about it,' he said in the pause that followed. Too much to hope the man might speak, he supposed, but there was a definite added light in the eyes, some form of perception: he'd certainly got through. 'We'll be on our way now.'

Ivan would have liked to offer his hand, but he didn't push further, opting for a comforting pat of Stan's shoulder instead. 'My sympathies to you, Stan,' he said. 'I know how hard it is, believe me I do.'

Stan watched as Ivan Krantz walked off to join his wife and son. You don't know how hard it is at all, you dumb bastard. Stan's mind had been jolted into action and was now working overtime. Look at you there with that prick of a son of yours who never got drafted, who never went into battle – what have you ever had to fear? And the puerile attempt to jolly him along, a renewed business drive would be seen as a tribute to Neil, 'and Alan will join us', the dumb bastard had said. Alan isn't Neil! Alan can never be Neil!

Lots of things were coming back to Stan as he watched the Krantz family bidding farewell to Hilda at the door.

'I won't come downstairs,' Hilda said. 'I do hope you don't mind seeing yourselves out, but ...'

'Of course we don't.' Gerda Krantz kissed her on the cheek. 'Please take care, Hilda,' she said, 'of yourself as well as others.'

Look at them chatting as if nothing's happened, Stan thought. Your son's dead, Hilda, don't you know that?

He glanced around the room. Max was at the sideboard placing several empty bottles in a cardboard box. Ivy and Kate and Alan were collecting the glasses and cups that were scattered all over the place on coffee tables and mantelpieces, even the escritoire in the corner.

There's been a party, he thought, and then the images came back to him. He'd seen it all, Max swanning around with sherry for the ladies and Scotch for the men, Ivy offering platters of food, Hilda serving tea and biscuits. They've been having a party and my son's dead!

He stood. 'What the hell do you all think you're doing?' he demanded.

Everything stopped. Hilda had just closed the door following the Krantzes' departure and she turned to him. They turned every one of them, Kate, Alan, Max, Ivy, and there was a moment's stillness as they stared at Stan.

'You're having a party?' His voice was a combination of disbelief and outrage. 'Neil's dead and you're having a party!'

'It's a wake, dear,' Hilda said crossing to him, 'we held a wake for Neil. It was the proper thing to do.'

'Proper!' Stan roared his anger. 'What's proper about my son's death?'

Hilda gave a brisk nod to Max and Ivy who quickly departed the drawing room leaving the family to themselves. Stan didn't even notice them go.

'What's proper about that, woman?! You tell me. What's proper about that?!'

Hilda wanted to weep with relief. She had thought her

husband might be going mad. He'd spoken to no one, appeared to see no one, but he'd been living in mental agony: she of all people knew that – the gnashing of his teeth kept her awake every night. She had suggested time and again he see a doctor, but he hadn't heard her. Now at last he'd come back. His rage was an excellent sign. She could comfort him now, and they could share their grief.

'We must be strong, Stanley,' she said. 'But we will manage, we have one another to lean on, we can bear the pain together.' The line between romance and reality, a difficult delineation for Hilda at the best of times, now blurred into one as relief at her husband's return to sanity mingled with the several sherries she'd discreetly imbibed while serving tea to her lady guests. 'We must weather the storm, you and I, my dear, just as Grandmother Ellie and Big Jim did when Edward and George were killed at Gallipoli.' She raised a hand and gently touched her fingers to his cheek. 'It was the great love they shared that saved them,' she said, 'just as our love shall save –'

'Shut up, you stupid woman!' Stan bellowed. He could take no more of his wife's idiocy and grabbing her by the shoulders he shook her like a madman. 'Shut up, shut up ...' she was a rag doll in his huge, strong hands '... you stupid, stupid, stupid woman!'

'Stop it, Dad!' Alan leapt forwards. Grabbing his father's arm he wrenched with all his might, managing to break Stan's grip. 'Stop it,' he yelled.

With one hand Stan thrust Hilda aside and caught off balance she fell to the floor.

Kate rushed and knelt beside her. 'Are you all right, Marmee?' She took her mother's arm, about to help her to her feet, but Hilda waved her away.

'Yes I'm perfectly all right, thank you, dear.' Hilda preferred to stand on her own without assistance. She was undeterred by her husband's anger. Better his rage than his resignation from life.

Stan looked down at her and, horrified to see his wife on the floor, was instantly brought to his senses. Then as Hilda slowly stood, unassisted and unhurt, he registered the hand that was holding him back. He turned to see his son still locked onto his arm. Alan was maintaining a firm grip as if to prevent him from attempting any further attack. Stan ripped his arm free.

'Why did it have to be Neil?' he said, glaring accusingly at Alan. 'Why couldn't it have been you!' Then he stormed from the room.

Kate and Alan looked at each other. Kate's eyes registered the shock she felt that her father should say such a thing, but the exchange between brother and sister signalled a great deal more. Without sharing a single utterance, both knew exactly what the other was thinking.

'He didn't mean it, dear. He's upset as you can see ...' Hilda tried desperately to reassure her son.

Alan gave a shrug as if he didn't care, which wasn't true. Despite the knowledge that Neil had always been his father's favourite, the words had cut deeply. But his eyes remained locked with Kate's. They were thinking of the diaries and the extraordinary fact that Big Jim had said the same thing in very much the same way over fifty years ago.

Chapter Fourteen

Jim told me last night that of all his three sons, he would rather have lost Bartholomew. 'The wrong boys died at Gallipoli,' he said, 'why couldn't it have been him?' Shocking words, unforgiveable words, but at least he does not say them in Bartholomew's presence – for that I am thankful.

It is grief speaking of course: Jim remains inconsolable. As indeed am I. Every day that passes is empty without my two beautiful boys. But I must continue to be strong as I have these past months, for it is my strength alone that will save Jim from the blackest of despair that threatens to destroy us all. And there is my darling Bartholomew, whom I must protect at all cost, and his dear wife, Mary, and their baby son. We still have a family, if only I can convince Jim of this. There is a reason to go on.

Big Jim Durham had been inordinately proud of his sons when they'd volunteered. And they'd done so without his bidding – they'd surprised him with the news. 'We're off to war, Dad,' they'd announced, and Big Jim had been fit to burst. In his opinion every able-bodied man in the land should enlist.

'I envy you lads,' he'd said, 'off to fight for King and Country as you are. What an honour, what an adventure, dear God, if they'd take a man in his fifties, I'd be going with you I swear.'

Bartholomew had also volunteered. All three brothers had ridden their horses into town and presented themselves at the recruitment centre that had been set up in Bundaberg. Recruitment centres had sprung into being in every country town throughout the land, and young men were queuing by the thousands. But as things had turned out, when it came to the physical Bartholomew had been found wanting. A weak heart, the army doctor had told him. He'd been a nice enough man in his brusque way. 'Nothing to worry about unduly, son,' he'd said, 'but enough to make you ineligible, I'm afraid. Can't have hearts that are going to conk out on us under the strain of battle now, can we.'

'What a rotten thing to happen.' Young George had been most sympathetic. 'Who'd have thought it, eh?'

'It was probably that bout of glandular fever you had when you were little, Bartholomew,' big brother Edward had said; he too was sympathetic. 'Not to worry,' he'd added in an attempt to make amends for the injustice that had been served upon his brother, 'someone has to stay here and protect the home front.'

The brothers had always been close, although sibling rivalry repeatedly raised its head between Edward, the eldest of the three, and George the youngest, both of whom were assertive by nature and fiercely competitive. Given the four-year age difference, Edward had been the uncontested leader during their childhood, George frustratingly mounting challenge after challenge only to lose, while Bartholomew, in the middle, had taken the position of peacemaker.

Things had not changed as they'd progressed to manhood – indeed the rivalry had become more intense. George had grown stronger and bigger and as the playing field had evened out Bartholomew's peacemaking skills were regularly called upon. The balance had always been a good one and continued to be so.

Big Jim was not in the least surprised to learn that Bartholomew had failed to pass the army's medical examination. He made his views evident that very same night as he and his wife prepared themselves for bed.

'Well, it's to be expected, isn't it.' he said when Ellie voiced her worries about the discovery of Bartholomew's weakened heart condition. 'He might not be the youngest, but he's always been the runt of the litter.'

Ellie detested the way Jim was so disparaging of Bartholomew, even speaking at times with contempt. Throughout the boy's childhood he had considered Bartholomew's peaceful nature a character flaw. He was proud of the aggression his other sons displayed and openly encouraged their competitiveness, pitting one against the other. The fact that Bartholomew chose not to compete he saw as the epitome of weakness. Ellie didn't. Ellie saw it as a show of strength, a silent rebellion from a boy who had no desire to conform. She admired her son's resilience, and did her best to protect him whenever possible from his father's bullying.

'I take it you're not at all concerned about the doctor's report,' she said icily, staring at him in the dressing-room mirror as she sat brushing her hair.

'Why should I be? The doctor told him it was nothing to worry about.' Jim could see from the cold green glint of her eyes that his glibness annoyed her. He didn't like it when Ellie was annoyed. 'I'm not being heartless, my dear,' he assured her. 'They have to select only the very fittest, you must understand that. They can't afford to accept men who might let others down under pressure. It's a safety measure only, believe me. Now come to bed.'

Ellie allowed herself to be mollified. 'I'm very glad he's been turned down,' she said, 'and I'm sure dear Mary is too. Bartholomew should be by her side when the baby comes.'

Jim laughed. 'By her side? I don't think so. Hardly a place for a man – childbirth is women's business.'

'I didn't mean literally of course,' she said crossing to the bed where he was propped against the pillows waiting for her. 'But what if Bartholomew had passed the medical test? What if he went off to war and didn't come back?' The thought sent a chill down Ellie's spine. 'His child would be deprived of a father.'

'I would be the child's father, Ellie,' Jim said heartily as she climbed in beside him, 'we'd have another Durham and I'd raise it as my own.'

This time his glibness bewildered rather than annoyed, she found his cavalier attitude to the war mystifying.

'Do you not fear for our sons, Jim?' she said resisting just a little as he drew her to him, looking into his eyes, trying to fathom his reasoning. 'Do you not worry for their safety?'

'You worry enough for both of us, my love.' He buried his face into the curve of her neck, breathing in the smell of her, running his hands over her body, feeling the flesh beneath the nightgown. 'Let the boys have their adventure. The war will be over in no time and they'll be home with such stories to tell.'

Now, four months after the deaths of Edward and George, Big Jim continued to despise Bartholomew for surviving his brothers. He didn't say so out loud in his son's presence – not through any concern for Bartholomew's feelings, but rather in order to avoid incurring Ellie's displeasure. He had no wish to further upset the wife whom he adored and who, like he, was grieving deeply. It was true, however, that he had always disapproved of the way Ellie had mollycoddled their middle son. The boy was spineless and should have been whipped into shape years earlier. Now, Big Jim couldn't stand being in his presence, couldn't stand the very sight of him. Bartholomew was a constant reminder of all he had lost.

Bartholomew was fully aware of his father's feelings. Big Jim's contempt was nothing new to him: he'd suffered it for years. He'd long ago acknowledged he was a disappointment to his father and had refused to feel guilt, but he did now. Bartholomew felt guilty that he should be alive when his brothers were dead, and Big Jim's silent, ever-present condemnation compounded his guilt tenfold.

Big Jim's escape was the Burnett Club, where he had the sympathy of all and where he drowned his sorrows in imported Scotch or rum produced by the Bundaberg distillery, dependent upon his mood at the time. Huge man that he was and with a high tolerance for alcohol, he rarely displayed overt signs of drunkenness, but the liquor proved a welcome distraction and the club kept him away from the son he couldn't bear to look at.

Bartholomew's escape was work. Work and family – baby Stanley was now nearly one year old, having been born while Edward and George were still in training camp. But above even family, it was work that took precedence. While his father wallowed in self-pity and liquor at the Burnett Club, Bartholomew threw himself into the running of the mill, shouldering the burden of management in the absence of Big Jim and personally taking on the tasks of skilled workers, all the while pushing himself tirelessly, day after day after day.

His wife and his mother worried for his health. 'You mustn't overtax yourself, my darling,' Mary said time and again.

Ellie echoed her: 'You must slow down, Bartholomew.' But all their protests were to no avail. Bartholomew was insistent that with a wartime shortage of skilled labour it was imperative he take on whatever job he could, and he was right. Without his intervention on all levels, and most particularly his inspiration to his workers, Elianne's production would have been drastically diminished. Indeed the mill may well have ceased to function at all during that crushing of 1915.

Necessity, it was true, had dictated Bartholomew's devotion to duty, but he was also without doubt assuaging his guilt. Here was a way of proving his worth, to himself and perhaps also to his father. It was an ethic that was to remain with him throughout the whole of his life.

During the slack season that followed, Ellie continued to tolerate Big Jim's maudlin moods and his lengthy bouts at the Burnett Club, but as the months passed and the crushing once again drew near she decided it was time to rectify the situation. Bartholomew could not be expected to work a second time at such a pace and under such pressure.

'It's well over a year now since the boys died,' she said meaningfully as the two of them lingered over the breakfast table. Mary was upstairs feeding the baby and Bartholomew had gone into town to purchase fresh hardware supplies from Wyper Brothers.

'So?'

'So I think it's time you returned to work,' she said crisply. 'The mill needs you.'

He gave an uninterested shrug. 'The mill appears to be managing quite adequately without me.'

'Only because of Bartholomew,' she said, curbing her irritation. 'Without Bartholomew it might well have ceased functioning at all last season – he kept Elianne alive for you, Jim.'

'And so he should,' Big Jim sneered. 'He owes me that much.'

Ellie felt an uncontrollable surge of rage. She could no longer bear her husband's self-pity, nor his contempt and the way he spoke as if Bartholomew was personally responsible for the deaths of his brothers.

'What, would you have all three of them dead?' she demanded loudly, almost to the point of yelling, her eyes gleaming angrily. 'You have a son, for God's sake! You have a son and a grandson – can you not see that? You have a family! You have a reason for living!'

Big Jim stared back at her. He was shocked, stirred from his apathy. Ellie never raised her voice, Ellie never displayed anger.

Ellie was thankful that she appeared finally to have broken through his wall of self-pity. 'You must resume the mantle of responsibility, Jim,' she said. 'You must do your duty by your family. If you cannot love your son, then love your grandson, but do your duty by your family or you will lose us all.'

Lose us all? Was that what she'd said? Lose us all? But he dared not lose Ellie. He could cope with the loss of his sons, he could live without them, but Ellie, never; he could not live without Ellie. He would kill anyone who threatened to take her. Why, he would kill Ellie herself if she were ever to leave him. Ellie was his life.

Big Jim had been shaken back to reality and from that moment on his attitude changed. He even admitted his gratitude to Bartholomew, albeit begrudgingly.

'I appreciate all you have done over the past year,' he said stiffly when his son had returned from town. 'Your mother has impressed upon me how hard you have worked to keep the mill going in these difficult times.'

'I was doing no more than my duty, Father, my duty to both the family and the nation.'

Bartholomew's surprise at the change in his father's attitude was evident, and he glanced at his mother, wondering what had brought it about, but Ellie's face betrayed nothing. 'Sugar is vital to our men at the front,' he continued. 'The government has urged the mills to keep up production, despite the shortage of labour and fuel.'

'Quite, quite,' Big Jim said, 'and your dedication to duty has been most appreciated. We shall work as a team from now on, you and I.'

They did work as a team, father and son, but work was the only true connection they shared. Big Jim could not warm to Bartholomew, who remained in his eyes 'the runt of the litter' and a constant reminder of his loss.

He did, however, warm to Bartholomew's son. Heeding Ellie's advice he took an interest in his grandson and, as the years passed, young Stan filled the void in Big Jim's life. Here indeed was a worthy heir to the Durham throne. And little Julia too, pretty and beguiling. Ellie had been right, Jim realised. He had a family and a reason for living. But most of all he had Stan. Stan was Edward and George reborn.

Ellie watched with trepidation as Big Jim took over Bartholomew's son. She watched as Stan grew to idolise his grandfather – what boy wouldn't? A figure so much larger than life. Bartholomew could not have competed even had he wanted to, but then true to his nature Bartholomew did not try.

She felt somewhat to blame for her husband's preoccupation with his grandson, remembering the advice she'd so sternly given that morning years ago. 'If you cannot love your son, then love your grandson,' those had been her very words. But Big Jim would never have grown to love his son. As things were now, with his affection focused upon the boy, perhaps his son would be spared his contempt.

Ellie knew only too well that Big Jim could destroy Bartholomew, and she had no doubt that if he wished to do so, he would. It remained her mission in life, as always, to protect her family from her husband.

Chapter Fifteen

Following Neil's wake, the Durham family with the exception of Bartholomew proceeded to get drunk all four in their own particular way.

Hilda displayed no visible effects of the several healthy nips of medicinal brandy she downed in order to help her sleep, but without them sleep would certainly have evaded her.

Stanley Durham was discovered by Max slumped over the desk in his study, a near-empty bottle of Scotch before him. Upon being awoken, he did not appear overly affected and waved Max away, offended by his offer of assistance, but there was a distinct unsteadiness in his gait as he took himself off to bed.

Kate and Alan practised no restraint whatsoever, setting out openly and unashamedly to get drunk. After raiding their father's liquor supply, they sat at the table in the breakfast room swigging back Scotch and talking about Neil.

A half an hour and two swift Scotches later, Kate wisely decided to tell Alan about Yen before the alcohol took its effect. She recounted faithfully and in detail everything Neil had told her, concluding with her promise that she would look after his wife should anything happen to him.

Alan listened in silent and utter amazement, bottle forgotten, empty glass unheeded on the table, astounded to hear of his brother's marriage.

'I'm sorry I couldn't tell you before, Al,' she said finally, 'but Neil swore me to secrecy. He didn't want anyone to know until the end of the war when he could bring her home to Australia. I think he was worried that word might get back to the army.'

'And it would have for sure,' Alan replied, 'if Dad had ever heard about it.'

'Exactly. Which is why we must keep this strictly between ourselves until we can bring Yen to Elianne as I promised. What do you say?'

'You're on.' He poured them a third hefty Scotch and they clinked glasses.

'I want to show you something.' She stood. 'Don't go away, won't be a tick.'

She disappeared to return a minute or so later with an envelope that she handed him.

He recognised the writing immediately. 'It's from Neil,' he said.

'Yes. His last letter to me. Read it.'

Alan read the letter slowly, drinking in its every word. He was moved, hearing so clearly the voice of his brother.

When he finished he looked up at her. 'Neil never wrote to me like that.'

'He never wrote to anyone like that,' Kate said and her eyes welled with tears.

She's crying, Alan thought. He couldn't remember the last time he'd seen Kate openly cry. Even at the funeral she'd shown a restraint that most others hadn't. 'It proves how much he loved you, Kitty-Kat.'

'Yes. Yes, it does.' The tears spilled out to course down her cheeks and she did nothing to stop them.

The Scotch started to kick in very quickly after that. They told stories and wept together, the two of them, stories of Neil and stories of their childhood, on and on, until several hours later, exhausted and all cried out, they seemed to have drunk themselves sober, or they felt they had.

Kate studied the half-empty tumbler on the table before her, closing one eye and then the other, checking her vision, wondering if she was starting to see double. 'That was a terrible thing Dad said this afternoon.' She'd wanted to somehow make amends for the hurt her father's vicious comment must have caused, but she hadn't known when or how to bring up the subject. Now seemed a rather good time, she thought and a reference to the diaries seemed a rather good opening. 'He's not the same as Big Jim, Al. It was just grief speaking; he didn't mean it.'

'Course he did.' Although the words were a little slurred Alan's reply was brutally honest, he was not prepared to be fobbed off. 'Sure, Dad's not the same as Big Jim, he's not a bad man, but he can be bloody hurtful.' He gave one of those shrugs that Kate knew was never as careless as it was intended to appear. 'You can put things down to grief as much as you like, Kate,' he said, 'but Dad's sentiment is the same as Big Jim's. If he had a choice between who should have copped it, you can bet your bottom dollar it'd be me. People can't help having favourites. It's only natural.'

'Maybe it is, but people don't have to make things that obvious, do they?' she replied harshly.

As he gave another supposedly nonchalant shrug and topped up their glasses from the last of the bottle Kate felt a sudden and intense desire to punish her father.

'Let's get back at him, Al,' she said. 'We can you know. We can give him the diaries first thing tomorrow.'

'Nah,' Alan shook his head, aware it was the drink that was talking, 'we can't do that, not now. One day, sure, he has to know the truth. But not now – he's too bloody vulnerable.'

Kate studied her brother with affection. 'How funny,' she said, 'I used to think that Neil was the big softie and that you were the tough one.'

'I am, always have been,' he said with a smile.

A half an hour later they weaved their way off to their respective bedrooms.

Alan stayed on at Elianne for a further month. There were plans he needed to set in place, having decided his future must now take a different path. He had secret and lengthy discussions with the three older Fiorelli brothers and he took mysterious trips into town, where he visited a number of businessmen and looked at properties for sale. He told only Paola of his plans. Apart from the brothers no one else knew, certainly no one in the family, not even Kate. The household was in mourning and it was no time to discuss his personal future.

Christmas came and went without anyone noticing. Cook observed tradition and prepared the customary feast, but no one was hungry. It was a sombre affair.

Alan returned to Brisbane in the New Year, presumably to resume his apprenticeship and his studies, but in actuality to tie up his affairs there.

Kate, however, did not return to Sydney. She'd passed her final year with honours (1st class) and had applied for a Vet Science PhD scholarship funded by Vesteys, the large meat-producing company that, among its many international interests, owned cattle stations in northern Australia. While waiting to learn if her application was successful, she decided to stay at Elianne in order to provide some added comfort for her mother, and most particularly to be with her grandfather.

Bartholomew was dying. It was generally agreed that the shock of Neil's death had pushed him over the edge. That and the physical trip to and from town for the funeral, but in any event the past two months had seen a rapid decline. He was skeletal now, confined to his bed, even his favourite armchair in the corner by the window tantalisingly out of bounds.

Stan had employed a live-in nurse who specialised in palliative care to look after his father during the last weeks of the old man's life, but he took no personal interest himself, making the occasional token visit to Bartholomew's quarters with his wife simply in order to appease Hilda, who insisted it was proper. Stan didn't consider it proper at all. Why should one bother with the elderly and infirm when one had lost a healthy son in the prime of his life? Stan was functioning these days, but with difficulty. He spent a great deal of time at the Burnett Club, where the combination of men's sympathy and the downing of Scotch afforded some level of escape if not comfort.

Bartholomew was quite ready to die. In fact Bartholomew considered death long overdue. Seventy-nine this year, he thought, good heavens am I really that old? And over seven years since Mary went. It's certainly time I joined her.

They'd shifted his bed so that it faced the windows, affording him the view he'd so treasured from his armchair. He never tired of the sight. Unfolding before his eyes was the endless expanse of cane that had been his life. He was looking at the past, the present and the future all in one.

Bartholomew loved the timelessness of sugar cane. Over the years he'd seen many changes with the introduction of mechanisation and new methods of production and there would no doubt be many more, but the cane itself remained constant, re-generating itself with a hardy persistence he found admirable. Even after the normal four-year growth period when a field was ploughed and left briefly fallow, it was not long before the freshly-planted cane emerged to grow tall and strong, starting the process all over again. The cycle of life itself, Bartholomew thought contentedly. Cane was so reliable, so predictable, a most satisfying crop.

Kate sat with her grandfather most afternoons. Very often he was sleeping and she would sit holding his hand, staring out at the beauty of the view, and when he awoke, he would smile and squeeze her hand gently with the little strength he had left. Sometimes she would chatter about inconsequential things and he would nod, appearing interested in her every word. And other times they would sit in silence, sharing the panorama of the cane fields.

The experience for Kate was never in the least upsetting. Her grandfather was at peace. He made no complaint and appeared to be suffering no undue pain, except when the nurse moved him, rather brutally at times, in order to correct his posture in the bed and straighten his spine. He winced then, Kate noticed. It's probably murder when she bathes him and changes his pyjamas and rolls him around to put fresh linen on the bed. Poor Grandpa, she thought.

When she'd offered her assistance, however, the nurse had politely but brusquely refused.

'Thank you, Miss Durham, but this is what your father pays me to do, this is my job –'

'I just thought that perhaps with the two of us –'

'No, no, it's better this way, believe me.' Norma Pendlebury was a professional to her fingertips. Family members had a habit of interfering with her routine and she needed no assistance from amateurs, however well meaning.

Kate could only presume that Nurse Pendlebury, highly qualified as she was, must be right, but she was a difficult woman to warm to, big and bossy and seemingly insensitive. All of which no doubt comes with the territory, Kate thought.

Then, early one Saturday afternoon, the most remarkable thing happened.

Kate was sitting in the bedside chair looking out at the view and holding Bartholomew's hand as he slept. She was feeling rather sleepy herself. The sun through the open shutters and the gentle stirring of air from the ceiling fan formed a soporific combination and she was close to dozing off when all of a sudden she could swear she heard her grandfather's voice. At first she couldn't believe it. She'd not heard her grandfather speak for years, no one had, and she turned to stare down at him, presuming her imagination was playing tricks that surely the voice belonged only in her mind. But no, although his eyes remained closed his lips were moving. He's talking in his sleep, she thought. Leaning close, she tried to make out the words, but there seemed to be none: the sounds were unintelligible, no more than a gentle murmur.

She stayed watching and listening intently, holding his hand, hardly daring to breathe. The murmurs became intermittent, stopping and then starting again as if he was having some sort of conversation, and Kate strained to discern any meaning in what he was saying. Then finally on the gentle exhalation of his breath, she heard the words, quiet, barely audible, but to Kate, listening with such care as she was, quite distinct. 'Not long now,' he said in little more than a whisper, 'not long.'

He went quiet after that and minutes later the nurse bustled in with his medication. She was about to wake him, but Kate stopped her.

'Nurse Pendlebury ...' Gently releasing Bartholomew's hand, careful not to disturb him, Kate rose to her feet. 'He spoke,' she said. 'My grandfather spoke.'

'Oh yes,' Norma Pendlebury replied, 'he speaks quite a lot in his sleep, just gobbledy-gook, no sense to it –'

'But he hasn't spoken for years, not since the stroke he suffered after my grandmother's death.'

'Of course, Miss Durham, I'm fully aware of your grandfather's medical history,' the nurse replied pleasantly enough, but in her usual brisk manner. 'Who can tell what the brain does in these final days, the strangest things happen, believe me they do. But I wouldn't read too much into it if I were you, they're just sounds he's making, no more than that.'

Oh no, you're wrong, Kate thought, you're very, very wrong, they're not sounds at all, he's speaking. She did not correct Nurse Pendlebury, however. Instead she stepped to one side and watched as Bartholomew was awoken and propped up higher in the bed in order to be fed his medication, which had been ground up and mixed with water for ease of swallowing.

'There we are, Mr Durham.' Nurse Pendlebury handed him the glass of fruit juice she always brought to wash away any after-taste. 'Now I'll leave you two to yourselves,' she said checking her watch, 'and I'll be back with your afternoon tea in three quarters of an hour.'

Bartholomew nodded his thanks, he was always most courteous to Nurse Pendlebury, and he smiled up at Kate, pleased to see her. He had no idea she'd been sitting holding his hand for the past forty minutes.

Kate waited until the nurse had left and the bedroom door was closed before once again sitting beside her grandfather. Bartholomew handed her the glass automatically; he didn't want the fruit juice, he never did, but fruit juice following medication was part of Nurse Pendlebury's routine. Kate placed the glass on the bedside table and took his hand.

'Grandpa,' she said. 'You spoke.'

His expression was one of bemusement, as if to say did I? Did I really?

'You were talking in your sleep. Nurse Pendlebury says you do it quite often.' As his eyes darted to the door Kate thought she detected a tiny flicker of alarm. 'She thinks you're not really talking at all, she thinks it's only sounds you're making.' The flicker of alarm had gone now, Kate noted. 'But we know better, don't we Grandpa. You *can* talk, can't you.' She looked into his eyes, making it very evident that she was not asking a question at all, that she already knew the answer. 'I'm right, aren't I?'

The reply came after several seconds, as if Bartholomew had given the matter a little thought. 'Yes, Kate,' he said, slowly and with care. 'You are right. I can talk.'

In throwing down the challenge Kate had expected some form of response certainly, but she found herself nonetheless taken aback. His voice, although weakened by his condition, was just as she remembered, a gentle voice, a kind voice, like the man himself. She was moved, but fought against showing it.

'I would have thought, after all these years, you'd have been a bit out of practice, Grandpa,' she said with an element of accusation. 'How long have you been able to speak without letting any of us know?'

'I'm not quite sure, to be honest. After Mary went, I had no desire to speak and I think for some time I forgot how. Then one day, or rather one night I recall, I started talking to her out loud and I've been doing so ever since. She's always nearby. I can feel her presence.'

'Why didn't you talk to any of us?'

'I had nothing to say.'

'Even to me?'

'You and I never needed words, my dear.' Bartholomew gave her hand the lightest squeeze and as he turned away to gaze out at the cane fields Kate felt a rush of guilt for having intruded upon his silent world.

'I'm sorry, Grandpa. I won't tell anyone your secret, I promise. I'm truly sorry.'

'Why?' He turned back to her. 'Why are you sorry?'

'I had no right to confront you the way I did. If you don't wish to speak that's your business, I should never have –'

'Ah but now you have discovered my duplicity, Kate, I should like to speak. Just to you, no one else. There are messages you can pass on for me when I'm gone, my dear. Letter-writing is so wearying. I can no longer hold the pen.'

'Anything Grandpa, tell me anything. I'll be a willing messenger, I promise.'

'Tell Julia she is all I could have wished for in a daughter. I know she reproaches herself for not visiting me more often, but she mustn't. She has a family and responsibilities of her own. Tell her I love her very much.'

'I will.'

'And your father. Tell your father how deeply I feel for him on the loss of his son.' Bartholomew looked down at their hands resting entwined on the bed, the flawless fingers of a young woman clasped in the wizened claw of an old man. 'Had I chosen to speak, Kate, I could never have found the right words to express my sadness about Neil.'

'No,' Kate too gazed down at their hands, finding the sight beautiful, just as she was finding the sound of her grandfather's voice beautiful, 'no, I don't think any of us could.'

'I've gathered from the odd exchange between your father and mother when they've visited me that Stan is very bitter. I've gathered also that he would have preferred to have lost Alan than Neil.'

Meeting her grandfather's eyes, Kate was amazed by the perceptiveness she saw there, and by the matter-of-fact tone of his voice, weak as it was.

'That too is sad,' Bartholomew said, 'and destructive, in some ways more so for Stan than for Alan. Alan has always been strong.'

'Yes, he has.' Kate, riveted, waited for him to go on, but he didn't. He simply looked away once again to gaze out the window and she presumed he was tired and that the time for talking had passed.

Bartholomew was tired, but the time for talking had not passed. 'I was strong too, Kate,' he said after a full minute or so. 'I was strong like Alan, only Big Jim didn't know it, just as Stan doesn't recognise Alan's strength.'

Kate remained breathlessly still, realising that as he looked out at the cane fields Bartholomew was re-living the past.

'When my brothers were killed at Gallipoli, Big Jim made it quite clear that I should have been the one to die. Grief is such an illogical emotion I believe he even in some way held me responsible for their deaths.'

'Yes,' Kate said with deliberation, 'I know.'

'You know?' Bartholomew turned to her, puzzled. 'How could you possibly know, my dear?'

'I've read Ellie's diaries.' Kate had decided in that instant that the time was right. She would seize this opportunity and test her grandfather's knowledge. Just how much had Ellie shared with her son?

She told him about her discovery of the ledgers. 'Ellie wrote very intimately of her family,' Kate explained, 'and with complete candour, I might add, she held nothing back.'

'Really?' Bartholomew found Kate's own intimacy charming, that she should refer to the great-grandmother, whom she had known only briefly as a very old woman when she herself was a very young child, as 'Ellie', the way she would a contemporary or a friend. The diaries had clearly had a strong effect upon her. 'I am surprised that my mother should so risk retribution at the hands of Big Jim. He would not like to be written of intimately, and he could be a very harsh man.'

'She wrote in French,' Kate said.

Bartholomew heard himself laugh, no more than a throaty chuckle that threatened to become a cough, but how long had it been since he'd laughed, he wondered. 'How very like Mother,' he said, 'she was so clever.'

'She felt it was you who suffered at the hands of Big Jim, Grandpa. She thought your father was cruel to you.'

'He was, indeed he was, but he had his reasons. He saw me as the runt of the litter, and he was quite right. I never had the strength or the stamina of my brothers, certainly not as a child.'

'It must have been very hurtful. Surely you must have grown up hating your father for so openly displaying his favouritism?'

'No, Kate, not at all. Big Jim's bias towards my brothers only provided me with an even greater love from my mother. I was the lucky one.'

'So you were her favourite.'

Bartholomew shook his head. He was tired. He'd forgotten how exhausting talking could be. 'No, I don't think so, she was just being protective. But it was her love most certainly that made me strong.' Reflecting upon his mother, he smiled fondly. 'She was a person of great strength herself. My father would not have survived the deaths of his sons without my mother's love, Kate, and yet she had love to spare also for me. Ellie had love for us all. She was the true strength of the Durham family.'

You're right, Kate thought, Ellie was indeed the strength of the Durham family. But you don't know the truth, Grandpa. You know only the lies Ellie wished you to believe, the lies she invented for your own protection.

'I've exhausted you, haven't I?' she said.

'Yes,' he replied, closing his eyes and giving her hand another light squeeze, 'but in the nicest of ways. Do wake me, my dear, when the tea gets here.'

Bartholomew died five days later and another family funeral took place at Christ Church the following week. Alan drove up from Brisbane and Julia flew out from Canada.

'Why didn't you let me know?' Julia demanded of her brother when she learnt that their father had been lingering on the brink of death for some time.

'Dad wouldn't let me,' Stan barked back, annoyed. 'He wrote a note saying under no circumstances were you to be informed. He didn't want you leaving your family to rush to his bedside. Christ alive, I told him you'd come home for the funeral anyway so what difference would it make, but he refused to listen. You know what a stubborn bastard he could be when he felt like it.'

There was a large and impressive turnout at the funeral, members of Bundaberg's oldest families, the business elite, and representatives from every area of the local sugar industry. The attendance was not only a tribute to the social standing of the Durham family, but a personal testament to the respect accorded Bartholomew over the years.

At the wake which followed, again upon Hilda's insistence, Kate gave Julia her father's message.

'He said that you were all he could have wished for in a daughter, Julia. Those were his exact words.'

Her aunt made no attempt to mask her tears. 'The wily old bugger,' she said, 'he could speak. He could actually speak.'

'Yes, and he said to tell you he loved you very much.'

'Oh damn,' delving in her handbag, Julia came up with a handful of tissues, 'there goes the mascara.'

Alan had arrived home, his car packed with his belongings and the day after the funeral he announced he was not returning to Brisbane.

'I've chucked in my apprenticeship at Evans Deakin and I've chucked in the Diploma course,' he said over breakfast, 'I'm back to stay.'

Kate and Hilda both glanced at Stan, waiting for the fireworks they presumed would follow, but after a long and suspenseful pause, his reaction came as a total surprise.

'Good for you, son,' he said a little stiffly, 'you're doing the right thing. I'm proud of you.' Stan the Man appeared uncharacteristically at a loss for words, but in truth he was having trouble expressing himself without betraying emotion. Alan was coming home to assume his brother's responsibilities and take up the position that was now rightfully his. Bugger the apprenticeship indeed, Stan thought, and bugger the Diploma, the boy was doing his duty. This was just as things should be.

He cleared his throat. 'I was a little hurtful last time you were home, Alan,' he said awkwardly, 'grief makes a man say things he shouldn't ...'

Good God, Alan thought, don't tell me the old man's actually apologising!

That, however, was as close to an apology as Stan was prepared to go. 'But we can put any unpleasantness behind us now, son,' he continued. 'You and I will make a good team. Elianne will be in safe hands with us at the helm ...'

Oh no, he's making a speech. Alan's mind went into overdrive. He thinks I'm going to replace Neil as heir to the throne. Oh no, Dad, no, you've got hold of the wrong end of the stick altogether.

'Actually I won't be going into management, Dad.' He dived in quickly, trying to sound casual, but knowing he had to set things straight right from the start. 'I aim to open up an engineering workshop in Bundaberg.'

Stan stared uncomprehendingly at his son. What on earth was the boy talking about?

'I have tremendous plans,' Alan went on enthusiastically, 'and I'll be much more use to Elianne this way, I can promise you. You don't need me to manage the place, that's not what I'm good at and the Krantzes handle the business side of things anyway. Honestly, Dad, with the plans I have Elianne can become the most efficient, productive, cost-effective mill in the region.'

'The breakfast table is hardly an appropriate place to discuss business,' Stan said coldly, and he stood. 'I suggest we adjourn to my study.'

'But your eggs, Stanley,' Hilda protested, 'you've hardly touched your eggs.'

Her husband made no reply, however, marching off without a word, and as Alan followed he shrugged an apology to his mother.

Once in his study, Stan settled himself behind the large mahogany desk he'd had specially imported twenty years previously and demanded a full explanation of his son.

'So,' he said, 'tell me about these grandiose plans that are of such proportion you would relinquish your duty and your status as manager of Elianne.'

Sitting in the hardback chair feeling as if he was at a job interview, Alan ignored his father's sarcasm. 'I aim to concentrate on chopper harvesters, Dad,' he said. 'As we both know they've been around for a few years, but they've yet to replace whole-stalk harvesters in this region.

They need to be adapted to the local conditions and this requires quite a deal of expertise ...'

Stan said nothing. He wasn't particularly interested, recalling that the original disadvantage of chopper harvesters as opposed to the whole-stalk design had been the deterioration of the cane caused by bacterial infection through the cut ends of the billets. The problem had eventually been rectified by controlling the length of the cane to produce longer billets, and also by ensuring speedier delivery to the mill, but Stan had nonetheless avoided the change to chopper harvesters. They seemed to spell trouble.

Alan presumed from the silence that his father was waiting for him to go on, and he did so eagerly. He'd spent every spare moment at his disposal over the past two years researching and studying the revolutionary chopper harvester design.

'There's no denying the chopper will change the industry and radically increase production as it already has in the north,' he continued, 'but it's a far more complex piece of machinery than the whole-stick harvester. It requires a great deal more adaptation to suit our local conditions. The Bundaberg mills and cane growers want the chopper, Dad, but it has to be modified and streamlined to work efficiently –'

'And that's where you and your engineering workshop come in, I take it,' Stan finally interrupted. He didn't like being lectured about the business he knew so well, although he had to admit he was a little in the dark when it came to chopper harvesters.

'Yes, that's exactly where I come in. I've already bought several second-hand lathes, they're being delivered next week, and I've lined up an ideal workshop location in East Bundaberg on the corner of Quay and Kendall Streets.'

Alan, normally so attuned, and indeed accustomed, to his father's displeasure, didn't notice the tell-tale signs as he carried on earnestly.

'So you see, Dad, I'll be able to make modifications for Elianne. You get the choppers and I'll adapt them. You can be one of my very first customers. We'll lead the market in a successful changeover from long-stalk to chopper harvester. What do you say?'

'I say, who the hell do you think will pay for all this? I presume you expect me to foot the bill? That's it, isn't it? I'm to fund your enterprise while you shirk your filial responsibilities.'

Alan finally registered his father's disapproval. But his father didn't understand. 'No, no Dad, that's not it at all,' he said hastily, 'I already have the finance. Enough to get myself set up anyway: I have investors.'

'Oh? And who exactly would these investors be?'

'A number of local cane growers who are keen to make the changeover,' Alan replied a little warily. He knew his father would be none too happy to discover who, but what the hell he thought, it was only a matter of time before word got around. 'The Fiorelli brothers actually.'

Stan's burgeoning anger turned to sheer outrage. 'You're abandoning your family and your duty in order to ally yourself with Luigi and his brothers!'

Oh God, here we go, Alan thought, the full histrionics, I should have seen it coming. 'Luigi doesn't even know, Dad,' he said patiently, 'the arrangement is strictly between the brothers and me. They'll have a share in the business when it takes off, and we all agree it's bound to, in fact Tofts have already expressed interest in the regular supply of sprockets and adaptations for various chopper designs –'

'You ungrateful young bastard, this is nothing short of betrayal!'

'No it's not. It's common sense. As I said before, I'll be of far greater use to Elianne with my own business than I would –'

'You'll be of no use to Elianne whatsoever,' Stan rose angrily to his feet, 'and don't think you're going to live here while all this is going on! Don't think for one minute you're going to live here!'

'I won't actually, Dad,' Alan said as if politely declining an invitation. 'There's a flat above the workshop, so it'll be easier if I stay in Bundy. Saving on travel time will give me more daily work hours.' He stood. 'Now if it's all right with you, I'll go back and finish my breakfast.'

Burning with impotent rage, Stan watched as his son walked out of the study, gently closing the door behind him. Alan's implacability had always managed to infuriate. The boy did it on purpose of course.

Kate's application for PhD scholarship funding proved successful. It was hardly surprising. A company like Vesteys was only too keen to acquire the services of a talented young honours graduate eager to specialise in livestock. She returned to Sydney in early April to take up a laboratory position conducting research for Vesteys, while embarking upon her PhD thesis at Sydney University.

'Welcome back.'

She'd rung Frank shortly after her arrival, and they'd arranged to meet in the park on Saturday. Saturday lunches in the park, dependent upon the weather, had become quite a fixture the previous year.

'How's everyone coping at home?' he asked sympathetically when they'd bought their ham and salad rolls and coffee and were settled on their usual bench. He hadn't seen or heard from her since her brother's death over four months earlier.

'So-so,' she said with a shrug, 'Mum's better than Dad, but ...' Another shrug.

'And how are you coping?' He was concerned. She looked tired and under some strain, which he supposed was understandable.

'I'm fine.' She took a healthy bite of her bread roll as if to prove she was, and Frank, assuming she didn't want to talk about the situation at home, changed the subject.

'Great about your PhD scholarship,' he said, she'd told him the news over the phone, 'you must be really pleased.'

She nodded a 'yes' with her mouth full of food and he started on his own ham and salad roll after which they lapsed into a companionable silence, chomping away together.

'What an irony,' he said after a while, 'that Vesteys should prove your champion. I mean you of all people.'

'Why me of all people?'

'Your commitment to the cause,' he said, taking a sip of his coffee, 'you and Vesteys are pretty strange bedfellows, you have to agree.'

'In what way?'

'Oh,' he could see she was puzzled, 'sorry, I presumed you knew.'

'Knew what?'

'About Vesteys and the Gurindji Strike ...' She looked at him blankly and he went on to explain. 'In 1966 two hundred Gurindji stockmen and house servants together with their families walked off the Wave Hill Cattle Station, one of Vesteys' properties in the Northern Territory. They settled at a sacred site near Wattie Creek not far away and they've been there ever since, over two and half years now. You haven't heard of this?'

'No,' she shook her head, 'no I haven't.'

'The strike was originally presumed to be about conditions,' he continued. 'Vesteys are notorious for denying their Aboriginal labour even the most basic of human rights, but the campaign is really far bigger than that. The Gurindji are after the return of their land, or at least part of it, and rightly so. Vesteys, like most of the big northern pastoralists, have deprived the local people of their hunting grounds and traditional way of life, leaving them no alternative but to accept work on the cattle stations, where they serve as cheap labour. The Gurindji have a particularly strong case in this instance. They petitioned the

Governor General in 1967 and their claim was rejected, but they don't intend to give up. And nor should they.'

'How terrible,' Kate said. She felt shockingly guilty. 'I'm appalled that I didn't know about all this.'

'Don't be. Most of Australia doesn't. Besides, your work's been based principally here. The Northern Territory's a long way away.'

'That's no excuse, I should have known. And I certainly can't accept funding from Vesteys now that I do.'

'You most certainly can,' he said emphatically, 'in fact that's exactly what you must do.' She was about to protest, but he continued. 'For goodness' sake Kate, take their money and put it to good purpose. Get everything you can out of Vesteys – you'd be mad not to.'

She looked so troubled that it was Frank's turn to feel guilty. 'Kate, please,' he insisted, 'if I'd known this was going to upset you I wouldn't have said anything. I presumed that you knew, and I was only making conversation to take your mind off your worries anyway. Refusing funding from Vesteys would have no impact on the situation whatsoever. Please, please, don't make any foolish decisions that could jeopardise your future. If you do, I'll end up suffering guilt for the rest of my life.'

She gave a wan smile. 'Well, we wouldn't want that, would we?'

'You promise me?'

'I promise,' she nodded, 'principles out the window as of now.'

Frank thought how forlorn she looked, how insecure and vulnerable, quite unlike the Kate Durham he knew, always so forthright and strong. He wanted to protect her, to gather her in his arms and kiss her and tell her that everything would be all right.

'Do you need to talk, Kate?' he said instead. 'Do you need a shoulder?'

'Nope.' She took a swig of her coffee, which was by now cold and decidedly unpleasant. 'No, really, I'm fine.' How could she tell him about the emptiness of Christmas at Elianne without Neil? How could she tell him about her mother's cupboard drinking and her father's hideous moods and her younger brother, who'd been banished from the family home? Things were getting to Kate, but they were not things she could talk about.

'Have you seen *Planet of the Apes*?' he asked.

The non sequitur surprised her. 'No,' she said.

'Good, neither have I. Let's go tonight. It's on at the State,' he added, knowing that he was offering an added incentive. Of all the cinemas in Sydney the gloriously ornate State Theatre was Kate's favourite.

'All right.'

They sat in the first row of the dress circle, eating chocolate-coated ice creams and loving every minute of the Hollywood epic.

'Now that's what I call a movie,' Frank said as they walked through the main atrium and out into the street. 'You've got to admit, the Yanks know how to make them.'

They strolled to the car, which was parked half a block away. 'We're off to the Cross now,' he said, 'we're going to have supper at the B & B – all right by you?'

'Sure, sounds fine.' Kate allowed herself to be swept along by his plans, aware Frank was going out of his way to distract her from her worries. And it was working.

'You seem a lot happier,' he said as they sat by the windows at the Bourbon and Beefsteak, sipping wine and gazing out at the throngs revelling in the heady nightlife of Kings Cross on a Saturday.

'Well I must admit I found it rather difficult to stay dismal,' she said, 'eating a chocolate ice cream and watching *Planet of the Apes*.' She smiled gratefully and raised her glass to him. 'Thank you, Frank.'

'My pleasure.'

After supper he drove her home.

'Do you want to come in for a coffee?' she asked when he walked her to the front door.

'No thanks.' He would love to have come in for a coffee, but he wasn't sure what it might lead to; he had a feeling it could be dangerous. 'Think I'll call it a night.'

'Right you are. Thanks again, Frank, I had a lovely evening and I really am grateful.' He was a tall man and Kate, although not short herself, was forced to stand on tiptoe in order to kiss his cheek. 'You're a very good friend,' she said.

It would have been impossible for him not to kiss her. As their lips met he guarded against any overt show of passion, but the desire was there – they both knew it – along with the tenderness.

'I'm sorry,' he said as they parted. 'I'm really sorry. That shouldn't have happened.'

'Yes, it should.' She smiled reassuringly. 'Don't be scared, Frank – *I'm* not. Good night.'

Chapter sixteen

Alan had opened his workshop in mid-April and by the start of the crushing season barely two months later word had spread that this young man knew his business. Now six months down the track the enterprise was proving an unmitigated success, particularly as Toft Brothers had become a regular client. Alan supplied spare parts and adaptations as required to Tofts, specialising in steel sprockets made to order for cane harvesters.

His property in East Bundaberg appeared a bit of a shambles at first sight. It sat just across the Kennedy Bridge, which forded a small tributary of the Burnett River, and constituted a rather messy front yard, always littered with machinery, beyond which was an extensive workshop with modest living quarters above. The sign on the wire gates of the yard said in letters big and bold, *DURHAM ENGINEERING* and beneath in smaller letters *Mechanical Harvesting Specialists*. Alan had opted for the plural in the belief that it sounded more impressive and in the hope that the business would burgeon, as indeed it had. With orders pouring in it wouldn't be long before he'd need to employ assistant fitters and turners, although for the moment he was enjoying working on his own.

Stan the Man detested the fact that his son had chosen to use the family name. How dare the boy so presume!

The sight aroused his anger whenever he was in town and drove past the place, but he never confronted Alan. He refused to speak to his son, even disappearing from the house on Sunday afternoons when Alan visited his mother.

'It's so surly and childish of him,' Hilda would complain as she and Alan sat in the small drawing room taking afternoon tea, 'but don't worry, dear, he'll get over it eventually.'

Alan would nod as if he agreed, but he did not share his mother's confidence.

Hilda had developed a strength of late, which had come about through the only true confrontation she had had with her husband during their twenty-six years of married life.

'I have lost one son, Stanley,' she had said defiantly when he'd tried to forbid Alan's visits to Elianne, 'I am not prepared to lose another. If you attempt to force this separation upon me I will leave you.' Her boldness had shocked them both, particularly Hilda, and from that day on their relationship had undergone a subtle but distinct change. Stan had realised that, despite the fact he'd taken his wife for granted throughout their entire marriage, he did not dare lose her. And Hilda, in recognising her husband's fear, had become empowered, just a little, sometimes even enough to risk annoying him.

'Barbara told me at the bridge club the other day that Alan's business is doing remarkably well,' she said one morning. 'You should be proud of him, Stanley.'

'Don't push me, woman,' he growled before stomping away to his study. Stan was sick of being told he should be proud of his son. He'd heard the same thing again just the night before at the Burnett Club.

'You must be proud of young Alan, Stan,' Garnet Buss had said as they'd shared a couple of rounds at the bar. 'What a clever young businessman he's turned out to be.'

Everyone offered the same hearty congratulations, Rob Black, Stewart Pettigrew, Carl Nielson and those others of

Bundy's elite business set who met at the Burnett Club. 'I'll bet you're proud of your boy, Stan,' they'd say. He knew why, of course. They'd commiserated with him over Neil for months, every one of them, and they were now trying to give him a boost. Well, it didn't work. Alan's success was no compensation for the loss of Neil. Alan's success and above all his use of the Durham name for his business venture was a mockery to Neil's memory.

Nearly one year after the death of his eldest son, Stan was still blinded by grief, his pain as raw as ever.

Despite working long hours, often from dawn until dusk, Alan led an active social life. He didn't frequent the Burnett Club, respecting it as his father's domain and wishing to avoid any possible unpleasantness, but the Burnett Club was hardly necessary in any event. The younger male set with whom he mingled, sons of prominent businessmen for the most part, were members of Apex.

Apex was a club for young men aged eighteen to forty, its principal function being to raise funds for charity and perform good works for the community and the disadvantaged, none of which prevented its members from having a good time. They would meet once a fortnight in the upstairs dining room at Lewis Brothers Palais where, while discussing the club's latest project, they would demolish enormous steaks. As no alcohol was permitted at an Apex meeting, they would liquor up beforehand at the Commercial Hotel, then after the meeting and the steaks they'd adjourn to 'The Met' just up the road, where they'd scoff back more beers. The Apex boys knew how to enjoy themselves.

The highlight of Alan's social existence, however, was Saturday night, which was always reserved exclusively for Paola. He saw her regularly during the week, in fact nearly every day. She worked as a filing clerk in the office of Wyper Brothers main emporium in Bourbong Street and during her one-hour lunch break she'd bring sandwiches to his workshop. She'd make them a pot of tea in the upstairs kitchen and sit chattering away happily while she watched him work – he never took more than a fifteen-minute break himself – and they would discuss what they'd do the following Saturday. Saturday nights were precious to them both. Occasionally they'd go out for an early dinner and then on to the pictures, but as a rule they preferred to go dancing, sometimes as far afield as the Bargara Surf Club, although more often than not it would be the Lewis Brothers Palais, which was closer to home.

The Lewis Brothers Palais was above Harry Lewis's Milk Bar in Bourbong Street. A set of stairs led up from the milk bar, at the top of which to the left was the dining room, famous for its steaks, where the Apex Club met each fortnight, and to the right was the Palais, which came alive every Saturday.

A circular bandstand sat in the centre of the dance floor, a local band pumping out old favourites and popular songs of the day while dancers whirled all about them, graceful or frenzied dependent upon the choice of music. Doors led to a balcony overlooking the street where exhausted couples could take a breather now and then before returning to the fray. The Lewis Brothers Palais was a buzzy place for Bundy's younger set on a Saturday night.

After the dance, Alan would drive Paola home to Elianne and they'd share a final good-night kiss outside the Fiorellis' cottage, Alan fighting to control his own passion and also hers, which threatened to further enflame him. Then he would return to town and his little flat in East Bundaberg.

At first it had seemed strange not to stay at The Big House, odd indeed to feel like a visitor on the property that had been his childhood home. But he'd quickly grown to enjoy his independence. He loved the poky little flat above the workshop and the fact that the life he led was one totally of his own choosing, unaffected by the dictates of his father. It was a strangely double life too: only Paola knew the true contradictory nature of his existence. His friends from the Apex Club, Anglicans to a man, had no idea of his secret and the members of his family were most certainly unaware.

Alan had embarked upon his conversion some months previously and was shortly to be accepted into the Catholic Church. He'd attended the requisite series of initiation classes with the priest at the Holy Rosary Catholic Church, he'd read his bible and catechism as instructed and had even attended Sunday-morning Mass on a number of occasions, although he'd been required to leave before Holy Communion as he couldn't receive the Eucharist until he'd been officially welcomed into the fold.

During the Mass he would sit alongside the Fiorelli clan, of which he was already considered a member. The families would drive into town and meet up outside the huge towering white stone edifice on the corner of Woongarra and Barolin Streets, its grand entrance marked by six stately Greek columns; and when they had all congregated, the brothers, their wives and their children would march into church together, the sheer force of their numbers a statement of their faith. Sunday Mass was of great importance to the Fiorellis.

Alan often wondered, as they milled about outside the church in clear view of those gathering at Christ Church just down the road, whether one or more of his friends from Apex might spy him in the crowd. He wondered also whether reports had got back to his family. The idea did not in the least bother him for his family and friends were all destined to know at some stage, but he kept awaiting comment from one quarter or another. As yet, however, there had been none. Perhaps people don't see what they don't expect to see, he thought. And with his dark hair he probably looked like one of the extended Fiorelli family anyway, a notion that he found immensely pleasing.

The conversion exercise itself had had little effect upon Alan. He remained a non-believer at heart, which made him feel something of a fraud, but the importance of the Fiorelli connection could not be underestimated. He loved Paola as deeply as it was possible to love and he also loved her family. If being accepted into the church and following its practises made him one of them, then so be it.

Paola knew her fiancé had not embraced the faith and from time to time she teased him about it. 'You're a terrible phoney, Alan,' she said.

'Yes,' he admitted, 'I am.'

'You don't have to do this, you know,' she added in all seriousness.

'I want to,' he said, 'I want to do everything that pleases your family. If they were Buddhists I'd become a monk.'

She laughed. 'That'd make our marriage interesting,' she said. Then she gave a mock frown. 'You'd better watch the blasphemy though: you're about to face baptism and Communion, which is a pretty daunting prospect.' Paola's teasing was nothing more than a cover. She couldn't find the right words to express how touched she was that he should go to such lengths for her and her family.

'I'll manage,' he replied with an easy shrug. 'And just think, by the time we get married I'll have been a good practising Catholic for a whole year. That'll impress your dad no end.'

'Yes,' she replied a little distractedly, 'it will.'

Paola was shortly to turn twenty and they planned to marry the following year after her twenty-first birthday. But Paola didn't want to wait another whole twelve months. In fact Paola wasn't sure if she could. Already she was wondering how she might go about changing the course of events. No one was receptive to her suggestions that perhaps they could speed up the process. Everyone including Alan himself seemed prepared to wait until she was twenty-one. 'I promised your father,' Alan would say, albeit reluctantly, and she would spend hours lying in her sleepless bed staring into the black hole of night, pondering a course of action. She must be bold, she knew that much.

She decided to carry out her plan on the Saturday following his baptism and Communion, which marked his official acceptance into the Catholic Church. The timing seemed right, although she wasn't quite sure why.

'Let's go to Bargara this Saturday afternoon,' she said lingering over the second half of her curried egg sandwich (he'd already scoffed his down and was back at his workbench). 'I could make us up a picnic lunch.'

'Sure, if that's what you'd like – sounds good to me.'

'Don't come and collect me though,' she said, 'I'll get the bus into town. It'll save time.' Paola had Saturdays off, but Alan always worked through until at least midday.

'Rightio, but don't bother packing picnic stuff, we'll grab some fish and chips, easier that way.'

She arrived carrying a shoulder bag stuffed with swimming togs, hat, beach towel, after-swim robe and a miscellany of other items that from the size of the bag appeared quite unnecessary.

'Crikey, you've come prepared,' he said. Alan had his togs on under his shorts and a towel slung over his shoulder.

'It's the girl scout in me.' She gave a disarming grin. 'Well, no,' she admitted, 'it's probably just the girl.'

The weather was glorious, November but not yet scorching, and they drove with the windows down as usual, the wind whipping at Paola's hair until with her customary deftness she tied it up in a knot.

Once at Bargara they headed directly for The Basin, where they cooled off among the families and young children wallowing in the shallows.

'Let's go to the surf beach,' she suggested as they lay side by side on the sand soaking up the sun.

'Why?'

'So you can catch some waves of course – this is far too tame for you. I'm happy to watch.'

'Nah, can't be bothered.' Propping on an elbow he leant down and kissed her. 'Besides I don't want to let you out of my sight.' It was true, he didn't. She looked glorious in the bright red one-piece costume that set off the silky-olive of her skin and the raven-black of her hair. 'Anyway I'm starving,' he jumped to his feet, 'come on,' he said, offering her his hand, 'fish and chips time.'

They bought their fish and chips wrapped up in newspaper and drove to the surf club, where they sat on the grass and looked out at the beach. From somewhere nearby came the sound of a transistor radio. Frank Sinatra was building to the final crescendo of 'My Way'.

'This is where I fell in love with you,' she said matter-of-factly, blowing on a chip that, fresh from the vat was still blisteringly hot, 'right there.' She waved the chip at the vast expanse of beach. 'That very spot.'

Alan laughed at the incongruity. 'That very spot, eh?' he said wolfing down a steaming mouthful of fish.

'Absolutely, I swear it. I can still see the dent in the sand. You told me I looked like Natalie Wood, don't you remember?'

'Of course I remember.'

She bit into the chip. 'I was fifteen years old,' she said looking down at the engagement ring no longer kept hidden but living permanently on her finger, 'and I knew right then that I wanted to marry you.'

'Me too,' he said. 'I felt exactly the same way.'

They kissed, tasting the salt and the oil of each other's mouths. Nearby, the transistor radio was no longer playing Frank Sinatra but Stevie Wonder, who was singing, rather aptly 'My Cherie Amour'.

After demolishing the fish and chips, they sunbaked and had another swim, Alan catching a few waves while Paola dabbled near the shore, and then they drove back to the flat at East Bundaberg, where she made them a pot of tea.

'Do you mind if I have a shower before you take me home?' she said. 'I'm all sandy.'

'Of course I don't mind.' He fetched a fresh towel for her and sat in the kitchen finishing his tea.

'Oh my God,' he said when she reappeared to stand before him fifteen minutes later. He rose and stared at her in shock, mesmerised by the sight. She was wearing a knee-length cream-coloured nightdress, lace-trimmed and of the sheerest silk. With shoe-string shoulder-straps and a deep décolletage nothing was left to the imagination and, although the fabric was not altogether transparent, from the way it caressed her skin she was clearly naked beneath. He remained speechless, unable to do anything but drink in the sight of her.

'Do you like it?' she asked, but went on without waiting for an answer. 'It's a nightie, but the lady in the shop called it a *chemise* – it's French. I told her I was buying it for my trousseau and she said it was exactly the right thing for a bride on her wedding night.'

Paola was aware she was probably talking too much, but she didn't dare risk a pause that might appear like uncertainty. She was not asking a question, she was making a statement. 'It's time, Alan,' she said, 'I can't wait any longer,' and she crossed to him, arms outstretched, offering herself. He was powerless to resist.

As they made love on the little single bed with its threadbare mattress, Alan tried to be as gentle as possible and, surprisingly enough, despite his own mounting passion, it did not prove difficult. Looking into her eyes, watching the wonderment unfold, feeling the response of her body after the initial pain of penetration, he was lost in his love of her. And even more, he was lost in her love of him. The touch and texture of her body was as thrillingly sensual as he remembered a woman to be from his experience in

Brisbane, but this was not like the sex he'd had with the girl whose name was long forgotten. This was not sex he and Paola were sharing at all: this was something far greater. The willingness with which she gave herself to him and the responsibility with which he embraced her trust was a sharing of love, an exchange of vows.

'We really are married now,' she said as they lay naked, her head resting on his chest.

'Yes.' Alan refused to feel guilt, at this stage anyway. He knew that would come later, and he knew it would hit him hard, but for now he could live only in this moment. 'Yes, Paola, we're married.'

He was surprised when she told him she was staying the night.

'Of course I am,' she said with a laugh when he queried the fact. 'This is my wedding night. A bride doesn't go home on her wedding night.'

'No I mean how have you managed it? What will your parents say?'

'I told them I was going to a Wyper Brothers pre-Christmas staff picnic at Bargara,' she coolly explained. 'Wypers always have a staff party in November. And I told them one of my girlfriends at work suggested I stay overnight at her flat.'

'And they believed you?'

'Of course. I said I'd meet them in town for Mass tomorrow morning.' She smiled at his open incredulity. 'My church dress and scarf and shoes are in your wardrobe,' she said.

'You really did come prepared, didn't you?'

'Oh yes. I've had this planned for a fortnight.'

They ate Heinz baked beans on toast for dinner – as this was the bachelor meal of Alan's choice there was always a healthy supply of tins in the kitchen cupboard. Then they made love again. This time, free of any pain and discomfort, Paola's response was unrestrained. She was a sensual girl to whom sex came naturally.

They made love again in the morning, languidly, with no sense of urgency, luxuriating in each other's bodies. It was as if they'd been lovers for years.

'I like being married,' she said.

She made them toast and a pot of tea, but as she set breakfast out on the kitchen table before him, chattering away and glowing like a young wife serving her husband's first meal, guilt started to creep over Alan.

'We'll have to arrive at the church separately of course,' she said, oblivious to his concern as she poured the tea. 'How exciting that this morning's your first Communion service,' she beamed happily, 'that's why I planned things the way I did. We get married and you get accepted into the church all at the same time –'

'But we're not married, Paola.' She was halted abruptly by the sternness of his voice. 'We're not married and you know it. I've betrayed your father's trust. I gave him my word.'

For the first time she recognised his genuine worry. 'Everything will be all right,' she assured him, keen to allay his fears, 'Papa doesn't need to know. We'll just tell him we want to marry sooner. I'll tell him myself. I'll say, "Papa, I can't wait any longer, it's not fair you should ask me to." He'll understand, I promise ...'

Aware that he was not convinced, Paola went on to tell him a secret. 'I've heard my mother and father over the years, Alan,' she said. 'I admit these past few years I've listened. I've listened as hard as I could for the noises, wanting to know what it's like, imagining it's you and me. They think they make no sound, but they do, and the walls in our house are thin. I've heard them making love.' She smiled knowingly. 'Papa and Mamma will understand, truly they will.'

'Ah well,' he smiled in return, not wishing to worry her, but despite her worldly confidence he remained dubious, 'we'll see.'

Papa and Mamma will probably understand only too well, he thought. Luigi will anyway, I'll bet on it. The moment we ask permission to marry earlier than planned, Luigi will know I've betrayed his trust. And what of the other possibility, what if she's pregnant? That hasn't even been mentioned. We made love three times without protection.

As he sipped his tea Alan made a mental note that first thing tomorrow he must buy some condoms.

They arrived at the church separately to meet up with the family, kissing each other on the cheek in greeting as they always did, and upon entering the church they sat side by side in the pew as usual, although he was aware that she was snuggling up to him a little closer than normal.

When he rose to take his first Holy Communion, Alfonso and the brothers patted him on the back as he joined them in the queue, but kneeling before the priest, Alan was barely aware of receiving the Eucharist, by now he was so riddled with guilt.

Throughout the service he'd been unable to meet Luigi's eyes, which he knew were upon him and had been from the moment they'd entered the church. He felt wretched and now that he was taking Communion doubly so. Not only was he a liar who had broken an oath sworn to the man who'd saved his life, he was a fraud. How dare he pose as a Catholic, what right did he have to deceive these good people?

As young Alan Durham went through the motions, accepting the body and blood of Christ, he didn't know where to look or how to hide his shame.

Luigi and Maria had recognised the signs. Maria particularly had known in an instant and she'd nudged her husband, whispering in his ear. Alan's guilt had been readable from the outset, but Paola's boldness had been the true giveaway. Paola had met her parents' eyes with a defiance that was undeniable, an expression even of triumph. It was obvious to them both who had been the true seducer.

At the conclusion of the service, when the families filed out of the church and were heading for their respective vehicles, Paola accompanying her parents, Luigi waved Alan over.

'You will come back to the house?' He posed it as a question, but Alan rightfully took it as a command.

'Of course,' he agreed, and he followed them to Elianne in his Holden.

When they were gathered in the Fiorellis' kitchen, Georgio once again discreetly absent, Luigi, Paola and Alan sat at the large wooden table while Maria brewed the coffee.

Luigi solemnly addressed the young couple. 'There is something you wish to say to me?'

'There is, Papa.' Paola took it upon herself to answer, coming out with her prepared response. 'I don't want to wait a whole year before I marry,' she said rebelliously. 'It's not fair you should ask me to. Alan and I wish to marry as soon as possible.'

'Yes,' Luigi's reply was not directed to his daughter, but to his future son-in-law, 'I believe that you should.' His wife nodded agreement as she set the coffee pot on the table.

Alan couldn't believe things had been resolved so simply. It appeared Paola had been right: Luigi and Maria really did understand.

Stanley Durham, however, did not. How could such a situation have come about without his knowledge, he demanded when his wife informed him of the news. The world had gone quite mad.

'You've had your head in the sand, Stanley,' Hilda said with her newfound confidence, 'everyone knows Alan and Paola have been officially engaged for some time, and with her parents' approval.'

'I thought that nonsense had been long forgotten.'

'No, you just wished that it had.' Hilda's confidence occasionally bordered on courage.

'Is that right? Well how the hell are they going to get married when she's a bloody Mick?' Stan growled triumphantly, 'you tell me that!'

'Alan has converted to Catholicism, or so he has confided to me – rather difficult to believe, I know, but there we are.'

Stan, rendered speechless and already maddened by his wife's complacency, left the room.

He did not go to the wedding, which was held a month later, refusing to set foot in the Catholic Church. But Kate did. Kate flew up from Sydney. And she brought Frank Madigan with her.

'Would you mind an extra house guest for a few days, Marmee?' Her query over the phone had been deliberately casual. 'Frank's a good friend and I've told him so much about Elianne. I'd love him to see the place for himself.'

'Of course, darling,' Hilda had replied, 'any friend of yours is most welcome, as you well know. And Cook will be overjoyed. With Alan now living in town and your father at his club more often than not, she has no one to cater to these days.' Hilda had been most intrigued. 'I look forward very much to meeting your friend.' So Kate is bringing a young man home, she thought, surely that must mean something.

Kate had been far less circumspect when she'd telephoned Alan. 'Mind if I bring a friend to your wedding?' she'd asked.

'Someone special, I take it?'

'Yes. Someone very, very special.'

Kate and Frank were lovers and had been for six months. They both agreed that their affair had been a foregone conclusion ever since *Planet of the Apes* and their first kiss, although in Kate's personal opinion it had been eminently predictable for quite some time before that.

The affair itself may indeed have been predictable, but the strength of their love and the speed of its growth neither could possibly have anticipated. Very early on, when Frank had voiced his concern about their different backgrounds and the reaction their relationship would arouse in others, Kate had been instantly dismissive. She cared nothing for public opinion, she told him. And then she'd talked. She'd talked with a passion that to Frank was revelatory. She'd held nothing back. And after that, nor had he. The two had continued to share their most intimate secrets and innermost feelings, developing a trust and understanding both knew could weather any storm that might confront them.

Nevertheless, Frank was surprised by her suggestion he should come to Elianne.

'Really?' he said as they languished in bed one Sunday morning. Sometimes they spent the weekend at his Surry Hills terrace and sometimes at the little house in Campbell Street; today it was Surry Hills. 'Meet the parents?' He raised a deliberately comical eyebrow. 'Already?'

'Why not? I'd say you're going to have to face that ordeal at some stage, wouldn't you?'

'Yes.' He kissed her lightly. 'I would say so, most definitely.'

Marriage had not once been mentioned, nor as yet even contemplated by either, but there was a recognition their relationship was destined to last.

'Besides, I'd like you to see Elianne,' she said, 'and Alan's wedding is the perfect opportunity.' She added wryly, 'Even though Dad's boycotting the whole thing. Al told me he's refused to set foot in the church. He's locked himself away in a world of his own and won't even acknowledge that the wedding's happening. No one can get through to him. He really has turned into the most terrible ogre.'

Frank ran his fingers lazily over her right breast. 'If your father's so incensed by his son's marriage to an Italian what on earth will he have to say about us as a couple?'

'Nothing,' she replied, 'not yet anyway. As far as my parents are concerned you're just a good friend. Shall I get the coffee?' She was about to sit up, but he stopped her.

'Later,' he said, 'much later.'

She was only too willing to acquiesce. 'There'll be none of this at Elianne though,' she warned him regretfully. 'Dad'd blow a gasket if he found out we'd slept in the same room.'

'Then we'd better make the most of things while we can,' he murmured.

Frank proved an instant hit with Kate's parents, despite, or perhaps surprisingly because of the uncomfortable circumstances surrounding Alan's impending nuptials. The atmosphere that pervaded The Big House was certainly strange. Stanley Durham refused to mention his son's wedding, now only two days away, and he turned sullen if anyone else did, which meant that his wife also avoided the topic, although in fact she was most excited by the prospect. The arrival of a stranger in their midst brought about a whole new range of conversation that was eagerly embraced, particularly by Hilda, who loathed any form of social awkwardness.

'Kate tells me you have a plumbing business, Frank,' she said as Stan carved the roast lamb that Cook had delivered to the table and Ivy arrived with the platter of vegetables. How splendid, Hilda thought, to feel like a family again. 'She says it's in the very heart of Sydney and that it's highly successful.'

'The business is in the heart of Sydney, yes,' Frank said, 'but I can't take any credit for its success I'm afraid. That I owe to my father.'

'Who is Irish, I believe.' Stan passed a plate of lamb to his wife.

'That's right.'

'So you're a Catholic.'

Frank registered the hint of accusation in Stanley Durham's tone and at the same time felt Kate's eyes on him from across the table, but he did not return her gaze, choosing to answer the man directly instead.

'I must admit to being nothing in particular, Mr Durham,' he said. 'I align myself to no specific religion.'

The answer went down exceedingly well with Stan who, apart from a distinct aversion to the Roman Catholic faith, cared little for the church in any form. 'A man after my own heart,' he said passing a plate of sliced lamb to Frank, 'too much bloodshed and strife brought about by religion –'

'Do help yourself to vegetables, Frank,' Hilda said before the diatribe could begin. She pushed the platter his way and started serving herself from the bowl of roast potatoes. 'We don't stand on ceremony here, dear.'

The evening progressed very smoothly after that. Upon Hilda's enquiry they talked about the theatre and the concerts Frank and Kate had recently attended in Sydney, after which the two men discovered their mutual love of rugby union football and then the conversation turned to the obsession they shared, like most Australian males, with all forms of sport.

To Hilda, Frank Madigan presented a romantic figure with his black hair and piercingly grey-blue eyes. Such an intriguing-looking fellow, she thought, and impressively tall. I do hope Kate is in love with him, they make a handsome couple.

To Stan, Frank Madigan was a man's man. You'd never pick him for a Southerner, Stan thought, he's more like one of us. If this is Kate's choice then she's done very well for herself. An excellent match indeed.

The following day Kate took Frank on a long walk around the estate. Cobber plodded along behind, not attempting to match their pace, just hoping to keep them in sight, and on the occasions when they slowed down Ben rounded them up in his customary Cattle Dog fashion with a mock nip to the heels, but it was habit only. At nine years of age, Ben too was less active than he'd once been.

As they went, she gave him the full guided tour explaining the history of Elianne, but in a way she'd never done before, so much now relating to her personal knowledge of Ellie and Big Jim. She had told him all about the diaries and how they had so dramatically changed her life. Kate found it extraordinarily liberating to talk so freely of her family and the past.

They finished up at the mill, standing in its eerie stillness, the toffee smell clinging to the air, no sound from the giant machines but the metallic clink here and there of a maintenance mechanic's tools. Frank was in awe: he'd never seen a sugar mill.

'You should be here during the crushing season,' she told him.

She introduced him to Luigi, who was working alongside the several others.

'You come to my daughter's wedding tomorrow, is good,' Luigi said, shaking Frank's hand enthusiastically, pleased to meet Kate's new friend.

'Yes, I'm very much looking forward to it: thank you for inviting me, Mr Fiorelli –'

'Luigi, Luigi ...' The Italian turned to Kate, arms outstretched in a typically flamboyant gesture. 'Who call me Mr Fiorelli, eh? Who call me Mr Fiorelli?'

Frank grinned. 'Thank you, Luigi.'

'Yes, yes, you come, you come. After we have big party at my brother's home, much singing, much dancing, is big day tomorrow.' Luigi was excited beyond measure at the prospect of his daughter's wedding.

The next morning, Stanley Durham stood on the front verandah, watching the exodus. Look at them, he thought, all deserting me, the whole bloody household, and probably every staff member and worker as well. He had made no complaint about the fact, however, even allowing Max the use of his Mercedes. But he'd refused to acknowledge the occasion. They might just as well have been heading off for a picnic at Bargara. Stubborn to the end, Stan the Man was making a statement with his silence.

Max opened the passenger door for Hilda while his wife, Maude the cook, and young Ivy, both dressed in their Sunday best, piled into the back seat. Frank was driving one of the mill's Land Rovers, which he and Kate had collected from the garage the preceding day, and he climbed into the driver's side, leaving Kate to linger on the verandah as he knew she wished.

'You could still change your mind, Dad,' she whispered in her father's ear.

Stan ignored her. 'Have a pleasant time,' he called loudly for the benefit of all, and Kate gave up. She pecked him on the cheek. 'See you later,' she said and started down the steps.

Ben bounded ahead, presuming he was coming along for the ride. 'Stay,' she ordered, and the dog dropped, dejected but obedient. 'Where's Cobber?' The Labrador was nowhere to be seen. She looked up at her father. 'Where's Cobber?' she asked.

'No idea,' Stan said. 'Go on now.' He shooed the whole lot of them away with an annoyed wave of his hand as if they were insects. 'I'll find the dog, Kate, go on now, go on.' And he walked off into the house.

The church was crowded not only with family and friends of the bride: the groom's party too was well represented, for Stanley Durham was alone in boycotting the event. His friends did not shy from attending a Catholic wedding. A host of Elianne employees was there alongside the Krantzes and many business acquaintances of Stan's who now had dealings with his son. And the young Apex Club members were of course present in force, led by Alan's closest mate Charles Watford, who had accepted the role of best man.

'You sly bastard,' he'd remarked when Alan had asked him, 'you never said a bloody word. Why didn't you tell us?'

Alan had shrugged off the enquiry with his customary nonchalance. 'Didn't think it was necessary, Charlie.'

'You were scared we'd take the mickey out of you being a Mick, I'll bet that was it.'

'Yep, something like that.'

Following the wedding, the bride's party, beribboned limousine to the fore, led the troops to Alfonso's home where the reception was to be held al fresco in the rambling grounds surrounded by cane fields. The gathering was once again eclectic, but with a flavour purely Italian.

Volare oh oh
Cantare oh oh oh oh

Cousins Lucia and Gio were the featured vocalists of the so-called 'Fiorelli Family Band' but whenever a favourite song was played no one could stop the whole clan from joining in and, 'Volare' being a favourite, Gio's solo performance was rather lost in the sea of boisterous voices.

The huge backyard of Alfonso's house was festooned with white. The magnificent giant fig in the western corner was swathed in white streamers, Gio having climbed to the top to fling them about with gay abandon; white satin bows hung like unripened fruit alongside the lush orange spheres of the mango tree; the bushes and shrubs that lined the yard's perimeter were draped with satin ribbons, some artistically, some haphazardly, depending upon the personality of the family member who had draped them; and in pride of place on each of the white-clothed trestle tables set up to accommodate a hundred guests was a massive floral decoration of Christmas lilies. Alfonso had certainly succeeded in his determination to do his younger brother proud.

The Fiorelli family had agreed that, given Stanley Durham's antipathy to the marriage, it was advisable the reception be held at Alfonso's house rather than Luigi's, which was part of the Elianne estate, but the choice of venue had proved advantageous. Popular as Luigi's home was for family gatherings it could never have accommodated such numbers.

The band segued on to 'Ciao Ciao Bambina' at Alfonso's insistence, Domenico Modugno being a personal favourite. Lucia sang the lyrics in Connie Francis fashion, but she too was drowned out by the other clan members, 'Ciao Ciao Bambina' being another family favourite.

The five-piece band consisting of drum kit, bass and rhythm guitars, piano accordion and violin, was set up on the verandah. The Fiorelli cousins were not untalented and played regularly at family functions, Alfonso often joining in on his harmonica and his brother Enzo occasionally featuring on the mandolin. The five younger members were in particularly fine form on this most auspicious of occasions, having been diligently practising for weeks.

Paola and Alan were not joining in the family sing-along. They were on the dance floor that had been laid out on the grass beside the verandah, swaying gently in time to the music, oblivious to anything but each other, Paola the picture of bridal beauty in her classical lace wedding gown. Never had she been happier and never had Alan seen her more radiant. He'd been greatly relieved when she'd announced two weeks previously that she was not pregnant, although she'd boldly added that she wouldn't have cared in the least if she were.

'*Canzone Napolitana*,' Maria called out when 'Ciao Ciao Bambina' came to an end. She and the other wives were mingling about with trays of hors d'oeuvres prior to serving the main meal, while Luigi and Alfonso stood at the drinks table refilling glasses of beer and red wine.

Alfonso's wife Claudia took up the call. '*Si, si*,' she cried, '*Canzone Napolitana*.'

Young Georgio who was on the piano accordion obligingly struck up with 'O Sole Mio' and the other members of the band joined in. No Italian wedding was complete without a bracket of Neapolitan songs, certainly no Fiorelli wedding anyway.

Several songs later, after 'Santa Lucia', the band took a break, the wives and daughters disappearing into the house to fetch the food while several of the younger men cleared the floral arrangements from the tables.

Paola automatically joined the women as they set off for the kitchen, but her mother waved her away, telling her to mingle with her guests.

'A bride does not serve food,' she said.

Alan also mingled, finding himself at one stage chatting to Ivan Krantz, who was uncharacteristically open in expressing himself.

'Your father will come to his senses before long, Alan,' he said. 'Stan can't keep closing himself off the way he has since Neil's death. He needs you.'

Alan was surprised by Ivan's show of concern, although as usual he gave away very little himself. 'Maybe, maybe not,' he said, 'I personally doubt he needs me at all, but there's not much I can do about it anyway.'

'You can be there for him when he finds out he's no longer cock of the yard,' Ivan said, 'I've a feeling it might come as a bit of a shock.'

Alan found the remark jarring. He'd presumed the man's concern had been directed towards him, but he'd obviously been wrong: Ivan's show of sympathy had been intended for his old friend Stan Durham. His manner and choice of expression, however, seemed unnecessarily arrogant. Ivan Krantz has certainly changed over the past year or so, Alan thought.

'Sure, I'll be there for him,' he replied with a shrug that said why should I? If upon Ivan's advice Stan chooses to sign the estate away to investors, then let him, Alan thought. Elianne was Stan the Man's to do with as he wished. And if Stan the Man remained ignorant of the fact that he was losing control, then that too was his choice. Any warning he'd been offered had long gone unheeded – Stanley Durham had been living in the past for years.

'If my father ever decides to talk to me again, Ivan, I'll certainly be there for him,' he said, 'in the meantime ...' Another shrug sufficed and he wandered off to mingle elsewhere.

The women brought out the food – giant platters of meat, bowls of steaming pastas, salads and breads, wave upon wave – the guests were called to table and the feast began.

The speeches were as abundant as the food, and the wine also flowed freely. Bottles and dishes were unceremoniously handed around tables, fresh supplies fetched regularly by those members of the family elected to keep an eye on the proceedings and the afternoon grew progressively raucous.

Toast after toast was made from the bridal table, and following dessert when the speeches had finally run out and the meal was drawing to an end, the young band members leapt for the verandah to start up afresh, this time with a *tarantella*.

Alan and Paola were once again first on the dance floor, others quickly joining them and Luigi, prompted by a nudge from his wife, rose and offered his arm to the mother of the groom.

'You would like to dance, Mrs Durham?' he asked.

'Why thank you, Luigi.'

Hilda was having a splendid time. She would have preferred champagne to red wine herself and, unaccustomed as she was to the style of food served, she'd initially found it all a little rich. But as the day had worn on, she'd realised that everything seemed to go very well together and that the lack of table service at a function she'd assumed should have a formal tone didn't matter in the least, in fact it contributed to the freedom of the atmosphere. Even the raucousness, of which she'd been somewhat critical to start with, was a display of affection, she'd decided, and really quite uplifting.

'What a lovely reception, Luigi,' she said as they danced. Hilda had always loved to dance although it seemed such a long time since she'd last stepped on to a dance floor. The Italian was light on his feet, she noted, and led well: he was a good dancer.

'*Si si*,' Luigi happily agreed, 'much food, much music, Italian wedding is good.' He glanced at the newlyweds nearby and when he looked back at her his expression was serious. 'I am proud that my daughter she marry your son, Mrs Durham,' he said. 'Your son he is a good boy.'

'Yes, he is.' Hilda smiled. 'I am proud too that my son is marrying your daughter, Luigi. Paola is a fine young woman. And from now on as your daughter's mother-in-law I insist you call me Hilda.'

Luigi gave one of his irrepressible grins. 'Very good, Hilda.' He twirled her under his arm and passed her along to Alan. 'Now we swap – you dance with your son,' he said breaking up the couple and gathering his daughter in his arms.

It was mid-afternoon when the newlyweds left, Paola in her pretty, floral going-away dress waving out of the open car window as Alan drove off, the tin cans that Charlie and the Apex boys had tied to the Holden's rear bumper bar rattling away noisily. Alan laughed at the racket and gave Charlie a wave, but he would rid himself of the cans before reaching the main road for there was a five-hour drive ahead. Not that that in the least daunted him. Alan loved driving.

'See you at Christmas,' the Fiorelli cousins called after them.

Alan and Paola were off to the Gold Coast for a one-week honeymoon at the Surfers Paradise Hotel and would return several days before Christmas in time for the family festivities.

After the couple's departure, many of the older guests left, including Hilda, whom Max drove home to Elianne together with his wife Maude and young Ivy. Ivy was most reluctant to leave. She'd danced at least a half a dozen times with Gio Fiorelli and could have gone on all night, he was by far the best partner she'd ever danced with, and Ivy was an excellent dancer. He'd said he was going to the Palais on Saturday night, however, and had suggested they meet there, a proposition which Ivy had graciously deigned to consider, although in truth the prospect excited her no end.

Kate and Frank, who had also danced themselves into a state of near exhaustion, made their farewells towards the end of the afternoon. The numbers had by then halved, but the party was still in full swing, the younger set clearly intending to go on until all hours.

They arrived home at The Big House as dusk was falling to discover Stan the Man seated in one of the cane armchairs on the front verandah with Ben curled up asleep at his feet. Kate was most surprised to see her father apparently waiting for them, but she took it as a good omen.

'Hello, Dad,' she greeted him as she trotted up the stairs. Ben rose to meet her at the top, tail wagging, but in a rather subdued mood. 'We had a marvellous time –'

'Your dog's dead,' he said tersely.

'What?' She halted before him.

'Your dog's dead. I shot him.'

Halfway up the stairs behind her, Frank also halted. Is this some sort of sick joke? he wondered. Stanley Durham was a tyrant given to unreasonable behaviour, that much was plain, but the man surely hadn't shot his daughter's dog in some act of malice.

'You shot Cobber?'

'Yes.'

'Why?'

'Nothing else I could do.' Her father's shrug appeared careless. 'I looked for him as soon as you'd gone. He was down in the bushes outside the laundry, still alive but paralysed – had to be a snake.'

'Where is he now?'

'On the floor in the laundry,' Stan said. 'I knew you'd want to examine him.' As she turned to go, her father reached down and grasped Ben's collar in order to prevent the Heeler following her.

Kate glanced at Frank as she went back down the stairs and he accompanied her around to the rear of the house where the laundry was situated.

She turned on the lights and they stepped inside to where Cobber lay covered by a tarpaulin.

They both knelt and Frank watched as she lifted aside the tarpaulin and examined the body. The dog had been neatly shot through the brain.

She inspected the snakebite wound high on the right shoulder. 'An Eastern Brown, I'm sure of it,' she said. 'Browns can be aggressive and they hold their necks high when they strike.' She stroked the dog tenderly. 'Poor old Cobber,' she murmured, 'good old boy, I hope you didn't suffer too much. I'm glad Dad found you.'

Frank watched as she crooned to the animal who had been her companion since childhood days. 'Good old boy,' she said continuing to stroke him, 'good boy Cobber.' He could tell she was moved and waited for the tears, intending to comfort her when they came. But they didn't.

'Goodbye, old friend.' She gave the dog one final caress, replaced the tarpaulin and rose to her feet. 'Well, he had a fine innings,' she said as Frank rose to stand beside her. 'Thirteen years – you can't complain about that.'

'It's sad though,' he said, 'it's very sad.'

'Yes,' she agreed, 'it's sad.' Kate sensed he was expecting her to shed a tear, and she could have if she'd wished,

Cobber's death was indeed moving, but a rebellious voice inside was saying, We're tougher than that up here, mate, we're Queenslanders. 'At least I didn't have to shoot him myself,' she said, 'it's painful when you have to kill your own dog. At least Dad saved me that.'

'All right, I get the message,' Frank acceded with a smile, 'you're tough and I'm a city slicker.'

She gave a light laugh acknowledging the way he'd read her mind, but then they always seemed to know what the other was thinking. 'Exactly,' she said.

Kate did not know what Frank was thinking, however, when five minutes later they joined Stan on the front verandah, where he remained sitting in the gloom, his hand still resting on Ben's collar.

'Thanks, Dad.' Kate bent down and kissed her father on the cheek.

'Said your goodbyes?'

'Yes.'

'Right. I'll have a couple of the boys bury him in the morning.' Stan released his hold on the dog's collar and stood. 'Go to bed, Ben,' he ordered and the Heeler obediently set off down the stairs to the kennel around the side of the house, the kennel that would now seem so empty without his old friend.

'I'm going to my study,' Stan said, 'I've got work to do. Cook says she'll be serving up a light supper at nine.' He patted his daughter's arm. 'He was a good dog, Cobber.' Then he left the two of them alone on the front verandah.

Throughout the exchange, Frank had observed the closeness between father and daughter. They had not articulated their feelings to be sure, but there'd been no need. This martinet of a man who had alienated his whole family had waited the entire day to share his daughter's pain over the loss of her dog. And his daughter knew it. Surely that signifies something, Frank thought. The strength of their bond was strong, he could sense it, far stronger than Kate had led him to believe. And perhaps, he thought, stronger than even Kate herself knows.

After the boisterous festivities at Alfonso's the solemn air of The Big House was oppressive and everyone thankfully crept off for an early night after supper, during which no mention of the wedding had been made. The omission seemed bizarre to the entire household, both family and staff, but all continued to tread warily in Stan's presence.

Things were little better in the morning. Breakfast was a gloomy affair and as if to compound the misery Ben was fretful. He'd been sniffing at the laundry door all night and when the workers came to bury Cobber he followed them. His pining was painful to witness.

An hour or so later, Kate borrowed her father's Mercedes and drove Frank to the airport. He was flying back to Sydney that day while she stayed on at Elianne over Christmas and the New Year period as usual, although she would far rather have been returning with him.

'Pity about the gloom and doom,' she said, trying to sound light-hearted, although she found it a depressing state of affairs. 'Not much fun for you, I'm afraid.'

'No need to apologise, Kate,' he said, 'I feel very sorry for your family.'

'Yes, so do I.' She dropped the light-hearted tack, which obviously hadn't worked. 'Elianne used to be such a happy place, particularly for us kids. Our childhood was so carefree. Now Dad's bent on destroying everything we've shared. It seems if he can't be happy, then none of us can.'

'I believe you could change that, Kate.' Frank decided to speak his mind. 'In fact I believe you're the only person who could.' He was aware that he'd surprised her. 'Your mother can't,' he went on, 'and your brother obviously can't, but I believe that you'd be able to get through to your father. You share a bond that might be stronger than you know.'

'I hardly think so,' Kate scoffed, 'we're at war more often than not.'

'That's a bond of sorts, isn't it? Would you bother to pick an argument with someone you didn't respect? He respects and admires you, Kate, and he loves you very deeply – I sensed that last night. And you did too, didn't you?'

Kate nodded and fell silent and Frank did not pursue the subject. There was no further exchange until they arrived at the airport and pulled up in the car park.

'Don't come in to the terminal,' he said, 'we'll say goodbye here.' He kissed her as if they were making love and she responded in kind. 'I wouldn't be able to do that in there,' he added with a smile. 'God I'm going to miss you.'

'Me too,' she said quietly.

He thought how extraordinarily vulnerable she looked, and he kissed her again, very gently this time.

'How do I go about it?' she asked as they parted. 'What do I do, Frank? How do I get through to him?'

'The truth mightn't be a bad start,' he said. He could tell she was hanging on his every word, as if he might be able to supply the magic answer. 'I'm an outsider, Kate, and I've probably no right to offer an opinion, but sometimes an outsider's view can be valuable. There are so many secrets and lies in your family. You said that your father's locked himself away in a world of his own. Then shock him into the real world. Tell him the truth. Share the past with him.'

'I don't know if I can.' After all this time the prospect now seemed more daunting than ever. 'I wouldn't know how to begin.'

'Take your time ... don't rush things. You'll know when the moment's right, you'll sense it. But tell your father the truth, Kate, tell him everything.' He kissed her on the cheek. 'I'll see you in Sydney,' he said and he climbed out of the car and walked off towards the terminal.

He turned to wave before disappearing through the doors. 'Good luck,' he called.

Kate started up the engine and drove back to Elianne.

Chapter Seventeen

Perhaps it was Cobber's death, perhaps it was the fact that wedding fever had subsided, or perhaps it was simply Kate's presence in the old family home, but over the next several days Stanley Durham was less belligerent and the atmosphere in The Big House noticeably more relaxed.

'What a pity Frank couldn't stay on a little longer,' Hilda said over breakfast one morning, 'he could have spent Christmas with us. A guest would have added to the festivity.'

'Oh I think he would rather spend Christmas with his father, Marmee,' Kate said, 'they're very close.' It wasn't the first time Frank had featured in Hilda's conversation. She'd brought his name up on several occasions, either fishing for information or signalling her approval, Kate wasn't sure which, but the reference was never subtle.

'How nice,' Hilda said, 'Christmas should be shared with family. And with friends too of course, which reminds me, Stanley,' she added turning to her husband as she continued seamlessly, 'I would rather like to invite some friends to luncheon this Christmas, the Krantzes and several others.'

'As you wish, my dear,' Stan said amicably.

Hilda cast a meaningful glance at her daughter and Kate realised that this time around her mother had been not only subtle, but distinctly manipulative. The introduction of Frank's name had been purely in order for Hilda to steer the conversation towards a Christmas gathering. How clever, Kate thought, she's planning a family reunion.

'Lovely,' Hilda said. 'Cook will be so pleased having a party to cater for, I think around twelve to table would be ideal – it'll be just like the old days.'

Kate waited for her mother to list the other guests she intended to invite, presumably Alan, his new wife and his new wife's immediate family, but Hilda left things as they were for the moment.

'More tea, dear?'

'Yes, thank you.' Stan rose as she poured him a fresh cup. 'I'll take it to my study and leave you girls chatting,' he said.

When he'd gone, Kate leant in to her mother. 'Do you think he'll agree?' she asked quietly.

'We can only hope so, darling. He's been much more amenable of late. I shall ask him as soon as Alan and Paola return from their honeymoon. He must surely see that this schism in the family is so silly and so very wretched.'

'We'll front him together,' Kate said. 'He'll have to give in to the two of us.'

But as it turned out, even the combined forces of mother and daughter proved insufficient to budge Stanley Durham, who simply would not accept his son and his son's wife and family under his roof.

'Alan's made his own bed, let him lie in it,' Stan said when they approached him with the suggestion some days later. He was not angered by their request, but quite adamant in his refusal. 'The boy's a Fiorelli now. He can spend his Christmases with them.'

Kate found her father's obstinacy infuriating. 'For goodness sake, Dad,' she begged, 'don't you see what you're doing? You're tearing this family apart! You should embrace the Fiorellis. They were your friends once. They were like family to us as children – what in God's name has changed? What have you got against them?'

'I have nothing at all against them,' Stan said, his tone maddeningly reasonable. 'I am quite willing to accept them as friends on a professional basis. I like and respect the brothers and their sons, hard workers every one of them, and Luigi is immensely gifted, there's no one in the district with a greater knowledge of all things mechanical –'

'Except perhaps Alan,' Kate interrupted pointedly, but her father ignored her and went on.

'Respect and friendship, however, are one thing, Kate; marrying into a family is something entirely different. Alan is no longer a Durham, he has forfeited the right. He married a Roman Catholic and an Italian one at that, and such a marriage is a betrayal of his family.'

'He fell in love!' Kate fought against the urge to scream. Exasperated beyond measure, she wanted to physically grab her father and shake some common sense into him. 'You can't choose who you fall in love with!'

'Perhaps not,' Stan agreed, 'but you can most certainly choose who you marry.' He smiled benignly at his wife. 'Look at your mother and me, the perfect match. Two of a kind from families of like-standing in the community and we've been happy for years.'

The remark, although intended as a compliment, was an extremely backhanded one and Hilda returned a perfunctory smile in order to keep the peace. She'd opted out of the argument altogether by this stage. Hilda knew a lost cause when she saw one.

'In marriage it's important to stick to your own kind, Kate,' Stan continued, determined to drive his point home. 'Alan lost sight of that fact a long time ago, but you haven't and I hope you never will. Take your friend Frank, for instance. If Frank were to prove your partner of choice, I would approve the match. He's one of us. He may not be from a wealthy family, but then nor were we in the old days – Big Jim built Elianne from nothing. Frank's done well for himself and I admire a man like that. I'm prepared to be flexible, as you can see, Kate, but there are certain barriers which should never be crossed.'

Kate decided that now would probably not be a good time to tell her father Frank was black. It would ruin Christmas for them all, so following her mother's example she opted for silence.

Stan, however, demanded a response. 'You do get my point, don't you?'

'Oh yes, I get your point, Dad, I get it loud and clear.'

'Good. Enough said then.'

Christmas luncheon proved abysmal. The Krantzes were there, mother, father and son, Ivan with his recently acquired arrogance and Henry as pompous as ever. To flesh out the numbers, Hilda had offered a last-minute invitation to her bridge partner, Barbara Woodley, together with Barbara's husband Kenneth and daughter Susan. The Woodleys didn't really want to be there at all; Barbara would have politely reneged on the invitation, but she'd agreed to alter the family's Christmas plans upon her husband's insistence. Kenneth considered it advantageous that his business acquaintances should know he'd spent the day at Elianne as the guest of Stanley Durham.

Eighteen-year-old Susan was having the most awful time. Everyone was ancient. There was no one anywhere near her age at the table. Well there was Kate who was twenty-three, but Kate might just as well have been thirty she was so smart! Susan was sulky. She could have been with her cousins at the family party in Bundy instead of sitting around this stuffy table being waited on by servants and having to watch her manners every second.

Hilda, mindful of all about her and aware the day was proving a failure, dived into the Dom Perignon and as the luncheon progressed became overly gay in her determination that the festivity of the occasion should not be lost.

'To families and friendship ...' she said. Her first toast, and then ten minutes later, 'To Christmas and the spirit of peace and good will ...' The toasts went desperately on.

Hilda's guests presumed their hostess's performance normal, she was after all the mistress of Elianne and they were dining at The Big House, but Kate knew otherwise. Kate realised that this was the first time she'd actually seen her mother drunk. Hilda Durham had been in the grip of alcohol for years certainly, but never had the effects been so markedly evident. Poor Marmee, Kate thought, poor dear Marmee.

The agonising lunch eventually came to an end and Hilda farewelled her guests, propped up against the sideboard for support, seeing them out with a gracious kiss on the cheek or a shake of the hand like royalty, which was eminently acceptable to all who had no idea of her condition. Then when they'd gone she made her way upstairs for her customary afternoon lie-down with slow, measured step and a firm grip on the railings. Kate accompanied her, although she did not offer any physical support; Hilda was obviously determined to manage on her own.

'Thank you for being my daughter,' she said as she lay back on the bed and allowed Kate to take off her shoes.

'Thank you for being my mother,' Kate replied pulling up the coverlet.

Hilda was gently snoring as Kate closed the door behind her.

Stan had retired to his study, Max and Ivy were cleaning up in the dining room and Cook was scrubbing pots and pans in the kitchen when Kate returned downstairs. She took a chilled bottle of Dom Perignon from one of the ice buckets on the sideboard and walked out onto the front verandah where Ben was curled up half asleep.

'Stay,' she said as the dog rose and stretched in preparation for their customary walk

Ben sat watching dejectedly while she went down the stairs and, in the still-scorching heat of late afternoon, set off up the road towards South Mill Row.

She could hear the music from some distance away, a piano accordion and a male voice singing 'Viva Las Vegas', and upon arriving at Luigi's house she walked around to the rear to discover the back door open, the kitchen packed and the party in full swing, as she'd known it would be. The Fiorelli Family Band wasn't playing, but Georgio was pumping away at his piano accordion while Gio gave an excellent impression of Elvis Presley and the other cousins clapped along in time to the beat. Georgio and Gio, both devout Elvis fans, knew every one of 'The King's' hits and regularly teamed up as a duo.

'Kate's here,' someone called and Alan instantly appeared at the back door.

'Mind if I join the party?' She held up the bottle of champagne as an offering.

'That was the plan, wasn't it?' Alan had asked her to come along after the luncheon at The Big House. 'It'll be a damn sight more fun than the Krantzes,' he'd promised. 'Merry Christmas, Kate,' he said.

'Merry Christmas, Al.' They hugged each other then he ushered her inside, where she was warmly welcomed by all, and for the first time that day she felt it actually was Christmas.

'Champagne?' He raised his voice above the cacophony and was about to open the bottle, but she stopped him.

'No thanks, Al, leave it for the others, I'm a bit champagned out.' She glanced at the carafes of red wine that sat on the table. 'I'd much rather go a red if that's OK.'

'Red it is.' He fetched a fresh glass and poured her a wine.

The family meal was over. The wives were at the sink in the corner washing and drying dishes, while the brothers were seated on the wooden bench against the wall, puffing away at their Christmas cigars. Baskets of bread and platters of cheese and fruit remained on the huge wooden dining table, which was never left devoid of food and drink at any family gathering, but the table itself had now been dragged to one side to make room for the younger ones who wanted to dance.

And dance they did. At the conclusion of 'Viva Las Vegas', Georgio launched into 'Jailhouse Rock', Gio grabbed his cousin Paola and along with several of the others they started jiving while the onlookers belted out the lyrics.

Alan nudged Kate, indicating they should go outside where they could talk and, looking across at Paola, he pointed to the back door. Without breaking rhythm for one second, she smiled and nodded and blew him a kiss.

Brother and sister wandered out into the modest backyard, which was mostly taken up by a healthy vegetable garden either side with a path down the middle. Maria grew nearly all of the produce the family consumed. They walked down to the far end where a small bench looked out across the railway track that led from the pumping station to the mill, beyond which lay the ever-present expanse of cane.

The music followed them as they sat with their glasses of red wine – 'Jailhouse Rock' had become 'Shake, Rattle and Roll' – but at least it was quiet enough that they could hear one another speak.

'Was it as bad as you thought it'd be?' Alan asked.

'Worse. Poor Marmee got drunk – I've never seen her like that.'

'Oh.' Alan's face clouded. 'That's sad.'

'Yes, I found it sad. I don't think anyone else realised, strangely enough, except maybe Dad, but he didn't care.

He just couldn't wait for everyone to leave, and I must admit neither could I.'

'What a bugger. Poor Kate.' Alan raised his glass to her. 'Thanks for giving it a burl anyway. I suppose it was worth a try.'

'Thanks for giving what a burl?'

'The attempt at a family reunion.'

'Oh, that was Marmee's idea, I can't take any credit; although as I told you I did go into bat pretty hard.' She took a swig of her wine and shook her head in frustration. 'God, he's an obstinate bastard, he won't listen to sense at all. You've switched alliances and you're a Fiorelli, to Dad it's that simple.'

'Perhaps he's right.' A hard note crept into Alan's voice. 'Perhaps I have switched alliances and perhaps I am a Fiorelli. I can tell you one thing, being a Fiorelli's a damn sight easier than being a Durham.'

'Oh Al, don't give up on us. Please!' Sensing a distance in her brother, Kate felt suddenly desperate. 'We're still a family. A dysfunctional one, I grant you, but you're still my brother and I don't want to lose you.'

'You'll never lose me, Kitty-Kat.' He grinned to put her at her ease. 'Hell, you're the only sister I've got. I'm never going to let you go. That's a promise,' he added seriously, once again raising his glass.

They clinked and drank a silent toast to each other.

'Hey, there's something I didn't tell you,' Kate said with a smile. 'Dad thinks Frank's the ideal man for me.' She punched the air theatrically and growled an imitation of her father. '"He's one of us!" That's what Dad reckons.'

Alan laughed outright. He knew of Frank's background; she'd told him some time ago. 'Crikey, that's a turn-up for the books.'

'Yes it is rather, isn't it?' There was a mischievous glint in her eyes as she added, 'I thought about dropping the bombshell that he's black, but decided it probably wouldn't be a good idea.'

'It'd be only one of many bombshells you could drop on the old man,' Alan said laconically. 'Come on,' he rose from the bench, 'let's go back inside, I need another red.'

She drained her glass and stood. 'Me too.'

'What are you doing New Year's Eve?' he asked as they walked down the path.

'No idea.' Her glance to him was wry. 'Something wildly exciting at The Big House, I should think.'

'Come into town and spend the night with Paola and me. We're going to a party at Charlie Watford's, there'll be heaps of people you know.' She appeared hesitant so he added, 'You can get as drunk as you like, there's a spare room at the flat.'

'Well that makes the offer irresistible,' Kate replied, 'I would naturally intend to obliterate myself.'

'You know what I mean,' he said. 'I want you to spend time with us, Kate. We both do, Paola and me. You don't have to stay locked out here at Elianne – come into town and see us.'

'Thanks, Al, I will.'

New Year's Eve proved most enjoyable and over the week that followed Kate took Alan up on his offer, regularly driving into Bundaberg to spend time with him and Paola. Not wishing to disappoint her mother, she had resigned herself to staying on at Elianne until mid-January as planned, but she was thankful to escape The Big House, which had become increasingly oppressive, even prison-like, its atmosphere tense and laden with things unspoken. She missed Frank and longed to be in Sydney with him, sharing the freedom of their existence.

How strange, Kate thought. Elianne's vast landscape and grand house and clear, unpolluted air had always embodied to her the very essence of freedom and yet here she was longing for the grubby city with its lines of poky little terraces. Prison came in many forms, she supposed.

She spoke regularly to Frank. Each telephoned often simply in order to hear the other's voice. He missed her as much as she did him.

'Happy 1970,' he said when he phoned several days into the New Year. They exchanged New Year greetings and then he asked, very casually, 'Said anything to your dad yet?' It was the first time he'd made the enquiry, being careful not to nag her.

Gentle though his query was, Kate was nonetheless confronted. 'No,' she said guiltily, 'somehow I haven't been able to find the right –'

'Don't worry, Kate,' he assured her. 'Like I said at the airport, you'll know when the time's right, don't worry.' Frank resolved not to ask the question again. 'Now tell me what you got up to on New Year's Eve.'

Things came to a head in the second week of January, just when Kate was finally starting to count the days.

'G'day, Stan, haven't seen you for a while.'

It was a Wednesday afternoon. Stan had gone into Bundy to buy some supplies and had stopped off at the Burnett Club for a beer on the way home.

'Hello, Albert,' he said, reluctantly joining the man lounging at the bar near the door; Albert wasn't his favourite of the Club's members. 'No I haven't been around, been a bit busy lately.' He'd avoided the club since early December; he'd got heartily sick of the constant references to his son's impending wedding.

'Heard the wedding went well,' Albert said. Albert wouldn't step foot inside a Catholic Church himself, but that hadn't prevented his son, an Apex mate of Alan's, going. 'Craig reckoned the reception was a real beauty.'

'So I believe.' Stan gritted his teeth and signalled the barman, who was serving a group at the far end of the bar.

He'd grab a beer and find someone else to talk to, Albert Atherton got on his nerves at the best of times. He was a fussy old fart who gossiped like a woman.

'Heard Kate had a bloke from Sydney in tow,' Albert said, 'fella called Frank Madigan. A friend of hers, is he?'

Stan resisted the urge to say, What bloody business is it of yours, you nosy prick?, but his irritation showed nonetheless. 'If she had him in tow he'd obviously be a friend of hers, wouldn't he?'

'Yes, yes, of course, of course he would.' Albert was quick to back down. It wasn't wise to antagonise Stanley Durham. 'I was just a bit surprised, that's all. Hadn't thought he'd be the sort of bloke you'd want Kate hanging around with.'

'Oh? And why would you think that, Albert?' The stupid old fart's determined to dig a hole for himself, Stan thought, I'll deck him any minute.

'Well, you know ...' Albert hesitated as if trying to find a delicate way of putting it '... him being a half-caste and all that.'

'A what?' Stan looked at the man as if he was mad.

Albert Atherton was pleased to discover he was right. He'd been sure that Stan couldn't possibly know, and it was only proper he should be told, a person of Stanley Durham's standing certainly wouldn't want his daughter going around with a boong.

'Oh yes, he's an Abo all right.'

'What the hell are you talking about? The man's as white as you and me.'

'Yes, that's exactly what Craig said, he reckons you'd never know.'

'You're spouting a load of rubbish, Albert.' Stan ignored him and looked about the bar for whoever else he might gravitate to when his beer arrived. 'For your information, the bloke's parents are bloody Irish.'

'One of them may well be,' Albert's tone held an irritating edge of superiority, 'but it doesn't stop him being some sort of half-caste throwback, does it? He's an Aboriginal activist, that's what Craig told me.'

The barman had arrived to take his order, but Stan waved him away. The words 'Aboriginal activist' held a ring of truth. Propping against the bar, he turned to Albert, his full focus trained upon the man. 'And how exactly would Craig come to know this fact?'

Albert basked in the knowledge that he now had Stanley Durham's undivided attention. 'It was back in 1967,' he explained, prepared to make a meal of the story, 'when Craig was in Sydney playing for the South Sydney Rabbitohs ...' Albert Atherton boasted endlessly to all and sundry about his youngest son, a talented rugby league player who'd been signed up by South Sydney, but this time he didn't get very far.

'Craig didn't play for the side at all,' Stan barked, 'he played in the reserves for a year and then they dumped him. Get to the bloody point.'

How rude, Albert thought, rude and ungrateful. He was offering valuable information that could only serve Stanley Durham's best interests and the man chose to insult him. 'There was a national referendum on Aboriginal rights that year,' he said waspishly.

Stan nodded. '1967, that's right.' The referendum to which Kate had been so committed, he recalled. Albert once again had his full attention. 'Go on.'

'Frank Madigan was a high-profile campaigner on the referendum,' Albert continued, his tone peevish, 'there was an article about him in the Sydney newspaper and a picture of him with another black activist Charlie Perkins. Craig said Madigan was quite famous at the time.'

Albert had intended to elaborate a great deal further about his son's surprise upon seeing Frank Madigan at the wedding with Kate, but still piqued, he stopped there.

'I see.' Irritating though the garrulous old fart was, he'd proved useful, Stan thought; the facts certainly rang true. 'Well, I must thank you, Albert,' he said. 'I'm most grateful for this piece of information.'

Albert, pride salved, was instantly mollified and forgave the insult. 'Yes I thought you would be, Stan. I naturally considered it my duty to let you know. I mean you wouldn't want to see Kate take up with a man like that, would you?'

A dark cloud passed over Stanley Durham's face and Albert once again beat a hasty retreat. 'Oh not that I'm insinuating anything of course, the relationship is quite innocent I'm sure, but even as a friend –'

'The relationship is most certainly innocent, Albert, my daughter does not "take up" with men, be they black, white or brindle.' Stan ceased to prop against the bar and, drawing himself to full height, towered threateningly over Albert Atherton. 'I'll tell you something else you should know about my daughter, Albert. She's an extremely intelligent, highly qualified young woman devoted to her academic studies and to the many social justice causes she embraces as an activist, particularly the issue of Aboriginal rights. It is only natural she should form an alliance with a man like Frank Madigan. Kate has my full support and I'm proud of her. I'm proud of her stand for human rights and I'm proud to be her father.'

Stan was aware that his speech in his daughter's defence contained an element of double standards, if not an outright lie. He was indeed proud of Kate, but he'd never supported her causes. In fact he'd been scathing of her activism on many an occasion, but he would not have his daughter maligned by the likes of Albert Atherton.

Good heavens, Albert thought, he'd obviously misread Stanley Durham – the man appeared to have extremely liberal views. Albert did not at all approve, as he was sure most wouldn't, but he didn't dare say anything.

Stan leant down, his face close to Albert's, his eyes glittering dangerously.

'So you feel free to chatter all you like about Kate and Frank Madigan, Albert, as I have no doubt you will,' he said, his voice low and menacing. 'But get your facts right, mate, because if I hear the slightest smutty innuendo your life won't be worth living.'

Albert made an attempt to stammer his assurance, but in vain. Stan the Man was already striding out of the bar.

'What's going on between you and this bloody half-caste?!'

Stan's approach was altogether different forty minutes later when he confronted his daughter. He'd sought her out as soon as he'd arrived back at The Big House and called her into his study.

'What on earth do you mean?' Kate replied coldly. She'd known there was going to be a showdown the moment she'd seen him.

'You know bloody well what I mean: you and your Abo mate, Frank bloody Madigan. Why didn't you tell me he was a half-caste?'

They stood facing each other across his desk, their eyes locked like combatants about to do battle.

'He is not a half-caste,' she said scathingly. 'His grandmother was a Wiradjuri woman.'

'That makes him a bloody half-caste in my book. So what's going on between you?'

Kate refused to lose her temper, attempting to reason instead. 'Since when did you become such a racist, Dad?' she asked, her tone not aggressive but genuinely seeking contact. 'You have Kanaka friends here at Elianne. You've always been proud of your relationship with your black workers. Why do you feel the need to degrade Frank?'

'You're buying time, Kate, and you know it. Tell me the truth. Are you two having an affair?'

'Yes.' She didn't flinch for one second. 'Frank and I love each other as much as I believe it's humanly possible to love.' From his stunned reaction she might just as well have struck him a physical blow. 'And I'm afraid there's not one thing you can do about it, Dad,' she said, again without aggression, simply stating her case. 'You can disown me as you have Alan if that's what you want, but I promise it won't make a shred of difference.'

He stared back at her and she met his gaze directly, expecting him to fight on, but he didn't. He sank into his chair instead.

'What's happening to this family?' he said shaking his head, bewildered. 'Everything's falling apart ... things are not as they should be ... not as they were ever intended to be.'

He appeared to be talking to himself as much as to her, and he looked so lost that Kate felt a rush of sympathy.

'Times have changed, Dad.' She sat in the chair opposite and leant forward hands on the desk, still trying as best she could to make some form of connection. 'You're right, things are not as they were, but they're not meant to be. Times are changing more as each year passes. The post-war immigration, the breakdown of the White Australia Policy, the Vietnam War – we're not the isolated country we once were. People are becoming more tolerant.'

'Not this tolerant,' Stan continued to shake his head helplessly. 'They haven't become this tolerant, Kate. I mean you and Frank ...' He halted as if further words were unnecessary.

'You liked him. You liked him a lot.'

'I did, yes I did. But he's black.'

Now was the right moment, Kate realised. Frank himself seemed to be pointing the way. She could hear his voice; he might as well have been in the room, right beside her.

She stood. 'There's something I have to show you, Dad. Don't go away.'

Stan had no intention of going away, he had no intention of doing anything, and when his daughter returned five minutes later with an armload of paperwork he was still staring blankly into space.

Along with the folders containing her typewritten translations Kate had also brought one of the original ledgers, and circling the desk she placed it before her father. It was the last of Ellie's diaries, the one that was only half filled before Ellie had put down her pen, never to write again. The rest of the ledgers Kate had left in the suitcase under her bed, where they'd remained since she'd brought them home to show Alan.

She placed the stack of folders on the desk too, all but the final one, which she retained, and then she opened the ledger.

'I found over a dozen of these under Elianne House before it was destroyed,' she said. 'They're Grandmother Ellie's diaries, or rather her scribblings, as she preferred to call them; this is the last one.'

Stan looked down at the open page, which was utterly unintelligible to him. 'It's written in French,' he said.

'Yes. I spent nearly two years on the translations.' She tapped the pile of folders. 'You need to read them in their entirety, Dad, but start with this one.' She picked the ledger up from the table, tucked it under her arm, and replaced it with the final folder.

'Why?' A touch of the old belligerence returned. 'Why should I?'

'In order to learn the truth.'

'What truth?'

'The brooding Durham look that Marmee's always been so proud of, Dad, *that* truth. You and Frank have more in common than you think.'

Stan gazed blankly up at her.

'Look at your eyes, look at your skin and your hair,' she said. 'Look at the eyes and the skin of your sons, look at me. I may have the eyes of Grandmother Ellie, but look at my skin. I never burn from the sun, my tan never fades.' Kate smiled to soften the blow. 'We all have black blood in us, Dad.'

'What the hell is this bullshit?' Stan countered angrily. 'What kind of cock and bull nonsense are you trying to tell me?'

'I'm trying to tell you that your father was the son of an islander.'

He looked at her uncomprehendingly.

'I'm saying your grandfather was a Kanaka, Dad. A man of New Hebridean and French blood called Pavi Salet.' Kate opened the folder. 'Read for yourself,' she said and left the room.

Chapter eighteen

I have determined this will be the last of my scribblings. At sixty years of age it is tiring living a lie while recording the truth – much easier to give oneself over wholeheartedly to the lie, I feel. However, I cannot leave off without recording my final confession. If there were someone in whom I could confide I most certainly would, for I long to share the burden. But I dare not. In the absence of a confidant, I am therefore compelled to confess to myself.

I have known love, love of the purest kind. Only once, but it has lasted me a lifetime and given me my greatest gift.

Ellie was distraught that morning when she arrived at the Salets' cottage. Upon Big Jim's departure, she'd left baby Edward in Bertha's charge and had run to the only place she could think of, seeking support, needing desperately to voice her terrible suspicions.

Pavi was across the road at the stables, but Mela was there in the front room with little Malou, rocking the wooden cradle that her husband had made and singing a lullaby to the baby in her native tongue.

'Mrs Ellie, Mrs Ellie.' She sprang to her feet, deeply concerned to see her mistress and dear friend in such a terrible state.

Leading Ellie to the sofa, Mela sat beside her and gathered her in her arms, shushing her as she would little Malou. 'Hush now, Mrs Ellie, hush, hush now,' she said stroking her mistress's hair while Ellie sobbed and gasped for the breath that seemed so unattainable.

When the attack of hysteria had passed, Mela brewed a pot of her special herbal tea, which she made Ellie drink, and then she listened as Ellie poured out her terrible fears.

'He couldn't have killed little Beatrice, he couldn't have,' Ellie said over and over as if to convince herself of the impossibility. 'No man could commit such an atrocity, not even a man like Jim, who is capable I know of terrible things. He could not have killed my daughter.'

'No, no Mrs Ellie, the Boss, he would not kill your daughter,' Mela assured her, although in truth Mela believed otherwise. Mela believed this was exactly what the Boss would do. It was the first thing that had sprung to her mind when she'd heard the news of the baby's mysterious death in the dead of night. The Boss would not want the little girl with the twisted mouth, no matter how precious the child was to his wife.

'But he was so cruel, Mela, so heartless. He said any child with such a deformity would be better off dead.'

'The Boss does not mean to be cruel.' Mela knew it was important she come out with the right words so she took her time, speaking in a slow, deliberate tone. 'The Boss does not understand women's feelings – some men are like that. The Boss, he loves you very much, Mrs Ellie,' she said comfortingly, 'he would not hurt your baby.'

Mela's assurances had the desired effect, and as Ellie calmed down she found herself sharing all sorts of truths, truths she had admitted to no one.

'He doesn't love me, Mela,' she said, 'he never has. Oh he believes he loves me, certainly, he believes he loves me to the point of worship, but what Jim perceives as love is not love at all. I am a possession to my husband, something he prizes and takes for his pleasure. I have no complaint and can live such a life, for he will give me children to love and that will be enough ...' As the image of Beatrice returned, so too did the threat of a fresh onslaught of tears. 'But I cannot live with the thought that he could have taken my daughter from me.'

'No, no, Mrs Ellie, you are wrong,' Mela insisted. 'You think this thing in your head, that is all.'

'Yes, yes, of course it's my imagination, of course you're right, Mela, I know you're right.' For the sake of sanity, Ellie thought, Mela had to be right; the other path led to madness.

'You drink your tea, Mrs Ellie.' Mela poured her another cup and rose from the sofa. 'And you look to Malou for me. I will not be long.'

She walked out the front door and across the road to the stables. She was gone less than ten minutes and upon her return, she poured a cup of tea for herself. While she sipped it, she kept glancing out the window at the dusty street as if waiting for something. Then several minutes later she gave Ellie her instructions.

'You go now and see Pavi,' she said. 'I have told Pavi what you tell me. Pavi he will comfort you. Go, Mrs Ellie.'

Their relationship now seemingly upside down, Ellie did as she was told like a worker obeying her mistress.

She entered the stables to be greeted by the familiar smell of fresh hay and harness and the acrid odour of horse dung, the mixture that strangely enough she'd always loved and which now seemed so soothing. The stables were all but deserted, even of animals. There was only one horse there, a mare in foal. The Clydesdales were out in the field, Big Jim was being driven to the train station in the buggy and pair-in-hand and the stable boy had taken the workhorse and dray to fetch chaff from the regular supplier's farm five miles away.

Pavi was waiting for her. He said nothing as he took her in his arms and held her to him. No words were necessary between them, just as words had never been necessary all those years ago. The dearest friend she had ever known was aware of her pain.

They stayed silently locked in each other's embrace for some time, the past and the present becoming one, and then he kissed her. Surprising though the kiss was, it neither shocked nor alarmed her, but seemed a natural progression of the love they had always shared. And as they lay together in the fresh straw, so too did the lovemaking that followed. Never in her life had Ellie experienced such tenderness, and never before and never again would she give herself so freely.

Only when it was over did she feel shame. Swept away by her emotions and the response of her body, she'd not once thought of Mela. She did now. Now she thought of nothing but Mela.

'Oh, Pavi,' she said, 'what a terrible thing I've done.' It was the first words that had been uttered since she'd entered the stables. 'How could I have so betrayed Mela?'

'You have not betrayed Mela,' he replied, gently stroking her arm as they lay side by side in the fresh straw. 'Mela sent you to me.'

'Yes, she sent me to you,' Ellie said, sitting up in order to break away from his caress, 'but she sent me so you could comfort me, not –'

'And she wished me to comfort you in the way she felt necessary.' Pavi sat up and faced her. 'Mela intended this to happen, Elianne.' He called her by the old name, the name that now belonged to a grand estate, but the name which to Pavi would always be hers. 'She told me to send the boy away to fetch the chaff in order that we should be alone.'

Ellie stared at him speechless.

'You see, in the culture of Mela's parents a man may have several wives,' he went on to explain, 'and Mela has always considered you my first wife. In a way she is right,

Elianne. We have loved each other you and I in the purest of ways, and in our hearts we always will. But this day will never be mentioned again.' He kissed her gently and chastely, like a brother. 'I wish you to be happy with your life,' he said, 'so does Mela, who also loves you dearly.'

He rose, turning his back while she dressed and brushed the straw from her clothing. Then he opened the stable door for her and they parted as wordlessly as they had met.

No more was ever said about that day. Not a word was uttered, not a look of complicity exchanged. There was no sign of acknowledgement that the incident had ever occurred as their friendship resumed its normal path. But Mela and Pavi had given Ellie the love and the strength she needed to carry on.

Upon Big Jim's return, she accepted his nightly embrace, but when she gave birth nine months later, she knew the child would not be her husband's. The freedom with which she had given herself to Pavi had invited conception.

To Ellie's profound relief the baby was born white. Pavi was olive-skinned rather than dark, given the French blood of his father, but Ellie had feared the child might bear the physical traits of Pavi's islander mother. If such had been the case, she knew that Big Jim would have killed both her and her baby.

Though the child's skin and features appeared Caucasian, Ellie could see in the baby so much of Pavi, the same fine chiselled bones, the same soft brown eyes and, as the boy grew, the same sensitive nature.

During the years that followed, she wondered more and more how others didn't see the similarity when to her it was so obvious. How could Mela fail to recognise her husband in little Bartholomew? How could Pavi fail to see himself in his son? But from neither was there ever the slightest flicker of recognition.

Strangely enough, the only one who seemed to sense a distinctive difference in Bartholomew was Big Jim. Big Jim found the boy's gentle disposition uncharacteristic of a Durham and so unlike the competitive personalities of his other two sons that he accepted the fact as indisputable evidence that Bartholomew was 'the runt of the litter'.

Ellie felt safe with her secret, which for many years she had thought was hers and hers alone, and then the day came when she discovered there was another who knew, one who had always known.

'Goodbye, Mrs Ellie.' Mela waited for her mistress's handshake on that terrible morning of the final farewells. With Big Jim standing by, there were no hugs shared.

But Ellie did not offer her hand. She embraced Mela instead, holding her fast in the hope that Mela would know she was embracing them all. And when they parted, she said, 'Thank you,' in the hope that Mela would understand all that was meant by those two small words.

Mela certainly understood. Mela understood far more than Ellie had ever realised, and now that the danger of discovery was past she was happy for Ellie to know that they shared the secret. Just the two of them, for she had said nothing to Pavi.

'Your sons will be a comfort to you, Mrs Ellie,' she said, her glance taking in the Durham brothers one by one, but her eyes coming to rest on Bartholomew as she added, 'They are fine boys.' And when she turned back to Ellie her smile held a special meaning.

Ellie realised then that Mela knew the truth and was telling her so. But Mela's smile and her expression as she'd looked at Bartholomew had signalled something else, something only two women could share. Mela was happy that her friend had been blessed with a child born of a loving union, and that Ellie would be left with an ever-present reminder of the man she truly loved.

As Ellie stood in the dirt road waving goodbye to the dray, she couldn't help wondering about the turn of events. *When Mela sent me to Pavi that morning all those* years ago, was it in the hope that I might conceive? It seems strangely possible somehow. But I will never know.

There. I have purged myself. I have no regrets and make no apologies, but I rejoice as I always have in my gift of Bartholomew.

I have never quite forgiven God for taking Edward and George from me for whatever Divine purpose intended, indeed God seemed to have deserted us all in those dark days. But I will always thank Him for Bartholomew, and now in the fullness of time for Bartholomew's children, who grow so healthily to adulthood. There is much to be thankful for.

I will now leave off writing and concentrate on the lie that is essential to my family's safety, the lie of the love shared between Big Jim and me, for if Jim were ever to discover the truth I have no doubt he would kill us all.

I intend to destroy these scribblings before I die, but I must admit that for the moment it is something of a comfort seeing the words on paper. I have enjoyed my confession.

Chapter nineteen

Kate sat in the breakfast room with a cup of coffee awaiting her father's reaction, unsure what to expect, but presuming he would seek her out after reading Ellie's confession. An hour passed, however, and he didn't appear. Good, she thought, he's decided to read the diaries in their entirety: much better he learns the whole truth in one hit even if it takes him all night – and it probably will.

While waiting, she'd looked through the final ledger that she'd brought with her from the study, re-reading the words in their original French. She'd often wondered in the past why Ellie had not destroyed the diaries as had been her intention. There'd been plenty of time in which to do so. Ellie had lived a further twenty years, and death had not caught her by surprise: according to all accounts she'd known she was dying for some time. Furthermore, she'd had her wits about her right to the end, so she would not have forgotten of the diaries' existence.

Kate had come to only one conclusion, the simplest explanation of all. Ellie had wanted the diaries discovered. In the last stages of her life she'd made a conscious decision. She'd packed the ledgers away herself beneath her precious books or, if in a weakened state, she'd ordered their packing and storage. The diaries were meant to be found. Perhaps well into the future, perhaps generations on, but one day, when the family was safe from the threat of Big Jim's vengeance, the truth was to be known. And Ellie had been right, Kate thought. The truth needed to be told.

'Hello, my darling, how unusual to see you cooped up inside.'

Hilda appeared at the door. Following her customary nap, she'd come downstairs to take her late afternoon tea in the front drawing room. 'Are you not feeling well?' she asked concerned. At this time of day, Kate was usually out walking with the dog or swimming in the dam.

'I'm fine, Marmee, absolutely fine, thank you.'

'Oh I am glad.' Hilda beamed. 'Would you care to take afternoon tea with me? Do say yes, dear,' she urged, 'I would so enjoy your company.'

'Yes, I'd very much like to.' Kate decided in that instant to prepare her mother for the worst. 'As a matter of fact, there's something I want to show you, something of great importance.'

'How terribly exciting. Pop into the kitchen and tell Ivy we'll need two cups, there's a dear. I'll see you in the drawing room.' Hilda sailed away.

Kate joined her a minute or so later and pulling up a hardback chair beside her mother's she placed the ledger on the coffee table in front of them.

Hilda looked down at it in surprise. Hardly an item of great importance, she thought, book-keeping held little interest for her. 'This is what you have to show me?' she asked, her disappointment readable.

'Yes. I found a whole pile of these under Elianne House when I was clearing out Grandmother Ellie's books.'

'Really?' The reaction was instantaneous, the mere mention of Elianne House and Grandmother Ellie enough to garner Hilda's rapt attention.

'They're her diaries.' Kate opened the ledger.

'Oh. Oh my goodness.' A hand fluttering to her chest, Hilda gazed down at the page. 'Her diaries,' she said breathlessly as if any moment she might have a heart attack. 'Grandmother Ellie's diaries,' she traced her fingers across the paper with gentle reverence, 'written in her very own hand.'

'That's right.'

Hilda's look to her daughter was puzzled, even a little hurt. 'But Elianne House was destroyed years ago,' she said. 'Why did you not tell me about the diaries earlier?'

'It took me a long time to translate each of them, Marmee.' Kate answered with care. 'There were over a dozen ledgers and I wanted to –'

'Of course, my darling, of course, you wanted to surprise me. I'm sorry if I sounded in any way accusatory, how shockingly ungrateful of me,' Hilda's eyes sparkled with excitement, 'and how wonderful that you've gone to the trouble of translating them. I shall be able to read them all to myself.' She glanced down at the open page, once again tracing a finger over the words. 'I wonder why she chose to write in French – that's most mysterious, don't you think?'

'No, it's not actually, she had very good reason.'

'Oh?'

'Grandmother Ellie wrote intimately, about quite a lot of things that she didn't want others to read.'

'My goodness, how riveting.' Hilda clapped her hands in delight. 'But where are your translations, my darling? I can't wait.'

'Dad has them in his study, I gave them to him an hour or so ago.'

Ivy had arrived with the tea tray and was about to set it down on the coffee table beside the open book.

'Careful, Ivy, careful.' Hilda snatched up the ledger and closing it with care clutched it to her chest. 'I'll pour thank you, dear,' she said and the maid left the room.

Passing the ledger to Kate, Hilda started to pour. 'When we've had our tea, I shall join Stanley in his study,' she said. 'We can read the diaries together.'

'I don't think that would be a good idea, Marmee.'

'Oh your father won't mind, my darling,' Hilda gave a light laugh. 'I virtually worshipped his grandmother, as everyone well knows. Stanley won't find my interest at all intrusive.' She passed Kate a cup of tea and started pouring her own. 'In fact I believe this could prove the perfect bond, something the two of us can share.'

'It'll be something you can share all right,' Kate replied drily, 'but I doubt it'll prove the perfect bond.'

'That's rather enigmatic of you, dear,' there was a mild rebuke in Hilda's voice, 'and a little cynical I might add.'

'I'm sorry, Marmee, I didn't mean to be rude.' Kate very much wanted to prepare her mother for the inevitable, but she remained circumspect. There was no point in revealing the truth, far better Hilda should read Ellie's own words than be told second hand. 'It's just that Grandmother Ellie unveiled a lot of family secrets, some of which are rather shocking, I'm afraid.'

But Hilda was in no way disheartened by the prospect of what might lie ahead. 'How very intriguing,' she said and took a sip of her tea. 'So I shall just have to wait then, shall I?'

'Yes, you'll just have to wait,' Kate replied firmly, 'and for some time, I should think.'

Kate was right. The wait was a long one.

When Stan the Man didn't appear at the dinner table that night, Hilda went to his study and knocked on the door, but received no answer. She tried the handle. The door was locked. She knocked again. 'Stanley, it's me,' she said.

'Go away,' her husband called. 'I don't wish to be disturbed.'

'But Cook has served dinner.'

'I'm not hungry.'

'As you wish.'

Hilda made no argument, although she was a little put out. A well-run household revolved around meal times and the observance of ritual.

She retired shortly before midnight, a good two hours later than normal, having waited up for her husband, and before she did she knocked once again on the study door.

'Do you intend to stay in there all night, Stanley?' she demanded.

'Yes,' came the brusque reply.

'Very well.' Her voice assumed the edge of command. 'I shall have Ivy deliver breakfast to you first thing in the morning. If you choose not to open the door to her, she will leave the tray here on the floor outside. You cannot be so foolish as to starve yourself. Good night.' She sailed off without waiting for an answer, but none came in any event.

The breakfast tray remained untouched the following morning and Stan the Man remained hidden behind locked doors.

He finally surfaced at lunchtime, just as Hilda and Kate were sitting down to their chicken salad.

'Ah there you are,' Hilda said, as if her husband's prolonged absence was perfectly normal, 'I was about to have Ivy deliver a luncheon tray.'

Stan dumped the armload of folders and their contents unceremoniously in the centre of the table, where they slithered to a halt among the condiments and salad servers.

'Read that lot and discover the truth about your precious Grandmother Ellie,' he said to his wife, then without drawing breath he addressed his daughter. 'Who else knows?'

'Only Alan and Frank.'

'Frank!' Stan stared at her in dumbfounded amazement. 'You shared the Durham family skeletons with a total stranger!'

Kate nodded guiltily, although she couldn't help thinking it was surely better she shared their secrets with a stranger than one who knew the family well. 'I needed to tell someone.'

'Why not try your father?' His voice was icy.

'I'm sorry, Dad. I wanted advice and I turned to Frank. It was Frank who told me I should –'

'I don't give a shit what your boyfriend told you.' Stan waved a hand at the offending folders. 'So you and Alan have known about this since the destruction of Elianne House nearly six years ago.'

'I have, yes,' she admitted. 'I worked on the translations before I told Alan. He's known for two years.'

'And neither of you said a word to me. You kept the truth to yourselves, both of you, for two whole years.' Stan seemed to be suggesting that the joint silence of his offspring had been some sort of conspiracy.

'Yes. We were going to tell you, Dad, but ...' She tailed off. *But Neil died. Do you remember the state you were in after Neil's death, Dad? Do you think you could have handled the truth then?* She didn't say the words out loud. They remained in her brain as she tried desperately to fathom her father's mood. He was scathing certainly, cold and disdainful, but she had no idea what he was truly feeling. *Is he angry about the lies he's been fed all his life?* she wondered. *Is he hurting at the discovery, is the truth as painful as Alan and I feared it might be?* Kate found it impossible to decipher what might be going on in her father's mind.

'Do sit down, Stanley,' Hilda insisted, 'and have some lunch, you haven't eaten for –'

'Read that,' he interrupted brusquely indicating the folders. 'When you have, we'll talk together as a family and decide what action we take. I'm going into town. Be close at hand for your mother, Kate,' he added caustically, 'she may well need your support.'

They didn't see Stan for the rest of that day. He headed directly to the Burnett Club, where he sat in a haze of Scotch and fractured thoughts, chatting with old friends, wondering what they would say if they knew even a shadow of the truth. His daughter was not alone in her inability to fathom his mood. Stanley Durham was having trouble deciphering his own feelings. The one thing of which he could be sure was the fact that the world he had known for the whole of his life would never be the same.

Hilda spent the entire afternoon and quite a deal of the night in the front drawing room, having retired with the armload of folders that Kate had carried there for her.

'Call me if you need me,' Kate had said, but as the day wore on she'd received no summons.

It was well beyond midnight when Hilda finished reading the last of the diaries, after which she crept upstairs and into bed beside her husband, who had returned from town less than half an hour earlier. She could smell the alcohol on him even though his back was turned to her and as he wasn't snoring she wondered if he might be awake.

Stan was. He'd felt her slip quietly in between the sheets. But as they lay there in the dark, their thoughts simultaneously racing, neither said one word to the other.

Kate had rung Alan during the afternoon.

'Dad's read the diaries,' she said bluntly, 'I gave them to him yesterday and he stayed up all night.'

'Oh hell. What was his reaction?'

'I have no idea. He's keeping things to himself, so it's impossible to tell. I think he might be in a state of shock.'

'Yep, I'd bet on it. How about Mum?'

'She's reading them as we speak.'

Alan sensed his sister's concern. 'Don't worry about Mum, Kate,' he said, 'she's much tougher than you think. Mum's a true survivor. Dad's the one who'll go under.'

'I think you should come around tomorrow, Al.'

There was a pause. 'You reckon that's wise?'

'Dad knows you've read the diaries. He said when Mum had read them we should talk together as a family. And family includes you.'

'Did he say that?'

'No, but he should have.'

'My coming around is a bold choice.' Alan's voice sounded a warning.

'I know.' Kate had given the matter a great deal of thought. 'But the diaries are such a leveller, Al. They put a different perspective on our entire world – Dad must see that. This is an opportunity to reunite the family,' she urged. 'We've all been fed lies, every one of us. We should face the truth together and support each other. We'll be stronger for it if we do.'

'Yes, we need to front the old man,' Alan said, which was surprising, for he'd made a point of avoiding confrontation the whole of his life. 'It'll be a make or break situation, but even if it severs any bond I might still have with him at least I'll know where I stand. Anything's better than this endless, bloody stalemate.'

'I agree.' Kate too was relieved the situation was to be brought to a head. 'Let's hope things go our way.'

'What time will I turn up? I'll take the morning off if you like.'

'No need; around midday will do. That'll give Mum and Dad time to talk. I'll tell Dad you're coming, we won't spring a surprise.'

'Good thinking, 99,' he replied, one of his favourite catchphrases, and Kate could hear the wry smile in his voice as he added, 'Given some warning the old man can shoot through if he wants to.'

The talk that Kate had presumed would take place between her parents proved remarkably brief.

Hilda awoke to an empty bed the following morning, her husband having risen early to take himself off to his study, but he made an appearance at the breakfast table an hour or so later. Stan obviously chose to confer with his wife in the presence of their daughter, a fact which rather surprised Kate, who had assumed her parents would have a private talk before the subject was introduced for general family discussion.

'Nothing, thank you,' he said to Cook, who was serving Hilda's cheese omelette. Cook herself was waiting table. Ivy had every second weekend off and was currently being driven to the station by Max, where she would catch the train to Brisbane to stay with her sister.

'A piece of toast at least, Stanley,' Hilda insisted, 'you haven't eaten for –'

'Yes, yes, very well, very well,' Stan said tetchily and he took a slice from the rack on the table. He helped himself to a pat of butter and spread it on the toast, wondering why he was being forced to perform such a trivial action when his world was disintegrating about him, and wondering also how his wife could sit there calmly eating a cheese omelette. The sight irritated him intensely.

'So,' he said when Cook had returned to the kitchen, 'I take it you've read these "diaries" as Kate calls them?'

'I have,' Hilda replied.

'And what was your reaction to their many revelations?'

Hilda put down her knife and fork. 'I was shocked.' She dabbed at the corners of her mouth with her linen napkin. 'I was deeply shocked, I must admit.'

'Hardly surprising,' he said drily.

'To think that for all those years the great love shared between Grandmother Ellie and Big Jim was a lie ...' Hilda shook her head, perplexed. 'Who could have dreamt such a thing possible?'

'I see.' Stan studied his wife with disdain, as if she was some form of sub-human species. 'And this revelation proved a greater shock than the discovery that you'd married into a family with black blood in its veins?'

Hilda knew that she'd come up with the wrong answer, but in the face of her husband's derision she remained surprisingly unflustered. She had formed her own conclusions and refused to stray from her path.

'Naturally, the relationship with Pavi Salet and its outcome is the greatest shock of all, Stanley,' she said. 'I understand the ramifications that this entails for the family. But I cannot personally find Grandmother Ellie's actions reprehensible. She was lost and alone, cast adrift after the death of her daughter –'

'That's enough,' Stan barked and Hilda lapsed into silence, aware that she was being judged, but not particularly caring. Stanley had never understood matters of the heart. Most men don't, she thought as she picked up her knife and fork and re-addressed her omelette.

Kate had found her parents' exchange fascinating. She understood her father's reaction to his wife's apparent superficiality, for her mother's fixation with romance could indeed be irritating. But something in their brief dialogue, and particularly in Hilda's response to her husband's contempt, had changed the views of a lifetime. In the past, Kate had considered her mother's fey other-worldliness a sign of weakness, a trait that left Hilda vulnerable and prone to ridicule. She realised now how wrong she'd been. Hilda's ability to romanticise was her greatest strength.

Just look at you Marmee, Kate thought, studying her mother, whose focus was now solely upon the omelette before her, you've provided yourself with the perfect escape. Alan's quite right. You're a survivor. More than a survivor, you're indestructible.

Stan wanted to hurl something at his wife. Watching her eat, so imperturbably and with her perfect table manners, he wanted to upend the impeccably laid table and send things crashing to the floor. But what was the point? He looked down at his buttered toast, knowing that if he attempted to eat it he'd choke.

He stood. 'I'm going into town,' he said and walked out of the room.

Kate jumped up and ran after him, cornering him before he got to the front door.

'Don't go, Dad,' she begged, 'please don't go, we need to talk.' She stood between him and the door as if her mere presence could prevent him from leaving.

'Why? What is there to talk about? No one seems to know what's happened to this family.'

'I do. Alan does. He's coming around. He'll be here at midday.'

Her father said nothing, his reaction unreadable.

'Please, Dad, please, I'm begging you. We have to talk! You said so yourself, we have to talk as a family and decide what action we take –'

'What action is there to take? We burn the diaries and pretend this whole thing never happened. We go back to the way we were: that's what action we take.'

'We can't and you know it.' She fronted him boldly, calling his bluff. 'We can't bury the past, Dad. We need to confront it and accept the truth, all of us. You know we do. Stay and talk to Alan. Please.'

Kate saw a flicker of something in her father's eyes, something that appeared to her like recognition. He knows I'm right, she thought, he knows the truth has to be faced. Then the eyes went dark and the wall was up again.

'I'll be in my study,' Stan said, 'tell me when he gets here.'

He walked off. It was a little after nine in the morning, but Stan felt in need of a Scotch.

Alan arrived at ten past twelve. He'd dropped Paola off at her parents' house, where he would join her later.

'You're late,' Stan called as his son climbed from the gleaming new Belmont utility.

'G'day, Dad. G'day, Kate.'

Alan patted the dog that had trotted down to meet him

then climbed the stairs, Ben following, to where his father and sister were sitting waiting on the front verandah.

'She told me you'd be here at midday,' Stan said with a jerk of his head to Kate.

'Yeah, give or take a few minutes.'

Alan wasn't sure whether his father was joking or not. Stan was lounging comfortably in one of the wicker armchairs and seemed relaxed, but Kate didn't look comfortable at all. He noted the half-empty bottle of Scotch on the table, and the quick look he exchanged with his sister told him yes Stan had been drinking. As usual, it was difficult to tell whether or not he was drunk though – Stan held his liquor well.

There was an awkward moment as Alan stood before his father waiting to see if a hand would be offered. It wasn't, so he pulled up a wicker chair and sat.

'New ute,' Stan said.

'Yep. Bought it for work; won't stay shiny for long, you can bet on that.'

'The sprocket business must be booming.'

'Yes, yes it is thanks, Dad,' Alan chose to ignore the sneer in his father's tone, 'business is going exceptionally well all round.'

'Good on you, Al, that's great news,' Kate interjected before Stan could respond with another barbed comment. She wished her father would be a little more welcoming. 'I adore the ute, can I have a drive later?'

'Course you can.'

'Hello, darling.'

The door had opened and Hilda stood there; she'd been watching from the front drawing room for her son's appearance. Alan stood and kissed his mother.

'Would you like a cup of tea?' she asked.

'No thanks, Mum, I'm fine.'

She was about to offer him a coffee or a soft drink, but Stan the Man got in first.

'Perhaps you'd like something stronger,' he said, indicating the Scotch bottle.

Alan shook his head. 'Not for me thanks, Dad, bit too early in the day.' The moment the words were out he realised they sounded wrong and that his father would probably take it as a criticism.

'Suit yourself.' Stan leant forwards and topped up his glass. He was drinking his whisky neat.

'Well if there's anything you want I'll be in the front drawing room,' Hilda said brightly. 'Just give me a call.'

'Rightio, thanks Mum.' Alan plonked himself back in his chair.

Hilda smiled at the sight of the three gathered around the table: her family was finally together. She wished Stanley didn't look quite so grumpy, but at least he'd agreed to meet with his son.

'Your father was so keen to see you he's been waiting out here on the verandah for over half an hour,' she said with the intention of getting things off to an amiable start, 'isn't that so, Stanley?' She beamed directly at her husband, who made no reply, taking a swig of his Scotch instead, so she spread the radiance of her smile around the table in general. 'I'll leave you to it then. Have a nice chat.'

Closing the door behind her, Hilda retired to the front drawing room where, although not privy to their conversation, she would at least be able to see them through the windows that looked out over the verandah.

Stan had barred his wife from the family discussion. She had nothing to offer but romantic claptrap he said and they didn't need any of that bullshit. 'Besides,' he'd added, 'this doesn't concern you. You're not a Durham.'

Hilda had refused to take umbrage. She hadn't even bothered countering with the fact that she'd borne him three Durham children. When Stan dug his heels in like this there was no getting through to him and if the discussion were to turn unpleasant she didn't want to be part of it anyway.

With the departure of his wife, Stan turned his full focus upon his son. 'So,' he said, lounging back in his armchair, tumbler of Scotch in hand, 'what are your thoughts on all this? I know your sister's, but how do you feel?'

'About the diaries you mean?'

'Jesus Christ, boy, I don't mean about the bloody weather.'

Alan and Kate shared another look. They could both see that their father's aggression was fuelled by more than alcohol. Something else had triggered a rage that seemed to be simmering beneath the surface. Kate gave the slightest shrug, signalling to her brother she had no idea what had brought about this black mood. She knew it had not been Alan's appearance, for she'd seen a difference in her father the moment he'd emerged from his study. Over two hours of drinking and thinking had proved a potent combination and something was stewing in Stan's brain.

'Where is he?' he'd demanded. 'Where's your brother?'

'It's only half past eleven, Dad, he won't be here until twelve.'

'I'll wait on the verandah. I need some air.'

When Stan had gone back to his study for the Scotch, Hilda had suggested, diplomatically, that they should have tea and scones on the front verandah as soon as Alan arrived.

'With Ivy away I shall serve it up myself,' she'd said, the prospect pleasing her, 'a real family affair.'

'No tea,' Stan had flatly announced and then he'd informed her she was banned from the discussion.

To Kate, things had not appeared promising. 'I'll wait with you, Dad,' she'd said, and the two had sat in stony silence.

Ignoring his father's brief outburst, Alan answered with positivity. 'I think it's a good thing the diaries have come to light.'

'You do, do you? Why?'

'Because it's high time the truth was revealed. In fact the truth's been hidden for far too long: we should have known all this years ago.'

'So like your sister you believe we shouldn't destroy the diaries. That we shouldn't pretend they never existed and go back to the way we were.'

'We can't, Dad.' Alan was amazed his father could even suggest such a thing. 'We can't go back to living a lie.'

Stan made no reply, but gazed steadfastly at his son, his expression unfathomable.

'You can't be serious,' Alan protested. Still no reply … 'We've been living a lie for the whole of our lives, Dad,' he argued, 'every single one of us. For four generations! The Durham legend is a myth. We're not the people we thought we were. Everything's been a tissue of lies right from the start.'

'I know this,' Stan snapped, 'do you think I don't know this? I know also that you've been aware of these lies for the past two years and that you and your sister have been hiding the truth from me.' He cast a cursory glance at Kate. 'Your sister may perhaps have been attempting to protect her mother or her mother's misguided view of the world,' he said scathingly, 'but what's your excuse? You're my son, damn it! You're my son! You should have told me!'

Alan felt a surge of irritation so intense it bordered on anger. Oh, I'm your son now, am I? he thought. Since when did that come about?

'He was trying to protect you, Dad.' Kate found her father's accusation so unjust she jumped in before her brother could answer.

'Protect me from precisely what?' Stan demanded.

'Neil had just died and you were vulnerable …' Kate's reply was wary: they were approaching tricky ground. 'Al thought you might have trouble handling the truth.'

'The truth about my slut of a grandmother, you mean?' Stan knocked back his Scotch in one hit. 'The truth that there's black blood in the Durham veins.'

'No.' Alan didn't need his sister to answer for him, nor did he feel the need to tread warily, better to have it all out in the open, he thought. 'The truth about Big Jim being a dreadful human being,' he said.

Stan the Man's eyes locked with his son's and his very silence seemed to hold a challenge.

It was a challenge his son took up willingly. 'We all know how much you idolised Big Jim, Dad.' Alan's response was reasonable, his tone calm but firm; he'd controlled his irritation. 'Everyone knows. Hell not just the family, the town, the region, the whole sugar industry. Big Jim was your lifetime hero. You modelled yourself on the man. Discovering the truth was bound to shatter you – Kate and I both knew that.'

Kate wondered momentarily whether Alan might be taking the wrong tack, she would not have pushed the Big Jim issue herself. But neither she nor her brother could have foreseen the reaction that followed.

'You should have told me,' Stan roared at the top of his voice. 'You should have told me!' He stood and hurled the whisky tumbler over the verandah railings with all the force he could muster; it shattered against the side of the brand-new Belmont.

Alan and Kate both sprang to their feet. Had their father gone insane?

'What kind of a son are you,' Stan yelled. 'You knew the truth and you kept it from me! You knew that my life had been made a mockery and you said nothing! What kind of a goddamn son are you!'

'I'm a damn sight better son to you than you ever were to your father!' Alan stood his ground. Normally he would have turned and walked away, but not this time. This time he needed to hit back. He didn't even care that his father's lunatic rage was not directed at him at all, but at Big Jim. Alan had had enough.

'You're right, Dad,' he said cuttingly, 'you're dead bloody right. Your whole life's been a mockery. You modelled yourself on a hideous man! You lauded him to the skies! "Big Jim built Elianne from nothing", how many times did we hear that as kids. "Big Jim created this empire!" Well bugger that! Your *father* made Elianne, and what thanks did he get from either Big Jim or you?!' Alan, who never lost his temper, was now angry. 'Bartholomew saved Elianne from ruin through two world wars and you ignored him the whole of your life because you were so busy worshipping Big bloody Jim!'

'Get out,' Stan roared, 'get out of my house!'

'You idolised the wrong man, Dad! Well I'm glad you know what a bastard your hero was! I hope the truth hurts! I hope it hurts like hell!'

'Get out of my house!' Any minute Stan would launch himself at his son. 'Get off my property!'

Alan's anger was spent. 'Willingly,' he said and as he turned to go, he saw for the first time the group huddled at the open front door, his mother, together with the two household staff. Max had a protective arm around both Hilda and his wife, Maude the cook, prepared to usher the women out of harm's way should the situation turn violent, as it certainly threatened to.

'And don't you ever come back to Elianne again,' Stan yelled, 'you hear me? Don't you ever set foot on my land again!'

'That's perhaps something else you should know, Dad.' Alan turned back to his father. 'This isn't your land. It hasn't been for some time. You don't own Elianne. The investors do. A bunch of businessmen in Amsterdam hold the majority of shares – former Dutch East-Indies traders, I believe.' Stan stared blankly at his son. 'You're not even aware of that, are you?' Alan continued, not maliciously, but in the knowledge he was twisting the knife. 'You've been selling off shares in Elianne for years. This land is no longer the exclusive property of the Durham family. In fact, except for this house, nothing belongs to you. You're no more than a glorified manager.'

'You're lying.' Stan continued to stare at his son in disbelief. 'You're lying, you bastard.'

Alan shook his head. 'You should have checked all those papers Ivan gave you to sign. He asked you often enough, we all did. But you preferred to let the minions do the work while you played Lord of the Manor. Just like the old days. Just like Big Jim. Crikey, Dad, you accuse Mum of living in a world of her own making – look at you! You're a dinosaur. You've been living in the past for years.'

Stan finally erupted. He grabbed the heavy wooden table and hurled it across the verandah, sending the dog scuttling down the stairs, the bottle of Scotch smashing and chairs crashing to the floor.

'Get out! Get out all of you,' he roared as he caught sight of the group huddled in the doorway. He picked up one of the chairs as if he was going to hurl it at them. 'Get out of my house!'

Alan grabbed his mother's hand. 'Come on, Mum,' he said, and they set off down the stairs. 'You don't need to be here if he's going to smash the place up. Come on, Kate,' he called, 'we'll go to Luigi's.'

They piled into the cabin of the utility, Alan hefting Ben into the tray. 'You can come too, mate,' he said.

As the car drove away, Stan dumped the chair he was holding and turned to see Max still hovering in the doorway, shielding his wife but uncertain what was required of him.

'Piss off, Max,' Stan growled. 'Take the Land Rover, go for a drive, take your wife into town, I don't care what you do, but piss off both of you and leave me alone.'

He pushed past them on his way to the study and another bottle of Scotch.

'Get your handbag, Maude,' Max muttered.

The Fiorellis were having lunch when the Durhams arrived, Maria and Paola busily dishing out huge bowls of ravioli to three hungry men. Young Georgio and his cousin Gio had just returned from Saturday-morning footie practice in South Kolan and Luigi had come home from the mill for his midday meal break, as he always did during the slack season.

Places were immediately set for Alan and his mother and sister, who were welcomed to the table, although none of the three felt in the least like food.

Hilda shook her head apologetically as Maria tried to ply her with a bowl of ravioli. 'I'm so sorry, Maria, but really I couldn't.'

'Is no matter,' Maria said in her broken English, 'you is no hungry, I understand.' Maria could see Hilda Durham was upset. She wondered what had happened, but tactfully did not enquire and would have signalled the men to do likewise, except the men had not noticed anything amiss. The men were too busy shovelling down their food. 'I make you tea, yes?'

'That would be lovely, thank you.' Hilda nodded gratefully.

Paola had known the instant she'd seen them that Alan's meeting with his father had been disastrous. They had discussed the possibility that it well might.

'Things didn't go as you and Kate had hoped,' she murmured, serving up his bowl of ravioli and edging in beside him on the communal wooden bench.

'Understatement of the year,' he muttered. 'Dad went berserk.'

'Oh. I'm so sorry.' Paola cast a sympathetic glance across the table to Kate, who nodded and gave a helpless shrug. She squeezed her husband's hand reassuringly. 'You did all you could, Alan,' she said, 'at least you tried.'

Paola knew the whole story. Alan had told her about the diaries' revelations before their marriage, feeling it only fair she should be warned of his ancestry. 'Just in case you want to call the whole thing off,' he'd said, only half-jokingly. She hadn't.

Alan gazed vacantly down at his ravioli. Paola's right, he thought. I really have done all I can. I've given it my best shot. There's no point in agonising any further. It's over. All of a sudden he realised he was extraordinarily hungry.

'God, I can't tell you how good this looks,' he said, much to Maria's delight.

After lunch, Luigi returned to the mill and the women cleared away the dishes and washed up, Hilda insisting upon drying. The young men went outside into the back garden, where Giorgio and Gio rehearsed the Rolling Stones bracket they planned to perform at Alfonso's fifty-fifth birthday in two weeks' time. Gio's father loathed rock and roll, but that didn't matter, the younger members of the family all adored the Stones.

Alan sat on the little bench at the end of the garden, looking out at the cane fields, listening to 'Honky Tonk Woman' and feeling the whole situation was somehow surreal. What should he do next? Would it be safe to return his mother and sister to The Big House or would his father still be rampaging about the place like a maddened bull? Should he drive them into town so they could stay at the flat? The world seemed to have gone insane and he was unsure about the course of action he should take.

With the kitchen chores out of the way the women too gravitated to the music and Alan lifted chairs out onto the little back verandah. The question of what to do was by now fading somewhat; the afternoon had a happily balmy feel.

It was four o'clock before they knew anything was wrong. Gio was setting off for home when he saw it. He left via the backyard and the side gate as the family always did, the Fiorellis' front door being rarely put to use, but in walking down the path to the street where his battered old ute was parked, he saw the smoke. It was coming from The Big House, barely half a mile away.

He raced back to alert the others. 'Fire,' he yelled, 'fire! It's your dad's place, Alan. The Big House is on fire!'

They all ran out into the street to where they could clearly see the smoke billowing into the air.

Alan took command. 'Go to the mill, Gio,' he ordered, 'tell Luigi to bring the fire truck and a team; Georgio, you come with me.' He caught sight of his mother's panic-stricken face and knew she feared for her husband. 'Don't worry, Mum,' he said, 'we'll get him out safely,' then in an aside to his wife, 'look after her for me, Paola.'

Kate joined her brother as he raced for the utility. 'I'm coming too,' she said and she piled in beside Georgio. Alan raised no protest. He hadn't presumed for one minute that Kate would stay behind with the women.

Having decided to burn down The Big House, Stan had set about his task with methodical precision. The use of the diaries as a prime source of ignition had seemed to him not only apt, but intensely satisfying.

After the others had gone he'd sat drinking morosely in his study for some time, his son's hard-hitting home truths still ringing in his ears. Then he'd roamed the house, whisky bottle in hand, swigging from its neck, swinging it about with drunken abandon, sending crystal and fine china flying from shelves, smashing Hilda's favourite objets d'art from the sideboards and mantelpieces of the main lounge and front drawing room and causing whatever general wreckage he could, his mind all the while raging. So this is all I own, is it! This house is all that belongs to me? Well to hell with them! *Crash*. To hell with the lot of them! *Crash*. To hell with Ivan Krantz and his prick of a son! *Crash*. To hell with my son and my father! *Crash*. To hell with Big Jim! Yes, most of all, to hell with Big Jim!

But as the image of Big Jim had come into his mind, something had changed. The need to destroy had taken on a greater significance than the mere release of pent-up hostility. Everywhere he looked Stan could see his grandfather's influence. He was surrounded by the man. This very house had been built in order to impress Big Jim. At the time he'd pretended it had been for Hilda, but it hadn't been at all. He'd wanted to show off to his hero. He'd wanted to build a home that was bigger and grander than Elianne House, a home even more opulent than Big Jim's. And oh the pride he'd felt upon receiving his hero's stamp of approval!

'Well, well, isn't this grand.' He could hear Big Jim's voice still, he could see him filling the house with his giant presence. 'A new mansion for a new generation of Durhams: you've done well, Stan my boy. You've done this family proud.' How he'd basked in his idol's praise!

The memory, still crystal-clear, had aroused in Stan a potent mix of hatred and shame. This house was a monument to his worship of Big Jim. It stood mocking him, a permanent reminder that in emulating a man whose cruelty had destroyed his family, he'd destroyed his own. This house was a symbol of his humiliation. He'd decided in that moment that he needed to do far more than vent his anger at the world. He needed to burn down this house. He needed to raze it to the ground and obliterate all it stood for.

That was when he'd seen the folders. An armload of the things, piled high, each thick with the pages of Kate's translations, sitting right there on the front drawing-room desk where Hilda had left them. Grandmother Ellie's diaries ... How fitting, he'd thought. Indeed how perfect.

He'd felt a great deal calmer having come to his decision and after gathering the necessary equipment together, everything had gone very much to plan. He'd scattered the folders and their contents in strategic positions around the house, beneath curtains and on rattan and wicker chairs, anything that was likely to prove flammable. Areas that would be more difficult to ignite, he'd doused with petrol. Then he'd gone from room to room systematically setting everything alight with a trickle burner, just as he would the cane.

Now, standing on the verandah watching the blaze grow steadily stronger, Stan's anger returned with a vengeance. He wished this could be Big Jim he was burning ... Big Jim the man himself ... he wished he could see his grandfather among the flames ...

He looked through the window to the front drawing room, now ablaze, trying to imagine Big Jim, there inside this house that was his monument. He tried to see him screaming in agony, begging forgiveness. But Big Jim wasn't there. Big Jim was still mocking him.

'Dad! Dad!'

Stan didn't hear the utility pull up. He didn't hear his son calling out to him. The more intense the flames grew, the more so did his rage. If he couldn't burn Big Jim the man then he'd burn all Big Jim stood for. He'd burn Elianne! He'd burn it all to the ground – the plantation, the mill, the entire estate. He'd destroy everything Big Jim had created. This house was just the start.

'Go around the back, Georgio,' Alan ordered, 'there's a hose by the laundry.' He didn't need to issue orders to his sister. Kate was already unfurling the hose that serviced the front garden. There would be an adequate water supply, Alan knew, to have both hoses running at full strength for some time. The household tanks were always kept well stocked from the dam. The overall effectiveness of hosing, however, was doubtful, for the fire had considerable hold. *Our only hope*, he thought, *is to keep the blaze under control as much as possible until the arrival of Luigi's team and the fire truck.* In the meantime, what the hell was his father doing on the front verandah?

'Dad,' he yelled at the top of his voice. 'Dad, get down from there!'

But his father took no notice. He didn't even appear to hear. His father seemed to be revelling in the spectacle of the blaze.

The hoses were now on at full force, Giorgio manning the rear of the house while Kate concentrated on the front.

Alan raced up the stairs to his father, copping a blast from the hose as he went. He grabbed Stan by the arm.

'Dad, what the hell are you doing?' he yelled trying to haul him away. 'Get off the verandah!'

The arrival of his son meant nothing to Stan, who shook himself free of Alan's grasp, staggering drunkenly as he did so, but managing to stay upright. The jet of water that hit him, however, was a different matter altogether.

'No, no,' he roared angrily, 'let it burn! Let it burn! Let the whole place burn!'

Despite the smoke, which was reaching suffocating proportions, Alan could make out the trickle burner lying on the verandah and realised with a sense of horror that his father had deliberately lit the fire. Through the window of the front drawing room he could see the blaze raging inside and even in that split second the window itself shattered, to be quickly followed by several others as the heat intensified. The place was becoming an inferno. The hoses were having no effect. The fire was out of control.

'She's going to go up, Dad,' he yelled as the flames licked hungrily through the open windows at the verandah's timber. He made another desperate grab at his father. 'Get down the stairs while you can! For God's sake get down the stairs.'

Clasped in each other's embrace, they struggled like clumsy dance partners, Alan managing to catch Stan off balance enough to haul him to the top of the stairs. But upon regaining his footing, Stan once again flung him aside with ease. Even in his drunkenness, Stan the Man's size and strength far outmatched that of his son. Alan found himself skidding along the verandah on his back, shards of glass cutting through his shirt and into his skin, while his father kept screaming like a madman.

'Let it burn! Let it burn! Let the whole place burn!'

He's insane, Alan thought, struggling to his feet. He's demented with the drink. What the hell does he think he's doing? Does he mean to incinerate himself along with the house?

'You're drunk, man,' he yelled, 'get down the bloody stairs,' and he hurled himself at his father in a rugby tackle, grabbing him around the knees and holding on for dear life.

Stan fell as if in slow motion and Alan went with him, all the way down the stairs, father and son locked together.

They landed in a heap at the bottom and Kate dropped the hose, leaving it to snake about like a live thing as she ran to help.

'Are you all right?' she said squatting beside her brother who, winded, was fighting to regain his breath as he shakily sat up. 'Oh hell, look at your back.' She saw the blood seeping through his tattered shirt.

'I'm fine, Kate, I'm fine,' Alan replied, his voice husky, the smoke catching in his lungs. 'Check out Dad – how is he?' Stan was not moving.

Kate made a quick professional examination of her father. 'Nasty cut to the forehead, but he's breathing and there doesn't appear to be anything broken.'

'He's probably passed out – he's as drunk as a skunk.' Alan hauled himself painfully to his feet. 'Let's get him out of the danger zone.'

They took an arm each and as they started to drag Stan away from the house other willing hands were suddenly there lending assistance. Luigi and his team had arrived in the fire truck, Gio in his utility close behind them.

With the fire now raging out of control, Luigi instantly assessed the situation and took command. 'We must let her burn,' he said to Alan. As the Boss was unconscious he sought permission of the next Durham in line. 'Better we contain the blaze so it do no more damage, *si*? The house she must go. Cinders in the cane, Alan, no good: we could lose all of Elianne.'

'Yes, Luigi, I agree.'

'You stay, look after your father, I have men enough.' He stopped Kate who was about to return to the hose she'd been manning. 'You stay also, Kate,' he said with a meaningful nod at Alan's bloodied back, 'you stay, look after your brother.'

Luigi left them and upon Kate's instruction Alan removed his shirt, which was in tatters. As she crossed to the garden hose now being manned by Gio, Alan sat naked-chested on the ground beside his father's inert form. He watched Luigi's team set about their work. A half a dozen men armed with shovels and cane knives were busily creating a fire break, while Luigi and his co-worker had started circling the perimeter in the fire truck, saturating all in their path. Alan was thankful for the fire truck, which was a recent innovation. A Bedford fitted with a water tank and powerful hose, it proved useful enough in the control of burnings, but was invaluable in a situation such as this.

Kate returned with the sleeves of her own shirt, which she'd ripped off to form two rags, both now drenched. 'Here,' she said, handing one to him, 'you do Dad and I'll do you.'

Cradling his father's head on his knees, Alan started to bathe the blood from Stan's forehead, while his sister knelt behind him, dabbing gently at his back.

'God, you're a mess,' she said, peering closely. 'The cuts aren't deep, but we'll have to get at you with tweezers later. I can feel glass splinters everywhere.'

'So can I. Ouch! Go easy.'

'Don't be a wimp.'

She cleaned the blood off as best she could, then they sat together watching The Big House burn. The blaze was now at its peak, hungry tongues of fire devouring balcony railings and licking at walls like an insatiable beast revelling in its prey.

'Quite a spectacle,' Kate said. 'The end of an era.'

'He did it deliberately you know.'

'*What?*'

'Dad. He lit the fire himself. There was a trickle burner on the verandah, he wasn't mucking around.'

'Good God.' Kate looked down at Stan, whose head was still resting in his son's lap. 'I expected him to burn the diaries, but not the whole damn house.'

'Yep, pretty radical,' Alan agreed drily. 'A bit excessive to my mind, sending everything up in smoke.'

'Not quite everything.'

Her brother looked a query.

'Not the diaries,' Kate said, 'not the originals anyway. The ledgers are in the boot of my car: I didn't want to risk Dad destroying them.

As if he knew he was being talked about, Stan suddenly stirred. His eyes opened and he regained consciousness to find his head cradled in his son's lap. He sat up, disoriented. What had happened?

He looked at his son, and then at his daughter, and then at the house that was burning like a funeral pyre. Of course, that's what happened, he vaguely recalled. He'd burnt down The Big House.

Kate and Alan exchanged a glance. They could both see that the madness had left their father. In fact he seemed extraordinarily sober.

'It's over, Dad,' Kate said.

They sat together side by side, the three of them, and watched in silence as the fire devoured the past.

Epilogue

1974

The early seventies ushered in many changes for Australia and its people. After twenty-three years of Liberal–Country coalition government, the Labor party was voted into power in 1972 under the leadership of Edward Gough Whitlam.

Although the Vietnam War was to drag on for a further two years, the last Australian troops were finally withdrawn and the country's participation in the conflict formally declared at an end with the delivery of the Governor General's proclamation on 11 January 1973.

The Whitlam Labor government announced an official end to the White Australia Policy, proclaiming its intention to eradicate racial discrimination. It appeared, without doubt, that Australia was a country on the move.

As if in a bid to keep pace with the rapid changes of the new decade, the sugar industry continued to capitalise on the technological breakthroughs of the sixties and production kept rising. Australia was a major sugar-producing country and had for some time been a respected world authority on cane-harvesting mechanisation. The central focus of this latest technology was the heart of the Queensland southern cane-fields region itself, Bundaberg. Bundy had become famous. And in the thick of it all was Alan Durham.

Alan's prescience had paid off. His company had expanded dramatically, business was booming: he was a wealthy young man. But the fulfilment of his private life far exceeded that of his commercial interests, for Paola had recently given birth to their second child, a baby girl whom they'd named Sophia after Luigi's mother. The birth of little Sophia had brought joy to everyone, not least of all the child's paternal grandmother. Hilda Durham had embraced grandparenthood with a passion.

Christmas 1974 was looming and Hilda couldn't have been happier. In fact she felt she'd never been quite this happy. Christmas was now the true family occasion that in her opinion it should always have been. She recalled the Christmases of old when Elianne's senior staff and families had been entertained in the formal dining room of The Big House, elaborate affairs, impressive certainly, but stilted and with far too many speeches. Then there'd been those several years following Neil's death, those terrible years when Christmas had ceased to exist. She didn't think about those years any more: she'd put them behind her; these were happy times. She adored being a grandmother and Christmas in the new house, so ideally suited to family gatherings, was the highlight of her year.

The home that Hilda and Stan now shared wasn't really new at all. Situated not far from the site of old Elianne House, it was a gracious Queenslander in true classic style and had been home to one of the estate's senior staff members in bygone days. Hilda actually preferred it to The Big House. She'd said as much to Stan.

'I did find The Big House just the tiniest bit ostentatious, dear, I must admit. We really didn't need that amount of space.' Her intention had of course been to ease her husband's mind about the change in their lifestyle, but she'd been nonetheless honest. She found her new home pleasantly reminiscent of old Elianne House, stylish but at the same time warm and welcoming, an elegant home and as such a constant reminder of Grandmother Ellie herself.

Grandmother Ellie still featured a great deal in Hilda's conversation, although Big Jim had become notably absent. 'Sacrifice' rather than 'great love' was Hilda's theme these days. Indeed Grandmother Ellie's strength and devotion to family throughout her entire life had become the stuff of legend. Grandmother Ellie had been a true matriarch, and Hilda's only wish was that she herself might one day prove worthy of such a title, which was why Christmas was so very important.

This Christmas promised to be particularly fulfilling with a new grandchild present. Alan and Paola would of course be bringing little Sophia, barely a month old, along with their son, Ricky, just turned four. Luigi and Maria would be there too, and Paola's brother, Georgio, accompanied by his new young fiancée, who was most welcome, as Cook always said 'the more the merrier'.

Hilda knew that following the luncheon the Fiorellis, together with Alan and his family, would join the rest of the clan at Alfonso's house for their customary raucous get-together, but she didn't mind in the least. On the contrary, she very much approved. Family was family after all, and it was good for the grandchildren to experience both cultures. Why little Ricky could already speak Italian, just imagine that. Hilda found it a tremendously exciting sign of the times.

And Kate, too, would be home for Christmas, with Frank. Hilda did so wish that Kate would have a baby. She'd be twenty-eight years old in only a month or so and had been married for two whole years – surely time was running out. But Kate had declared that career took precedence until she was thirty. She'd even announced, and with Frank's approval, that after having had children she would continue to work! Hilda wasn't sure she understood the modern woman. According to recent press reports, Kate was *of significant importance to the country*.

The youngest member ever appointed by the Australian Government to the Advisory Committee on Livestock Breeding, Control and Distribution, Dr Kate Durham also heads a private consultancy firm advising the Australian Quarantine Inspection Service, the CSIRO and the Australian Livestock Breeders Association. Dr Durham is clearly a young woman of significant importance to this country.

Hilda was proud of her daughter's achievements certainly, but when it came time in a young woman's life to embrace motherhood, surely men could take over those jobs of *significant importance to the country.*

She naturally did not express such views to her daughter, who she knew would simply scoff and call her old-fashioned. And she had to admit, after all, that Kate's contacts in high places had certainly proved beneficial for the family.

Hilda could barely contain her excitement at the thought that Kate and Frank were bringing with them a new member of the family. The three were due to arrive on the afternoon of Christmas Eve and she and Alan would be eagerly waiting to greet them. They'd kept the news from Stanley though. They'd both agreed with Kate that it should come as a surprise.

When Kate had made general enquiries about bringing her brother's widow to Australia, she'd confronted more difficulty than she'd anticipated, a fact which she'd found most disappointing. For all Whitlam's declaration of 'no more White Australia Policy', it appeared the government was not as keen as it had professed to be in welcoming the Vietnamese to Australia, even those married to Australian citizens. There still seemed to be a guard up against Asian immigration including, at this stage anyway, those of refugee status.

Annoyed at the bureaucratic red tape confronting her, she'd unashamedly used her government contacts, and in doing so had discovered that she couldn't bring Yen to Australia anyway. Yen was dead, along with most of her family, killed two years previously in a Viet Cong raid upon her village. But Yen's child had survived, a boy now five, the son Neil never knew he had. Yen had been in the early stages of pregnancy when her husband had died.

The boy had been brought up by Yen's aunt, a widow who, living some distance from the village, had escaped the massacre. The widow was poor and illiterate, but had received assistance from a Catholic priest who was a close friend of the family. The priest had arranged with the bank in Vûng Tàu for her to draw funds from the monthly deposits that arrived from Australia in order that she might adequately support her dead niece's child. He had also taken it upon himself to continue the boy's education, teaching him English, as Yen herself had been doing. It had been Yen's greatest wish that she and the child might one day go to Australia and meet her husband's family. She had wanted her son prepared for that day.

The Catholic Church in Vûng Tàu had proved of great assistance in Kate's application to bring the child to Australia. The priest, only too eager to see the boy afforded a better life, had produced all the necessary documentation, marriage and birth certificates, records of the child's baptism – there was every proof to hand that this was the legitimate son of Neil Durham.

Kate had nonetheless encountered bureaucratic obstacles on the home front. She was told she must bide her time, she was fobbed off, but she'd refused to be daunted. Using her stellar status, she'd gone directly to federal level. A favour asked had been granted and she'd succeeded in her aim. She had brought her nephew to Australia and the legal adoption process was currently under way. She and Frank were about to become parents well before they'd planned, and were now bringing the child home to meet his new family.

They drove up from Sydney in Frank's Land Rover, staying overnight in Ballina, showing the boy the countryside, watching him relax more and more with the passing of each hour. He'd been understandably guarded when they'd first met, trying very hard Kate could tell to disguise the fact that he was frightened. She could see so much of her brother in the child and she'd desperately wanted to hug him, to feel Neil's flesh and blood in her arms. But hugs would come later, she'd told herself, and she'd offered her hand instead.

'Hello, I'm your Aunt Kate,' she'd said.

'Hello.' He was a good-looking boy, tall for his age, and he'd shaken hands very solemnly, doing his best to be grown up. But after a second or so, his eyes had flickered nervously to the ground, avoiding further contact.

Now, after only several days of their acquaintanceship, he was becoming simply an excited little boy enjoying new sights and the company of people he liked. He particularly liked Frank. Frank's laidback personality and man-to-man attitude made him a winner with little boys, who wanted to be just like him. It was happily apparent to Kate, although no surprise, that Frank was a born father.

The trip north served to bring them closer together, all three, and as they turned off the Bundaberg–Gin Gin Road onto the dirt road of Elianne, they felt to Kate already like a family.

She looked out at the passing cane fields and the giant mill in the distance, recalling how, just ten years earlier, when she'd returned after her first year at university, everything, familiar as it was, had appeared on the cusp of change. She'd presumed this was because she herself was changing. She'd been wrong, she now realised. Elianne *had* been changing. But she hadn't known then to what an astonishing degree; the canecutters a dying breed mechanical harvesters replacing them; fewer people living on the estate, most commuting instead from Bundaberg; merchants closing up shop and moving from Elianne's village into town; the changes had been endless. Yet now, as they passed by the mill and the mill dam and the sugar shed, and then on past the stables and the old hall and the once-busy village green, everything appeared as it had in her childhood. It seemed as if nothing at all had changed.

Frank sensed her reflective mood. 'Good to be home, I take it?'

She smiled. 'This is no longer home, my darling,' she replied. 'Home is with you, home is wherever we are, you and I.' She turned to look behind her at the boy who was leaning out the open window drinking in the sights and the smells. 'But yes,' she said, 'yes, it's good to be back.'

They pulled up outside the family home in the late afternoon glow.

Hilda, Stan and Alan were gathered in the sitting room, Cook having just delivered a fresh batch of scones to go with the afternoon tea she'd served. Cook and Max had remained in Stan's employ, but the household was without a maid these days since Ivy had left to get married.

There was only the one sitting room at Durham House, big and airy with shuttered windows looking out over the front verandah. The main door and the shutters were now open wide, giving access to what little breeze there was – the day had been stifling – and Stan heard the four-wheel drive pull up outside.

'They're here,' he said, rising from the throne-like chair that even at first glance clearly belonged to the patriarch of the house. 'Let's go out and meet them.' He always bellowed a greeting from the front verandah: it was his habit.

'No, no, dear,' Hilda insisted, 'sit down, please do, we have a little surprise in store.'

As she crossed to the door, she cast a quick glance at her son, a mixture of nervousness and excitement.

Alan stood, returning an encouraging smile, while Stan, intrigued, seated himself back in his armchair and waited for his surprise.

'Come in, my darling, come in.' Hilda embraced her daughter warmly, and offered Frank her cheek, which he kissed. 'Hello, Frank dear, how lovely to see you.' Then she stepped back, fingers lightly to breast in breathless anticipation. 'Well, well, who do we have here?' she said and she looked down at the little boy who was clutching Kate's hand as if it was a lifeline.

They all looked at the boy, whose guard was instantly up, his eyes flickering around at the strange faces and then down at the floor.

Kate gave his hand a quick squeeze. 'Don't worry,' she whispered, 'they won't bite.'

Stan stared long and hard at the child. He was obviously Asian, or some sort of half-breed, but he seemed oddly familiar. There was something about him: what the hell was it? Stan was puzzled. Why had Kate brought a Chink home, and why did the boy remind him so strongly of someone?

There was silence while they all waited for Kate to make the introduction. As they had expected, she did so directly to her father.

'Dad, there's a special person I'd like you to meet.' Hand in hand she and the boy crossed to Stan's armchair, where they halted in front of him. 'This is Neil Durham,' she said.

Stan's eyes left the boy and he glared up at his daughter. What sort of sick joke was she playing at?

'Neil was married. His wife, Yen, died in the war,' Kate went on. 'She named her son after her husband. This is Neil's boy, Dad. This is your grandson.'

Stan's eyes returned to the boy, and he knew that this was no joke at all. The resemblance was uncanny. He was looking at an Asian version of his son. For one of the few times in his life, Stanley Durham found himself utterly dumbstruck.

'Hello, Neil,' he said finally.

The boy's eyes flickered up from the floor. 'Hello,' he replied. Normally his gaze would have returned to the floor, but something in the eyes of the big man in the big chair compelled him to retain focus just that little bit longer.

Introductions were then made all around, after which Hilda fetched some lemonade for Neil. He sat on the edge of his chair sipping his drink and refusing a scone with jam and cream, mainly because he was sure he'd drop it. The others talked among themselves, trying not to place any pressure on the child, for he was obviously nervous.

Frank noticed, after a while, that the boy's eyes kept darting towards the open door where Ben lay curled up on the verandah.

'Do you want to go outside and say hello to Ben?' he asked.

Neil looked at him, confused.

'Ben, that's the dog's name, Ben. Do you want to go outside and pat him?'

The boy nodded.

'Why don't we all go outside?' The suggestion came from Stan. He stood. 'It's cooler now, let's sit on the verandah.'

They trooped outside to where a miscellany of chairs constituted the verandah furniture and Neil knelt beside Ben, patting the old dog, who responded with a thump of his now threadbare tail.

Stan chose to sit in one of the canvas deck chairs, which was surprising for, like Hilda, his preference was always a hardback at the table. The particular deck chair he chose, however, happened to be the one closest to the dog.

'We're going to get Neil a dog, Dad,' Kate said as telling looks were exchanged. Stan's eyes hadn't left his grandson.

'That's good,' Stan replied, 'a boy needs a dog.'

'He is old this dog.' The child's English was good, but stilted.

'Yep,' Stan said. 'He's fourteen now. That's old for a dog.'

Neil looked up and gave a solemn nod. 'Yes,' he agreed, 'it is old,' and he returned his attention to the dog.

Conversation dwindled away and they sat, relaxed and comfortable, watching the child and the dog. Then after a little while, Stan stood.

'I need some exercise,' he said.

The child looked up once again, sensing the comment had been made to him.

It had been. 'Ever seen the inside of a sugar mill, son?'

Neil shook his head.

'Do you want to?'

The boy gave a vigorous nod.

'Come on, then.' Stan reached out his hand and the boy stood and took it. 'We'll go for a walk.'

The two set off down the stairs.

As they reached the bottom, Kate rose from her chair and called after them. 'You'll have to take the car, Dad – it's too far for him to walk.'

'What's wrong with a piggy-back,' Stan called in reply and he swung the boy up onto his shoulders.

Neil squealed excitedly. 'Ben can come too?'

'Sure, why not, if he can make the distance. Come on, Ben.'

The dog obediently hobbled down the stairs. He would go a hundred metres or so before turning back for home.

Kate's image of Stan the Man striding off towards the mill, his grandson on his shoulders, a boy from Vietnam, would stay with her forever. How times had indeed changed.

Author's note

My sugar mill and plantation of Elianne, although loosely based upon the grand estates of old, is fictional, as are all of Elianne's family members and the workers employed upon the estate.

In writing of the township of Bundaberg, I have referred to some of the well-known early entrepreneurs and local businesses for the purposes of authenticity, but these only in passing. All major characters in the novel are fictional.

I have tried to be consistent as far as possible, but it's difficult to be spot-on when neither the locals nor the historians can say exactly why the grand, main thoroughfare of Bundaberg was named Bourbon Street and exactly why and when it became Bourbong, which I find very amusing. Theories abound, one being that the original surveyors, who were inspired by many Aboriginal words in their naming of streets and sites, euphonised *'boorbung'*, the local term applied to a string of nearby waterholes. Some believe 'bourbong' is the phonetic spelling of the French *bourbon*, the name given to a particular variety of cane grown in the area before 1875. And there's even the theory that Bourbon Street was changed to Bourbong during the years of prohibition. That one sounds a bit dicey to me, but take your pick – it's all part of the colourful world that is Bundaberg.

Acknowledgements

My thanks, as always, to my husband, Bruce Venables, and also to those loyal stalwarts who continue to lend support and encouragement: big brother Rob Nunn, Susan Mackie-Hookway, Sue Greaves, Colin Julin and my agent, James Laurie.

A special thank you to other friends and family who offered invaluable research assistance in their specific areas of expertise: Dr Meredith Burgmann, Dr Christopher Bradbury, Ros Forrest, Paul Ham and my niece Cory Kentish.

I could not have written this book without 'the Bundaberg connection'. My sincerest thanks to Ian Gibson for sharing his vast knowledge of the sugar industry and for his infinite patience in spelling out so much detail to a novice, even to the point of providing personally hand-drawn maps. My thanks and gratitude also to Sue Gammon of Bundaberg Library, who not only provided invaluable research material, but so willingly shared her extensive knowledge of, and her passion for, the region.

Thanks also to Peter Lamond of Fairymead Sugar Museum; to the helpful staff at the Bundaberg Visitors Information Centre; and to the many friendly citizens of Bundy who so warmly welcomed me to their beautiful part of the world.

My thanks to Beverley Cousins, Brandon VanOver and Kate O'Donnell. Thanks also to Brett Osmond, Gavin

Schwarcz, Jess Malpass and all the hard-working team at Random House.

Among my research sources, I would like to recognise the following:

Bundaberg: history and people. Janette Nolan, University of Queensland Press, 1978.

Southern Sugar Saga. John Kerr, Bundaberg Sugar Company Limited, 1983.

History of the White Australia Policy to 1920. Myra Willard, Melbourne University Press, 1923.

Control or Colour Bar? A proposal for change in Australia's immigration policy. The Immigration Reform Group, Melbourne, 1960.

Welou, My Brother. Faith Bandler, Wild & Woolley Pty Ltd and Aboriginal Artists Agency Limited, 1984.

Vietnam, the Australian War. Paul Ham, HarperCollins, 2007.

Bundaberg in Pictures: 140 years of history. Bundaberg Newspaper Company, 2000.

100 Years of News: Bundaberg in the 1900s. Ed. Sandra Godwin, Bundaberg Newspaper Company, 2000.

The History of Bundaberg. J.Y. Walker, Gordon and Gotch, 1890.

Summer Memories Through Winter Eyes. Betty Bull, Fiona Drews, Margaret van Hennekeler, 1987.

The Story of Kolan. Don Dignan, M.A., Dip.Ed., W.R Smith & Paterson Pty. Ltd., 1964.

Other titles by Judy Nunn

Beneath the Southern Cross

In 1783, Thomas Kendall, a naïve nineteen-year-old sentenced to transportation for burglary, finds himself in Sydney Town and a new life in the wild and lawless land. *Beneath the Southern Cross* is as much a story of a city as it is a family chronicle. With her uncanny ability to bring history to life in technicolour, Judy Nunn traces the fortunes of Kendall's descendants through good times and bad to the present day . . .

Kal

Kalgoorlie. It grew out of the red dust of the desert over the world's richest vein of gold . . . From the heady early days of the gold rush, to the horrors of the First World War in Gallipoli and France, to the shame and confrontation of the post-war riots, *Kal* tells the story of Australia itself and the people who forged a nation out of a harsh and unforgiving land.

Heritage

In the 1940s refugees from more than seventy nations gathered in Australia to forge a new identity – and to help realise one man's dream: the mighty Snowy Mountains Hydro-Electric Scheme. From the ruins of Berlin to the birth of Israel, from the Italian Alps to the Australian high country, *Heritage* is a passionate tale of rebirth, struggle, sacrifice and redemption.

Territory

Territory is the story of the Top End and the people who dare to dwell there. Of Spitfire pilot Terence Galloway and his English bride, Henrietta, home from the war, only to be faced with the desperate defence of Darwin against the Imperial Japanese Air Force. From the blazing inferno that was Darwin on 19 February 1942 to the devastation of Cyclone Tracy, from the red desert to the tropical shore, *Territory* is a mile-a-minute read.

Pacific

Australian actress Samantha Lindsay is thrilled when she scores her first Hollywood movie role, playing a character loosely based on World War II heroine Mamma Tack. But on location in Vanuatu, uncanny parallels between history and fiction emerge and Sam begins a quest for the truth. Just who was the real Mamma Tack?

Other titles by Judy Nunn

Maralinga

Maralinga, 1956. A British airbase in the middle of nowhere, a top-secret atomic testing ground . . . *Maralinga* is the story of Lieutenant Daniel Gardiner, who accepts a posting to the wilds of South Australia on a promise of rapid promotion, and of adventurous young English journalist Elizabeth Hoffmann, who travels halfway around the world in search of the truth.

Floodtide

Floodtide traces the fortunes of four men and four families over four memorable decades in the mighty 'Iron Ore State' of Western Australia. The prosperous 1950s when childhood is idyllic in the small city of Perth . . . The turbulent 60s when youth is caught up in the Vietnam War . . . The avaricious 70s when WA's mineral boom sees a new breed of entrepreneurs . . . The corrupt 80s, when greedy politicians and powerful businessmen bring the state to its knees . . .

Tiger Men

Van Diemen's Land was an island of stark contrasts: a harsh penal colony, an English idyll for its gentry, and an island so rich in natural resources it was a profiteer's paradise. Its capital, Hobart Town, had its contrasts too: the wealthy elite in their sandstone mansions, the exploited poor in the notorious Wapping slum, and the criminals who haunted the dockside taverns. Hobart Town was no place for the meek. *Tiger Men* is the story of Silas Stanford, a wealthy Englishman; Mick O'Callaghan, an Irishman on the run; and Jefferson Powell, an idealistic American political prisoner. It is also the story of the strong, proud women who loved them, and of the children they bore who rose to power in the cutthroat world of international trade. A sweeping saga of three families who lived through Tasmania's golden era and the birth of Federation and then watched with pride as their sons marched off to fight for King and Country.